THE ADULTE

Noëlle Harrison was born in England a
1991. While based in Dublin in the early 1990s she wrote and
produced plays. She has written extensively on visual art in
Ireland. Her first novel *Beatrice* was published in 2004, followed by *A Small Part of Me* in 2005 and *I Remember* in 2008.
She lives in Oldcastle, County Meath.

Praise for *A Small Part of Me*

'Harrison is an intriguing and sensual writer, confidently
charting out her own distinctive territory' *Sunday Independent*

'The search for redemption and the simple heartbreaking love
of a mother for her child imbue this novel with echoes that
you won't forget'   *Irish Independent*

Praise for *Beatrice*

'Harrison has written a stunning book'   *Irish Times*

'Vivid and powerful, *Beatrice* is a novel told in gleaming
moments, like a string of pearls brought one by one out of the
dark. It has the compelling power of a detective story, following a trail of ghosts into the past'   Niall Williams

THE ADULTERESS

Noëlle Harrison

MACMILLAN

First published 2009 by Macmillan
an imprint of Pan Macmillan Ltd
20 New Wharf Road, London N1 9RR
Basingstoke and Oxford
Associated companies throughout the world
www.panmacmillan.com

ISBN 978-0-230-70988-1

1 3 5 7 9 8 6 4 2

A CIP catalogue record for this book is available from
the British Library.

Typeset by Intype Libra Ltd
Printed and bound in the UK by
CPI Mackays, Chatham ME5 8TD

Visit **www.panmacmillan.com** to read more about all our books
and to buy them. You will also find features, author interviews and
news of any author events, and you can sign up for e-newsletters
so that you're always first to hear about our new releases.

For the apple gatherers

They bite from the same apple. It drops from her hand and rolls across the uneven floorboards. The crumpled bed sheets smell like a summer orchard. He kneels before her and presses his face in her soft belly, inhales her scent. He wraps his arms about her waist, his fingers making temporary indentations in her skin. She takes his hands in hers, and pulls him up so that he stands above her. She goes up on her tiptoes and kisses his lips lightly. She tastes of apple still – bitter, sweet, tart, true. He holds her in his arms, and they rock gently backwards and forwards. One pure moment passes and then he lifts her up. They tumble back onto the sheets, fragrant with their lingering desire. They are laughing, joy burning through their sweat. Together they are their whole sensual world. Perfectly complete, utterly fragile.

JUNE

We walk the land, Robert and I, his hand in mine, and I try to say something to comfort him in his loss. We have been married for five years and yet he has never spoken about his father to me, and since I have never met the old man, it is hard to know what to say. I cannot help wondering why it is we never visited him.

I catch sight of the house. It is a balmy day in September. There is warmth in the sun, a rare occurrence in Cavan. The thatch gleams in the sunlight, dazzling me as if it is real gold. I have never seen such a friendly-looking abode, so different from the house I was raised in.

My husband's family home sits before me, with whitewashed walls, a bright-blue door and window ledges like two little eyes and an open mouth welcoming us in. It looks like a quaint cottage from a time long past. There are hens running across the yard, a mayhem of squawks, and even though we are here because Robert's father has just died, there is such a celebration of life all around us. Hedgerows full of a variety of little birds, and red berries and blackberries peeking out of the greenery, brown cows and one dapple-grey horse grazing in the fields, a profusion of bright-pink fuchsia bells bushed around the side of the house. Something about the place is familiar, as if I have seen a picture of it in one of my childhood storybooks. The woods are Little Red Riding Hood's, and the cottage Hansel and Gretel's, and there is even a round tower on a distant hill, which looks like Rapunzel's home.

Robert and I have always loved the city, vowed we would never leave it, but as we walk through his father's fields and into the wood, something happens to us. I do believe we are bewitched by the landscape. Sunlight diffuses through the canopy of trees, still rich with leaves, showering us with amber warmth. I remember the sun of my childhood, how I loved its rays on my bare skin, how I felt the sun kissed me when my mother did not. We can smell the crisp whisper of autumn beginning as Robert and I pick sweet blackberries, feeding them to each other until our lips and chins are stained with juice. My husband appears more sensual to me than ever before. He softens, looking younger somehow, and less weighed down with all the worries he carries home from work every day. And the war . . . he is always talking about the wretched war. Is it being here, in Cavan, his real home, that makes him seem instantly happier, lighter, somehow more mine? Am I hoping he might forget about armies battling, bombs dropping, the possibility that Ireland might join in the war?

The air around us is humming with life, late lazy bees droning, dragonflies hastily mating, perhaps for the last time, and tiny tabby butterflies, dozens of them, fluttering around us. Everything surrounding us is light, and fast, thrumming in our ears, and yet we slow right down, each footstep measured in the dewy folds of grass. We walk beneath the trees, breaking through cobwebs, leaves spinning from their tendrils so that we know we are the only two who have passed this way in a long time.

I am not surprised when Robert suggests the move. On this glorious autumn afternoon, as we lie in a meadow overlooked by his newly inherited cattle, it seems the most natural thing to do to agree. More than anything I want to live somewhere that reminds me of nothing apart from fairy tales, and the sweet sugary side of childhood. Here, I say to myself, we can live in a dream world.

As we walk back up to the cottage we come across a rose bush bursting with velvet blooms, their sultry perfume arresting us. Ignoring my protests that he will prick himself with the thorns, Robert gathers a bunch of crimson roses, every now and then pausing to suck the tiny beads of blood off his fingertips. He presents them to me with a kiss, his lips blessing my forehead. I cradle a single scarlet rose in my palm, wishing to protect this symbol of our love. I look down at it. On one red petal is one red drop of blood.

NICHOLAS

The old house in Cavan is in pieces. Nicholas can see that once it was a pretty little cottage; however, years of neglect have turned it into little more than a derelict barn. And yet when he first saw the house he knew he had to buy it, even though it was practically uninhabitable and he was certainly no builder. But the cottage was familiar to him, as if he knew all the rooms by heart before he walked into them. He felt at home here, more than he had ever felt in the nine years they spent in Dublin. He tries to banish the memory of all the hard work he put into their home in Sandycove. The hours spent sanding the floors, choking in the dust, his eyes red-raw. There was the tiling that he had to redo because Charlie said he got the pattern wrong. The bloody bathroom. He never even liked it when it was done. Now here he is, starting all over again. Charlie said it was his choice to leave, but she gave him no choice. Nicholas has his pride.

He guts the house. The roof is good and the old stone walls are beautiful, but inside is a mess. The staircase up to the attic has woodworm and is completely rotten in places. The walls are wet with damp and mould. He tells himself he can do this. It is spring. He has the whole summer stretching ahead. Somehow it is his duty to bring this cottage back to life. Can a house have a heart and soul? he wonders. His piano stands lonely in the back room. Untouched.

He cannot bear to play, although soon he will have to teach to make some money.

He looks out of the window at the green fields rolling away to infinity. He is in a landlocked county now and Nicholas misses the Irish Sea, those days when he and Charlie would walk all the way from Sandycove into Dun Laoghaire, and then down the pier to watch the ferry leave, discuss should they go too. He remembers looking across at the marina, and the bobbing yachts, and wondering what it would be like to spend your life sailing the sea, being as free as the seagulls wheeling above them.

'The light is amazing here,' Charlie would say and force Nicholas to quickstep so that she could get back home and paint, immediately translating the wide sea sky, grey, aqua and white, onto canvas. He preferred those early paintings, although he never dared tell her that. She thought she was getting better, but her pictures became more self-conscious, technically good, but they lost something.

Nicholas thinks of the Pacific Ocean crashing onto the beach at Turtle Bay and their honeymoon in Hawaii. They are lying in bed, entwined around each other like the limbs of a fantastical plant, and gazing at the huge waxen head of a flower outside the window. Its outrageous lushness, its dazzling pink brilliance seduces them. He rolls Charlie over, and her blue eyes sparkle the same colour as the ocean.

'I love you,' he says.

'I love you too,' she gazes at him with her true blue eyes, wrapping her legs around his waist and guiding him into her.

He was so young he thought this love was enough to keep them together forever. Yet it was only nine years ago. Not such a long time.

Nicholas sits back on his heels and closes his eyes, still holding the spirit level in one hand, a pencil in the other. Pieces of wood

The Adulteress

lie about his feet, and he wonders what the fuck he is trying to do, buying a wreck in the middle of nowhere. Beads of sweat break out on his forehead, although it is damp in the attic. He can feel his heart beating fast, and the pain everywhere: behind his eyes, in his throat and chest, his legs, his groin and his back. His whole body pulses with need and he cries out like a wild animal. No one can hear him, in this crumbling old house in Cavan. Nicholas has chosen it as his place of refuge, his exile away from his old life, away from Charlie. He opens his eyes. Dust motes spin in the air, and a spider scampers across the splintered and rotten floorboards. He breathes in deeply. He can smell the heady fragrance of flowers. Hawaii. They are snorkelling together, their eyes beneath the surface of the crystal-clear blue, holding hands, floating, watching a sea turtle as she swims by. Then their minds are as one, in awe of the creature's preternatural wisdom, the way she glides slowly through the water, taking all the time in the world to live. She looks at them – eyes so gentle, knowing, forgiving.

Nicholas snaps the pencil in half. Charlie. He cannot believe he will never hold her again, never touch her breasts, or feel her legs around his waist, her hips on his. But he would have to see her, yes. With the new face she wears, the distant, patronizing look in her eyes, detached smile, friendly as if he is a stranger. She behaves as if it were his fault. Has she no shame? Sometimes he wishes she were dead. Would it be easier then? She said that once. 'Nick, you're killing me.' He didn't understand what she meant, but he never asked.

Nicholas stands up, kicks the pile of wood across the attic. Suddenly he is filled with such a fierce rage he wants to destroy this house, pull it apart bit by bit, smash it up. He picks up the hammer and throws it through the window. The glass shatters, spraying him with tiny shards of glass. He is suddenly cold, shocked by his anger. He looks at his arms, speckled by little drops of blood. He is shaking, colder now than he has ever been in his life, his teeth are chattering. There is a huge hole in the window, and he will have to push all the glass out, get a new pane. More money. He stands by the broken window and again the aroma of flowers surrounds him. He recognizes the scent – roses. It is too early in spring for summer roses, red roses like his mother used to grow in her English country garden. Yet the smell is most definitely roses, over-powering, but not unpleasant. It calms him down. And then, as he is looking at the window, the rest of the glass falls in suddenly, as if someone has pushed it from the other side. He takes a step back, looks around the attic. Something doesn't feel right.

He goes downstairs and takes a beer out of the fridge. He downs it in three gulps, each one gradually making him feel less spooked. He sits on the step of the back door, holding the empty bottle in his hand, and looking at his solitude, green fields, woods, an orchard. And yet he doesn't feel alone. He is shivering again although it is warm in the sun. He twists around to look back into the shadows of the old house. The wind whispers through the hall, blowing some leaf skeletons, slowly dissolving residents since last autumn. His back is chilled and Nicholas places his hand on his heart, feels its faint beat through his shirt. He is surviving without Charlie – barely though, barely at all.

JUNE

I miss the sea. It is so very quiet here. Robert says I will soon get used to it and the place will grow on me. This is what he tells me, but I find it hard to imagine. There is a permanent chill in the air. I can feel it in my bones. And it is so damp my hair is in a constant frizz. The skies are filled with grey clouds, promising to rain, or having just rained, and a dark gloom enshrouds me all the hours of the day. I even miss London, but more so I miss the sea, the waves, its open lunacy, so different from the brooding corners of this country.

In Cavan the grey blanket of mist and rain has not lifted once since we moved in. Of course it rains in Dublin too, but the weather there can be brilliant sunshine one moment, strong sea breezes the next, and then a short, sharp burst of hard, drenching rain. There is nothing monotonous about it.

I was the wife of a city man, and now I am a farmer's wife. We no longer live in a small rented flat, but in a thatched farmhouse on about fifty acres of land. We have ten bullocks, two cows, three little pigs, one horse and about thirty hens. I am a little daunted by this, for the farm is a kingdom all of its own and one I know nothing about. Robert rises early, returns for dinner and then goes back out again until dark. I am constantly busy learning all the duties a farmer's wife has. If it were not for Oonagh Tobin, a neighbour's daughter, I would be completely lost. She is a kind and patient teacher, but sometimes I feel so frustrated when I see her doing something easily and quickly, yet I cannot get the grasp of it. I am sure she believes I am a useless article. The first morning she had to show me how to bake a loaf of the brown soda bread they like to eat here. I will never forget her expression of surprise and then pity when she realized I had never done it before. I wanted to run away from her into my room and hide. I wanted to read a book.

She thinks I cannot cook. But I can. It is just that I make food with ingredients we cannot get here. I can bake so many different kinds of cakes – Madeira, rich fruitcake, chocolate gateau, Battenberg, Bakewell tart, Victoria sponge. I can even make a perfect lemon soufflé. Oh gosh, I can smell it now, taste it melting in my mouth, the light angelic spongy topping, followed by rich creamy-lemony filling. But what use have I of a lemon soufflé in Cavan? I have not seen a lemon since I came here. And when I think of the lemons in Italy – the size of grapefruit – and their scent in the air in Sorrento, the bittersweet taste of limoncello still lingering on my lips. It is almost a form of torture to remember such sensory delights.

Ireland is at economic war with England. Robert warns me there will be an awful lot more work once the spring comes. There is compulsory tillage because of the emergency, so he will have to plough most of the land. He has no help apart from the Tobins. They live further away from the village than us, towards the large lake, which I can see on a clear day if I climb a little rise of land at the back of our house. Of course the glimmer of water makes me think immediately of the sea.

Our closest neighbours are the Sheridens. They live on the outskirts of the village. At the edge of our land there is a small wood, and it is this that separates us from the Sheridens' property. If we were to walk through the wood, we would end up in their back garden. Their house is quite different from ours: tall, and grey stone with a slate roof. I noted to Robert that it was large.

'That may be so,' he said, 'but we are better off in our house. When it gets really cold, our thatch will keep us cosy and snug. The Sheridens will be freezing.'

He said this with such satisfaction that it made me think he is not too fond of these Sheridens.

Some days as I churn the butter, my hands sore, my shoulders and back stiff, I wonder what I am doing here and remember my old desires and dreams. How can I bear this? For a brief moment I feel like throwing the churn to the floor and watching its golden entrails spill across the flagstones, greasy, half-made, unfinished. Wasteful. I see myself running out into the yard, the hens flying about me in panic, the rain hammering down upon me.

'Robert!' I would cry out. 'Robert!'

I would find him in a black boggy field, battling against the elements, wet and old-looking in a coat of his father's. I would search for the dashing city man I married.

'Take me home!' I would command him, like my mother so often commanded my father.

I would see our old life in London, illuminating the donkey-grey sky like a celestial vision. Dinner parties, red buses, smoky tea rooms and train stations, the pictures, my sister Min laughing gaily and her husband Charles, smoking a pipe, stroking her hair affectionately, little Lionel the dog curled up asleep at her feet.

This second of regret is long. Its suppression is hard, for even if I did demand this of Robert, a return to our old life in London is impossible. Our London is gone forever. Our London has been destroyed by the war.

On these days I stop churning for a moment and look out at the lines of rain as they appear horizontal in the sky. I shiver in the damp kitchen. I scold myself. *Remember, June, how lonely you were until you met Robert. Remember how you envied Min her married life. Remember how you longed for a husband too.*

I repeat my farmer's wife's refrain like a prayer. 'I will be a perfect wife. I will be *the* perfect wife. I will be Robert's perfect wife.'

I have always put one hundred per cent into everything I do. Mummy, and maybe even Minerva, thought I would be a dusty spinster for the rest of my life. A classical scholar. A bluestocking. How surprised my mother was to learn that I had met the right match. My Irish English gentleman.

To be perfect is to be without fault or defect, to be perfect is to be complete. Let me tell you a story of imperfection, of a love's incompletion and a wife's undoing. Let me tell you about an adulteress.

It all began when my sister and I were children. How far from the tree does the apple fall? We grew up in Devon in a big white house, overlooking Torbay. What a fearless duo my sister and I were. We were like two little porpoises, splashing in the churning sea, rocked and cradled by the ocean. They were the summers when we were all together as a family. And Daddy would roll us along the beach, line us up saying, 'You two look like peas in a pod.'

Yet it wasn't true. We were the same height and proportion, but how different our colouring and our faces were. And our temperaments. One like Mother, and one like Father. When we were little, Father said we were the image of two angels by Raphael, with our curls – mine fair, Min's dark, but both mops refusing to grow longer than our collars, instead getting thicker and thicker. It used to drive Mother insane, trying to get the brush through our hair every night.

Min and I took it in turns to sit on Father's lap and he would play 'This is the way the farmer rides', and even though you knew what was going to happen, you didn't know *when* until you were dropped through his legs, nearly on the ground, screaming with delight and fear. But Daddy would be holding you in his hands, one in each armpit, as you howled with laughter, helpless, all his.

When I think of my parents, it is Mummy who is the stern one. In my mind's eye she looks like a column of marble, unblemished, beautiful, but too cold to touch, and Daddy is the vine wrapped around her. He needed her. But she didn't want him.

Here in Cavan it can rain all day, but sometimes the skies will clear by evening. A few fragile rays of sunlight attempt to break through the cloud, and the land will glisten magically. It is at this time I might take a walk. I go down to the lake to look at the two swans. Oonagh tells me they arrive every year. The same pair, to mate. Year in, year out, their offspring coming, going, but the pair beholden to each other, monogamous. So it is, animals are quite capable of fidelity, and we humans can act with animal instincts, without a thought for principles. We are capable of this. There is not such a difference between us.

It is five o'clock. Already I can see dark shadows creeping up the fields, swallowing the land. Robert will be back soon. I stand in the yard and I can hardly see any sign of human life at all, just the slate roof of the Sheridens' house, the woods, the fields and the lake in the distance. How the land rolls all the way down to the lake like a green ocean, waves of grass surging in the wind, drizzle like sea spray on my face. When you live somewhere like this, it is hard to imagine there is a war going on. But I do think of it every day. I think of my sister Min in London. I think of Mother.

Yet here in Ireland people appear to ignore the war. Oonagh says the robin hasn't come this year and this is a sign the Germans will invade, yet she doesn't seem too perturbed by this possibility. What most people seem more preoccupied with is the fact that England won't take our beef. Times are pretty hard here, but we are lucky, all the same, to be living in peace. Indeed, we seem to live in a forgotten world in our nook in the country, and it is hard to imagine anything disturbing it. Robert loves the solitude, but for me, I do miss company.

Yesterday Robert finally noticed my low spirits.

'I think we will call on the Tobins this Sunday night,' he announced at dinner. 'Great fun is to be had with the singing and the dancing at their house of an evening.' He smiled at me, his eyes soft caramel, creasing at the corners so that I longed to touch his laughter lines.

'Do they have a piano I could play?'

His eyes widened and he laughed at me, so that I felt like a fool. 'No, of course not, June, these people could hardly afford a piano!' But when he saw the look on my face, he changed his tone. 'Do you miss playing the piano with your sister, darling?'

I nodded, a lump in my throat preventing me from speaking.

'Well,' he sighed, 'the Sheridens have a piano. They have been abroad for a few years, but I heard they were back. Maybe we could call on them as well.' He spoke without enthusiasm, not looking me in the eye.

'That would be wonderful, Robert.' I grabbed his hand and squeezed his fingers.

'There won't be too much to do once it's winter, so we may as well occupy ourselves, and not think of other things.'

I knew he meant Minerva, maybe Mother even, as he spoke. I couldn't reply at all, just nodding again, trying in vain to hold back the tears, and touched by his concern.

Robert let go of my hand and stood up, his back to me, staring out the window. 'The Sheridens are different from most folk around here. She is French, and . . . well . . . a little strange. Phelim is an artist, of sorts.'

'Do they have any children?'

'Just one, a girl, Danielle,' he paused. 'She's your age. But she is married and living in France.'

'So the Sheridens are quite old.'

Robert walked away from me. 'Well, only if you think I am. They're my generation.'

'Oh, darling . . .'

But he left the house to go back to work without looking round, without another word, and I am not sure whether he was offended. Surely not, for he knows it means nothing to me how old he is?

Robert. Are you still out in the fields? Tell me it is true. You have seen him, haven't you? Tilling the land. His sure hand on the plough, walking steadily behind the dapple-grey horse, making drills in the heavy, cloying earth. Back and forth, for evermore.

It is at night I am afraid. I am a ghost afraid of the dark. During the day I forget about time, and I live in the past. I expect any moment to see Robert returning, striding across the fields in his father's coat, rain glistening in his hair like fairy gems, smelling of the earth and hard work. I spend daylight hours imagining I am cooking. The sweet aroma of my country baking soothing me. But at night I remember he does not come. He will never come back and I am lost in my loss. I try not to haunt you, but I am lonely, and sometimes I lie next to you on your bed and give you my dreams. This is what adultery can be – two lonely souls drawn together. This is the first lesson I can teach you.

All that I miss. All that I long for. My family. I remember every night I used to light a candle for Minerva and her husband Charles, praying for them. I wonder will you light a candle for me?

NICHOLAS

Nicholas strikes the match and lights his cigarette. He has not smoked for ten years. He coughs, inhales, coughs again, and then throws it down on the grass and stubs it out with his foot. The cigarette has made him feel sick, so he takes a swig of beer. He is going to drown his sorrows.

Oh God, why can't he get Charlie out of his head? She had slept with someone else and he would never forgive her. He imagines her now. Where is she? He looks at his watch. It is one in the morning. She is probably in bed, but not on her own – no, in bed with someone else. He closes his eyes and sees her naked body and some faceless bastard beneath her, and she is sitting on him. He can see the dimples in the small of her back, and the curve of the side of her breast as she pushes up and down. He can hear her laugh. Nicholas throws his beer bottle and it smashes against the wall of the house. He still wants Charlie and it makes him angry. Just thinking about her fills him with desire. No, he isn't going to let her do this to him, frustrate him. He wants to feel her. He remembers the last time he gave Charlie an orgasm.

'Play me,' she said, 'like you play the piano.'

She told him that his touch was like no other, because of his piano fingers, because of his dexterity.

That night they had made music, you could say, the power of his hands making her sing. But that was nearly a year ago. When had she stopped wanting him to touch her?

Nicholas sees another picture. A different Charlie. She is sitting up in bed, her knees pulled up close to her chest, so that the sheet falls away like snow on a mountain, and she is crying. Her face is red, her eyes swollen and her nose drips. She shivers and she sobs. She looks at him beseechingly, but he turns his back on her and says nothing. He goes to sleep in the spare room. And when he remembers this image, Nicholas knows that it is unlikely Charlie is in bed with another man. She is asleep. And in sleep there is still innocence.

The moon is full, and it is not too cold. Nicholas walks around the house, thinking about the roof and whether he should try to restore it to its original thatch or stay with the slates. It depends on money. The house has cost him nearly all of his savings already. Really he should make Charlie sell Sandycove and split the profit with him, but he can't bring himself to do it, not yet.

He sits down on a ledge, which protrudes from the old stone wall, and looks at the fields that spread out before him, glistening in the moonlight. He doesn't own the fields, and he can see the shadows of cattle, still in the darkness. A bat swoops in front of him, making him start. He doesn't belong here. It is too far away. And yet he doesn't want to go home. The moonlight turns the fields into a meadow of silvery water, the long grasses rippling like waves in the sea. He imagines he sees two girls jumping in the water, and he thinks of Charlie as a little girl, Charlie telling him about her summers in West Cork by the sea, and playing with her sister. How happy she was then. But the picture he sees now is from a different era, like a snapshot from the past, like looking at an old black-and-white movie and the negative has been overpainted in colour. One of the girls runs towards him and he sees quite clearly her face, as if she is real. He blinks and the image is gone.

Nicholas looks down at his hands. They are shaking. He fans them out on his knees, forcing them to be still, palms up to the moonlight, the skin pale, more lines and cuts on them than when he had arrived one month ago. He flicks them over suddenly and gets up, turning back towards the house. He feels pulled by something, someone. He walks through the dark kitchen and into the tiny back room, which is lit by one lamp. His piano takes up the whole room. He opens the lid and sits down on the stool. He stares at the keys. Then he lifts his fingers and begins to play. He doesn't know what he is playing, for he is detached from the notes. All he knows is that his body is swaying and his stiff fingers are racing across the keys, and blood is beginning to pump inside his veins again. He feels like he is awakening from a deep, dreamless sleep.

A finger traces his spine. He stops playing, tenses. The door of the room bangs open and the lamp flickers. Nicholas stands up, spins on his heels.

'Who's there?' he calls out, but he knows the house is empty. A dog barks in the distance, he can hear a cow lowing in the field.

I have only one regret.

The voice is grainy and cracked like a voice from the radio. He gets up from the piano and crosses the room without thinking, the old floorboards creaking. He pulls back the curtain and undoes the latch on the window. The frame is stiff, and wood and paint break off as he pushes it free. As soon as the window swings open, he hears a sigh. And he knows it is not a trick of his mind or even the voice of his ex-wife haunting him, because in an instant he sees a woman standing, looking in. She is slender, boyish almost, with light-brown hair curling about her face in a style from a bygone era, and she wears a pale blue top and skirt that glimmers in the moonlight. She is ephemeral, all shadows, insubstantial, and shifting in the silvery light. She raises her hand to her face as if protecting her eyes from the light in the room. Her gold wedding band sparkles, hypnotizes him. He wonders if he is dreaming and if he will wake up in bed, cocooned in his own miserable loneliness for another long day.

She speaks again and now her voice is quite clear. She has an English accent, posh, distinct, but not haughty.

I have only one regret.

This is the only time Nicholas sees her. It is later that he discovers who she is. But for now he sees a stranger, a fragile lady in blue, a picture from the past, a woman trapped in the memory of one regret, and appealing to him, hoping he will understand. But she has chosen the wrong person, for when she speaks again her words are inside his head and she is invisible.

Let me tell you the story of an adulteress.

Adultery. The word stings him, wounds him. He steps back from the window, shaking, raging inside his skin so that he is blistering, his throat dry with anger. He doesn't want to hear this phantom's tale for he swears he will never understand, let alone forgive, his adulteress wife's betrayal.

JUNE

In the centre of our house is the kitchen. It is large, yet cosy, with an open fire at one end on which I do all the cooking. There are four bedrooms, all small, but perfectly sweet. We only use one of the bedrooms at present. It was Robert's father's room, which I wasn't too keen on as the old man died in the bed, but then it is the largest room, with the nicest view. All the windows are very small in the house, but the largest one is in our room. I suggested we turn one of the empty bedrooms into a parlour, but Robert said there was not much point, as we need to conserve our fuel and we spend most of our time in the kitchen anyway.

Then he smiled at me and, almost blushing, he said, 'We might be needing one of those rooms very shortly . . .'

I looked at him and his expression was questioning, hopeful.

'When we start having a family . . .'

His voice petered out and I nodded hastily, relieved that it is not now at least.

There is no running water in the house, and this is the hardest thing to cope with. It is amazing how one takes for granted turning on a tap, and a lavatory inside, rather than in the stable, so that you can hear the horse right next to you, chomping his straw.

Also we still don't have electricity here. So the nights are blacker than anything, and once it is dark the house becomes full of shadows. There is a shortage of both candles and oil for the lamp, so we have to be very careful about how much we use. Sometimes we just sit by the light of the fire unable to read, or even see each other's face clearly. Just listening to each other breathe. In this darkness I learn to understand my husband through the tone of his voice rather than the expression on his face. The fire makes shapes on the walls. I can't help thinking about Robert's mother and father, and whether their spirits haunt this house.

My favourite place is the loft. It is here I will retreat to when I feel lonely for company, and lie on the bare boards, staring at the thatch, dreaming my mind away. It is like a secret hideaway, and when I am lying under the straw, listening to the wind's hush, I feel cocooned under the eaves of my husband's house, as if I am a little girl again. Here I feel safe.

The place I fear is the orchard. Although it is so close to the house, it is quite a forgotten-about place. Robert told me his father planted it for his mother when she was a bride. It was his gift to her, and indeed their wedding party took place under those trees when it was just an infant orchard full of young slender saplings. Now the trees are ancient, gnarled and unpruned, huddled together in a canopy of old bark, and mottled leaves. There is a foreboding about the place.

I asked Robert why no one uses the orchard. I can see apples on the trees, and littering the ground, and now with the emergency and food shortages it seems criminal not to pick them. He said that his parents hadn't collected the apples for years, not since his brother died in the First World War. Apparently the orchard had been James D.'s domain and he had always made it his business to pick the apples. He made cider out of them or gave them to his mother to cook with. But since the very day James D. died, his parents had not had the heart to touch the orchard. I thought about this – how a mother could be so wounded just by eating an apple, and how the taste of it might have brought back the scent of her son.

When I asked Robert what we should do with the apples, he made excuses. 'I am just so busy with everything else, but we will get round to it, I know it's a disgrace.'

He looked very anxious then, and I felt so sorry for my poor Robert. All of his family are gone. Maybe the orchard is filled with memories for him, too.

Sometimes in the middle of the night, when I have to go out of the house to use the lavatory, I stop in my tracks, hypnotized by the moon throwing light on those old apple trees. In the dark they could be witches and hags watching me. Some are practically bent double. They seem ancient and hostile, old sentinels of the land, reminding me that I am an intruder, and I don't belong here. How silly to feel frightened by an orchard of apple trees!

But Cavan is such a different world to mine. Years of city life are slipping away from me, as if they are old skins, but all the same there is so much I miss. The pictures, for instance, when Min and I sank back into those red velvet seats and entered the world of moving fiction. I imagined I shared the lives of my favourite heroines. I too would some day meet the man of my dreams. How Min and I loved Bette Davis in *Jezebel* – 'half-angel, half-siren, all woman' – and we chanted those words all the way home, arm in arm, so that we alarmed just a few passers-by. We *knew* she must have been wearing a red dress, although the film was in black and white. And we never mentioned her name, but of course we were both thinking of the same person: Mother.

One afternoon I brave the orchard. I am going for a ramble inside the woods, and the only way into them is through the apple trees. I open a little kissing gate, all overgrown and rusty, and there I am in the middle of a jungle of apple trees, loaded with fruit. It is shocking to see such waste. I forget all about my fear of the orchard, or my walk in the woods, and turn tail back to the house.

'Do we have a basket?' I ask Oonagh as I come in the back door.

'What for?' She looks at me curiously.

'For the apples.'

'The apples . . .' she repeats in a whisper, as if I have blasphemed.

'Yes,' I reply, irritated. 'There is a glut of apples in that orchard. It's shameful. We must pick them.'

'The orchard is haunted, Mrs Fanning.'

'Please call me June,' I say to her for what must have been the hundredth time. 'My husband and I do not believe in ghosts.'

She raises her eyebrows. 'No one goes in that orchard.'

'Well, that's ridiculous – the apples are going rotten. We are throwing away food, Oonagh.'

'They say that not one of those apples is good.'

She speaks quietly, but all the same opens a cupboard beside the hearth and takes out a large basket made of rushes.

'All rotten,' she adds, handing me the basket.

But I cannot be dissuaded. I have it in my head now, and in my tastebuds. I am longing to taste apples again. I don't care how tart they are. I want so much to smell them, and touch them, and crunch them between my teeth. It is the most all-consuming craving. Rosy red apples, solid green orbs, crisp, tangy, full of life. I am going to make my husband the most delicious apple pie he has ever eaten. For the first time since I moved to this house I feel happy, because I am going to bake a pie. I remember watching Mother bake, a talent incongruous with her glamorous image. But cooking was my mother's best-kept secret. I close my eyes, and I can picture our kitchen at home in Torquay the winter Mother did all the cooking. There is poor Father in my picture, a crooked smile on his face, his pipe in his hand as he watches Mother whizz around the kitchen in a flurry of flour and spices. Daddy loved my mother when she made him apple pie.

'I have a surprise for you.'

'Oh,' Robert raises his eyebrows, a smile forming on his lips, as I pour him an extremely weak cup of tea from the pot. 'A surprise, you say?'

I nod, so excited I can hardly wait for him to put down his cup.

'I can smell something baking.' He sniffs dramatically.

I kneel down by the hearth and reveal the pie, steaming and fragrant. I pick it up and bear it in my arms as if it is treasure from the pharaohs. Robert's brow furrows.

'What is it?'

'Apple pie,' I announce, 'made with apples from our orchard. There are so many of them, Robert, I spent the whole afternoon picking.'

He looks at me, none too happy, and I think, *Gosh, he doesn't want those apples picked*. But of course he knows what an unreasonable thing that is, especially the way things are with shortages. So all he says is, 'I don't like apples. You know this, June.'

I feel as if he has slapped me, and tears prick my eyes as I set the pie down on the table.

'Will you not have a slice?' My voice wobbles. 'I made it specially for you.'

'I am sorry, dear,' he says icily, 'but apples make me quite sick.'

He gets up, saying he wants to try to tune into the wireless in the back bedroom, find out what is happening with the war. He walks out of the kitchen.

There is my pie steaming on the table, but I have such a lump in my throat that my appetite is completely gone. I stare at my creation, and I cry for all the things I am missing, my sister and the old Robert.

My husband has become so solemn. The war. He is obsessed with news of the war. Why is he concerned with events so far away from us, when I am here, in front of him, needing him? Each day I feel he is becoming more distant. Is he disappointed in me?

Then it dawns on me. If I had placed that hot apple pie in front of him, and then sat down by the fire to nurse his child, he would have eaten it all. Robert would have watched the baby feeding, and cleared his plate, his eyes on mine, full of pride and joy. He would have made himself sick for love of me, the mother of his child.

I clench my fists and sit back in the chair. I push the hair off my face; my cheeks are burning, and not just from cooking. I look at my beautiful pie, and then I pick up the knife and dig it in, watching the apple heat spurt out. I slide a huge slice onto my plate.

I eat slowly, a quarter, and then another quarter of the pie, but I am not tasting it. The light pastry, the soft sweet innards of the pie are lost on me. I still keep eating, all the while staring out of the window. It is quite dark now, and a single candle flickers on the table, while the lamp remains unlit. I sit in a pool of moonlight, watching a giant harvest moon ripen. I do not notice when I am full because my anger makes me want to go on and on. As if I am somehow being defiant.

I eat that whole pie. I eat the whole damn thing. And when I am finished I sit as still as one of those ghostly apple trees lit up by the moon, my stomach groaning, and bloated, as if I really am pregnant.

NICHOLAS

He is lucid in his nightmare when he sees the Adulteress look at him, her legs wrapped around her lover. Her honey eyes turn as cold and grey as clay, for he is the husband who is no longer a lover like this man can be for this wife. Nicholas watches her with her lover, sees the changing landscape of her face, open skies, gentle rain, loving waters, nature itself, expecting no more than what can be given in each moment. The wind rattles the window, branches claw at the glass, and all the dark spirits of jealousy clamour to enter the bedroom.

Nicholas wakes wet, sweltering, sobbing, and feels as if he is dying. He sits up in bed, trying to slow down his breath, pressing his hand to his chest. He listens to the wind's lamentation outside the house, shaking the blossom off the apple trees in the orchard. He remembers his mother telling him that a storm always heralds a new death. Could lost love kill him?

In his murky bedroom Nicholas feels the depths of his anger, and it frightens him. He presses his arms against his body, holding his elbows with his hands, trying to stop himself from shaking. Gradually he sees a light, a fragile radiance emerging from the shadowy corner by the window. He lies back against the pillow, and it comes towards him, gleams above him, a translucent haze. He shivers, and yet this light is a comfort. He imagines he can feel a hand brush his

26

cheek, tiny fingertips like a child's following the contours of his face. The fingertips press down on his eyelids and he drifts back into a dream-filled sleep.

When he wakes in the morning Nicholas doesn't feel so lonely. The duvet is not wound around him tightly like usual, but spread across the whole width of the bed as if he had a partner sharing it with him. He remembers his dreams and they were strange. The ghostly woman he had seen outside the window was lying next to him and speaking softly in his ear. *I miss, I miss, I miss,* she whispered, and he cried back. 'What? What is it that you've lost?' But she shook her head dolefully and faded away.

Nicholas is hungry. He gets up and goes into the kitchen. The fridge is empty apart from milk and eggs, so he makes a huge omelette with all four of them. He sits down at the table, chewing his golden eggs and looking out the window. The sun is shining and pink blossom is out on two cherry trees in the front of the house. He picks up his plate and steps out the front door, sitting on an old rickety chair he was going to chop up for firewood. In Dublin he had never really noticed the seasons changing, but here summer is bursting all around him. The air smells good, and he feels optimistic about his renovation project. Yes, it will take a while, but when he is finished his home will be perfect. Just how he wants it. He imagines keeping bees and making honey, and then he starts to think about the apples. He gets up and walks through the little gate into the orchard.

The trees haven't been pruned in years. Some branches are bowed so far over they appear to be growing back into the ground. But some of the younger trees look healthier. He wonders if he will get many apples this year, enough to make cider even. He could travel around to those farmers' markets with his cider and sell it.

He picks some white blossom up off the ground and fingers it. He thinks again of the strange woman of his dreams. The phantom spirit from the past. Maybe he should get the place exorcised or something, but in truth he doesn't mind. Is he so pathetically lonely that he enjoys the company of a ghost? This makes him laugh. He realizes it is the first time he has laughed out loud since he came here. He stops laughing and kicks the ground. Charlie took away his happiness. Why would he ever want to laugh again?

Nicholas strides back into his house, banishing his ex-wife from his mind and instead filling his head with plans. He could make this place work for him: honey, cider, piano lessons. He likes the idea of living simply. He turns the kettle on to make coffee. He can smell something baking. He opens the oven, but it isn't on and it's empty. He opens all the cupboards. They're empty, but still he can smell it. He steps into the yard, but it's not coming from outside. He goes back into the kitchen and the smell is stronger than ever. He feels a wave of astonishment. Either he is going mad or his ghost has been cooking. He sniffs again, and the aroma makes his tummy rumble. It is his favourite pudding. She has baked him an apple pie.

He taps the kitchen table with his fingers, playing 'Clair de lune' on the mottled wood. The aroma of baked apples swells around him and again he is pulled towards his piano in the back room. He tries to remain in the real world, but something else seizes him, an urge to be part of a story, even if it isn't his own.

He sits down at his piano and he can feel her arms about his chest, squeezing him, as if his heart is an accordion and she demands music from his pain. His hands are shaking, but slowly he places his fingers on the piano keys. He plays her 'Clair de lune' like he used to do for Charlie, and yet he has never played it like this before. Each note is torn from him as if he made them himself from his very own lost love. As Nicholas plays, he decides he will find out who she is, and what happened to her. He wants to know the tale of the Adulteress because he wants to understand.

JUNE

Today when I wake I feel quite terrible. Not surprising, since I ate a whole apple pie before I went to bed. My head is pounding, and I only just make it across the yard to the lavatory in time to be sick. I am as weak as a puppy. I manage to clamber back into bed, and lie quite still in an attempt to quell the nausea swirling around my stomach. It is only just beginning to get light, but Robert is awake. He will soon be up and gone for the day. The thought of this makes me feel even worse. He always goes out to work early and it never bothered me before, but this particular day I do not want to be alone, with all my chores laid out in front of me, stretching endlessly into dusk.

'Are you all right, darling?' Robert is looking at me.

'I do feel rather peaky.'

'Have you been sick?'

I nod, tears pricking my eyes.

'Now don't be such a silly old thing.' Smiling softly he adds, 'I am sure it is only all that pie you ate.'

I cast my eyes down, ashamed of my greed, when I could have given the pie to the Tobins.

He makes to get up, and pull on his trousers. I lean over and tug at his hand.

'Robert, please stay with me today.'

'What on earth is the matter?'

His eyes scrutinize me. In the morning light they look almost ginger, and striped, like the coat of a marmalade cat.

'Please, darling, can we spend the day together?'

I feel such a deep need, like a child every time your mother leaves you after blowing out the candle and you are left lying in the dark. You pray she will return, and hold you until you fall asleep, but she never does.

Robert surprises me. Bending down and pushing the hair out of my eyes, he speaks so very politely, the way he used to do in London when we first met.

'It was very selfish of me to marry you.'

'What do you mean?' My cheeks colour in confusion.

He cups my face with his hands, and kisses me on the lips. 'I suppose I can get up a little later for once,' he says, ignoring my question, turning his eyes away from mine and, climbing back under the covers, he takes me into his arms. I nuzzle up to him and let him cradle me, his long legs tucking me up next to him. Immediately I no longer feel sick, and with his hands on my belly I drift off to sleep.

When I wake the room is cascading with golden light, the walls dappled with reflections from leaves outside. I can hear the wind washing through the trees. Robert is kissing me. I turn, and he holds me by the shoulders.

'Can we try to make a baby?'

He asks me so sweetly. In his eyes I can see the boy he once was. I nod.

He kisses me again, all the while undoing his underclothes and helping me take off mine. I close my eyes, and my husband puts himself inside me. He is so quiet, and gentle, and steady. It is like being lapped by the ocean.

Afterwards is always the best. Robert holds me in his arms and closes his eyes, dreaming of goodness knows what. I look at him, trace each line on his face, count the grey hairs in his thick black hair, and wonder what our child would look like if we were to have one. But it is a fantasy, because it is so long since we have been trying that I cannot imagine actually having a baby now.

'I love you,' I whisper into his ear, which is surprisingly small and dainty for such a big man.

He mumbles softly and goes back to sleep.

By the time we rise it is terribly late, and Robert hurries out to milk the cows. I prepare the dinner. I am glad Oonagh isn't here today. It is just the two of us. For once I feel contented to be in my Cavan home. I look at a miracle rainbow arching the wet land in the distance, and smell the scent of turf fire spinning out of the top of the chimney. Robert returns to the house for dinner, but after we have finished eating, instead of going back out to the animals, he leans across the table and takes my hand.

'Let's pick the rest of those apples,' he says, pressing his thumb into the soft flesh of my palm.

'Are you sure you want to?' I glance nervously out of the window, across the yard, towards the tangled orchard.

'Absolutely.'

As we approach the apple trees, I feel his body stiffen next to mine. I know he doesn't want to pick those apples, but he is forcing himself to make me happy. That is enough for me and, taking his hand in mine, I turn to him.

'There are plums, over there,' I point. 'Will we pick those instead?'

'Yes, that's a wonderful idea,' he says gratefully. 'You can make jam.'

I close my eyes now and all I can see is purple. It is a sea of regal, promiscuous, empress purple, wound around my hand, bandaging my eyes, enfolding me in its rich, sensuous shades.

We eat and we pick, and while we do all this, we stroke each other, on the backs of our hands, our shoulders, the smalls of each other's back, making lovers' imprints with our palms. Our lips are magenta, and our fingers stained indigo from our labours, but we are happy about this. Our markings make us one, united, together in the work our marriage makes. I think of Mother and Father and how I never saw them do anything together, not once. I am determined Robert and I will succeed.

When I was a little girl I was frightened of my mother, and I adored my father. I did not understand how he could love my mother, for she was often angry and cruel to my sister and I. I remember one time in particular. Min and I had gone down to look at the sea, just look, but of course we had got carried away as usual. Mother was there waiting for us on the front lawn as we came scampering back up the garden.

'Look at the pair of you,' she cried out, the perfect mirage of her face cracking with anger.

I spoke quickly, 'Mother, I'm sorry . . .'

But Min interrupted me, 'We were racing on the beach.'

There was no apology in her tone, no explanation, and now it was too late for me to tell the neat lie I had created in my head. We had slipped down a dune, while looking for shells, to make a necklace for her – for her, our beautiful, imperious mother.

Mother's lips twitched and she hissed, 'You are not boys, you are girls, and girls don't race.'

I remember the fear, the pain of this dreadful anticipation. Who will she choose? But I knew deep down that I would not be the victim. I never was. It felt like the most awful treachery, never to be chosen.

'Why not?' Min's voice rang out clear as the sparkling sunlight, insolent and challenging. Immediately afterwards there was the

32

sharp sound of Mother's hand, slapping my sister's cheek. I winced, although my sister stood rigid, with heat in her bones. I could feel her ire.

'Miss Sinclair, you are a dreadful creature.'

Mother always adopted this formal tone when she was angry with us, and always spoke to my sister directly, never to me. It was as if I was invisible.

'And a liar too,' Mother added. 'A simple race on the sand would not reduce you to that state. It looks to me as if you were in a rugby scrum! For goodness' sake, we have people coming to tea!'

Min was shaking beside me, but she was not crying, she was laughing. Mother slapped her again, but it only made Min worse.

'Stop it!' Mother shouted, 'stop it!'

My mouth was dry with fear.

'Mummy, please, we're sorry,' I begged, beginning to cry, as if it was I who was being hit, not my sister, so fearless, her eyes dark with pride and rage. But Mother ignored me.

'Stop laughing at me this instant.'

She raised her arm high, as if she was about to serve in a game of tennis, but there was no racquet in her hand, just her rings on her spread fingers, glittering in the afternoon sun. She was wearing a printed chiffon afternoon dress in shades of pink, its waist dropped to the hips and detailed with a black satin bow, collar, cuffs and hem. The skirt rose to just above the knees to reveal her slim legs in flesh-coloured stockings, and tiny ankles and feet in a pair of black patent-leather pointed shoes. Her dark, glossy hair was cut short, as was the current fashion, and her fine face was framed by a black silk hat, with a red velvet ribbon.

When I compare my mother to other mothers, I realize how very different she was. She had the perfect form, and was still able to wear the clothes she wore as a young bride (although she never would, of course). Mother's knowledge of fashion was encyclopaedic. Her desire to be in the latest season's clothes was her only passion – that and the attention of other people's husbands. But even if Mother had worn an old sackcloth, and was twice the size, she would still be stunning, for it was her charming visage that stopped most people, men and women alike, in their tracks. Arched brows, long lashes and crystal-blue eyes, a small fine nose and rosebud lips. Her skin was pale and creamy, and her hair was jet-black. She was created for adoration.

At that time it was as if she always despised us. Her daughters were reminders of her age and the frailty of all her desires. As we got older it got worse, for our breasts were beginning to bud, and it was apparent that one of us had inherited her looks, although one of us had not.

The hand came down, and later Min claimed it had not hurt, not one bit. But there was still a red mark on her face even then, and surely it had, because even though Mother was small, she was strong and had sent my sister flying across the grass.

Mother took a step back, shocked at her own actions. I could hear the bell ring inside the house and knew the guests had arrived. It was another world, all neat and clean, and nice manners. Out here on the sunny lawn was high drama.

Mother walked over to Min, her tiny ankles and slim legs mesmerizing, and I marvelled at how gracefully she bent down so that you might feel sorry for her, not my hurt sister, flung to the ground.

'Are you all right?' she asked her daughter.

Min sat up, rubbing her chin. 'I'm fine,' she replied brightly. 'I suppose I deserved it.'

Mother pulled Min up by the wrists, dusted her down. 'I'm sorry, darling, but just look at what you did to those new dresses I ordered for you both. And it's the Sandersons coming to tea, and you know how Daddy likes to impress Captain Sanderson.'

I looked over at the house, the study window dark against the sunlight, but I knew my father was sitting there, looking at us, indifferent to Captain Sanderson's arrival, ignoring my mother's behaviour.

Mother took Min's hand and squeezed it in her own, and they began walking briskly towards the house. I stood, willing my father to open the window, shout out at Mother, tell her she was being a tyrant. But nothing happened and in the end I trotted up the lawn behind my mother and Min, their arms linked. I knew what Mother was trying to do. It made me feel sick, and I dreaded the forth-coming tea, the sly asides at my expense and the praise of Min. She was trying to split us, but she never would, not ever.

The lawn rose in a slight incline as we approached the veranda, and I tripped as I hurried behind them, only just managing to regain my balance without falling onto the gravel. Mother noticed.

'Clumsy foot!' Her voice rang out, soft and mocking, and Min turned round, and giggled at me. I forgave her though, for Min had taken my punishment for me, had she not?

All summer long we had to endure tea on the lawn with this young gentleman or that, prospective husbands that my mother had selected for us. She would flirt with the fathers, the mothers rigid with disapproval, and our father was sometimes there, sometimes not, but so distracted it hardly mattered. There was my sixteenth birthday and yet another tea party with the Sandersons. That was the afternoon when the seeds were sown for all the bad things that would happen to my family.

It was a sweltering June day, and there was nothing I would have rather done than gone down to the beach with Min, and swim in the sea. We could even have begged Mrs Wyatt to give us a small basket filled with egg sandwiches, two small bottles of her tart lemonade and a slice of fruitcake each. It would have made the perfect birthday afternoon. Just the two of us, lying on the sand, tickling each other's toes and talking about our dreams for the future. But Mother interfered and told me that my sixteenth birthday meant I was grown-up now, too old to be building sandcastles, the right age to get used to polite society. Min thought it hilarious that Mother would describe the Sandersons as 'polite society', but Mother's attention made me nervous. I was bound to disappoint.

For the special occasion of my sixteenth birthday Mother had decided to buy me a new dress, which had given her an excuse to go into town and spend an afternoon in Hooper's admiring her own reflection in the new season's fashions. She announced that with the advent of the Thirties there was, thank goodness, a return to more feminine contours: a normal waistline, a lowering of the hem, curlier hair and more attractive hats. All of these trends Mother had adopted.

'It's important,' she said to us, 'for the matriarch always to look smart and up to the minute.'

Min smirked in the corner. 'But, Mother,' she said sarcastically, 'there would never be any fear of it being otherwise.'

Mother sniffed, and turned her attention to the dress she had chosen for me. 'Yes, that will do.'

I looked at my reflection in the mirror of the dressing room, and out of the corner of my eye I could see the assistant's unsure expression, Min's hand over her mouth and Mother's stern face.

'Oh, June!' Min blurted out, 'you do look a sight!'

The dress was buttercup-yellow with a bright-orange print, shades that looked fabulous on my raven-haired mother and would, next year, look equally super on Min, but were not suited to my complexion, not at all. I have the colouring of my father, light-brown hair, pale skin and ginger freckles spattered across the bridge of my nose. My best features are my eyes, which are the only thing I inherited in looks from my mother. I opened them wide in that dressing room in Hooper's, staring in horror at the vision of myself in the tight yellow dress.

'Mummy, I think it is too small.'

'Not at all. You just need to eat a little less. You've put on far too much weight recently.'

It was true that for the first time in our lives I was larger than Min. I spent as much time as possible reading, with secret supplies of Mrs Wyatt's ginger cake in my pockets, whereas Min had no interest in books or cake, but liked to roam outside, picking up tiny blue birds' eggs, shells from the shore, leaves and stones, which she would bring back to the house and draw. All the same, it was not so much my waist as my chest that was too large for the dress. It was the only part of my anatomy that I believe my mother may have envied.

'You need to keep covered up,' Mother warned me. 'A bosom of your proportions, if revealed even to a tiny extent, will give a man the wrong idea.'

But I had seen the flash in my mother's eyes as she glanced at my bust, sensed her irritation, and it pleased me slightly. Now she had done her best to make one of my only assets look its worst by squeezing me into a garish, georgette dress, with a very fussy bow at the front and a high collar, which strained at the seams every time I sat down.

'Mother, I don't think this dress suits me at all.'

But she ignored me, a cerise crêpe evening dress for herself already being packaged by the assistant, its price three times that of my dress.

The only item my mother bought me that I liked was a pair of cream kid gloves. These did make me feel sophisticated. They were incredibly soft, and felt like a protective second skin. My mother was a huge fan of gloves. She described them as possibly the most erotic part of a woman's wardrobe. For to peel them away was to reveal the most delicate part of a lady's anatomy, her tiny hands. With gloves you could remain mysterious, for who was to know whether the lady was married or not?

I stood for an age in my underwear, looking out of my bedroom window at the perfectly blue sky, the seagulls wheeling about, the dress lying on a chair next to me, wishing I could be free like those birds.

Min came into the room. 'Come on, Juno, everyone is waiting.'

'Oh, what the hell, it's only the Sandersons.' I grabbed the dress and pulled it on over my head.

Min helped me with the buttons at the back. 'Poor you,' she said. 'How is it our mother doesn't have a maternal bone in her body?'

I knew exactly what she meant, for what mother would wilfully try to make her daughter look like a fool?

What made wearing the dress even worse was that it was such a hot day. The yellow material clung to my sticky body, and the high neck made me feel even more choked. I longed to rip it off and sit under the weeping willow tree, fanning myself with its long green fronds, dressed solely in a cool cotton petticoat. It had taken me so long to get ready, so much time begging Mother to be allowed to wear something else – anything else – that by the time I was walking across the lawn to the tea table the rest of the company were already seated.

Horror of horrors, there was a stranger at the table; and not only that, but he was a boy! I stumbled forward, aware I was perspiring, and the panic of this making me redden. Min had gone on ahead and was sitting on the chair closest to me, her black hair tied back loosely with a pink ribbon, dressed in a plain white linen dress. She looked up at me sympathetically.

'Well, I was wondering what happened to the birthday girl!' said Father, standing up and pulling out a chair for me. 'Happy birthday, darling.' He handed me a small, neat package, which I knew instantly was a book, and my fear and embarrassment melted away.

'Oh, thank you,' I said, to my dear sweet father.

I knew what it was. He had promised it to me months ago. *Myths and Legends of Greece and Rome*, an edition all of my own. It was my grandfather's book, published in 1880, and illustrated with engravings from antique sculptures. Suddenly the silly yellow and orange dress was forgotten about, and all I could think of was getting back to my bedroom to open the package up and start reading it, all over again, like revisiting an old friend.

My mother's voice broke through my thoughts. 'June . . . June . . . you haven't said hello to our guests.'

Captain Sanderson leaned forward and shook my hand. 'Happy birthday, young lady.'

He was so very tall he nearly blocked out the sun. Min called him Prince Charming because he was dashing, and handsome, with a fine moustache and chestnut-brown eyes. He was also young, much younger than his wife, who was a quiet, dumpy woman, completely in awe of Mother. She nodded at me now, and wished me a happy birthday.

'This is Meryl and Charles's nephew, and he is called Charles as well,' said Mother. 'So it will be a very confusing afternoon,' she twittered.

Charles Junior extended his hand and shook mine firmly.

'Charles is about to follow in his uncle's illustrious footsteps and join up,' said Mother.

'The navy, rather than the army,' Captain Sanderson interrupted.

'I hope I can live up to my uncle's fine reputation,' Charles Junior said earnestly, glancing curiously at Min, as she raised a hand to hide the smile that spread across her face.

'Well,' Captain Sanderson said, dramatically slapping his left thigh, 'unfortunately I didn't have the chance to serve my country for long.'

Every time they came to tea, Captain Sanderson's war story was brought up. His grim experience in the cavalry, and how he was only three weeks at war in Belgium when he was thrown off his horse in combat, and was lucky to survive with his leg still attached to his body.

'I'm no good to anyone now,' he said, looking at Mother.

'Oh, that's just silly, dear Charles,' she replied, patting his wife's knee. 'You wouldn't be without him, would you, Meryl?'

Mother looked magnificent, completely outshining poor Mrs Sanderson. She wore a new Chanel dress with a matching bolero jacket, a striped sash and a small hat in the same material tilted on the side of her head. The overall effect was fresh and sporty, while at the same time remaining ladylike. On her hands were, of course, a pair of cream gloves. I watched Captain Sanderson ogling her; even Charles Junior could not keep his eyes off her. It was funny how Father never seemed to notice.

Mrs Wyatt appeared with the tea, and because it was my birthday she had made my favourite cake – apple sponge, even though apples weren't in season yet. She must have used some of the precious hoard, stored in straw in the cellar since last winter.

'Quite delicious,' said Father, cutting another slice of cake. 'Quite, quite delicious.'

We sat back in our chairs, bathing in the bright sunshine, and for a moment everyone was quiet.

'June, open up that present, will you?' Father asked impatiently.

'All right.' I ripped off the paper to reveal just what I had hoped for.

'*Myths and Legends of Greece and Rome*,' Captain Sanderson read as he leaned over and took the book out of my hand. I was annoyed, but said nothing, sitting demurely with my hands in my lap.

Mother sighed. 'How boring,' she said. 'I would think a girl of your age would rather have a novel of some sort.'

'Oh, I don't know,' said Captain Sanderson. 'I loathed Latin at school, but I did enjoy hearing all about the wrangles of the gods and goddesses – lots of passion there.' He chortled. 'And so very different from our religion.'

'They are a reflection of our humanity,' Father spoke up. 'Everything the gods and goddesses did, or said, was a way of illustrating man's condition to the Ancients.'

'Whatever you say, old man,' Captain Sanderson said, but Father was not to be put off. I could see his eyes sparkling behind his glasses. He was the most animated I had seen him in weeks.

'Their stories can make us think of all our human foibles, in particular our moral dilemmas. It is the exact opposite of our Christian religion, which tries to suppress the human experience.'

Yes, that is just so, I thought, but I did not speak up and neither did anyone else. There was a pause. Mrs Sanderson coughed, and Mother picked up the pot, offering more tea.

My birthday always heralded the beginning of the summer holidays, when Min and I were at our most euphoric, for we faced day after day of freedom. Although we had schoolfriends aplenty, neither of us was fond of boarding school. But Father had high hopes, although Mother said a governess at home would do. He wanted his daughters to be pioneers in academia. He wanted his world of ancient ruins, dead tongues and pagan glories to live on through his offspring.

But my sister Minerva, despite her name, had no interest in ancient history. She lived in the present. Her only interest in the past was inspired by art, her favourite painter Delacroix, and music, her great love, Strauss. Min refused to be weighed down by Father's obsession, and many times, while I had my nose firmly in a book – I was spending the summer reading Virgil's *Aeneid* upon Father's instructions – Min appealed to me to come and dance in the garden, catch the sunlight through our fingers, accompany her on the piano while she sang, and abandon my studies. It was hard for me to refuse my pretty, dark sister's entreaties, but burning inside me – shy, plain June – was ambition, which had nothing to do with the things I talked to Min about. I wanted to go to university, and spend my life studying the Romans. This was how I felt when I was sixteen. Min, however, was a romantic, and although a year younger than me she was far more interested in boys.

'What did you think of Charles Junior?' she asked me, that night after the birthday tea.

We were both squeezed together on the windowsill, our feet hanging over the edge and dangling in the wisteria. It was so thick and high we were hidden from the road, and were able to watch people passing by, going in and out of other houses, sitting or working in their gardens. In the distance we could see the lights of Torbay winking at us, and imagine the inky sea, its promise of somewhere else other than home. To sit on the windowsill was a favourite hobby of ours since we were little. 'Spying on the neighbours,' Min called it.

'Oh, Charles, he was all right, I suppose,' I replied reluctantly.

'Not for you then, Juno?' Min swung her feet backwards and forwards. 'Now you're sweet sixteen, Mummy will want you married off as soon as possible so that she can save on the school fees, get herself a fur this year.'

'She's not that bad, Min.'

I shuddered at the idea of being married. To have a husband, and to have to sleep in the same bed as him, horrified me. Actually I did like Charles Junior, but he had hardly noticed me. What was the point of even thinking about him, when he was, quite obviously, smitten with Min? He was a boy who wanted a beauty. Maybe one day I would meet someone like Father – a great mind whom I could admire – and help in his work.

'But just think, if you were married you would have your own money, and you could have your own house, and never have to see Mother again, ever, if you wanted to,' Min said.

'Is that how you feel, honestly?' I looked at my sister. Min remained staring ahead, her profile reminding me of a drawing of a Red Indian I had seen in one of my history books. Everything was perfectly straight: her forehead, and nose, her fine cheekbones, and her neat lips pressed together. Her black hair was loose, her baby curls had turned into languorous waves, which fell straight and then swept her shoulders.

'Oh, look,' she said pointing, 'there's Mrs Webster going off out, all dressed up to the nines, I wonder where she can be going.'

'Min, do you really want to get married so young?'

'Of course I do. I want to fall madly in love – that's what artists do best, apart from paint.'

'Oh, you are silly.' I put my arm around my sister's narrow shoulders.

'It's different for you,' said Min, looking intently at me. She was smiling, but her eyes were black, hard. 'Mother doesn't actually hate you.'

'But she doesn't hate you, either.'

'Yes, she does.' Min leaned forward and plucked a tendril of buds out of the wisteria.

'Of course Mummy loves you, Min. She adores it when you sing, and she loves your paintings. She is always praising you.'

'I suppose,' said Min, pushing wisteria through her bare toes. It was a warm night, with no breeze. I thought of the indigo sea, heavy beneath the night sky, thick as treacle, but deliciously cool. I shifted my hot legs.

'I can't bear to get into bed,' I said listlessly.

'Imagine being married.' Min's eyes were twinkling, her mood less serious. 'I wonder what *it* is like . . .'

'Oh, I don't know. Vivien said it can hurt, and that it's awfully messy—'

'Oh, stuff Vivien. What does she know! I can't wait to be kissed properly and to touch—'

'Oh, do stop,' I interrupted, irritated. I didn't want to think about being kissed, or touching or being touched. I wriggled on the windowsill, bringing my knees up and hugging them. I wanted to stay where I was, firmly planted in the past.

'Do you remember that time we saw Mr Gregory?' Min whispered.

'Of course I do!'

It had been on a similar night to this, two summers ago, when we had watched our neighbour across the street taking a bath. It was like a strange vaudeville show. His curtains open, the bare light bulb on, and the silhouette of this middle-aged man, naked, climbing into the bath. We had convulsed in giggles, holding onto each other and nearly falling through the wisteria onto the veranda. But deep down inside I had been appalled at our voyeurism, and shocked at what I had seen. I had always wondered: did Mr Gregory know we were spying on him?

Min loved bringing the story up, talking about the size of his thing, and did I think it was average, or big? I didn't like to think about it at all. Yet I could never forget what it looked like, and it seemed strange that this body part belonged to half the population, yet was something I had never seen before. It was a secret to all the girls I knew.

'Come on,' said Min clambering back into the bedroom. 'I'll draw you.'

She turned on a lamp, and pulled her sketchbook and pencils out from under the bed.

'Oh, do we have to?' I moaned, turning round and sliding into the room off the sill.

'It's so hot we can't sleep anyway – please, Juno.'

'All right, but can I read?'

'I suppose so. Sit in front of the window, that's it. I think I'll make a painting of this, put the wisteria in behind you.'

I sat facing into the room, Virgil's epic spread on my lap. Min came over and arranged my hair.

'Dear Juno,' she whispered, carefully curling my hair around her ring finger. 'I will marry young, you know, and have lots of children, lots and lots, and *all* of them I'll love.'

THE ADULTERESS I

He is stabbing her. She lies on the bed, her arms outstretched, cru-
cified, her fingers curled around the cold, metal bed-frame, and
licks his breath off her lips.

It feels like a wound, the way she seeks him. It comes beyond
her will, this desire. The agony of her need has ripped away all her
decency. She is living by her instinct, her resolution in tatters.

She releases her fingers, and suddenly grips his shoulders, pale
and gleaming in the half-light of early evening. He lifts his bent
head, and smiles. Her accomplice. He reaches down, neither gentle
nor rough in his movements, but with authority, for she has given
that to him, has she not?

Her lover puts his arms behind her back and pulls her up to greet
him. He takes her in. And his hips move in unison with hers, stabbing, deeper, deeper, so that they are no longer a mere man and a
woman, but one writhing entity, showering bedclothes about them.

She closes her eyes, suddenly reminded of a scene from her
childhood. She is racing along the beach with her sister. She
remembers the sensation of their flesh smacking together as they
fall in a tumble on the sand. They are fighting and loving, all at the
same time. Two lonely girls, fierce in their loyalty to one another,
and fierce in their competition. Who had won the race? She cannot
remember now, nor can she think which of them pulled the other

down so that she would not be beaten. The chase was forgotten, became an intimate scrum along the beach, not caring about how they were scratching their limbs, and tearing their clothes, not caring about the sand in their mouths, as they kept spitting it out. She believed she loved her sister more than any other human being on the earth, and she her.

The Adulteress always feels as if her husband is wearing kid gloves when he touches her. She is often surprised when she looks down to see his bare hands, as they tentatively dab at her skin. He looks at her as if she is a miracle, yet her lover always looks her straight in the eye.

She paints a picture in her head. The sparkling sun showering a crowd of jostling children dancing at the edge of the sea, splashed by the waves, the summer light casting bright haloes about the children's heads. They are excited and noisy, for they are waiting for their fathers' boats to come in. It is a moment of pure innocence and joy. It is the sensation of her lover's flesh tipping her inside.

The blustery seaside day spills out of her mind, illuminating her lover's studio. On the beach there are no shadows. The sea is clear and full of life, the sky is wide and open, yet here in his den she has never looked into all the corners. Cobwebs hang between the ceiling and picture rail, and the window is grubby with green mildew.

Her lover lies on top of her, and his weight pushes her down into the soft mattress. She can smell how old it is. She wonders how many souls it has held in suspense. She tries to look away as he lifts a strand of hair out of her eyes.

Why are you crying? he asks, his eyes amber in the near-dark, his hand cupping her chin.

She shakes her head, unable to stop. She imagines how they look from above, lying in their tangled lovers' heap. They are art.

JUNE

When one walks one notices the detail in everything. Maybe this is why I miss cars. I am unable to turn a blind eye to my new environment. Walking to Mass, I cannot ignore it. Right here, in front of my nose, is glaring poverty. Barefoot children, and people with nothing at all, and I can't help thinking about all the hard times this nation has been through and how, in the main, my country is responsible. It is strange this is something Robert and I have never discussed before.

Robert even sounds *more* Irish here. In England his accent was hard to discern. Indeed, Min had to tell me he was Irish. Now, among the people of his youth, he is becoming more and more unmistakably an Irishman. I had not realized before how very proud he is of his country. My husband is a chameleon, and it is hard to imagine him and Charles together, the latter being such a quintessential English gentleman. But that is what I thought Robert was too . . .

None of our neighbours are concerned about an invasion. They are more afraid of bombs dropping on us by mistake. After what happened in Belfast, and Dublin, we all dread the sound of the terrible drone of the bombers passing overhead, echoing down the chimney into the kitchen. On those rare nights it is as if we are all frozen into a tableau. We are a Dutch interior, dark corners, small windows, and bare plastered walls reflecting light onto our pale faces. The men at the table stiffen, gripping their cards tightly in their hands, while we women breathe shallowly in the stillness, our fingers suspended above our crochet, needles poking out at angles.

At these moments I survey our company as if from above, like the ghosts of Robert's parents. The lovely Tobins who sit about our kitchen, so good and kind to us, and generous in everything they have. Yet although Oonagh chats away to me, and her sister, Teresa, asks me questions about the films I have seen, and sometimes gets me to practically re-enact the whole story, I also have to be careful what I say. In private I am sure the Tobins wonder how Robert came to be with me. I once overheard Sean Tobin teasing Robert that he seemed to have returned home with the very Queen of England as his wife. But I am no more royalty then anyone else in our kitchen. The women think me grand, but I cannot help the way I talk.

Things weren't so easy for us, either. Maybe it is worse to have a lot, and then lose it. Mummy was constantly struggling to keep up appearances, and poor Daddy never knew quite how to provide for his family.

'Education, that's the key to your future, girls,' he kept telling Min and I. He never wanted us to be dependent upon a husband, like Mummy, expecting him to fulfil her life materially, and more besides. At that time I do not think she would have been happy even if he had been a duke who owned half of England. Who would think that, years later, she would change to such an extent?

October ends and, with it, the incessant rain. At last the grey blanket has been lifted from the sky. Late autumn brings dramatic displays of light. The clouds are now purple, ringed by the frustrated sun, shooting through the woods like golden arrows into the earth. It looks like a storm might break at any moment, and yet it has not rained for one whole week. The earth is no longer boggy, but soft and springy, covered in carpets of verdant green moss. In London all seasons were the same, but here I can even smell the difference. Ireland's scent is bred from the earth, as if she cannot quite leave go of it, like a child clinging to her mother. There are rainbows nearly every day, arching the landscape, making me truly wonder whether this really is the place fairies come from.

Oonagh has plenty of stories for me about the fairies – none of them seem too nice, not the sweet sugar-plum fairy variety of my childhood imaginings. The one she says most are afraid of is the pooka. He most often appears as a sleek dark horse with sulphurous yellow eyes and a wild mane. He roams the countryside tearing down fences and gates, scattering livestock in terror, trampling crops and doing all sorts of terrible things to farmers.

It is the pooka that has brought the foot-and-mouth. He lives on top of the mountains and no one goes there. He is a restless, troubled spirit, endlessly moving, galloping up and down slopes, his hooves split, his whinny shrill. Is he the wild voice of the landscape, angry at our humble interference?

Someone in some small part of Ireland did not do enough to placate him, and the pooka has spread sickness among the livestock, destroyed the fragile livelihood of countless farmers throughout the country. Now no one wants Irish cattle. We are lucky in Cavan. The disease has not spread here yet, and the local defence force is out on all the bridges, trying to stop it entering this corner of the county. It seems that, to the Irish, this is more serious than a possible invasion by the Germans.

I would like to think these fairy stories are humbug. Are they not just a different kind of mythology from my own preferred Greek and Roman gods? I have heard neighbours in our kitchen speak regularly of encounters. They are ordinary people, without a need for drama in their lives. It does leave me wondering.

When I go walking in the woods it is easy to believe in such things. It is as if I am inside a painting and, if I ripped through the canvas, there would be another world on the other side, where I could see spirits as translucent as dragonfly wings, hovering above the bogs, waiting for me to slip in. I am not sure whether they are benevolent or not.

It has become a daily ritual for me, this walk in the small woods between our house and the Sheridens'. Although Robert promised we would visit our neighbours, we still have not done so. I miss my music so much. It is not just that I yearn to play. I want to listen as well. But Robert is wrapped up in the foot-and-mouth crisis, and my needs seem frivolous.

Today I saw Mrs Sheriden walking in the woods. I am so used to being on my own that I almost cried out with fright when I saw another person. It was getting dark, and since Robert was not back yet, I nipped out before it was time for tea. My hands were sore from the churning, and I longed so much just to push them into the damp moss, as soft as plush velvet. I was crouching down by a small pool, doing just this, when I heard a voice, more of a call. I looked up through the trees and saw a woman, small, with short dark hair. She stood quite still, with her hands in her pockets, and called again.

'Danny!'

I expected to see a dog bounding through the undergrowth, but nothing happened. There was something about the way the woman called that sounded so wretched that I crouched down further under the ferns, reluctant to be seen. I don't know how I knew it was Mrs Sheriden, but I did. Maybe because she walked off in the direction of her house, or maybe because there was something about her that looked French – her big dark eyes, or pale skin, or the way she dressed. I was intrigued. Who is Danny?

*

Robert is home late for his tea. He was with the Tobins all day, since one of their boys has joined the local defence force and they are short a hand.

'Sean thinks the foot-and-mouth mightn't last too long coming into the hard weather, but I don't think it works like that.' Robert shakes his head as he takes off his boots. 'I think the frost will preserve the disease, make it worse.'

He stands bolt-straight, staring at me, yet through me, out the door, at the orchard.

'God help us if it spreads to here,' he says quietly.

'We'll be all right, won't we, Robert?'

'Yes, it will be tough, but we will be fine. It will be worse for others, for those who've had to destroy their whole herd. It will be the final straw after the English sanctions,' he looks at me, and sighs. 'I don't know what to think any more.'

I go over to the hearth and check the dinner. I do not know what he can mean.

'I find it hard to forget what happened here in Ireland, the way the English sent over the Black and Tans, who ran roughshod over the countryside, murdering innocent people in cold blood. How much hatred that caused.'

I turn and watch my husband carefully. He has never before spoken about this to me.

'And yet,' he says, rubbing his calves, 'and yet I feel something else inside my heart, June.'

I follow him with my eyes as he paces the room, coming to stop with his back to me, looking at the picture of his mother on the dresser.

'That is why I left this place before, and why I came to be in England. I had to escape from——' He breaks off, and the fire sparks, making me jump.

I stamp out the embers with my foot.

'My brother fought for the English in the First World War,' he continues. 'He was a hero, but no one mentions it. My neighbours consider it best forgotten. But, June, I can't forget.'

He turns round, shoving his hands in his pockets and, to my horror, I think I can see a tear forming in my husband's eye. It frightens me. What should I say to him?

'Robert, that is the past.' My words are hesitant.

'How can you say that, you of all people, when you are so obsessed with history?'

'It's different. That is ancient Rome, not in our lifetimes.'

'I feel that I am burying my head in the sand, living in my father's house, surrounded by memories from my childhood, from those years when James D. was fighting. What happened to England, June?'

'What do you mean, Robert?'

But I know what he is saying. Our life is so different now from how it was when we first married. London was our city. We belonged to it, like Minerva and Charles, and we thought we would be part of it forever. Could my Irish husband feel the same shame I did? Were we deserters?

'I know that de Valera thinks we should stand on our own two feet, as a nation, and be independent from England, but this is wrong, June. It's not just about England and Ireland. It's about the whole world, it's about the future.'

His tone is deadly serious. As he speaks, the light has suddenly gone out of the kitchen as if day has turned to night at the turn of a dial. I go to the dresser, fumble around for candles.

'Here, let me do that, go back to the dinner.'

I return to the hearth, aware that I am illuminated while my husband is still hidden in the shadows of our kitchen looking for the candles. The fire hisses and spits. It is the only sound in our safe little house. I think of fires burning in London, houses in flames, and men and women destitute. Minerva. Charles. It makes my throat tighten, and I long to scream out loud. Again I feel an urge to shout at Robert, order him to take me home.

'What will we do, Robert?' I ask instead, my voice barely raised above a whisper.

'This is our home now, June, we will stay here.' He sounds resigned, and his tone is almost patronizing. 'But I do not know how long this war will go on for, and I fear it will only get worse.'

I feel sick when he says this. How can it get worse when London is already in smithereens, and people most dear to me are in daily danger? I try to think of something else, let my mind drift to thoughts of ancient gods and goddesses, and the battles of old empires, but it is silly to be doing this, standing on the flagstones of Robert's cottage, doing my woman's work. Those thoughts are the frivolous imaginings of a girl who had time on her hands, not a busy farmer's wife. That was my life before the war. An image of Claudette Sheriden comes into my head and, without thinking, I speak.

'I saw Mrs Sheriden in the woods today.'

There is a crash, and I turn round sharply, nearly knocking the stew onto the ground.

'Blast!' Robert is crouching on the floor, and I can see tiny shards of glass glistening under the kitchen table. 'I dropped the candlestick on mother's picture.'

He bends down, carefully picking up the photograph of his mother. It is a very old photograph, possibly the very picture her husband had been given when she was his fiancée. It is the only picture Robert has of one of his parents.

'Let me help . . .' I wipe my hands on a towel.

'No, it's fine,' he says tightly. And then under his breath, so that I nearly don't hear, 'Damn Claudette Sheriden!'

I stand quite still, wounded by being dismissed in such a manner, and by a new feeling. There is the presence of another woman in our kitchen, as cloying as the aroma of our dinner. It curls inside my stomach, making me feel suddenly nauseous. I feel like a fool. I feel how a woman like Mrs Sanderson must have felt when my mother's presence swallowed her up.

I remember the last time I saw her, sitting demurely at the white ironwork table, spattered by reflections from the weeping willow tree, sipping tea from one of Grandmother's china-blue cups. Mrs Sanderson never said much; instead she watched. Her eyes darting in her round face, always in the shadow of our mother. It strikes me how similar we are. We were always the observers, watching the drama of our family members unfold before us. The others were the principal characters, and Mrs Sanderson and I stayed backstage. What was she wearing when I last saw her? I can't remember, although I can recall vividly every dress Mother and Min wore each time the Sandersons came to tea. What colour was her hair? Was it brown, or more copper; or paler, even a mousy blonde? She had been such a nondescript woman. Even her illness and death had been without drama. She had just crept away, thinner, paler, diminishing until she was no more. It was shocking. And the memory of it makes me shake all of a sudden. I feel guilty about Mrs Sanderson. I regret I didn't pay her more attention, and that I used to laugh at Min's impressions of her. She was a woman who bolstered a man, but she was never adored. Not like my mother.

And her funeral. No, I do not want to remember that day. I lean over the stove, stirring our stew diligently, listening to Robert as he sweeps up the glass from his mother's picture frame. Yet still the images return. There we are, Min and I, standing in the cold church and Min whispering to me, 'Do you know that Mrs Sanderson is the first person we have known who has actually died?'

She looked almost excited about this, her cheeks flushed, and her hands fidgeting.

I stared back at my sister stonily. 'And so?'

'So . . . it's . . . important . . .' Min began hesitantly, but the rest of her words were drowned out by the organ striking up.

Even Father managed to come to the funeral. He said little, nodding and smiling weakly at us, and taking Mother's hand whenever he could. Once I saw her pull her hand out of his, and I was sure Father recoiled, as if slapped.

The priest droned on, and my mind wandered to the story of Halcyone, who plunged into the sea in despair after the shipwreck and death of her husband, King Ceyx. The goddess Thetis transformed both husband and wife into kingfishers, which always fly in pairs, symbolizing the tender love and unity of the dead couple. I thought about Isis and her brother Osiris, and how Isis was able to bring about the resurrection of her brother-husband through the power of love. She too transformed herself into a bird, a hawk, so that she could hover, and watch over her love. And then I thought about Mrs Sanderson and how like a little bird she had been, always watching, never speaking, her eyes shining with some other knowledge that she was never willing to reveal, yet behind them misery. The poor woman had always put a brave face on things. Even in my inexperience I could sense Mrs Sanderson's loneliness, and felt sorry for her. Had she lived her whole life with no great love in it? For I was beginning to think the grand stories of the Ancients were a mere wash over how mundane marriage really was. The myths created such false expectations, which could break a heart. I wondered whether this was what had killed Mrs Sanderson, really, and whether this was the true reason my own father spent days hiding from the world in his bed.

I turned my attention to the top of the church. Captain Sanderson looked the picture of bereavement, dignified, pale and smart. He was dressed in uniform, and stood as straight as a poker, his dark eyes expressionless, his mouth set in a straight line. Charles

Junior was there too, and at every opportunity looked round at Min, but she ignored him, staring down at the ground, muttering the verses of the hymn.

After the burial, everyone was invited back to the Sandersons' house for tea and sandwiches. Father excused himself, and walked home. He said he needed the air after being cooped up in the house for so many weeks.

'It is because he doesn't want to drink,' I heard my mother whisper apologetically to Captain Sanderson, who nodded distractedly before walking off to speak to his wife's relatives.

'Can I come with you, Daddy?'

'No, June, I prefer to be by myself. Besides, you must stay and keep your mother company.'

I watched him lumber off down the road. He was a tall man, yet he seemed crushed in stature, walking heavily, as if the weight of the world was on his shoulders. My eyes followed him down the street, a small pearl of rejection lodged in my throat, making me gulp.

It was the first cool day in August. I sniffed the air, aware that today was the last day of the holidays. The grass was still damp from rain the previous night, and a nipping wind was picking up. I shivered, pulling my light jacket tightly about my shoulders and watching the funeral guests milling about inside the house. It was surprising how small the Sandersons' house was. I had imagined them living somewhere much grander. But then, what exactly did Captain Sanderson do, now that he was no longer a soldier? Mother had told Min and I that the house had been Mrs Sanderson's; she had been widowed before she met her current husband. The couple had no children, and there was that exactness to the interior of the house – where there were no disruptions to the order – that Captain Sanderson had placed on everything. I was cold outside, but I couldn't bear to go into the house and attempt to balance sandwiches on my lap while talking to Mrs Sanderson's niece, or cousin, or other distant relative. I turned my back to the house and gazed at a row of poplars, which blocked the view of the sea. What a stupid place to plant them.

Min and Charles Junior emerged from the small potting shed at the bottom of the garden with croquet sticks and balls, waving at me to come and join them. Was it inappropriate to play croquet? Nobody in the house seemed to notice us, so we tried to play for a couple of hours, but they were half-hearted games. The garden was much smaller than ours and too bumpy to play properly. By six o'clock it was too windy and cold to stay outside any longer.

'I'm afraid I must be going,' said Charles Junior.

'Will you not come back into the house with us?' Min asked, touching his sleeve.

He smiled at her. 'No, I already said goodbye to my uncle . . .' He faltered. 'I don't think I can bear to do it again.'

We all nodded, saying nothing. Charles Junior suddenly reached forward and took Min's hand. I reddened. The couple said nothing, just stared into each other's eyes. How could Min embarrass me so? I began to walk briskly across the lawn away from them. They did not call after me. I wondered what he was asking her. He couldn't possibly be asking her to marry him? That would be ridiculous. Min was still only fifteen, and a schoolgirl. But then the way he looked at my sister, he was most certainly in love.

I entered through the French windows, thinking of school. We were going back the next day and the thought depressed me. I hated leaving Father when he was so low. I longed to have one afternoon discussing Classics with him. I felt suddenly cross with him. Why did he have to be like this?

There were no lights on in the house, and the clouds, which had begun to gather outside, blocked the sun so that the room was murky. There was no one in here, only half-drunk glasses of sherry, and crumbs on plates. I walked over to the sideboard and took a sandwich off an untouched pile, then picked up a small glass of sherry and knocked it back in one. I coughed. It tasted disgusting, but it warmed my chilled bones and made me feel a little less gloomy. I needed to find the lavatory.

I opened the sitting-room door and entered the cramped hall, heading towards the staircase. Where was everyone? The grandfather clock ticked solemnly, and I walked slowly up the stairs looking at the walls crammed with engravings of horses and dogs. On the landing I was faced with four white doors. I needed to go quite badly now, so I tried one door, but it wouldn't open. It was locked. I was terrified I might walk into Mrs Sanderson's bedroom. The body was gone of course, but I didn't want to see her things. I tried the next door and turned the handle slowly.

It wasn't the bathroom. And it wasn't Mrs Sanderson's room, either. I was looking into a bedroom, obviously unused, and I was looking at Captain Sanderson, who was standing facing me and holding my mother. That was what I could see. He was cradling her face in his hands, and he was crying. The two of them were completely unaware I was behind them, for his eyes were closed as the tears trailed down his cheeks. I had never seen a man cry before. I watched incredulously as their lips came together, and they kissed. It was like watching a moment in a film. Then I saw their bodies coming closer together, and Captain Sanderson put his hand under my mother's skirt. I saw him lift the light material, and I saw my mother's alabaster limbs, as one of her legs wrapped around Captain Sanderson's backside. I jerked my head back suddenly and stepped out into the hall. My breath came so fast I was almost hyperventilating. I ran down the stairs and back into the sitting room, out of the French windows and onto the grass. It had begun to rain, and I looked about for Min. Finally I saw her, sitting under an oak tree at the end of the garden. I ran towards her.

'Crikey, what's wrong with you?'

'I just . . .' I sat down, trying to catch my breath, 'I just saw Mother and—'

'Captain Sanderson?' Min finished the sentence for me. She turned towards me, held me by my shoulders and stared into my face. I saw her eyes harden. 'Were they at it?' she asked harshly.

'No, well, maybe . . . They were kissing?'

'Did they see you?'

'No.'

Min folded her arms, whistled through her teeth. 'I knew it,' she said emphatically.

I felt stunned. How could Min have known? Although my sister was a year younger than me, I felt naive and stupid.

'How did you know?'

Min pursed her lips into a smirk. 'I just did.'

'Oh.' I looked at my feet. I felt confused and strangely betrayed. Why had Min not said something before? How many secrets might Min have from me? I looked at her hands, half-expecting to see an engagement ring, but her fingers were bare. 'What did Charles . . . Charles . . . Junior say to you?' I asked, my anxiety causing me to stutter.

'Oh, nothing.' Min smiled serenely. 'Apart from the fact that he wants to marry me.'

'But you're only fifteen!'

'He wanted me to promise myself to him, until I am sixteen.'

I picked up a couple of acorns, which had already fallen from the tree. I separated one of them from its cup and pressed its smooth, round green body into my palm.

'What did you say?'

'Well, don't you know me well enough by now?' Min raised her eyebrows and laughed out loud. I smiled with relief, and then the fright of what I had just seen inside the house began to make me giggle.

'I can't believe it! Mother and Captain Sanderson! It's so—'

'Ghastly!' yelled Min with her arms outstretched towards the pouring heavens.

The two of us dissolved into laughter, as the rain beat down through the leaves of the trees, soaking us. I couldn't stop laughing. I danced up and down with mirth, made worse by the fact I still needed to go to the lavatory. Yet my heart was filling up with a new rawness. The biting reality of our mother's adultery confirmed the travesty of our family. I will never fall in love, I promised myself.

As we sisters laughed we held hands, swaying like two young saplings in the wet wind. This is love, this is intimacy, I remember as I uncurl from over the stove, and press my hand into the small of my back, standing upright, feeling suddenly fierce in my husband's kitchen, unnoticed by him. I look out into the black yard and I see Min and I, lit up and young. We have laced our fingers together and are rocking back and forth. How is it that Robert and I have never laughed together like this? But see, even our sisterly love is an illusion. Already I am beginning to detach, and Min becomes a wet hand, any hand. When I close my eyes I imagine I can feel that same rain streaming down my cheeks, and I see my father's face at Mrs Sanderson's funeral when Mother pulled away from him. I see his wounded expression and I understand what happened to him. In my memory there are no longer two girls laughing in the rain. Now there is only one girl, and she is crying.

THE ADULTERESS II

He is not a big man, her lover, but he is strong. He has the stamina of an ox. She stands inside his door, her arms raised above her head, her hands pressed into the splintering wood, and shivers with anticipation. She is completely naked.

She has never felt so exposed.

She had lain with him, and undressed in front of him on numerous occasions. She had even sat on him, but to be standing, and to know he is behind her, looking at her, all of her, is something different. For some reason it feels like the ultimate anarchy.

She smells him first, the damp sweat of him, which is so different from the odour of her husband. He smells of his life, resin and oil, and hard work. She tenses, excited, unsure of what he will do.

He takes her by surprise, just one finger, tracing it down her spine, right to the bottom of her back, and further, tracing underneath her, passing over her opening, wet, wanting him, until he stops. Then he presses her flesh with certainty, and she lets out an unexpected murmur.

Oh! she says.

Oh! he laughs softly. Oh, yes.

He begins to rub her and she twitches, pushing back into his stomach.

He peels the outside of her away, layer after layer, and each sen-

sation grows deeper, closer and closer to the edge. He is teasing
her, and impetuously she gropes behind her, finds what it is she
wants so badly, needs so much inside. She pushes him into her, and
then just as suddenly he is gentle no more. He surges forward,
and her face is pressed into the door, his hands grip her waist, and
he grinds into her. She wants this feeling – that now she is no longer
herself, but just an element igniting him, and they are fusing.

It is nature, and it is not something they can stop, for all nature
is art.

NICHOLAS

For three days it rains non-stop. At first Nicholas tries to get some work done, but he finds it hard to motivate himself. It is so dark and gloomy and the wet makes it too difficult. It is supposed to be the summer, but it feels like a winter's day. The second day of rain he tries to bake an apple pie, but he has no recipe books and is unsure how to make pastry. The result is a strange, doughy con-coction of apples, flour, butter and sugar, which is tasty if odd-looking. He decides just to bake the apples themselves, with the cores cut out and stuffed with raisins and honey. He remembers his own mother doing this when he was little, and the delight of Sunday dinner with his mum and dad, the three of them around the kitchen table and the aroma of roast meat, roast potatoes and sweet apples in the air. He wishes now he had paid more attention to what his mum had been doing in the kitchen, rather than hang-ing on to his dad's every word. He had been a great storyteller. Charlie had loved to hear about Nicholas's childhood Sunday din-ners and the stories his father told him. She said her family never sat around the table, apart from Christmas Day. They were a TV-dinners family, with two working parents and the four siblings fighting over the best seats in front of the telly, Birds Eye crispy pancakes and Angel Delight served up on trays.

'You're so lucky,' she would enthuse. 'You had such a happy childhood.'

Yes, he did. That is, until he was twelve, until his father died. His mum had been great, always putting his needs before hers. Charlie thought she was wonderful. She was always complaining about her own mother, and how she had ignored her when she was a little girl, and then broke up the family by leaving her father for another man. Nicholas guessed there was no such thing as an idyllic childhood, but he decided not to let himself be defined by his father's death. He didn't want to use it as an excuse. He hated telling people, he hated pity. And so he played along with Charlie. Yes, he had had so much happier a childhood than her, and that was why she was allowed to be more difficult than him, more demanding.

Nicholas waits for the apples to explode so that their insides are frothy and white and the skin is brown, and crisp. Had Charlie ever understood who he had been as a little boy? Charlie the child was always there in their relationship. He saw her in her paintings, and in her moodiness, and in the way she would react to him sometimes with no logic whatsoever.

'I'm not your bloody mother!'

He would yell back sometimes. She expected so much from him, but not any more. He is free. But although the baked apples melt inside his mouth, his new-found freedom doesn't taste so good.

And so he retreats into music. Since the day the ghost lady led him to the piano, Nicholas cannot stop playing. He plays for as long as his hands will let him. He plays his favourite Debussy, challenges himself with Rachmaninov, and then comes back to his mother's favourite, Chopin. Afterwards he drapes himself across the keys, his heart raw, his fingers sore, his back aching.

On the third day of rain he writes Charlie five different texts.

I trusted u but uve shown yr true colours now.

How long was it going on 4?

R u still seeing him?

Who r u fuckng?

Uve ruined my life will never 4give u.

He doesn't send them, deletes them all and throws his phone into a kitchen drawer, slamming it shut in disgust.

He is running out of money. Every day he wakes up wondering if he has made the biggest mistake of his life. He has no friends here, no income. And yet he feels relief that he is living somewhere nobody knows him, or what happened to his marriage.

It is still raining when Nicholas gets in his car and drives into town. He carefully negotiates the old Volvo around the potholes and deep puddles of boggy water up the lane. Town is one broad main street double-parked with tractors. There are five pubs, two hotels, one small supermarket and post office, a bookmaker's, a Chinese takeaway, a couple of clothes shops and a cafe. The falling sheet of rain makes the town seem dismal and depressing. Nicholas wonders what it must have been like growing up somewhere like this. He goes into the supermarket, but he can't think straight. It feels as if everyone is looking at him. He grabs a six-pack of beer, a loaf of brown bread, cheese, milk, eggs and bacon. There is a horrible smell in the supermarket, as if someone has been frying bacon in old cooking fat. He puts the bacon back in the refriger-ator unit and picks up a packet of smoked mackerel instead. The woman behind the till has weak blue eyes and straight blonde hair with dark roots. She doesn't seem to be in any hurry, although there is a queue behind Nicholas. Slowly and wearily she pulls the food across the scanner.

'Terrible weather,' she says casting her eyes bleakly at the grey sky outside.

'Yes,' Nicholas replies, fumbling with his wallet.

'The poor kids. They've no summer at all. Of course as soon as they go back, it'll be baking, you see.'

'Yes,' he nods, uncomfortably.

She takes his money, and hands him his change. 'So you're doing up the old Fanning place?'

Nicholas stares at her. Who is this woman? How does she know this? 'Yes,' he replies coldly, trying to shove his shopping into his bag as quickly as possible.

'And how are you finding it? Do you like living there?'

Nicholas stops what he is doing and stares at her. There is something in those weak blue eyes, some kind of intelligence. He wonders: does she know about the ghost?

'Yes, sure.'

He walks hastily away from her. Everyone in the queue is listening to their conversation. Everyone knows who he is and where he lives. Already his desired anonymity is shattered. He sees a noticeboard right in front of him by the exit to the supermarket. He digs into his pocket and pulls out a card he has already written and reluctantly sticks it up. He doesn't want to have to teach, but he has no choice. He senses someone standing next to him, at his shoulder and reading his card. It is a plump woman with long red hair. Her face is so pale it looks like white china, and it is moist-looking as if the dampness in the air has made her skin wet.

'Are you any good?' she asks, still staring at the noticeboard.

He bristles with annoyance. 'Well, I am professionally qualified, as you can see from my card.'

She nods, still not looking at him. 'How much?'

'Fifteen euros for half an hour.'

Finally she turns to look at him. He is startled by the colour of her eyes. They are such a dark brown they look almost black. The effect is unsettling.

'When can I start?' she asks, smiling. 'I've always wanted to learn the piano.'

'Oh, for you . . .' he stutters, presuming she had children whom she wanted taught.

'Yes, just me. I can only do mornings while my daughter is at summer camp.'

'Right, well, how about tomorrow? Around eleven?'

'Great. Where do you live?'

He describes where his house is. He has no address, just the name of the townland. She frowns, and her black eyes turn brown again.

'Oh, the old Fanning place.'

'Yes.'

She hesitates, and again he has the sense that she knows something about where he lives, like the woman at the till.

'See you tomorrow then.'

She picks up a basket laden with vegetables, a cabbage falls out, and Nicholas picks it up and hands it to her.

'Sorry, I don't know your name.'

'Oh, it's Geraldine. Geraldine Mulraney.' She looks up at the board. 'And you're Nicholas Healy, with a Masters in Music from London University.'

He blushes, feeling ridiculous. He doesn't want to teach this woman. He would rather teach children. Adults are nosey.

The next day Geraldine Mulraney brings the sunshine with her. As she pulls up outside his house in a dirty white Ford Fiesta, the sun breaks out from behind the grey clouds and illuminates rainbows in the puddles. She is wearing a blue summer dress with a green cardigan, the colour of the new summer sky, and the grass in the field.

'I just knew the sun was going to come out,' she says brightly as he opens the door to her. 'Sure it's hard to believe summer is nearly over and we've had no decent weather.'

Nicholas leads her through the kitchen to the back room. He senses her eyes taking everything in, looking at his handiwork.

'You've done an awful lot to the place.'

'Have you been here before?'

'Oh, years ago,' she says vaguely. 'It was derelict then. But my granny knew the family that lived here a long time ago, before the last owners. In fact she used to work here when she was a young one, before she got married.'

'Really?'

'Yes, she's always reminiscing. She loved Mrs Fanning. Adored her, so she did.'

Nicholas pulls out the piano stool and Geraldine sits down. He wants to ask her more about her granny and Mrs Fanning, but she is here to learn the piano. They only have half an hour and he can tell that this woman is a chatterbox.

'Right,' he says. 'Will we start?'

She nods, fingers the keyboards gingerly and then clasps her hands.

'This is so exciting,' she exclaims, smiling at him with shining eyes. Nicholas looks at her and he can see how sad she is, how lonely.

Geraldine Mulraney becomes Nicholas's friend. One lesson a week becomes two, then three. Geraldine is married, but she rarely mentions her husband. She has only one child. Nicholas thinks it odd because all of the mothers have at least two. He acquires six other pupils, ranging in age from six to thirteen. He discovers he is enjoying teaching, being with young people. They seem to like him. He had always thought children didn't like him.

Nicholas has no brothers or sisters. After his father died, it was just him and Mum, who had only remarried when Nicholas left home. He had grown up surrounded by his mother's adult friends and had always preferred their company to the other boys at school. Apart from the piano teaching, Nicholas had managed to avoid children most of his adult life. He had always wondered if God had never blessed him and Charlie with a baby because of his failure to like children. In Dublin his relationship with his pupils had been formal and aloof. But country kids were different. Somehow they managed to make him drop his guard. The day he actually said something funny and made Eamonn Bennett crease with laughter was a revelation for him.

Every day that she comes Nicholas bakes apples for Geraldine, and after her lesson they sit at his kitchen table, drinking coffee, eating hot sweet fluffy apples and chatting.

'Are you from Cavan?' Nicholas asks Geraldine as he pours cream over his hot apples.

'Yes, 'fraid so.' Geraldine digs her spoon in. 'These are just yummy.'

It is a dark day, raining outside. The kitchen feels cosy, scented with the cooked apples, and warm from the lit stove. Geraldine looks out of the window.

'Oh dear, I hope Grainne doesn't catch a cold. But she just adores the riding. The rain doesn't bother her a bit.'

The lights flicker, and Nicholas can feel that the ghost is there in the room with them. He wonders if Geraldine senses anything too. She shivers.

'Sorry, do you have a window open?'

He shakes his head. 'Here have some more coffee, it will warm you up.'

Geraldine sits back in her chair and sighs. 'This is so lovely,' she says. 'You go to so much trouble. I really do look forward to my lessons.'

'I enjoy it too. It's a good distraction from all the work I have to do on the house.'

The renovation is painful. Nicholas feels worn out most of the time. He wishes he had moved to France, bought an old farmhouse there, so at least he would be warm.

'My husband, Ray, is a builder. But he's better doing modern houses. I wouldn't want to let him loose on this place. He renovated our house, and I think he sort of took the soul out of it. It was my parents' homeplace, but it doesn't feel like home any more.'

Geraldine breaks open the skin on her second baked apple.

'I can't believe I'm still here,' she says suddenly.

Nicholas glances at his watch. It is half-past eleven. 'Are you late for Grainne?'

Geraldine laughs. 'No, I mean *here*. In Cavan still. I always thought I'd leave, live in a city like Paris or New York. Even London.'

'And why didn't you?'

'I was going to. I was heading off to London, had the boat ticket bought and everything, and then Daddy died sudden, of a heart attack. Mammy was in an awful state, so I stayed. It was only meant to be for a year, but she kind of lost it. She couldn't cope on her own, and my elder brother was living in Australia by then. There was no one else to mind her.'

Geraldine sighs.

'Poor Mammy. I got a job in a factory in Oldcastle and that's where I met Ray. We went out for ten years before we got married.'

'Is your mother still alive?'

'No, she died about eight years ago now.'

'So why didn't you leave then?'

Geraldine shakes her head and gets up. She picks up her dirty bowl and brings it over to the sink.

'It was too late. I thought about it, I really did, because I had a tiny bit of money left me and the house, but I was all entangled. And then Ray asked me to marry him, and he moved in. And that was it.'

Geraldine leans on the sink staring out the window.

'I got pregnant. I lent him the money for his business. Before I knew it, I was stuck.'

Nicholas is not used to having such a frank conversation with a woman, apart from his wife. But it feels safe. He doesn't fancy Geraldine, and besides, she is married to someone else. He is enjoying talking with her. He misses talking to a woman. But maybe she has told him too much? He doesn't know what to say.

'Oh, look,' Geraldine suddenly points out the window. 'Did you get chickens?'

Nicholas gets up from the table. 'Not as far as I know.'

Geraldine looks confused. 'It's gone now. I'm sure I just saw a chicken in your yard.' She laughs. 'I must be going nutty.'

Nicholas stands next to Geraldine and they look out of the window together. He can't see a chicken anywhere. The rain pounds the yard, and gathers in pools in the broken concrete. Geraldine smells of mimosas, a perfume similar to the one his mum used to wear.

'What do you think of it round here?' Geraldine asks him.

'I like it.'

'Why?' She turns to look at him, her eyes narrow so that she almost looks angry.

'Well, it's so peaceful and unspoilt, and the people are very kind.'

She huffs. 'That's what you think. It's all right for you. They leave you alone. You're an outsider.'

'What do you mean?'

'It's just that I always feel like I'm being criticized, by my husband's family mostly. And I'm just so . . . bored.'

'Bored?'

She laughs. 'Yeah, bored. Busy, but with what? Cooking, cleaning, looking after other people, but still bored.'

'Well, how can we make your life more interesting?'

As soon as he speaks, he regrets it. He turns on the tap at the sink and begins to wash the bowls and spoons. Geraldine doesn't move; he senses her looking at him.

'How?' she says in a small voice.

'You know, you've started the piano and you're really good at that, and isn't there anything else you're interested in?' Nicholas blusters. 'Now your daughter is older and at school, isn't there something you'd like to do? You could start your own business.'

'Ray wouldn't allow it.'

Then she brings her hand to her mouth as if she is trying to swallow the words she just said.

'Sorry, I have to go.'

She picks up her bag and almost runs to her car. He can see her scarlet cheeks as she drives away, and he wonders whether she will ever come for another lesson.

JUNE

I am under the eaves, catching strands of straw through my fingers,
listening to the rustling thatch and dreaming.

I remember when I was a girl, and I needed my mother to love
me and my father to be well. But all I had was Min, and we made
up for what we did not receive by giving more to each other.

I am going to have a baby.

There, it is said out loud. The fact of it. Spoken with my head
bent backwards, looking into the dark roof of my husband's house.
This is a good thing. I must tell Robert.

But I have not yet, because I am afraid he will not see any joy in
my face. He will know I am lying when I tell him how happy I am.
Then will he think it is a slur on him, for can I not love him enough
to want his child? Am I my mother's daughter?

I am thinking of my time in university when I was so attached
to my studies. All that work belonged to me, and I lived through
the lives of the pagans. I loved them. They made me want to carry
on, and show others what I knew. How I wanted to share my
Romans. Is this what it is like to have children?

Will I lose all the secret parts of myself to live through them?

I lie flat on my back, my fingers pressed down onto the bare
boards, and I am lying on a raft, drifting out to sea. There are birds

chattering in the eaves, but the music in my head begins to drown them out. It is Debussy, his song of the Sirens. Min and I went to hear his *Nocturnes* just before the war. Neither of us could speak once we left the concert hall. We sat opposite each other on the train staring into each other's eyes, both of us brimming with longing. I hear the female chorus, no need for words, just their sighs weaving like ether through the orchestra. It makes me feel like a particle of dust spinning in the golden light. It makes me want to sink to the bottom of the ocean. What is a life anyway?

Some things you cannot say, some things you cannot write, you can only feel them, for if my sister had asked me to jump off the cliff, there was a time I would have done so gladly. And the ocean would have applauded at my pagan abandon.

Sometimes when I look into a mirror I think I see Min's face, not mine. I think I am becoming more like her. I have lost a little weight and now my cheekbones are more pronounced, my eyes larger, my chin more pointed. Just eleven months between us, to the day, 11th May and 11th June, and we were like two little leaves from the same stem. I was the bigger baby. Mother said I sucked all the strength from her, and Min was born so tiny and frail. She called her Minerva, Goddess of War, because she was a little fighter. Mother said my sister earned her name.

I can hear footsteps below me. They stop, and pause at the bottom of the steps. Robert calls. I should get up. I want to get up, but the sea still holds me, and I am swaying on the cold floor, cresting waves, going home.

'June!'

He comes up the staircase, and pushes open the door.

'What are you doing in here?'

I open my eyes, surprised it is now almost dark. Robert's face appears before me, and it is so familiar and so safe that I feel a sudden surge of hopefulness at the news I am about to tell him. He crawls in under the eaves and comes towards me.

'It's all right, I'll come down,' I say.

But he is beside me now, and takes my hand, before saying, 'There is something I must tell you.'

He looks so serious that I am alarmed, shaken out of my own little world. 'What is it, Robert?'

He looks quite pale now.

'What's wrong?' I ask. 'Has something bad happened with the foot-and-mouth?'

'No, it's not that.'

Then he lifts my chin, and stares straight in my eyes. At least he does not look away. At least he lets each word pierce me one by one.

'I am joining up.'

I shake my head. I cannot believe what he has just said. 'But the farm, you can't just walk away from it,' I protest, the first silly thing that springs to mind.

'That is all taken care of,' he says. 'Sean Tobin and a couple of his sons are going to run it for me.'

'But, Robert, where are you joining up? Where?'

It is impossible to imagine there is a way off our little island.

'I am going up to Belfast, by train . . . tomorrow.'

'Tomorrow!' my voice wails under the eaves. I am on the verge of hysteria.

He wraps his arms about me. 'June, darling June, I have to do this.'

'But you're not English, Robert,' I say angrily. 'Ireland isn't at war. None of our neighbours are joining up.'

I try to calm down, breathe slowly. I cannot believe he would leave me here, all alone.

'But I spent many years in England, as you know, June, and it gave me an education, and work, and you . . .'

He looks at me, and I believe in the devotion I see in his eyes.

'Oh, Robert,' I whisper, 'I'm pregnant.'

'What!'

He sits bolt upright, clasps my shoulders.

'What did you say?' he repeats, stunned.

I flop like a rag doll in his arms. 'I am expecting,' I say tremulously, and my fingers grip his flesh, holding onto his muscular arms. 'So you can't leave now, not now . . .'

'Oh, darling,' he kisses me passionately, and I collapse into his embrace, relieved that the crisis has been averted. I would rather have a baby than lose Robert to the war and be left here by myself. Now I know why I have miraculously conceived. It is to save Robert, and to save me.

We kiss again, and he puts his hand on my belly, laying me down on the boards again.

'Don't be such a silly,' I giggle. 'You won't be able to feel anything yet.'

We make love in our loft, and it feels like such a naughty and such an innocent thing to do, all at once. The thatch murmurs above our heads, and we are as snug as if we live in it.

I had brought no lamp or candle up with me earlier, and now it is completely dark. We cannot see each other's faces. We are just able to discern the shadowy outlines of our bodies.

'June,' Robert says quietly, his voice in a hush. 'You mustn't speak about it to anyone, apart from the Tobins.'

'All right. I wasn't going to for a while, not at least until I am showing. I thought it might be bad luck.'

'No, darling,' he says, putting his arm around me in the dark, 'I didn't mean about the baby. I meant about me and the war.'

I stiffen in his arms. My heart begins to thump inside my chest. 'But, Robert, are you still going to fight?' I ask breathlessly.

'I have to.' His voice sounds desperate in the dark. 'I have to do my bit, June, surely you understand that? You, of all people, should.'

I slide back into the black attic, shaking. 'No, Robert, you can't leave me here.'

'It's not about us any more. I thought I could, but I can't hide away. It's what my parents would have wanted, and it's what James did.'

'So is this about measuring up to your brother? Do you think you have to prove something?' I raise my voice, furious that his dead family has priority over me.

'Of course not,' he says wearily, 'I am just doing my duty.'

Love versus duty. I think of Virgil's *Aeneid*. How I loved 'The Tragedy of Dido'. She was my heroine, the champion of love, and how indignant I was when Aeneas left her, for what? For duty, *pietas*. Dido cursed him, didn't she? She cursed him as she threw herself upon her very own funeral pyre. So I do not come first, and neither does Robert's child.

He continues talking. In the darkness he cannot see the look on my face, my unspeakable anger.

'I don't want to leave you, but my conscience won't allow me any peace. Every day when I go out to work in the fields I try to flog myself, and do three times the work of the others because I am ashamed. I know what is at stake, I need to help somehow, and now even more so, because I want to ensure that our child grows up in a world free from Fascists. We all have to make sacrifices.'

His words are swallowed up by a sob, and although I cannot see his face in the evening gloom, I am aware he is crying. I crawl back towards him, take his hand in mine, and kiss his wet cheeks. His tears dissolve all my peevish and selfish thoughts.

'I'm sorry,' I say, humbled. 'You are right. You are doing a brave and noble thing, and I'm very proud of you.'

He collapses then, flinging his arms around my waist. I put my arms about him, my first mothering role, and rock him. He does not have to say a word, for I know he is terrified.

NICHOLAS

After weeks of disturbed nights, Nicholas begins to sleep deeply. He surprises himself by waking up late every morning, the high sun blasting through the uncurtained windows, unwelcome on his face. He cannot remember what he dreams about, but he knows he dreams, maybe even speaks out at night. For a few moments as he lies in bed and looks about the room, it seems as if it is full of different things. He looks at his bedroom through the eyes of someone else. It smells different. Apples. The room smells of apples.

He gets up and goes outside into the orchard and looks at the apple trees and he can see the beginnings of a small crop. Soon he won't need to buy the apples to make the desserts he has been cooking for himself and Geraldine. Some of the trees are so old and rotten he cannot see any apples on them, but some are festooned with bright-red hearts, and others with fat green cookers. It isn't quite time to pick, but he will go to the library and get a book on making cider and other things to do with apples. He will phone his mother and ask her. He has a vague memory of her making some kind of apple jelly when he was little. Then he changes his mind. He dreads talking to his mother. She adored Charlie, and she doesn't know what happened. She blames Nicholas for the break-up and somehow he can't bear to tell her the truth. He's not sure why. It always irritated him how much attention his mother gave

Charlie. It makes him feel like she wished she had had a daughter, not a son. Stupid to think that way, because he knows his mum loves him.

It starts to rain in the orchard. The water tinkers on the leaves around his head, and he hums along to the sound. He shoves his hands in his pockets. He should start work on the second bedroom. The floors need to be sanded, but today he doesn't have the will to put his body through it. Without a second thought he pulls his car keys out of his jeans pocket, walks out of the orchard and gets into the Volvo. He reverses, swings the car around and heads up the lane. It is only when he hits the main road and is driving in the direction of Dublin that he knows where he is going.

It feels like he has been away for months, yet it has only been six weeks. He parks outside their house and sits in the car, breathing quickly. What is he going to say? He mustn't think too much, just do. He'll know what to say when he sees her. He gets out of the car, locks it, crosses the road, opens the black wrought-iron gate and goes down the steps to the basement flat. The curtains are closed. He stands in front of the door. His name is still there. 'Nicholas and Charlotte Healy' in thick black ink. She made it in fancy calligraphy. He looks through the wobbly glass panels on the door and he can see a distorted image of the red abstract painting in the hall. Charlie painted it in Barcelona on a residency a couple of years ago. It was her response to bull-fighting. It is a whirlwind of red and black. A very disturbing picture. The only thing that reveals what the inspiration is are two white horns in the centre of this pulsing blood-black whirlwind. He never liked that picture. Maybe because he associates it with a time she was away from him. Three months she spent in Spain. It hadn't even crossed his mind that she might have been unfaithful, but now, thinking about that picture, and all the energy and passion in it, it makes him think about sex. It makes him wonder what it is really about.

His throat feels scratchy as if he is coming down with a cold and now he thinks he shouldn't knock on the door at all. That bloody painting. He wants to rip it down, but he doesn't have his key any more. He had thrown it at her the day he walked out.

There is noise all around him – cars, people, life going on – but on this doorstep everything is still. He is frightened. He has come to say he is sorry, but what will he do if she isn't alone? He realizes that all these weeks he hadn't really believed his marriage was over. Even though she slept with another man. Even though he could never forgive her. What if she doesn't care whether he is sorry or not?

He turns around and almost runs back up the steps. He gets into his car, and he is shaking. He sits for a few moments trying to decide what to do. He picks up his phone and finds her number, his finger hovers over the call button and then it rings. He looks at the screen. Kevin.

'Hello.'

'Hey, Nick. It's Kevin. How you doing?'

'I'm okay.'

'Listen, I'm really sorry I haven't called. I heard about you and Charlie. Christ! I can't believe it.'

'What did you hear?'

'Well, you know, you left . . . Jackie told me all about it. I'm sorry, mate.'

'Yeah.'

'Listen, do you want to meet up? Go see a band, or have a drink?'

'I don't live in Dublin any more. I've a place in Cavan.'

'Yeah, I know. Jackie told me.'

'Well, actually I'm up in Dublin today. Do you want to go out tonight?'

'Shit! I can't – not tonight, but I could come down to you at the weekend, I'm a free man while the girls are away.'

'The girls?'

'Yeah, didn't Charlie tell you? She and Jackie have gone to Greece for a month – painting the sky and sea, or whatever. I think they just wanted to hang out together, after what happened . . .'

Kevin's voice trails off, and Nick tries to remember whose friend came first. Did he meet Kevin through Charlie and Jackie? Or did Charlie meet Jackie through him and Kevin? They had all known each other so long. Something about Kevin annoyed him, but at the same time Nick was sick of being on his own.

'Yeah, great, you can help me dry-line the house.'

'Sounds fun.'

'And then I'll take you to the local to meet the locals over a pint.'

'Sounds scary.'

Nick tries to work out what it is about Kevin that irritates him and then he remembers. Years ago he saw Kevin looking at Charlie in a certain way. Just before they got married. It makes him start to wonder. Was there something going on with Kevin and Charlie once? Was that something he didn't know about, either?

He rolls down the window and lights a cigarette. He needs to get a grip. Stop imagining things. He looks across the road at the house. Now he wishes he had kept his key. She's in Greece. He could go in there now and have a look. See what she is up to.

He sits up suddenly and flicks the cigarette out of the car window. He gets out of the car and watches it smouldering in the road. He can hear his wife telling him off for littering, so he bends down and picks up the butt and puts it in one of the bins behind the railings. He goes back across the road, down the steps and round the side of their flat. He climbs over the wall, which is only knee-height, and goes towards the back door. He pulls back the pot full of lavender and the back-door key is still there. He picks it up.

The metal is cold as ice on his warm palm. He turns it over and over in his hand, and then he shoves it into the lock. He turns the handle. It's too late now. He is doing this. It's his house as well, he tells himself. He has a right to be here.

The first thing he notices is that the place smells different and it's very tidy. There is a big bowl of potpourri in the sitting room (since when did Charlie start buying potpourri?) and when he sniffs it, the fragrance of roses fills his nostrils. This is not a smell he associates with his wife. It is an intruder in their home. He goes into the kitchen and everything looks more familiar here. The spice rack and the orange Le Creuset pots they got as a wedding present from his Aunt Betty are still hanging up. He should take them, they are his, but then she would know he had been here. He walks in a circle around the sitting room three times before he summons the courage to open the door and go into Charlie's studio. There is no carpet on the floor, and the window blind is up high so that the room is full of light. There is an unfinished painting on the easel. It is shades of white and grey. As if an abstract grey form is coming out of a fog, and there is a sense of fast movement in the brush-strokes, so that now Nick realizes the figure is running away, not coming towards him, and he wonders whether this painting is about him. Her laptop sits on the table and he thinks about turning it on. He could check her emails, see whom she has been communicating with, maybe even find out who he is. Is she still seeing him? Or what is she telling her friends about him? Will she tell them the truth. *I cheated on Nick, so he left me. He said he had never been unfaithful to me, and he can't forgive me. He said I was a slut.*

He winces when he remembers saying that to her. He didn't mean it. He was just so hurt. He turns and walks out of her studio. He doesn't want to read what she has to say about him.

He stands in the sitting room, looking at the place where his piano once stood and at the dents in the carpet, and he begins to

84

cry. If she were here now, he would take her in his arms and tell her he's sorry, let's begin again, he can forget about it – he can. But she is in Greece. He goes into the bedroom and looks at their bed. He bends down on the floor in front of it, sobbing with frustration because he knows it's not true. If she were here, he wouldn't say any of those things because he can't forgive her. She had been the centre of his world, and he thought he had been her centre, too.

A pair of pyjamas lie on the chair beside the bed. Nick picks them up and holds them to his nostrils. Oh God, he can smell her now. That mixture of ylang-ylang and vanilla. Sweet and sultry. He opens one of her drawers. If he could just take something that smelt like her, it would make him feel better. To have this part of her. There is a scarf at the bottom of the second drawer. He remembers giving it to her right at the beginning of their relationship. It is purple and black and silky. It smells of Charlie. He shoves it into his back pocket and then he takes one last look at the bedroom. He feels a fierce rage inside him. If she were standing here in front of him, he knows what he would do. He would make love to her and then he would tell her it was over. And he would let her crawl across the floor, begging him to take her back. But he would reject her because he wanted to hurt her as much as she had hurt him.

By the time Nick hits the Cavan road it is getting dark and the day has turned nasty. Wind whips across the road, and in parts it is flooded. There are warnings on the radio. But he drives on. He has to get back to his house in Cavan. It is his sanctuary.

He is driving down the hill the other side of Oldcastle when he sees a white shape on the side of the road. His lights sweep it as he drives by and he sees it is a dog. Without thinking he stops the car. He gets out and runs back, hoping the dog is dead and not suffering. But when he gets to it, the poor creature is conscious, yet unable to get up. Nicholas looks about him desperately, wondering who the dog belongs to, but there are no houses nearby and the dog has no collar.

He kneels down beside it.

'It's all right, boy, it's all right.'

He tries to see where it's hit. It looks like one of its back legs is broken. It is covered in blood and the dog keeps trying to bend back and lick it.

The dog looks at him, and he looks at the dog. It stops whimpering and he picks it up, not caring that blood is getting all over his jacket. He carries it gently to his car and puts it in the back. It is a relief to know that he still cares.

JUNE

1932 was a bad year for my father. He was only out of bed a week, returning to his studies, when he received a huge shock. All of his money was wiped out overnight. Grandfather had invested heavily in the railways, and Father had been living off the dividends all of his life. It never occurred to him that his investment should be managed. When the stock market crashed, he did not even think it would affect him. He was an effete scholar, and the grubby affair of making money was never a concern of his. But now everything changed: his whole way of life, his home, even his career was under threat. His response was to crash as well. He went back to bed.

At first Mother left him alone. She would disappear for hours on end, sometimes nights, but Father never seemed to notice, and there was no one else at home to mind, for Min and I were oblivious to our family's predicament, away at school. September, October, November passed in this way. My father became more unkempt, and uncared for, in the same way as the house. My mother was hardly ever there, and when she did return her cheeks would be flushed and there were smudges of dark circles beneath her eyes for the first time in her life.

And then one day in early December Mummy suddenly clicked into action. She swept into Father's bedroom and pulled the covers off him, forcing him out of bed.

'You are to be a man. Do something about the situation. Get yourself some work.'

She pursed her lips with determination as she pressed his best suit, did up his tie, plonked a hat on his head and forced him out of the door.

'Call on some of your old chums,' she ordered him, as he clambered into the car in a daze. 'Surely someone will be able to help us out.'

When Min and I came home for the Christmas holidays no one met us at the station. We had to walk home, along the sea front, in cutting winds and icy showers of sleet. We lugged our heavy suitcases along, moaning about our forgetful parents, and enviously looking into the windows of the houses we passed, gaily lit up with Christmas trees and radiating hospitality and fireside heat. By the time we were home, we were shivering and chilled to the bone. But it felt no warmer inside. We searched downstairs, walking from darkened dining room to an arctic sitting room. None of the fires were laid, and the house had never seemed so cheerless. There was not even a Christmas tree, not one decoration.

'Happy Christmas to you too,' Min whispered sarcastically, her words splintering the deathly silence surrounding us.

'Where are they?' I asked anxiously. 'What could Mrs Wyatt be thinking of, not to light the fires?'

'Let's go down to the kitchen and find out,' my sister suggested.

We went down the stairs, relieved to hear some noise as we descended. Sure enough, we could see a glow of light behind the kitchen door, and heard music, as if the wireless was playing.

'Thank goodness,' sighed Min. 'At least Mrs Wyatt is here.'

'Oh, do you hear that?' I said. 'How delightful. It's "Clair de lune".'

But to our utter surprise when we opened the door, we were not greeted by the familiar and comforting body of Mrs Wyatt, busy about her usual business; instead our mother stood in front of us, her hair bundled into a blue scarf, a matching apron spattered with flour, rolling out pastry on the kitchen table.

'I should have known Mrs Wyatt wouldn't listen to Debussy,' Min whispered into my ear.

'Mother!' I cried out in surprise. 'What are you doing?'

'Well, what do you think I am doing,' Mummy replied crossly. 'I am baking a pie.'

'But where is Mrs Wyatt?' asked Min. 'Is she sick? Has something happened to her?'

Mummy walked over and turned off the wireless. She clicked across the kitchen floor in her heels and went back to the table, picking up the rolling pin.

'Mrs Wyatt is fine.' She paused, pushing her hair back under her scarf, with fingers sticky with pastry. 'God, this is a beastly business,' she muttered to herself.

'But, Mummy, why are you cooking?'

In our entire lives I had never known my mother to do so much as boil an egg. She always claimed the kitchen was a disastrous place for the complexion, full of steam, and heat, and all that standing up so long ruined the calves. Anyway, she was so grand she absolutely had to have a cook.

Mother sighed, stared at us with her deep-blue eyes. Despite the fact that she was hot, and flushed, her face sprinkled with white flour, she looked beautiful all the same.

'I had to let Mrs Wyatt go,' Mother said briskly.

'But why!' Min exclaimed. 'How could you?'

Min sat down suddenly at the table and burst into tears. Mother looked at her, shocked.

'I never knew you were so fond of Mrs Wyatt,' she said coldly.

'I loved Mrs Wyatt,' Min cried dramatically, flopping her face forward onto the powdery table.

'And you?' Mother turned to me and regarded me icily. 'Do you love Mrs Wyatt?'

'Of course not,' I lied, speaking quickly. But I felt my stomach lurch. How would we cope now, without Mrs Wyatt to escape to? She was our safe haven when Mummy's temper flared, or Father's depression became too much to bear.

'I am sorry, Min,' Mother said, putting a hand on her shoulder, 'but I had to let Mrs Wyatt go because – well, we have had some pretty terrible news since you girls went back to school.'

Mother explained what had happened to our inheritance. Though they had a little money for the moment, it was imperative Father found employment. Until then he could not afford to pay Mrs Wyatt, or even to light the fires in the rest of the house.

'We shall have to live in the kitchen,' Mother said cheerily. 'It shall be quite cosy. I shall teach you both how to cook.'

'I didn't know you could cook,' Min said.

'Of course I can cook. Every young lady should know the fine art of cuisine, and it is something I have been remiss in teaching you.'

Our mother bent down, taking out a pie dish from below the stove.

'Indeed,' she said, 'I was sent to France to learn to cook properly.'

'But why have you never cooked for us before?'

'Because I didn't have to, darling. I am a very good chef, but I never wanted to end up with big red hands like Mrs Wyatt.'

Min burst out laughing, wiping her tears for Mrs Wyatt away with the back of her hand. 'Poor old Wyatt, she must have been awfully upset.'

Our mother rolled out the pastry and plopped it on top of the pie dish. She took out a fruit knife and began to trim the edges of the pastry. She worked fast, like a professional.

'Of course she was. Indeed, she shed more tears than you.'

She took up the cut-away pieces of pastry and rolled them up into a ball.

'But it is only temporary. We shall be back to normal soon, once your father has work.'

Min looked up from the table at me. Our eyes locked and we knew instantly what the other was thinking.

'But what can father do?' asked Min. We had never known our father go out to work. He had always been at home, in his study. He was a classical scholar, something that did not pay well, if at all.

'He is going to try and get work as a schoolmaster,' Mother said briskly.

'But doesn't that mean he would have to leave home and live on the school grounds?' I said, thinking of my female tutors, all of them spinsters, who lived a similar life to their young charges.

'Well . . . yes . . .' said Mother. 'But things are so bad, girls, we might have to sell the house and buy something a little smaller.'

'But you can't sell. It's our home!' Min exclaimed angrily.

Mother stayed calm. She wiped her hands on her apron and went into the larder. A sticky silence descended. I looked about the glowing kitchen. Suddenly home had never seemed so welcoming, and I could not imagine living anywhere else. Mother came back out of the larder with a large jar of Mrs Wyatt's mincemeat. She took a tablespoon out of the drawer and began to ladle it into the pie dish.

'You will be gone soon. Both of you girls married, and with families of your own. We have no son to leave this house to, and although you cannot believe it now, neither of you will want it. It makes perfect sense.'

She took up the small ball of leftover pastry and began to roll it out again. Then, taking up the knife, she cut it into thin slices, which she arranged on top of the mincemeat in a lattice.

I was still standing in my damp coat, my frozen hand gripping my brown leather suitcase. I dropped it on the floor and rubbed my hands together. Although the kitchen was warm, I felt freezing.

'What is wrong with you, June? Where are your gloves?' Mother looked at me crossly. 'Will you take that wet coat off and stop shivering.'

She opened the oven up and placed the pie inside it. I could see the flames at the back of it, orange, and blue. Instinctively I moved over towards the stove. My mother passed me by and sat down at the table opposite Min. She began to roll up tiny pieces of pastry.

'Get me a wet cloth, please, June.'

I went to the sink and turned on the tap. I leaned over the white porcelain basin and stared at the water swirling around the plughole. My head was pounding, for everything was changing. What would happen to Min and I? Would Min marry Charles Junior? I had been hoping to apply for university, but now it looked as if Father could never afford for me to go. I felt sick. I would do anything to get to college.

'Nothing is going to change overnight,' Mother said, wiping the table with the cloth I handed her.

'I can't see you as a schoolmaster's wife,' Min smirked, so that Mother stopped cleaning up and looked at her daughter harshly.

'I may not spend much time with him during the term,' she said slowly.

I looked up from the sink, turned my head and watched my sister and mother facing each other over the kitchen table.

'We may have some spare money from the sale of this house, and your father said I could travel a little, if I so wish. It is something I have always wanted to do, and never been able to, since I married so young.'

'What do you mean, "travel"?' asked Min.

'I want to go on a tour of Italy.' My mother closed her eyes, and smiled softly. 'It has always been my dream.'

'But who will go with you?' I asked incredulously. Mother had never said such a thing before, never expressed a wish to see another country. She had never even told us she had a 'dream'.

'You are leaving Father, aren't you?' Min stood up, pointing her finger at Mother.

'No, I am not,' Mother said emphatically.

'You are – we know, Mummy . . .' Min stuttered with anger. 'You are deserting Father, and you are going to run away with Captain Sanderson!'

Our mother's arm sprung out as if in reflex and she slapped Min across the cheek. Her fingers were still covered in mincemeat and flour, and Min's red cheek was now speckled with tiny dots of brown and white. Min put her hand up to her jaw and her lips curled into an ugly grimace.

'Yes, it was about time you hit me again. It hasn't happened in a while,' she said triumphantly.

Our mother looked wounded. She gripped her hands tightly.

'How could you suggest such an awful thing? The poor man is so recently bereaved.'

'I saw you.' The words left my lips almost against my will.

Mother turned her head abruptly, as if she had forgotten I was in the room at all. She stared at me, her blue eyes piercing me, and I searched them to see a flicker of maternal love. Now I wished more than anything I had kept my mouth closed.

'I don't know what you could mean,' Mother said hastily, clearing the table. 'My plan was to go to Italy with the both of you, once you have finished school.' She paused, scooping up tiny bits of pastry into her palm. 'I thought it would be invaluable for your education.'

'Mother, do you love Captain Sanderson?'

Min's voice was hideously loud, and jarred the atmosphere of the cosy kitchen. I expected to see Mother blaze again, and hit Min even harder this time. But Mother said nothing in reply. She washed her hands, took off her apron and hung it on a peg. Underneath she was wearing a white georgette evening dress with wine-coloured lace trimming. It fell in soft folds about her neat body, clinging to her hips. It seemed to me that she was even slimmer than when I last saw her. Mother took her compact out of her bag and used a damp cloth to clean the flour off her face. 'Well, this pie should be ready to eat in about half an hour,' she said calmly.

'Mother, did you hear what I asked you?' Min pushed again.

Mother put her compact away in her bag and picked up a pair of soft pink suede evening gloves, which she slowly pulled up each arm. She walked to the door and said, 'I chose to ignore it, for it was such an insolent question I was lost for words. What daughter talks to her mother in such a way?'

But as she spoke, her cheeks coloured.

'I am going out,' she said, taking her coat from a hook by the back door. 'I trust you can take that pie out and eat it yourselves. Your father is upstairs, if you want to bring him some.'

'She is, you know,' Min said as soon as Mother had left. 'She has fallen in love with Prince Charming!'

We could hear the car start up and crawl down the drive.

'Where do you think she is going now?' Min exclaimed. 'Straight into her lover's arms.'

I shook my head and sat down at the table, landing on the chair with a bump. My backside was still numb with cold.

'Oh, Min!' I put my head in my hands. 'Will I ever get to university now?'

'Is that really all you care about?' Min asked, her eyes widening in surprise.

I glanced at my sister. How like Mother she looked. I nodded.

94

'Of course you will, silly.' Min leaned over and squeezed my hand. 'Daddy would do anything for you to go to college. You are our big hope, June. You will be one of the first female classical scholars to be made a Fellow at Oxford, I'm sure.' She giggled then.

'Oh, how can you laugh, Min? Everything is just so terrible.'

'Well, I *am* upset about Mrs Wyatt, that's true,' Min said. 'But you know this is just a house, and were we ever really happy here?'

'But what about the sea, Min?'

'Oh, yes, it would be so sad to have to leave this place, but maybe they can buy a smaller house, still by the sea.'

'It will be awfully embarrassing.'

We contemplated this in silence.

'Do you think Mother was serious about taking us to Italy? Or do you think she is going to run away with Captain Sanderson?' Min asked suddenly.

'I don't know Min – it's all too dreadful to think she would leave Daddy.'

'She has been leaving him for years, June. Captain Sanderson is not the first; think of all the other friends our parents had, who suddenly disappeared. All the handsome husbands, and plain wives, who, once they got wind of what Mummy was up to, no longer wanted to come to tea. If Mrs Sanderson hadn't died, it would have happened with them too.'

Was our mother so bad? It seemed impossible, for I was so besotted with my father that I couldn't understand why Mother wasn't as well.

'Our father is a broken man, and it is Mummy who destroyed him,' announced Min in a solemn voice.

We could smell the pie now, and it made our tummies rumble. I went into the larder, and found some ham and half a loaf of bread.

We poured two large beakers of milk and helped ourselves to the bread and ham.

'Shall I bring some up to Daddy?' I asked.

'Let's wait a while.'

We ate quickly, stuffing the bread into our rumbling bellies.

'That pie will be ready soon. Gosh, I can't wait to eat it, it smells good,' said Min, looking cheerful again.

It always amazed me how my sister could bounce back, forgetting that Mother had hit her, or that now we had no money or inheritance, no rosy futures to look forward to.

'What will you do when you finish school, Min?' I asked her.

'Oh, I shall get married like I told you, June. And I shall make sure he has money and that he can pay for me to go to art school – that's what I shall do. I shall be *something*, June.'

Min picked up the oven gloves, took the pie out of the oven and placed it on the table.

'I wish I were as confident as you. Sometimes I feel like nothing at all.'

'But, June, no one is nothing if they are loved. And I love you.'

I looked at her, and her eyes blazed with emotion. I knew it was true that my sister did love me more than anyone else in the world, and I her. I could never imagine either of us finding a husband who would love us as much.

'Will you marry Charles Junior then?' I asked hesitantly, although he would hardly have the funds for Min's plans.

'No, of course not.' Min smiled, opening a drawer and taking out a knife.

'Well, how could you possibly know you're going to get married, if you haven't even met your husband-to-be yet?' I asked her teasingly.

'But I have met him,' Min replied with certainty. 'Mark my words, by this time next year I shall be a married woman.'

And she cut the mince pie with such aplomb that steam shot up into the air, like a fissure of a volcano, and I thought I could almost believe her.

I lie in bed in my husband's house in Cavan and I can almost taste Mrs Wyatt's spicy English mincemeat on my lips, and the scent of my last Christmas at home. I close my eyes. So long ago. I am in another country. I have my own family now. I put my hand on my belly, but I can feel nothing and I wonder who is in there. A girl. A boy. Loving. Cruel.

No one is nothing if they are loved. That is what Min had said. But now I am afraid I am not loved by anyone. My husband's declarations ring hollow, because I believe his actions are an indication of his heart. How can he leave me, voluntarily?

I do not understand this world, all of the violence of the war happening outside of Ireland. It seems unreal, like a hideous nightmare. I want to hide inside my nest, and I want him to hide with me too. He refuses. My husband cannot turn his back on the war because he has to live by his convictions, whatever the cost. What small sacrifice do I have to make, if he has to risk his life?

And so my brave Robert rises early in the hope I might not wake. He kisses my forehead and creeps out the door. I shiver under the warm bedclothes, curling up like a baby myself, my cheeks dry. I cannot cry, not yet. I am too stunned. I can hear his footsteps cross the kitchen, the clatter of a cup as he pours himself a drink and then the latch of the door. I pray he will stop. Surely he will turn round, come back to me? But the house grows deathly silent, and I know he has gone, and yet still I hope for a last-minute change of heart.

The hours pass. I lie in bed praying for time to go backwards. My eyes are wide open, bleak fear overwhelming me. Will my husband ever return? Will he live to see his child? Will I be left here, forever in Cavan, all on my own? Min always had such spirit. How I wish I could have just one little drop of it. I know my sister would not lie in bed feeling sorry for herself. No, Min would pack her bags and go back to London. She would follow her husband, even if it meant disobeying him. That's what my sister would do.

The room gradually fills with light. The hens are making a great noise, and I should get up, start working for the day. It would help to keep myself busy. But I can't. It is as if I am struck down by the hand of God, paralysed and suspended in the last few moments that Robert lay next to me in our bed.

Suddenly I hear the latch and I spring from the blankets.

'Robert.' I scramble across the room.

I charge into the kitchen, but my joy scatters about me as I come face to face with an alarmed Oonagh.

'Mrs Fanning, are you all right?'

'Robert!' I crumple onto the floor, hugging my sides, bent double.

Oh, the baby, I think, surely I will lose it now.

'Shush, shush.' Oonagh comes over to me and helps me up, makes me walk back into the bedroom. 'There now,' she strokes my hair. 'Why don't you get back into bed for a while?'

'Oonagh . . .' I gulp, tears flooding my face.

'I know, I know,' she nods, as wise as an old sage, yet her face is as open and unlined as a child's.

'I didn't say goodbye,' I whisper hoarsely, my throat so parched I feel as if I might faint from the thirst.

Oonagh passes me a glass of water from the locker. She pats my arm. 'Oh, but you did, Mrs Fanning. He understands.'

I sip the water and look at her. She has brown eyes the colour of bog water, and full cheeks, as rosy as apple skin.

'Do you think I will ever see him again?'

'Hush now,' she admonishes me. 'It's not good to think like that. You must trust in the Almighty that he will bring him back safely to you.'

'Yes.' I feel chastised. I wipe my eyes with my handkerchief, suddenly aware I have made a bit of scene in front of her. 'I am all right, now,' I continue. 'You can go.'

However, Oonagh doesn't leave the room. 'Are you sure, Mrs Fanning? Do you need anything else?'

'No, I want to be alone.' I try to rally myself.

She gives me a studied look. 'I'll put the kettle on. We have a little tea, don't we? I think this morning calls for a cup of tea.'

'Yes,' I say weakly, and nod. 'I'll get dressed.'

She goes into the kitchen, and I can hear her at the stove. I sit on the bed, looking at the side Robert slept on, pressing my hand down onto the creased sheets. It is already cold and his imprint is gone. I am shivering, but I cannot stir. I am unable to move because of the feelings raging inside me. It dawns on me that I have never lived alone before, not even when I was at university. The house creaks around me, already feeling larger, emptier, just in a few short hours. I have to pull myself together.

I get up slowly and go to the oak dresser on the other side of the room, pull out the top drawer and find a candle. I put the candle in the brass holder and light it. It flickers and I place it on the windowsill, where it flickers some more. I get dressed, not noticing what I am wearing, not bothering to brush my hair, and leave our bedroom, with the bedclothes still strewn all over the bed.

Oonagh has the tea brewed. She doesn't speak, just pours me a cup. It is as weak as dishwater, but with a little sugar it brings some warmth back into my body.

'Thank you, Oonagh.'

She says nothing, but looks at me with such compassion it makes me want to cry. I start to talk quickly, determined not to lose control again.

'Robert has asked me not to tell anyone he has gone off to fight. I believe some people might think it anti-Irish to do so.'

She nods. 'Some would. But most don't. We all think he's very brave. Daddy and the lads will do all the work for you, Mrs Fanning, you've no need to worry.'

'Please call me June. We are practically the same age.'

She looks at me curiously, the idea dawning on her that in fact there are only a few years between us, yet my husband is nearly the same age as her father.

'So we are . . . June!' She smiles slowly. 'Isn't it great to have a real cup of tea?'

'Absolutely.' I gulp the hot brown liquid down. 'I need to be busy today, Oonagh.'

She looks at me thoughtfully for a moment.

'Well, there is the orchard. It's still not completely cleared out.'

'You said the place was cursed,' I reply, surprised.

'Well, you must have broken the curse, so, because the pie we had the day before yesterday was delicious.'

She sounds quite upper-class when she says the word 'delicious', and it makes me smile. It is strange how one can find humour in such desperate times.

Oonagh stays with me the whole day, longer than she should. We break our backs in the orchard, but it is satisfying, and I am excited by our hoard of fruit. Apples are so very precious. We spend the afternoon writing down ideas of what we will make with the apples and some other things from the garden. *Apple & Blackberry Jelly, Apple & Beetroot Chutney, Apple Sauce, Apple & Rhubarb Tart, Apple & Elderberry Cordial, Apple Pie, Apple Crumble, Sloe Gin?*

We giggle like two naughty schoolgirls at the idea of making sloe gin. I had spied a tree heavy with sloe berries just outside the orchard walls. Oonagh tells me she has never drunk it before, and I tell her how Father used to make it. She would like to try some. She says it sounds much nicer than the poitín. My arms and legs are sore from all the picking, so we put our feet up by the hearth and hug our hot watery tea to our hearts, sitting in companionable silence. For a moment it reminds me of being with Min, and what a comfort she would be if she were here with me. I do so want to tell my sister what it is like to be pregnant. So before I think any better of it, I confide in Oonagh.

'That's great, so it is,' Oonagh beams at me, and then she looks suddenly serious. 'But, June, you should never have done so much work today. You must look after yourself now.'

'I feel fine, Oonagh, full of beans. It's just that I do so wish Robert had not left me.'

'Does he know you're expecting?' she asks, putting more peat onto the fire.

'Yes, of course he does.' I look at the turf crumbling into the flames, and the sparks shooting out of them. 'I told him, and he still decided to go . . .'

I did not mean to say this to her, because suddenly it sounds disloyal. But I can't help it, because I need someone else to reassure me, to explain to me just why my husband has left.

'The war is important to him, June,' she speaks gently, and pauses. I know she is going to tell me something significant. I look at her. Her face is as soft as the cosy room, her brown hair falling in fuzzy loops around her perfect skin. She is a little plump, what Mother would have described as fat, and there is nothing remarkable about her face, but somehow, in that firelight, with dusk creeping in through the open door, Oonagh looks like a goddess to me. I put my hands on my belly and wait for her to speak.

'I wasn't even born when Robert's brother James D. was killed, but I remember my sisters talking about him many a time. He was a legend in the locality.'

She takes a sip from her tea and then laughs softly.

'The way my sisters described him, I used to imagine this medieval knight in my head. I would dream about James Fanning, dressed in silver armour on a white horse charging off to war. Who he really was got mixed up with tales from my storybook. Robert was only one year and one month younger than James. I believe they were very close.'

How odd: Min and I, Robert and James so close in age, such sibling bonds. Oonagh shivers suddenly, and pulls her shawl tighter around her shoulders.

'You never met their father, did you?' She asks, turning her gaze away from the fire and looking directly at me.

'No.'

'He was very hard on Robert.' Oonagh looks back into the flames. 'I heard that after James died, he hounded Robert, comparing him to his brother. You would think he wouldn't want his other son to go off to fight, possibly die as well, but it was the exact opposite. I think that's why Robert finally left, because he never did follow in James's footsteps.'

'So why is he doing so now?' I ask hotly. 'When he has least reason to? His parents are dead, and he has me . . . and the baby . . .'

'I don't know for sure,' says Oonagh, 'but maybe it's something to do with the past. He could be wanting to be rid of his guilt for good.'

I stand up suddenly and slam my cup down on the kitchen table.

'How stupid!' I exclaim. 'How very stupid!'

'Come,' Oonagh reaches up, and pulls me down by the arm. 'There's no point in upsetting yourself.'

She sighs.

'This is the way it will be for women throughout time, is it not?

It is our work to stay strong, and mind the fort. You should be proud of Robert. He is a sound man, as my Daddy says.'

She says this as if she knows something else about him. I sit down.

'Sure, you know that already?' she asks me.

'Yes, of course.'

'I'd say he never expected the Sheridens to return after all this time,' she continues. 'Not after what happened all those years ago. People don't forget so easy.'

Oonagh obviously thinks I know what she is talking about. I feel embarrassed to tell her otherwise, so I let her go on, trying to guess what she must be talking of.

'Sure Mrs Sheriden's return, and how things were between Robert and her husband, all of that could have had something to do with his decision too, don't you think?'

She asks me this guilelessly, looking straight at me with her butterscotch eyes.

'Yes, possibly.' I avert my gaze, not wanting to reveal my ignorance.

'Well,' she says, suddenly getting up and going to the sink to wash her cup. 'I don't think you should dwell on such things. You need to be looking after yourself, and keeping your spirits up. We shall all say our prayers, and before you know it the war will be over and Robert will be home to mind you and the baby.'

She stands at the door, her shawl tight about her, her silhouette black against the grey sky, and I can no longer see clearly the features of her face.

'I'll see you tomorrow, so,' she says.

'But you're not due to come.'

'Well, I shall just check in on you, and rob some of those apples for Mam.'

'Thank you so much, Oonagh.'

I cannot tell her how grateful I am for her company because she would think me pathetic. Her concern momentarily lifts my spirits, but once I walk back into our bedroom it is as if someone has smacked me in the face. I survey the room and the symbols of our marriage: the bed strewn with bedclothes, the scent of last night's lovemaking still within it; a pair of Robert's socks screwed up into two little black balls on the floor; the wardrobe door hanging open, empty hangers and a few straggles of his wardrobe left. I walk over to the dressing table and pick up the picture of us both on our wedding day, walking down a street in London, his stride confident and mine compliant.

Where is Robert now? I look out at our land, and already I can see the moon illuminating the dark trees. The leaves are swirling like snowflakes in a soft breeze, like singed memories, spinning through my mind. I peer across at the road, dark with shadows from the row of sycamores that line its path, hoping I can see the image of a man, walking back, returning home. Maybe Robert has changed his mind, and the pull of his wife and child-to-be are just too strong for him. Maybe, when it came to getting on that train to Belfast, it became too impossible to abandon me?

I am confused by everything Oonagh and I have spoken about. I don't understand what Claudette Sheriden has to do with Robert going to war, but one thing I do know, call it woman's instinct — there was some kind of relationship between them in the past. Why could Robert not tell me himself?

I sit on the bed and shake myself angrily. I think of the terrifying world my sister has been occupying during the Blitz, and I pinch the flesh of my arms until it hurts. Selfish, silly woman! Robert has not abandoned me. He is protecting me from the evil of Nazism; that is what he is doing. Didn't he explain it to me, so that I would understand, be prepared to be a proud soldier's wife, a mother of the free-thinking world? How could I complain, when my own sister is trapped in the home front?

But I cannot ignore it, this seed of discontent, this feeling of abandonment. It is bitter and raw and tells me something. I am not cherished. I am not loved.

NICHOLAS

Geraldine does come back, but not on her own. Nicholas sees her car winding down the lane as he sits on the roof attempting to slip in some new slates. He has abandoned the idea of thatch – too expensive, too much commitment. He's not sure how long he will be here in Cavan. Yesterday and today have been dry, so he has taken advantage of the good weather before it gets cold again. The summer has been so short. Already he can feel an autumnal chill as he sits on the grey slate in his T-shirt, the wind slipping under the thin cloth.

It's now late afternoon and he has only been off the roof twice, both times to see how the dog is. The vet said it was lucky. If Nicholas hadn't picked it up when he did, the dog would surely have died at the side of the road. But it is a tough little mongrel, most likely abandoned, although Nicholas cannot think why. The dog is the most gentle creature he has ever come across. The first time he tried to stroke the animal, it flinched and began shaking. It was frightened of him, and Nicholas realized that the previous owners must have hit the dog. But it is beginning to trust him and starts to eat out of his hand. The vet had set its leg and the animal is now tentatively hopping around the kitchen on the other three. It seems it will have a permanent limp.

'Hello, there!'

Geraldine jerks her head up in surprise. She is getting out of the car. She stands with her hands on her hips, squinting into the sunshine.

'Hello, Nick. How are you?'

He swings his leg over the top of the roof so that they both dangle over the guttering. 'Great. Working hard.'

'I can see that. Sorry, I hope we're not disturbing you.'

Her passenger door opens and a little old lady gets out. Geraldine rushes round the side of the car. 'Here, Granny, let me get the door.'

The woman brushes Geraldine away. 'I'm not an invalid, Geraldine. Remember I wanted to cycle over.'

Geraldine sighs. 'I know Granny, but I'm not able for that.'

Nicholas twists his body around and climbs down the ladder.

'Nick, I want you to meet my granny.'

'How do you do? I'm sorry my hands are filthy,' he says, wiping them on his jeans.

'Delighted to meet you,' says Geraldine's granny. 'It's great to see someone looking after the old place.'

Nicholas sees her face light up as she looks around her. So this is Oonagh Tuite. Here is someone who knows about the woman in the house, who knows what happened.

'Come in, please, for a cup of tea.'

The white dog trembles in the corner as they enter the kitchen.

'Oh, you got a dog,' Geraldine exclaims when she sees him.

'Well, it wasn't intentional. I found him on the side of the road, run over.'

'How awful. The poor thing.'

She goes over to the dog and crouches down in front of him, patting him gently.

'Oh, he's a darling. Grainne is always on about getting a dog. But Ray doesn't want one.'

'Why ever not?' asks Oonagh sharply, and in those three words Nicholas can discern that the old lady might not like Ray.

'Oh, you know, Granny — too much work, too much mess.'

'Well, you'd be looking after the thing. It would hardly bother him. Everyone in the country should have a dog.'

She sits down at the table and places her bag on the floor, folds her arms and looks about her. She must be at least eighty, thinks Nicholas, but she doesn't look more than seventy. Her hair is pure white and thick, curling about her collar, and her eyes are as bright as a robin's. She is small, and he feels like getting her a cushion to sit on, as the table seems too high for her.

'Well, the place isn't that different,' she says, looking around her. 'Sure, it's the same warmth and cosiness in the kitchen. That was always the heart of the house.'

Nicholas puts the kettle on.

'Did you live here with the Fannings?'

'Lord, no. I was living at home on the farm. I had only just met Paddy, but we weren't even walking out then. To think that within the year I was married to him!'

Nicholas rummages around in the press, and to his relief he finds a packet of Jaffa cakes, opens them and puts them on a plate.

'I hope you don't mind us calling in on you like this,' Geraldine says, 'but it was rather spur-of-the-moment. I was taking Granny for a drive, and then I thought why not see if you're in. I thought she might like to see the old place.'

'I wanted to cycle,' Oonagh says. 'If I don't keep moving I seize up.'

'Yes, but we only decided to come once we were in the car.'

Nicholas pours boiling water in the pot and then sets everything on the table. He only has mugs. Does the old lady want to drink out of a teacup?

Oonagh points at the basket of windfalls on the dresser.

'I see you've been harvesting,' she says. 'I remember that first autumn when June arrived and we went into the orchard together. It was the day her husband left to fight in the war.'

'What was his name again, Granny?'

'Robert. Robert Fanning. Oh, my da adored him, so he did. Even though he thought Robert was plain mad to go off fighting for the English. He never understood that. But he didn't judge him and he never told a soul.'

'Did you have to keep it a secret?'

'Well, of course, because there were some round here who would have viewed it as treason to have gone off and fought for the English. Although many did fight for them, and many died and were forgotten about. Disgraceful.' She sniffs, and takes a hankie out from her sleeve, blowing her nose.

'Are you cold? Will I light the fire?' Nicholas offers.

'Not at all. I'm grand,' Oonagh says, taking a Jaffa cake and nibbling it delicately.

'Granny came to see June Fanning every day more or less, didn't you? It used to take you an hour to walk from your house to hers.'

'Yes, and I didn't have the bike then, because the tyres were gone and we couldn't get the rubber during the war. But it didn't seem like such a long walk. We were used to it. You young ones driving everywhere, it just makes you lazy and fat.'

Nicholas notices Geraldine reaching out for a Jaffa cake and stopping, hand in mid-air. She sees him looking at her and blushes.

'Go on, please,' Nicholas says.

'I shouldn't,' Geraldine replies, but takes one all the same. As she bites into it, he notices the orange filling is the same colour as her hair.

They sit in silence for a moment.

'Have you seen her?' Oonagh is looking directly at Nicholas, her eyes unblinking, youthful in her lined face.

'Her?'

'June.' Oonagh replies impatiently.

'Don't be silly, Granny,' Geraldine starts to say.

'Yes,' Nicholas replies, staring back at Oonagh. The old lady breaks into a smile and nods.

'Are you telling me you saw the ghost of June Fanning?' Geraldine's eyes are wide open, her face pale.

'I think so.' He can hardly believe he is telling this country housewife and her granny that he has seen a ghost. If he were telling anyone else, he'd feel like a fool. 'She didn't tell me her name.'

'She spoke to you?' Even Oonagh looks surprised now. 'I never heard of that before. I heard that people saw her. The Reillys, who lived here before you, I think the daughter saw her in the attic, but she never spoke to them. What did she say?'

Nicholas tries to remember. For some reason that moonlit night seems hazy and confused and he can't recall exactly what the phantom June had actually said and what he had imagined. 'She said she had only one regret.'

'Just one?' Oonagh asks.

'Yes, and I think she wanted me to play the piano.'

'Ah,' Oonagh says with satisfaction. 'She loved the piano.'

'Did you ever hear her play, Granny?'

'No. The Fannings never owned a piano.' She pauses. 'I would have liked to.'

'This is a very strange conversation,' Geraldine announces, helping herself to another Jaffa cake.

Nicholas looks at Oonagh's face, and behind the lines of her life he can see the young, energetic girl who worked side by side with June Fanning in his house.

'Have you ever seen her, Mrs Tuite?'

'No,' Oonagh says ruefully. 'She must have nothing to say to me. But then I haven't been in the house for years, not since—' And she breaks off.

'Since what, Granny?'

Oonagh shakes her head. 'Oh, since it all happened.' She looks out of the window. 'I remember we worked so hard that day picking apples, and I was so happy that finally someone had come here and broken that curse. It took another woman to take away the rotten actions of the woman before. My mother always said it. Claudette Sheriden was the biggest sinner in the parish. She said that woman killed Robert Fanning's mother just by breaking her heart.'

'Who's Claudette Sheriden, Granny?'

'You know where Gillian and Frank Creavy live?'

'Yes.' Geraldine gets up and points out the window through the orchard. 'Nick, see the back of the house through the small woods behind the orchard, well that's the Creavys' house.'

'That house used to belong to a family called Sheriden,' Oonagh continues. 'And they believed themselves a bit above the rest of us. Claudette Sheriden was married to Phelim. She was a very uppity French woman. They were living in that house when June was here.'

Nicholas looks at the tall grey house behind the woods. He hadn't really noticed it before, and yet now it stands out. Dark, and gloomy behind the bright-green leaves.

'I remember thinking how brave June was the day her husband left. And she didn't tell me she was expecting until the evening, and I was so cross with her because I wouldn't have let her do half the work if I had known.'

Oonagh squeezes her hands together, and her cheeks are flushed, her eyes sparkling with memories.

'I thought she was very posh, but kind too. And sophisticated. I remember being so impressed when she told me she could drive a car. Of course no one had a car then, apart from the people up at the big house and the Sheridens. But they didn't drive anyway because there was no petrol. Sometimes you might see army lorries coming down to collect turf, or a single rider on a motor bicycle from Mullingar, checking out a reported sighting of a German spy parachuting into the woods. June was so worried about the Germans invading.'

Oonagh laughs. It is a robust laugh and seems too loud for her tiny body.

'I told her that wasn't likely, even though I had seen a robin that winter. Sure sign of an invasion! And she asked whether any spies had been captured and I teased her, telling her that Paddy had told me he had seen a German spy walking into Oldcastle Square after Mart one day to get himself a cup of coffee. And then I told her that it was more likely poitín that had made people think they had seen parachutes landing in the woods. And she didn't know what poitín was, which made us even, because I had never heard of sloe gin.'

'Goodness, Granny, you never told me any of this before.'

'You never asked,' Oonagh says simply. Then she turns to Nicholas and fixes him with her beady eyes. 'Why is it June is still here?'

He can see she expects him to know the answer.

'Well, I thought you could tell me that.'

Oonagh frowns, and then shivers.

'Do you think she's in here, with us now?' Geraldine whispers.

'Don't be daft, child.'

'She said she had to tell me a story,' Nicholas says.

'What kind of story?' Oonagh asks him.

But Nicholas cannot bring himself to say the word 'adulteress'. It is too strong a word to say over tea with two women he hardly

knows. He shakes his head and looks away. 'I don't know. It's probably all in my head.'

He hears Oonagh Tuite sniff again and knows she thinks he is
lying.

'Where did June Fanning come from, Granny?' Geraldine asks.

'She was English,' Oonagh says. 'She was quite distraught
because all of her family were in England, and her sister, whom she
adored, was in London during the Blitz.'

'Did you ever meet her family?' Nicholas asks.

'No. She never told me anything about her childhood. There was
something sad about her, so I don't think it was too happy a one.
We may not have had much privilege, but I was always a happy-go-
lucky girl, like my sister Teresa, God bless her soul.'

The door gently blows open, and a light evening breeze fills the
kitchen with the scent of outdoors, a mixture of honeysuckle and
grass. Nicholas feels as if he is drifting back in time, as if the three
of them are not flesh and blood, but shape-shifting shadows. Fig-
ures from the past emerge around them – June Fanning standing
in her kitchen, churning butter and waiting for her husband to
come home; and another woman, the other side of the woods,
whose presence floods her with fear. The young Oonagh is there,
running into the kitchen light of step, and waking June out of her
reverie, making her laugh. Nicholas looks at Oonagh now and sees
a tear sliding out of the corner of her eye, and he knows that she
sees this memory, too.

Geraldine stands up suddenly, her red hair like a flame down her
back as she looks out the window.

'I wonder what happened?' she says.

Nicholas looks at Oonagh and they are thinking the same thing.
What has made June Fanning stay here all these years? Why is she
still trapped in her husband's house?

JUNE

I drift. By the window in the attic, lying on my back on the bare boards, and slipping through the cracks into the kitchen to bake again. If the door is open, the land calls me. When I first came to Cavan I did not belong to it, but now I do. The smell is in my skin, so that my scent is that of the red roses in the back garden, or the thick earthy mulch at the foot of the apple trees where some wind-falls have rotted, or in the Sheriden woods the spicy tang of bark in my blood, so that I am a part of it. When I am very lonely I run through the Sheriden woods and stop to look at the Sheriden house, and wonder and regret. The orchard I avoid, but more often I take my spirit through my husband's fields searching for him, and praying for time to repeat itself, so that I could return to those weeks before he went to war, so that I could prevent him from going.

In the autumn of 1941 after my husband left and joined the RAF I felt abandoned. The landscape I had resented when I first arrived in Cavan became my companion, and I spent many hours walking the fields as far as the lake. Can you see me? Walking on and on, in dusk, in dawn, always, I tell you, alone.

I follow the curve of the lake. The dark woods frame the shore, and in the afternoon the light is evanescent, hazy and uncertain.

The sun is so low in the sky that at times I am forced to close my eyes, and when I open them again the air is glittering. Jewels, I think, glancing at my engagement ring. The lake is the colour of a sapphire. It makes the grass all the greener, such a ridiculously bright shade of the colour that I can understand why Robert refers to his home as the Emerald Isle. The woods to the side of the lake are mostly spruce, but some of the other trees have lost their leaves now, and in the distance they look like hairy down, as if they are soft enough for a giant to lie upon.

I walk and I feel that I am going into a spiral. The leaves rustle in the undergrowth, alive with little birds and animals, but it is sinister to me, as if I am being watched. I pull Robert's greatcoat about me. I have taken to wearing it, not only because it is so warm, but because it is something of his. There are little twigs in the pockets, and I wonder why. I finger them, imagining his touch before mine, and just this makes me want to cry.

He has brought me here, to his country, and to his house where I am a stranger and where I know no one. The only person I can talk to is Oonagh Tobin. There is nothing to do: no theatre, no pictures and no concerts. I may as well be on a desert island. I feel a flash of rage, and a flare of rebellion. Maybe I should go home to England. Even in the middle of a war it would be better than this stifling existence.

It is so very different here. The smell of the earth decaying, the leaves fecund and cloying, and the land rolling in waves around me. It is at times like this I wish so fervently that I had a car and gasoline to waste, so that I could drive to the sea. It would not be the same as Devon, but it would be something. I have heard the Atlantic Ocean can be quite spectacular. Sometimes I imagine I can smell the tang of the sea, and the wind whistling is like a siren's call or the waves pounding the beach, early in the morning especially, but they are just tricks of my mind and memory.

Water soothes me. I sit on a large stone at the edge of the lake and look at its iridescent calm. I think how different it is from the sea, which is open, playful, yet omnipotent, able to snatch your life in one instant. The lake can be dangerous too, but it will yield none of its secrets. From my stone I can see the mushy bed, pale in colour, almost the same shade as sand, but then it drops suddenly and the water is a darker shade of blue, and although tempted to wade out and feel the sandy mud tickle my bare soles, I know I could be stepping out into the abyss. The power of the lake is hidden, and not meant for humans to explore, while the sea invites us to sail on her.

I listen to the moorhens coo, the rustle of the reeds behind me, and watch the two swans. They are fishing, their tails like two large white petals balanced on the water's surface. One comes up, and then the other. They do not touch, yet they move as if one, gliding in and out of each other, creating immaculate silhouettes against the opalescent sky, shifting water and floating woods. They know I am here, watching, but they choose to ignore me. I envy such containment within the partnership of two. I have always longed for it in my relationship with Robert. I know what it feels like, this unity of two, for I had it when Min and I were children until our paths diverged, until Min became a wife and I became a student. Is it possible to have a marriage, like our sisterhood, when you understand your husband's mind as perfectly as your own? I cannot help thinking about my conversation with Oonagh, and what she said about Claudette Sheriden being a reason why Robert might want to go to war. What could she possibly mean? Is it possible my husband was once in love with this woman, and now wants to avoid her? But to make him want to leave me, and fight – well, what does that imply? Could he still love her? The idea is just too frightful to contemplate.

I think back to the time I saw Claudette Sheriden in the woods a couple of weeks ago. She is not a beauty, like Min or Mother, but she is certainly striking, with sharp cheekbones, short hair and big eyes. I suppose there is something boyish about her, like Peter Pan. As I think about Claudette Sheriden, I realize I have been walking in these woods every day in the hope that I might meet her again. This time I will talk to her.

The wind rustles through the trees and it sounds like the sea. I remember the day Min and I danced on the beach at home like two Greek maidens of Isadora Duncan. All we wore were tunics – hers pearl and mine mule-grey – and no undergarments. The freedom! We danced the shape of clouds beavering across the sky, our dresses ballooning like sails, our bare feet sinking and kicking, sand oozing between our toes. We had no need of music – just the sound of the wind rushing over the tops of the waves, and the exhilaration of the spray making our hearts beat, creating our own internal rhythm. And without one leading the other, we managed to dance the same dance. Will we tell the same story too?

I see my sister and I making this dance, our hips pushing against each other and then breaking away, and letting our bodies lift our hearts. Our movements are pure joy. I remember that my husband has never danced with me like this. It pains me. And yet Min and Charles did. I think back to their wedding day and the first dance. I was still in shock, distraught by the idea of losing my sister, stand-ing against the wall, and looking blankly at the celebrations. At this moment the band struck up and I saw Charles take Min's hand and spin her in a circle, and her eyes were shining and she was looking at him in the same way she looked at me when we danced together on the beach. She believed she had found an immortal love, like I thought our sisterhood had been. In that moment I wanted to find it, too. I could not believe Min had found love so soon, so young – so fast and eager she was to break away from me.

Min's husband first fell in love with her over a game of tennis.

She was sixteen years and two months old. I had just turned seventeen. It was 15th July 1933. By the time the leaves turned brown the pair were wed. On that fateful day did Min fall in love with him as well, or was she just trying to save our parents' marriage? Was she trying to outdo Mother?

1933 also marked our last summer holidays at home. Although Daddy had managed to cling on to the house since Christmas, he had been forced to accept a position as a schoolmaster in a boys' boarding school in Gloucestershire. We assumed Mummy would go with him and they would sell the house. Yet despite his desperate financial circumstances, Father appeared to be in better form than the year before. Indeed, he was very enthusiastic when Mother suggested a tennis tournament with some friends and neighbours. Since we had come home from school he had not taken to bed once. He was excited about my forthcoming entrance to London University, using every spare moment he could helping me to prepare. It was the happiest holidays I had spent with my parents in years, for even Mummy left me alone. She had more work to do, with Mrs Wyatt gone, and therefore she had no time any more to persecute her daughters.

Our tennis court was in essence a lawn, with a rather grubby net slung across it. But Min spent the week before the tournament tidying up this part of the garden, cleaning the net and making sure the grass was mown by organizing a neighbour's boy to do it. She even got a tin of white paint from the shed, and painted out the lines of the court again. She pestered me to practise with her, but found a better partner in our mother. Although unable to spend too long in the same room before arguing, my mother and sister happily volleyed for hours on the tennis court. Sometimes I watched with envy. It was a relationship I had never experienced with my mother. But then these days I had Daddy more or less to myself, and my jealousy would swiftly dissipate as I turned away

from looking outside, at the pair playing tennis on the lawn, and
hunted Father down in his study.

Min had never been sporty, but there was something about
tennis that she loved.

'It's like a dance,' she claimed. 'I feel so graceful when I am playing tennis.'

'It is because you are very good at it, Min,' I said. 'I never feel
graceful when I try to play tennis. I am such a clut.'

'But you will play tomorrow, won't you? We do need the num-
bers.'

'Oh, Min, do I have to?'

'Of course, it will be fun!' Min squeezed my arm and grinned
at me. Although she had been wearing a hat every day she prac-
tised, she had still caught the sun a little, and with her dark hair
and bright-blue eyes she looked like an exotic princess.

'I shall burn in the sun,' I said mournfully, looking at the ginger
freckles littering my pale arms.

'Of course you shan't, if you cover up.'

Min got up off her bed and went to smooth out her tennis dress,
which was hanging outside the wardrobe. It was crisp white
cotton, sleeveless and short, as was the daring fashion of 1933. She
and Mother had gone to Hooper's to buy their new outfits on
credit. It looked like a strange, bodyless phantom, hanging up in
the dim bedroom.

'Besides,' Min said, 'Mummy has invited lots of dishy gentlemen
for us to play mixed doubles with . . .'

'And their handsome wives, Min!'

'Not all of them have wives.' She smiled mischievously, and
when she said this it was the first time that I noticed a difference
in my sister. Min was more agitated than usual. She tossed and
turned in bed, sighing and eventually exclaiming, 'Oh goodness,
June, I am just too excited to sleep!'

'Well, you had better, otherwise you shall be serving double faults and showing yourself up in front of all those fine gentlemen!'

Min giggled, then sighed again, and the sound was almost sad.

The 15th July dawned cloudy, threatening rain. Min could hardly eat her breakfast – every few minutes she kept getting up from the table and checking the skies, shaking her head and then returning to her now-cold kedgeree.

'Goodness, Minerva, you are like a jack-in-the-box!' Daddy complained.

'Do stop fretting,' Mummy said. 'It is going to be a beautiful day.'

'How do you know?' asked Min.

'I can smell it,' she said.

Mother was right. By noon the clouds had cleared and the sun beat down on the lawn, parching the grass. The air was dry, and hot. Playing tennis in this kind of heat was the last thing I felt like doing, but dutifully I donned my tennis clothes. I couldn't let Min down, even though I knew I compared badly with my sister and mother.

I dressed in Mother's old tennis outfit. It hung to below the knee, was waistless and extremely unflattering for my curvaceous figure. I wore white stockings, and on my head I tied a white bandeau, for I considered that I might as well complete the look. In for a penny, in for a pound.

We had a light lunch, because Mother had prepared an enormous tea for later on. Our mother's culinary skills were still a surprise to Min and I. She was a virtuoso baker, if somewhat erratic when it came to ordinary mealtimes. Thus a lot of bread, cheese and pickles were consumed in the Sinclair household, punctuated by the odd dazzling meal. The tennis tea was something to be looked forward to. Mother had baked a lemon-drizzle cake, a Bakewell tart and a fruit loaf, had griddled a stack of drop scones, had unearthed Mrs Wyatt's raspberry jam from last year, and for

savoury she had made cucumber sandwiches delicately cut into tri-
angles with no crusts, and Chinese eggs – Father's favourite.

The guests began to arrive. Firstly Dr Redwidge and his wife
Phyllis, followed by Matthew and Dolores Little, Ashley and Sarah
Judge, and finally Captain Sanderson along with Charles Junior. All
the men, apart from Charles Junior, were obviously besotted with
Mother. She flitted between them like an exotic and rare butterfly,
looking a mixture of boyish and fragile charm in her short tennis
outfit. It was sleeveless, and her perfect skin shimmered on her
slender arms, a paler shade of honey. Her legs were bare, and their
skin was flawless. She was wearing white ankle-socks and canvas
shoes, which emphasized her petite stature and tiny ankles. She had
styled her black hair into soft curls, which were arranged off her
forehead with a white scarf, making her face more open than usual,
its rare definitions even more attractive. She wore little make-up,
letting her bright-blue eyes – the same colour as the sky – dazzle
and bewitch her admirers. The only woman present able to out-
shine her was her own daughter, Min.

Of course I saw my sister day in, day out, and yet it was on this
particular day as we were getting ready that I noticed how much
Min had changed within the last year. She had always been pretty,
but now she had matured into a fully grown beauty, just like
Mother. Was this good fortune or a curse?

Our mother was chatting to Ashley Judge, her obvious favourite
in the group of her admirers, while his wife tried to ignore her husband's flirtations and talked animatedly to Father about a recent
visit she had made to Greece.

'There is nothing to parallel the Parthenon, is there not?' Sarah
Judge was saying, as our father nodded seriously in agreement
before launching into his theory on its classical proportions.

I noted that Mother had hardly spoken to Captain Sanderson, who
was sitting opposite her talking to Dr Redwidge, but occasionally

glancing over at Mother and then looking sadly away. Charles Junior seemed rather nervous. He caught my eye and smiled anxiously at me. I very nearly felt sorry for him, although I had never liked the way he usually ignored me in favour of my sister.

Min made an entrance. As she swung her racquet by her side, sauntering across the lawn towards the assembled party, I was thrown by what a fine figure she cut. I remember thinking she looked like a film actress, with her perfect features and slender frame. There was something about Min that was even more attractive than Mother. It was nothing to do with age, but more to do with her expression. It was her smile. Min was grinning from ear to ear. She exuded warmth and charm, and although our mother could be stunning, she was certainly not warm. All the men looked at Min, and the women too. My mother's eyes narrowed.

'My, how young Miss Minerva Sinclair has grown up!' Dr Redwidge said.

Min stood and swung her racquet up into the air, 'Anyone for tennis!' she trilled, and burst out laughing. She was like a child of the sun and a woman of the moon, all rolled into one. Of course all the men wanted to partner her, much to Mother's annoyance, but in the end Min chose Captain Sanderson, who had not taken his eyes off her since she had arrived down on the lawn. I could sense Charles Junior squirming in his chair beside me, and caught his angry glare at his uncle, but he was, of course, too well-mannered to say anything.

Unfortunately for Charles Junior, he was partnered with me and our first match was against Min and Captain Sanderson. Of course we lost, miserably, mainly thanks to my appalling game, but not helped by Charles Junior's own hot temper. He disputed every call, claimed the ball was in when it was out, and altogether displayed bad sportsmanship.

'Oh, do calm down, Charles, and behave,' his uncle admonished him several times. But Charles Junior was no fool, and what he could see being played out on the tennis court, in front of his very eyes, astounded him. He left after the first match, claiming he had to get back to Dartmouth, without saying one word to Min, or thanking Mother for the tea, or even apologizing to me for leaving me in the lurch without a tennis partner.

'Well, goodness, Charles, your nephew is in bad form,' said Mother, her racquet resting on her hip, giving Captain Sanderson a hard glare.

'Yes, I can't think why.'

Mother raised her eyebrows, but said nothing. She and Ashley Judge were playing against Captain Sanderson and Min. Though preoccupied in her flirtations with Ashley, our mother sensed something else carrying on, on the other side of the net.

Years later Captain Charles Sanderson admitted to my Robert over a late-night glass of Scotch that it was during this very match of tennis that he fell in love with Min. Like a miracle, she released him from his tortuous infatuation with our mother. He said he could see all Min's attributes on the court: her competitiveness, yet her fairness; her sense of fun, yet her ability to use her mind and play strategically. He said she moved as gracefully as a ballerina, her beauty beguiling him. She inspired him to play the best game of tennis he had ever played in his life, better even than before he was crippled with his bad leg.

In the short hour it took them to beat Ashley Judge and our mother, Captain Sanderson had shed the weight of his grief, which had been oppressing him since the day his dear wife had died, and which he had attempted to block by attaching himself to our mother, a married woman. But it was Min who touched a place within him that was tender, a part of himself he had only ever shown to Meryl Sanderson before. Within that hour Charles decided he had found a new wife, for he and Min displayed all the possibilities of a perfect union on the tennis court: energy, intuition, good communication, coordination, vitality and victory. As Dr Redwidge called out, 'Game, set and match', Captain Sanderson shook Min's hand and looked into her eyes. My sister smiled even more broadly than before, knowing that, yes, she had won.

NICHOLAS

Nicholas picks Kevin up in Virginia. His friend had never learned to drive, so he is taking the bus from Dublin to the Cavan town of Virginia. It's late. Nicholas waits in his parked car, the dog on the seat beside him, watching the cars as they drive through the town. It's six in the evening and the traffic is non-stop. He can see men in dark suits, driving silver BMWs and Mercedes as they power down the road, on the way home to their bored wives, and spoilt children. There are lots of women too, usually in people-carriers or shiny black SUVs, some with children, but the odd blonde in a coupé zips by. His car is an old Volvo estate. It is big, which has been useful for transporting builders' materials, and it is reliable.

Living in Dublin, Nicholas hadn't noticed it so much, but here everyone seems to be in new cars. Watching the Friday-night traffic he realizes that Ireland has changed dramatically since he first came over from England and got married to Charlie. He wonders whether Charlie wanted him to be more like those successful professional men in the big, powerful cars. Was his lack of ambition a disappointment to her? She had often commented how could they possibly consider bringing a child into their home when they lived so hand-to-mouth? He had tried his best, started to teach the piano privately and even got pupils in a couple of the local schools. She had lived off him, because she hardly made any money from her art. Yes, why was it that he was expected to teach, but when he asked her to do the same she said no, she wouldn't have time to paint?

'It's different for you,' she said. 'You aren't composing music. You perform. You can still do that if you're teaching, but if I'm teaching it takes up all of my creative brain.'

'And what would you do if I wasn't here, paying the rent, buying food?' he asked crossly.

She smiled at him, her eyes crinkling at the corners, and sashayed across the room towards him. It was early in the morning and she wasn't fully dressed. 'I guess I would starve, Nick.'

She put her arms about him and pressed her body, still damp from the shower, against him, her wet hair tickling his neck. His anger dissipated.

'You could always sell your body,' he joked.

'No one would want me. I'm too skinny.'

He pushed her back on the bed. 'Not for me.'

Nicholas grips the steering wheel, staring at Virginia high street, trying to banish the memory of that morning from his mind. He lets out an involuntary moan and the dog looks up at him, ears cocked.

On the bed with Charlie, peeling her damp pants off and leaning over her, and feeling rich because she was his. She was so light that when they made love she made him feel like a big man, powerful and strong, like those guys in the Mercedes. When was that morning they made love? It wasn't so long ago. Within the last year, but before – surely it was before – it had happened? Maybe even then she had been lying to him. Maybe he should have changed himself, gone out and made some money, although he didn't know quite how he would have done that. He grits his teeth. Where the hell is Kev?

*

Finally the bus pulls up, and Nicholas gets out of the car and waves over at Kev as he gets off.

'Christ, I didn't realize you lived so far away.'

'We've half an hour's drive yet. Wait until you see where the house is.'

'What's the dog called?' Kev asks as he puts his rucksack in the boot, and Nicholas moves the dog into the back.

'Hopper.'

'Cool. After the painter?'

Nicholas pauses. 'No, because he hops.'

The two men look at each other and burst out laughing.

'Bloody hell, you better help me get my head out of my arse. I've been hanging around too many artists,' Kevin says as he gets in the car.

Nicholas is glad Kev has come now, grateful even. None of his other friends had bothered to visit.

'Let's get a Chinese on the way home,' he says. 'I don't feel like cooking.'

A full moon fills the kitchen with light, as the two men sit on the doorstep smoking, Chinese takeaway boxes littered about them.

'This place is magic, Nick,' Kev says, taking a swig from his beer bottle.

Nicholas looks at the orchard, the trees lined with silver, shadows whispering between them, and listens to the solitude, the peace he inhabits. He imagines the ghostly June Fanning floating between the trees, young, beautiful and pregnant. A seed within her beginning to grow, her girlhood falling away, her womanhood ripening. Kev continues to talk.

'I love the trees. They are so twisted up, like bent old men. I've got to take some pictures of them tomorrow.'

'Don't forget you're down here to help me dry-line.'

'Oh, yeah,' says Kev unenthusiastically. 'Will we go to the pub?'

O'Mahony's is fairly full. Everyone looks at them as they walk in. Everyone knows who Nicholas is, but he doesn't recognize a soul. He wishes now they had stayed at the house and just drunk beer, but Kev doesn't seem to care what the locals think.

'How's it going?' he says cheerily to the assembled company as he makes his way to the bar and orders them two pints.

Nicholas sits down under the TV. All of the bar stools are taken up, and a small group of men are playing cards on the counter. There are three clusters of couples in different corners of the pub. The men on one side of the table, and the women on the other. Suddenly he is aware of someone looking at him. A woman. He realizes with a jolt it is Geraldine. She looks completely different with make-up and her hair hanging down around her face. She has an awful red lipstick on and too much blusher. She smiles and waves, and when she does this the man sitting next to her looks up and stares at him. Nicholas realizes he will have to go over now.

'Hi, I didn't recognize you for a moment.'

'Oh, yes – well, I have my glad rags on,' she says, shifting in her seat. She is wearing a shiny pink top, which is too tight for her. It looks terrible against her hair and skin.

'Ray, this is Nick,' she titters, and Nick can see she is a little drunk.

The man reaches out his hand, but he doesn't smile. He is a lot older than Geraldine, with wiry grey hair and thick grey eyebrows.

'Oh, you're the fella who teaches the piano?' he says. 'Bought the Reilly place? Belonged to the Fannings before that.'

'Yes,' Nick shakes his rough hand. 'Nice to meet you.'

Ray looks him up and down, and Nick knows he is assessing him.

'And do you make a living from teaching the piano?' he asks.

'Kind of,' Nicholas replies.

'Kind of?' Ray sneers, and Nicholas knows he doesn't like him. He can see Ray thinks he is weedy, just by the way he is looking at him. To be honest, Nicholas wouldn't like to get into a fight with him. Ray might be older than him, but he looks as tough as old boots. 'I don't know why she wants to learn the piano,' he says. 'It's a bit late now, isn't it, Geraldine?'

Geraldine colours, unable to reply.

'It's never too late,' Nick counters.

'Yeah, well, maybe if you've the time to be doing such things. Some of us have to make a living, you know. All right for these women, hey?' He gives Geraldine a jab with his elbow and she smiles weakly.

Kev comes up behind Nick, one pint in each hand.

'This is my friend Kevin, from Dublin.'

'Would you like to join us?' Geraldine asks, but Ray has already turned to the man beside him and is chatting away.

'Thanks, but we've seats over there,' Nicholas indicates. 'I enjoyed meeting your granny.'

'Yeah, she's great. She liked you too.'

'Who was that?' Kevin asks as they return to their table.

'One of my new piano pupils.'

'Right-o. Husband looks like a caveman.'

'Yeah, poor woman.'

'She doesn't seem your type though, mate.'

Nick pushes his glasses up his nose. 'What do you mean?'

'Your woman. She's a bit large for you, isn't she?'

'Kev. She's my pupil, not my girlfriend.'

'Well, she fancies you, it's obvious.'

'Great.'

'Come on, maybe you should go for it. When was the last time you had a shag?'

'Shut up, Kev.'

'I couldn't go without it for long. It's murder while Jackie's in Greece. I might have to stray.'

Nick looks at Kev in astonishment as he sips his pint, giving himself a white moustache.

'Last time she was in America for three months I had this hot weekend with this Spanish student over for the summer. What was her name? Monserrat – that was it. Loved her name. And her tits, for that matter.' Kev chuckles.

'Are you pulling my leg, Kev? Have you been unfaithful to Jackie?'

'It didn't mean anything, Nick. It was just sex. Christ, don't get so high-and-mighty. Jackie and me have been together since we were twenty. I mean, I love her – you know, want to have kids with her one day – but Christ, that's a long time. It's only natural you might have the odd slip-up. I'm sure she has.'

'But do you *know* she has?' asks Nick, his heart beginning to beat fast in his chest.

'Well . . . not for sure. It's always better not to talk about these things. If you don't mind me saying so, that's where you went wrong, mate. Never confess.'

Nicholas can feel his cheeks burning.

'What did Jackie tell you about me and Charlie?'

'She didn't tell me anything actually. She's loyal to Charlie, you know. But, I mean, it's obvious Charlie was crazy about you, so I thought – you know – that you must have done something—'

'Me!'

'Come on, Nick, don't tell me you've never been unfaithful to Charlie?'

'No, I haven't.'

There is a pause. Canned laughter and clapping floats down from the TV, and Nick can hear Geraldine's husband laughing loudly with the man he is sitting next to.

Kev looks at him. Nick can see he is a little drunk, but not so drunk that he cannot see that Nick is telling the truth.

'Christ! Are you serious? You're a bloody miracle.'

He pauses, and takes a drink from his pint.

'But then, if you didn't do the dirt, why did you guys break up?' Kev asks. But before Nick has a chance to reply he slaps his forehead. 'When Jackie said it was a matter of fidelity, I thought she meant you, but it was Charlie. Wow, I'm sorry. Do you know who he is?'

'No,' Nick says tightly. 'Some artist. She wouldn't tell me. It happened in London, when she went over for a show.'

'So that's why you broke up? Just because she screwed some guy in London?'

'She betrayed me, Kevin.'

'That's how you feel, is it?' Nicholas can feel Kevin's gaze penetrating him.

'How can you sleep with someone else, if you are in love with your partner?' Nicholas challenges him.

'Are you saying I don't love Jackie, then?'

Nicholas fumbles with his words. He knows that Kev loves Jackie, but they are different from Nick and Charlie. Those two were free spirits, open flirts – it wasn't surprising to learn that either one of them might have cheated on the other. They weren't even married. Kev had never made that commitment to Jackie. But he and Charlie were different. They had got married. They had promised themselves to each other. Of course he had been tempted, but he had never wanted to destroy what they had. And no woman had ever held a light to Charlie. She had been everything to him.

'Are you all right?' Kevin is looking at him, his eyes filled with concern. Nick puts his hand up to his face. His cheeks are wet. He's crying, and he doesn't even know it.

'Shit!'

'Here, I'll get us a shot each. I think you could do with it.' Kev stands up to go to the bar. Then he leans down and puts his hand on Nick's shoulder. 'Life's a bitch, sometimes.'

Nick looks up at him. 'Kev, do you know if she's still seeing him? Is she in Greece with him?'

Kevin looks taken aback. 'Of course not, Nick. Jackie and Charlie went to Greece on their own. She's not seeing anyone. She's in bits, Nick. When you left she was devastated. That's why Jackie took her away. She was worried about Charlie.'

Nick watches Kev go to the bar. He wipes the back of his hand surreptitiously across his cheek, hoping no one has noticed he was crying. It is dark in here, and no one seems to be minding them. But when he looks up he sees Geraldine looking at him, and he knows she has seen. She smiles at him kindly and he looks away. He doesn't want her pity. His head is wrecked. He doesn't understand why Charlie did what she did, if she was so upset when they broke up? She knew what he was like. She knew about his pride. When she slept with that artist in London, she knew she was ruining their marriage.

They wake late, heads hammered from too much drink. Hopper wants to go with them for a walk, but Nicholas is worried he isn't strong enough.

'We can always come back,' says Kev, slinging his camera bag over his shoulder. 'Come on, the sun doesn't look like it's going to stay out for long.'

It rained heavily during the night, and the ground is soggy as they walk through the orchard, the leaves still dripping with water. But it is warm already and there is a misty steam rising off the land.

Nicholas feels sweaty, although he has just had a shower. Hopper hops along, and Nicholas keeps stopping and waiting for him, but the dog seems happy sniffing in the roots of the trees and trying to raise his damaged leg to pee every so often.

At the back of the orchard there is a broken-down old gate.

'Did you know you've plums there, Nick?' Kev points to two trees beside the fencing.

'No, I didn't.'

'You can make us some jam when we get back!'

Kev laughs, pushing the gate aside and entering the cool woods. There is a very overgrown path leading through the trees. He goes on ahead, and Nicholas slows down to keep pace with Hopper. Flies buzz around his head, although it is early yet, and he sees a few rabbits dashing into the undergrowth. Hopper sees them, stiffens, but thinks better of chasing after them.

'Good boy.' Nick pats the dog and is rewarded by a lick on his hand.

The wood smells strongly, a tangy, fresh aroma like pine, although these are not pine trees. It is as if the rain has soaked all the scents of the wood and wrung them out in the air, which is thick and cloying, full of insects, and sunlight. Huge thistles line the path, with big purple heads, and there is an abundance of dandelions. It has only been a couple of weeks since he walked in the woods and yet it feels as if there has been a riot – all the rain has caused the vegetation to go wild.

He turns a corner and sees Kev taking pictures of the trees. It is a small gathering of beech trees on thick mossy ground, which looks like green carpet. Hopper pauses and looks at Nicholas. He sniffs the air. Nicholas looks behind him. He can hear someone, he is sure of it, pushing through the undergrowth, but when he steps back and looks again there is no one to be seen.

'Just a bird, Hopper,' he says.

But he can't shake this feeling of someone shadowing them, even when he reaches Kev and the two of them walk together through the trees.

'Can you hear anything?' Nicholas asks him.

'Like what?'

Nicholas turns around. 'I don't know, someone behind us.'

'Nope. These are private woods, aren't they?'

'Strictly speaking, they belong to the people who live in that house.'

They have reached the other side of the woods and are facing a thick hedgerow, behind which Nicholas can just see the top of the Creavys' house. So this was where Claudette Sheriden lived. Just a short walk between the Sheriden house and the Fanning cottage. He walks up to the bushes and pushes them out of his way. There is a huge wall of nettles within them, but he uses a stick to beat them down. Kev starts taking more pictures, close-ups of the nettles and leaves.

'What are you going to do with all these photographs?' asks Nicholas.

'I don't know. I can't help it, it's habit. I have to record everything,' Kev says.

Hopper seems tired. He lies down at Nicholas's feet. Nicholas crouches down by the dog. He doesn't feel well himself. He looks at the stone house facing him, and it makes him feel strange. It looks like so many houses in Ireland. A stone square, two up, two down, grey slate roof and a glass back porch. Yet he knows he has looked at this before – an overgrown back garden, a few apple and pear trees dotted about, a big oak tree with a broken old swing hanging off it, and the grey house staring down at him. Nicholas turns round suddenly and looks back through the trees. The sun speckles the ground between the leaves and he can see dust motes and cobwebs spinning in the light breeze. It is gentle and still, and yet he feels a sense of anticipation, as if at any moment he will see someone coming through the trees. And then for a second he does. Like an old movie, a black-and-white figure, walking briskly, her hands in the pockets of a man's coat, her head covered by a head-scarf, her chin tucked in, not looking at the woods around her, just wanting to get somewhere, quickly, without fuss or attention. Nicholas blinks and, when he looks again, she is gone.

'Did you see that?' he asks Kev.

'What?' Kev asks him, examining a phallic fungi jelly-formation on the ground.

'Nothing.'

Kev is too busy looking at the details of the woods to see beyond them.

Without warning the sun goes in and it starts to rain. They turn back towards Nicholas's house. Hopper hops between the two of them as Kev puts his camera away.

'How's the head?' Kev asks, not looking at him.

'Okay,' Nicholas says.

'Couldn't believe you played the piano when we got back.'

'Sorry?'

'I'm lying there in bed, God knows what time it is, and the next thing I hear you hammering away on the piano. Bloody lunatic!'

Nicholas feels a cold hand on his chest and he stops walking. It is as if the hand is holding him back, preventing him from going back home.

No. He hears a whisper in his ear.

He is about to say it – that he wasn't playing the piano last night and it must have been his resident ghost, June Fanning – but then he thinks better of it. He's not sure why he doesn't tell Kev. His friend would definitely have been interested. But then he might have shown him that it was all in his head, and that it was Nick him-self playing the piano, that he had been sleep-walking. He didn't want to believe that. He needs June Fanning's music to comfort him.

He steps forward, pushing against the cold hand, an invisible wall.

'Are you all right? You look like you've seen a ghost,' Kev comments.

Nicholas laughs, takes a cigarette out of his pocket and tries to light it in the rain. 'Yeah, I'm grand.'

Kev stops walking, looks at him, smiles. 'Jackie and Charlie are back tomorrow, you know. Why don't you come with me to the airport?'

Nicholas shakes his head in panic. 'No, I can't.'

'Come on, Nicholas, no one's perfect. You're a fool to chuck away Charlie.'

Nick inhales on his cigarette, shakes his head again. 'I've got to stay here. Finish the house.'

They have reached the orchard now. Kev goes through the gateway. 'You can't be serious about this place. You can't do all this on your own. Come back to Dublin, sort it out with Charlie.'

'No,' Nick snaps, pushing roughly past Kev. All he wants to do is get away from him, back to the house, and hide in his room. Suddenly he remembers that he heard the piano too last night. He thought it a dream. He had been unable to sleep. His head was full of memories of Charlie, and the image of Geraldine in her bright-pink top looking at him in the pub, and he had felt so sexually frustrated as well, twisting and turning in the bed. The notes from the piano had sawed through his heart, and he had lain on his stomach trying to shove his body into the mattress. The music had stopped then, and after a while he had felt a presence in his room, a slight shift in the temperature, a feeling of spinning in his bed. He turned over, lain on his side. Moonlight flooded the room. He could not see her, but he felt her next to him and he imagined this young woman, Robert Fanning's English wife, lying down next to him on the bed. They both lay on their backs, side by side. He held his breath, afraid that her ephemeral presence would disappear. He could sense her longing and pushed his hand out from his side. He imagined her tiny fingers holding his, reaching out from another world. When he closed his eyes he had a picture in his head. Himself and June Fanning lying face to face, the tips of their noses touching, resting their lips on each other, but not kissing, only giving. Giving succour.

Now, walking through the orchard, Nicholas feels more bereft than ever. He never knew it was so hard to live alone, to think that nobody in the real world cared about him. Had he invented June Fanning to fulfil his own lonely yearnings? Was he losing his mind?

The next morning Nicholas takes Kev to the bus. They have a late breakfast, eating eggs and bacon, sitting on the old chairs in the yard, looking at the orchard.

'Imagine what this place must have been like when it was a working farm.' Kev bites into a slice of buttery toast.

'A lot noisier, I would think,' says Nicholas.

'Yeah, chickens clucking and pigs snorting on Old Macdonald's farm.' Kev laughs. He takes a slug of his coffee. 'But seriously, Nick. Do you ever think about the people who lived here before?'

'Well, yes. In fact I would think most old places like this are haunted by their previous inhabitants.'

'Do you believe in ghosts?' Kev's eyes narrow, and Nicholas pauses. He isn't sure what he should tell Kev. He doesn't want to be mocked.

'Maybe.'

'Come on,' Kev snorts. 'Ghosts are the inventions of overactive imaginations. I put them in the same box as religion. The one labelled mumbo-jumbo.'

'Okay, Mr Cynic. But how can you be so sure that ghosts don't exist?'

Kevin picks up a piece of his bacon rind and chews it. 'I suppose it's like anything. It's only real if you believe in it.'

It is a warm day. Nicholas opens the sunroof and the car windows. Hopper pushes his snout out of the back window as they bump along the country roads. In this weather the landscape has never looked more charming. The green drumlins roll up and down on either side of the road, the blue sky is cloudless, and a heat-haze shimmers above the surface of the road. Tractors trundle along in front of them as they crawl along the road. Sometimes Nicholas has to remind himself that he grew up in England. Ireland has always been closer to his heart. His father was so proud of being Irish that it rubbed off on him. He wasn't from Cavan, but from the west, and they had spent most of their summer and Christmas holidays staying with their father's family in Connemara. Nick's mother hadn't liked it much. She said it was too damp and the landscape depressed her, too bleak. She was from the Cotswolds, where she lived still, with the honey-coloured houses, ancient village hamlets and gentle garden landscape. Populated and pretty. Ireland was too wild for Nick's mother. She had been encouraging Nick and Char-lie to move back to England for years. He knew she had been hoping for a grandchild, but she had never said a word to Nick, not once.

Most of Nick's Irish family were gone or dead now, but he had always intended to move out west. It was just that Charlie was from Dublin, and their lives had seemed permanently entangled in the capital city. Yet here he was now, living in Cavan, a place he guessed his mother would find even more desolate than the west. What would Dad think? He had been a farmer's boy, forced to emigrate to England when he was young, and always yearning for home. He thinks of June Fanning's spirit and wonders why it is that he can see her, sense her presence, but has never once felt his father around. Was that a good thing? Did it mean that John Healy was happy in the next world?

Under a different set of circumstances Nicholas believes his father was so full of stories that he could have been a writer. But he had been forced to make a living through more traditional ways as a bank manager. That was his upbringing. Nicholas feels grateful his parents had always encouraged his creative hopes and dreams. But maybe his father should have spent more time making him a man of the world, rather than filling his head with stories and songs about fairies from the west, and bog sprites and the dreams of his ancestors who wished to cross the Atlantic and conqueror America. Nicholas glances at the sky and sees a sparrowhawk hovering over a field. He had only been a little boy. Of course his daddy was only going to tell him tales. What must it be like to have your own child sitting on your lap, attentive, idolizing you? You are his world. Nick had always thought of his childlessness in terms of what Charlie was missing out on, but suddenly he realizes he would have made a good father, too. Who could he tell his father's stories to now?

They arrive in Virginia and Nick pulls up across the road from the bus stop. 'Listen, thanks,' he says turning to Kev.

'What for?' asks Kev.

'You know, coming to see me and everything.'

'I had a good time. Besides, I'm a lazy git, as you know — we didn't even do the dry-lining thing.'

'Oh, yeah,' Nick says unenthusiastically.

Kev gets out of the car and Nicholas gets out the other side. He opens the boot and takes Kev's rucksack out. They stand awkwardly on the pavement. Nicholas knows Kev wants to say something about Charlie. She is flying into Dublin this afternoon, and Nicholas can't get it out of his head.

'Well, bye . . .' says Nick.

The two men look at each other. Kev smiles and shoves his hands into his pockets. 'All right, mate?'

Nicholas nods. He gets back into his car.

'Hang on a minute.' Kev takes his camera out of his case. 'Let's take a picture of you and the mutt.'

Nicholas pulls Hopper onto his lap. He smiles at Kev's camera and his jaw aches. He knows the smile is false, but he can feel Hopper's heartbeat against his chest and that feels good. The dog suddenly licks his chin, his whiskers tickling his skin and making him laugh.

'That's better,' says Kev, taking the shot.

For a long while after the bus drives off Nicholas sits in his car with Hopper on his lap, the dog waiting patiently for his master to make a move.

'Just the two of us again, boy,' he says as he gently shoves Hopper onto the passenger seat and starts up the car. But as he drives back towards his farmhouse he knows that's not true. He is returning to June.

JUNE

The light drains slowly away here, not like at home when suddenly it is dark. By the time I am wending my way back up to the house I can see a lamp lit in the kitchen, and the sparks flying out of the chimney. Only then do I notice the strange bicycle outside the front of the house, and my heart does a tiny leap because a part of me hopes this could somehow mean Robert is home. A ridiculous fantasy, for only the day before I had received a letter from him telling me he had arrived safely in the south of England.

Why did he have to choose the RAF? Is it safer than the infantry, or the navy? I do not think so, for all I can think of are the stories of bombers going down, no crew surviving, and how they are in desperate need of men like Robert to replace them. At least he is not flying yet. I try not to think about it – Robert in his metal machine of destruction, up above France and Germany, dropping his deadly load. Things are beyond my control now and I should just carry on, as best I can. I should keep the place going, so that Robert has something to come back to.

But how I wish I were not pregnant. It makes me feel even more disempowered for I am now attached, irredeemably, to another entity. It is as if I am constantly off-balance, a strange surge and motion inside me like the swell of the sea, so I am nauseous half the time. It was my sister Min who wanted to have children, not I.

At moments I feel angry at this injustice, but then what did I expect – to sail through my marriage, without having children? That only happens to those who are barren, something my dear sister Min must be. How unfair it is that what she desired most was denied her. It makes me more determined to squash my apathy and accept things as they are now.

I think back to the night Mother gave Min the christening dress, and how thrilled my sister was. We were all certain that within the year there would be a new member of our family wearing it.

Min's wedding eve and our mother took us up to the attic to give her a trousseau. 'I did not think you would need this for a few more years. But as usual, Minerva, you have surprised us all.'

My mother regarded my sister coolly, knelt down and opened a plain trunk made of walnut. It was just over half-full of linen, crisp white sheets, pillowcases, napkins, tablecloths and handkerchiefs. In between each layer she had put small sprigs of lavender. The scent of clean linen, and musky lavender, wafted up from inside the chest.

'Oh, Mother!' Min spoke excitedly. 'Light another candle, so I can see!'

I leaned forward on my heels to look inside the chest. I reached out with my fingers and traced the outline of the embroidery on one of the table-tops. It was of a red rose and a white rose, their thorny stems entwined.

'I embroidered them myself,' said our mother, and I looked at her in surprise. 'Yes, you did not know what a little home-maker I can be,' she said sarcastically. 'But you will learn fast, Min, the things that please a husband.'

'Charles is more interested in pleasing me,' Min said proudly.

Mother smiled slyly. 'It is all attention and flattery before you are married, but once you are his wife, it is quite a different matter.'

I thought of all the wives that our mother had made sad by diverting their husband's attentions away from them. Even poor Mrs Sanderson, before she had got ill and died.

'It will be different for me, Mother,' said Min confidently.

'And how so, Minerva?'

'Because I am like you, Mama. I am a femme fatale!'

Mother burst out laughing. 'What rubbish have you been reading now? Or is your head turned by the picture that you and June went to see on Saturday? Femme fatale – my goodness, do you not know that femmes fatales never get married?'

She sighed, closing the chest and sitting back, her arms stretched out behind her, her fingers spread against the floorboards.

'Oh, I should stop you, really I should! But Captain Sanderson is adamant he loves you, and will provide well for you, and as you know your father is putting everything into June's education.'

She looked sharply at me.

'I hope you realize this, June, how much store your father has put into your academic career. You are this family's suffragette. There will be no room for romance in your life.'

Min giggled, 'Poor Juno!'

'I would not want to get married,' I said quietly. 'At least not yet.'

But Mother seemed not to hear me, and instead got up and walked over to a dusty old wardrobe in the corner of the attic. 'Now,' she said almost to herself, 'I think it could be in here.'

She opened up the closet and rustled around amongst the old clothes, eventually pulling out a small garment wrapped in yellowed tissue paper. The stench of mothballs was overpowering and made Min and I cough.

'Here we are,' Mother said. 'You should take this too, Min, you will probably be needing it before June.'

She unwrapped the tissue to reveal a baby's christening dress.

'Oh, how gorgeous,' Min swooned, taking it from our mother and fingering the tiny garment.

The robe was ivory, and made of thick silk, with delicate embroidery in white on the cuffs and collar. What made the dress so grand were its layers and layers of net skirt. It hung limply in Min's arms as she cradled it.

'This dress has been worn by each generation of the Sinclair family. I believe your father wore it, and his father before him.'

'Do you have your christening robe, Mother?' I asked, thinking she might give it to me.

She waved her arm away towards the sloping ceiling and spoke vaguely. 'Oh no, that was lost long ago.'

We were quiet for a moment, and I thought about my mother's family, whom she never spoke of. Her father had died young, and her mother had been unable to cope and had palmed her offspring off on various aunts. Our mother and her younger brother had ended up with a cruel old aunt. She never spoke of her mother now, and we didn't know whether she was dead or alive. Only once had Father spoken about her. He told me that apparently she had been very beautiful, and a socialite, unhappy to give up her lifestyle to look after her children.

'How old were you when you got married, Mother?' asked Min.

'I was seventeen, June's age.' She sighed. 'I was as excited as you, Min. I thought my life was going to change completely.' She turned abruptly, held Min's shoulders in her hands and stared at her for a minute, before speaking. 'Are you sure you wish to get married, Minerva?'

'Yes, of course,' Min replied, her voice rising.

'But do you love Captain Sanderson, or is it simply because . . .' Mother faltered, dropped her arms and looked away. 'He is so recently bereaved. He thinks he loves you, but maybe all he is looking for is comfort,' she said flatly.

'I have always loved Charles,' Min said shrilly. I felt a punch of surprise in my stomach. 'Since I was thirteen I have been in love with my Prince Charming. But it was always a dream that he would love me, because he was married, but now – now my dream has come true.'

'If you say so, Min.' Our mother sounded weary.

I looked at her expectantly. Why didn't she say something else? Could she not stop Min from marrying Captain Sanderson, from deserting me? I felt such a confusion of emotions: cross with Min for abandoning me, yet happy for her at the same time. She had found what she really wanted. It was like when I had found my love for ancient Rome.

'I suppose the birds must fly the nest one day,' Mother said sadly, and I was astonished that she would say such a thing, for she had always made us feel as if we were a burden to her.

'Mummy, when will you have to leave the house?' Min asked quietly.

'Soon, within the next month, I think, Min.' Mummy tried to sound upbeat. 'So I shall need you two girls to clear out some of your old things. But we shan't be here until the beastly end, shall we, June?'

I looked up at my mother. I did not know what she could mean.

'You will come to Italy with me, won't you, darling?'

Before I could answer Min piped up, 'And me too? I shall come too, shan't I?'

'But, Min, you are getting married tomorrow!'

'Yes, but Charles has promised to take me to Italy. So we can join you, can't we?'

Mummy looked uncomfortable, her cheeks reddening. 'I would rather not travel with newly-weds,' she said drily.

But Min was not put off. 'Oh, but I can't bear it if June goes and I don't, for I just have to go to Florence. I just have to. Why, I shall go with Charles first for our honeymoon, and then I can meet you when you arrive in Italy. How perfect that would be!'

'Maybe,' our mother said uncertainly. 'We shall think about it.'

I realized that Mother had not waited for an answer from me, but had assumed I would go to Italy with her. As if I belonged to her. I might not want to go, I might want to stay in England with Father. But then I thought about the chance to go to Rome, and to explore places I had only read about in books. It made my heart quicken – the possibility of stepping back in time.

'Now we had better go back downstairs, and go to bed. Tomorrow is an important day, and we all need to look our best,' our mother said.

Min grabbed her hand. 'Mummy, are you happy for me?'

My mother wriggled her fingers out of my sister's hand. 'Of course I wish you to be happy, Min, but you must know, as they all say, that marriage is not a bed of roses.' She paused. 'You may find it difficult at first in the marriage bed, but you will grow used to it, and I believe your husband will be gentle and attentive. He is a good man.'

She blew out the candle, and we descended the staircase in darkness.

Later, in bed, I could hear Min tossing under her eiderdown. We had shared one room for so many years, and slept in the same bed so many times, yet this night I felt a new distance between my sister and I. It made me want to cry.

'Are you all right, Juno?' Min whispered, as if by instinct she sensed my feelings.

'Can I get into bed with you?'

'Of course.'

I heard Min pull back her covers. I slipped out of my own bed and tiptoed across the chilly floorboards, climbing into my sister's warm bed as quickly as I could. We cuddled up together, like two peas in a pod, like two beautiful sea anemones, like two ship-wrecked sailors on a raft drifting out to sea.

'To think,' Min whispered, 'this will be the last time we share a bed.'

I felt a lump rise in my throat. 'Oh, Min, why do you have to get married?'

'Because I do,' my sister spoke into my ear. 'Don't you know I have always loved Prince Charming, and now I have made him fall in love with me. It is best this way, June, because now he can never take Mummy away from Daddy, can he?'

I froze in alarm. 'Oh, Min, you're not marrying Captain Sanderson for that reason, are you?'

'No, June, I know he loves me. He just fell under Mother's spell for a while.' She sighed. 'I can't bear to live here any longer, June. I have to make my own life now.'

'Are you not frightened?'

'Of what?'

'Of being a wife. Of having children?'

Min laughed softly, 'Oh, June, there is nothing to be afraid of, when you are in love. It feels so natural.' She sighed, and took my hand into her own, squeezing it. 'Dear June, when you fall in love you will understand what I am telling you, because you will feel how I do now, when all I want is to be in bed with Charles, and for him to caress me.' She shivered and kissed my wet cheeks. 'Now make me stop talking about Charles, because I shan't be able to sleep at all for thinking of how much I desire him.'

She released me from her embrace and turned on her other side. A few moments later I heard the steady rhythm of her sleeping breath. But I could not sleep. I lay on my back, and many images raced through my head. I remembered a time Min had made me pose naked for one of her life drawings, and how the cold air had made my nipples harden, and when that had happened I had felt a tightness between my legs, and a shortness of breath. This was what Min must have been talking about. This was the desire she spoke of. Instinctively I knew it was how Mother felt when she was surrounded by the young, handsome husbands she could never have. I understood it in the way my mother would twist her hips, her eyes become large black pupils, and you could see her breasts, firm and round as if pushing to get out of the fabric of her dress. I touched my own breasts. They were bigger than my hands, and I cupped them, imagining someone else's hands on them. Desire was not unfamiliar to me, but for me it was different. These stirrings would come to me when I was studying alone, and reading about the Roman women who rebelled against the patriarchs. Clever, spirited women who signed up as prostitutes so that they could have control over their own sexuality and not be used as political pawns in marriages brokered by male relatives. These historical imaginings excited me. As I sat at my desk, day after day, my head poring over a book, I would lengthen my legs, flex my feet and, without thinking, push my hands between my thighs, searching for a part of myself that would yield. Always, though, I stopped myself and clamped my legs tight, straightening my back, disgusted at my own perversion.

These memories trail me all the way back up to the house. How little I knew about love and sexual relations when I was a girl of seventeen. And yet possibly I was a more sensual being then. For there is a part of myself that I have long since shut away, and neither my husband nor my imagination is able to unlock it.

I walk across the nearly dark yard, bumping into Oonagh as she comes out of the kitchen door.

'June, there you are! Where've you been? I was looking for you in the garden, and the orchard, all about the place.'

She is flushed, and looks irritated.

'I'm sorry, Oonagh, I was down at the lake.'

'That's a very big walk. You shouldn't overdo it, you know.'

'I'm fine, Oonagh.' I bend down to take off my boots. 'Is that your bicycle?'

'Not at all. Sure we don't have a working bike between the lot of us.' She leans forward, whispering, 'That's why I was looking for you. It belongs to an old friend of James's.'

'James?'

'Yes.' She colours, as if it is her fault I cannot remember. 'James D., Robert's older brother.'

'Of course.' I shove my hands deeper into Robert's coat pockets, pausing on the threshold.

'He's waiting for you inside.' Oonagh puffs into the dewy air. 'Well, I'll be off so.'

'Are you not coming in for a cup of tea?'

It is so long since I have spoken to a man on my own, without Robert being there, that I suddenly feel very nervous.

'No, I'll get my tea at home. Mammy is expecting me.' She wraps her scarf about her neck. 'Well, you had better go in to him, don't you think?'

'Yes, all right, Oonagh, yes, I will.' I hesitate. 'What's his name?'

'Mr Sheriden,' she calls, running off into the gloom, as if she cannot tell me face to face.

Mr Sheriden . . . Phelim Sheriden – Claudette Sheriden's husband . . . The Sheridens who live in a big, cold house the other side of the woods, our neighbours and yet we have never called on them. The Sheridens who own a piano, and who are somehow part of a secret my husband has chosen not to divulge to me. How I hate secrets.

I take off Robert's coat and sling it over my arm, and then I smooth my hair down as best I can. The damp conditions here make it even more unruly than at home. I am sure I look a little wild after my walk by the lake, but there is nothing I can do about it now. The man is sitting by my hearth and it would be bad manners to dally any longer.

Colour – this is the notion that strikes me when I see Phelim Sheriden for the first time. He is the total spectrum of my twilight walk. Dressed casually, he is buried in a large green sweater the colour of moss, and his corduroy trousers are exactly the same shade as the beech trees I have just strolled through. He is standing by the stove, looking intently at the picture on the opposite wall, a crude landscape that belonged to Robert's parents. He turns as I enter the kitchen, a smile of welcome plastered on his face. But it is his eyes I am inevitably drawn to. They are a bright blue, the same colour as the sapphire lake, the same colour as Mother's.

He walks over, shakes my hand firmly and introduces himself. 'I was hoping to see Robert,' he says, smiling warmly.

'Oh, I am sorry, he's away . . .' I say hesitantly, still startled by his vivid hues.

'Has he joined up then?'

Before I can stop myself I nod my head, confused that Phelim Sheriden should immediately jump to this conclusion.

'I thought as much,' says Phelim pleasantly. 'When he called over last week, he said he was thinking of it.'

I redden, shocked to discover that Robert had in fact visited the Sheridens and never told me. I sit down suddenly, feeling dizzy and faint. I drop my head to stare at my feet, in their plain brown brogues. I feel dumpy, like Mrs Sanderson, stupid and plain.

Phelim coughs, and then says, 'So Robert joined up, eh? Like myself and James D., then?'

I look up, trying to compose myself, and hoping I sound normal. 'Yes,' I reply weakly, taking in what he has told me. Phelim Sheriden and Robert's brother, James D., fought together in the last war. It makes sense, for Mr Sheriden speaks and looks as if he comes from a different world to Robert. They would hardly have mixed socially.

I grip the table with my fingers and muster up some manners.

'Would you like a drink?' I ask, thinking of a dusty bottle of whiskey at the back of the kitchen cupboard. Tea will not do. I need something stronger to steady myself.

'That would be super.' He sits down in Robert's chair by the fire and stretches out his legs.

I get up, collecting two small glasses from the dresser, and kneel down to open the cupboard. I pour out the whiskey, handing Phelim Sheriden his glass first. We raise our glasses to the candle-light and both take a drink.

'Do you like it here in Cavan?' he asks me.

'Yes,' I lie, 'it's a very beautiful spot.'

'I suppose, although I always found it quite claustrophobic. I couldn't wait to leave.' His honesty startles me.

'But are you not based here permanently, Mr Sheriden?' I ask, remembering seeing Claudette Sheriden in the woods just two weeks ago.

'Please, call me Phelim.' He spreads his arms as wide as his smile. 'No, we have been away for a good few years. My wife, Claudette, insisted on returning recently, but for me . . .' he hesitates, his smile fading, '. . . there are too many memories.'

His words float out into space, and I feel tremendously awkward. He puts his hand inside his jacket pocket and pulls out a packet of cigarettes, offering me one. I immediately take it, thanking him.

'It's a while since I've had one of these,' I say as he lights it for me.

I sit back in my chair, inhaling deeply, almost closing my eyes with the bliss of it. I did not realize how much I missed smoking until now, puffing rings like a dragon in the Fanning kitchen.

'What do you do, Mr Sheriden?'

'I am an artist.'

He smiles again, as the smoke curls about his face, and I wonder why he has not come visiting with his wife.

'Oh, yes. Robert mentioned it.'

'Did he really?' Phelim's eyes flicker. 'Well, I try to make some sort of profession out of it.' He sips his whiskey. 'Although it was easier to do so in Paris than in Dublin.'

'Paris,' I murmur, as if it is the most sacred place on earth. 'Did you meet your wife in Paris?'

'No, oddly enough I met Claudette here, in Cavan.' He pauses. 'She knew James and Robert first.'

I feel a sudden jolt. Why has Robert never told me this? Possibly Phelim senses my unease, for he continues to talk quickly.

'I couldn't bear it here in Ireland during the civil war. It was a very dark time in our history, as I am sure you know. One moment we were heroes heading off to fight in the Great War, and the next we were traitors. So Claudette and I went back to her homeland, and it was there that I discovered painting. We moved to Paris so that I could train, and Claudette worked as an artist's model.'

'That must have been fun,' I say, immediately embarrassed by how silly I must sound.

'It was very different from here,' he says, sighing. 'We didn't have much to live on, and we didn't have our own house, or nearly as much space. But it was so stimulating to be in Paris, mixing with other artists, and writers. We wanted to bring our daughter up in France too, although this has proved to be a mistake.'

'Oh, why? '

I taste the bitter whiskey on my lips, imagining the Paris of the previous decade as he describes it, sitting in dusky cafes discussing art and poetry, fat on culture.

'Danielle is such a Francophile that she fell in love with a Frenchman. When we decided to return to Ireland, just before war broke out, they refused to come with us. It broke Claudette's heart, and she nearly wouldn't come with me.'

Danielle, Dani, Danny . . . so it was her daughter for whom Claudette Sheriden was calling out in the woods the day I saw her there. I suddenly feel sorry for the woman, for she is in the same position as me, worrying about someone she loves, trapped inside the horror of this war.

'Are they all right?' I ask gently.

'As well as can be expected. Contact is very difficult. We know they left Paris when it was invaded, and are living somewhere in the south of the country, but that is all. We are hoping they might be able to get out. Maybe through Spain.'

'Your daughter is very young to be married.'

'Well, my guess is she must be about the same age as you.'

He grins, and he looks cheeky, a lot younger than his age. I colour immediately, feeling gauche.

'So what has brought a young English girl all the way to Cavan? For I was so surprised to learn Robert had returned. He always swore he would never come back here.'

He opens up the stove and throws his cigarette in. I suck the last dregs from mine, and throw it in after his.

'It seemed a good idea at the time.' I am troubled that Phelim Sheriden seems to know my husband's sentiments towards his home better than I do. Yet the whiskey is warming me, making me more confident.

Phelim nods. 'Oh, really, it's not too bad a spot. At least I get seclusion here, to work.'

'What kind of paintings do you do?' I turn to safe territory again. My emotions about Robert's home are so mixed at the moment that I am afraid to talk about Cavan.

'Well, I'm an advocate of a new kind of painting . . .' He stands up suddenly, gesturing towards the dull landscape on the wall. 'My paintings would be very different to this.'

'Thank goodness!'

He looks surprised and laughs, in complicity.

'Great Scott, are you an admirer of the new art? Have I found such a rare creature, in the depths of the Irish hinterland?'

I speak shyly. 'I love looking at art.'

'Well, in that case, would you like to see one of my pieces?'

I take another sip of whiskey. 'Have you something here, with you?'

'Just a small watercolour. I was on my way back from the station. It has been with a gallery in Dublin for the past month or so. Unsold, unfortunately.'

He walks across the flagstones and picks up a leather folder, tucked behind the kitchen table. He unties the string wrapped around it and opens it out on the table. I get up and walk over, standing next to him as he bends down and hands me a small rectangle of paper, with splashes of paint on the back.

'I left the frame with a new, more conventional work,' he explains. 'It seems this piece is a little too modern for Dublin eyes.'

I turn the piece of paper over, and what do I see?

Nothing my eyes are used to, but shapes, and forms from another dimension, with such colour, and everything converging, vying for space. Underneath all this array of form and hue I sense control. It is impressive, and as strict as geometry.

'Is this Cubism?' I ask tentatively.

'You could say it is. Although I prefer the term "abstract". This is the style of painting I studied in France, but then we were forced to leave, as I told you. I tried London first, but the English are not so keen on the abstract artist.'

'And how about Ireland?'

He roars with a rich, deep laughter, making me jump. 'Let us just say that I do not think I will be making my fortune with abstract art in my homeland.'

'So why are you here?' I blush suddenly, aware of how rude I might sound. But why return to a place that did not appreciate his gift?

'I have seen my fair share of death and destruction in the last war. I would not want to be back in France, or even England now. And Dublin, well, I grew tired of it.'

He says this brutally, as if it is fine to say such a thing in front of me.

'And now I am here, in this small townland, because I am from here and Claudette is unwell. She wanted to come back.' He casts his eyes downward. 'Besides, the house was falling apart and I felt I should do it up a bit.'

I look back down at his tiny painting. It is very delicate, and I can see the lines of ink through the thin washes of paint. He has chosen golden colours: soft browns, rust, crimson and orange. They undulate in wavy lines, circles and columns of light.

When I look at his painting I think of my sister singing, holding one beat for two, dear Minim. How strange, I know, but this is what it makes me do.

I look back up at Phelim Sheriden and something about him reminds me of Father. Is it his golden hair, the green jersey he wears, or is it his gentleness, his interest in my mind? I think of the last drive I took with Father. Min was gone, and the house in Torquay seemed more desolate than ever, as my parents and I began to pack all of our belongings. I was to go to London after our trip to Europe, and I might never return to Devon. I felt orphaned, for this house, and the sea, had given me as much succour as my parents ever had. Of course I would visit Mother and Father in their quarters, at the school where father had attained a position as Classics master, but it was in Gloucestershire, and nowhere near the sea, far too far from Devon.

Daddy's summer-long depression lifted just in time to see the leaves drop and feel the chill of early autumn approaching in the air. Although it had not been as bad as 1932, he had still wasted many of the hot, blue sunny days of '33 in bed. I could not fathom it. I loved my father dearly, and yet I was hurt that he had not pulled himself together for me. Now infuriatingly, just as we were leaving, he had brightened up, full of banter about Rome and Greece.

Mother was in a whirl of excitement about our impending trip to Europe, and kept calling me into her room to show me one dress or another and to ask me whether she should bring it. I always said yes, and this seemed to exasperate her.

'You're no use at all. I don't know where you came from!'

She looked me up and down. I knew I was plain in my navy sweater and grey slacks, but I did not care what my mother thought. I was going to be an academic, and I had to look the part.

To this end, one night I cut my hair into a bob with the kitchen scissors, all the while smirking as I looked in the mirror, imagining what fun Min would think this was. It amused me to think that my mother's glamour would be compromised by my own ascetic presence, like a censoring nun, as we travelled across Europe. When I had finished I was surprised how like a boy I looked, just how I imagined Dickon from *The Secret Garden*, with his snub nose and freckles. It was a surprise to pass from my childlike face to my ample bosom. I was an odd hybrid of boy and woman.

At breakfast Mother dropped her cup of tea back down on its saucer and gave a tiny scream, while my father looked shocked.

'Your hair . . .' he stuttered.

'My goodness, June, what a terrible mess,' Mother said, regaining her composure.

'I like it short.' I cracked the top of my boiled egg with the back of my spoon.

My mother laughed. 'You look like Puck. I shall have to neaten it up for you, but maybe it can be sweet, and modern.'

I looked at Father, and to my horror his eyes were welling with tears. 'Your beautiful golden tresses,' he croaked. 'You had hair like a goddess.'

Immediately I felt terrible. I wished I could undo what I had done. I didn't want my mother touching my hair, turning me into a 'modern young thing'.

Mother snorted. 'And what goddess, pray? I think short hair for June is a great improvement. Long hair didn't suit her face.'

As she said this she pushed a strand of her own thick, curly black hair behind her ear.

The day before Mother and I were due to leave for Italy, Father asked me to take him for a drive.

'One last spin . . .' he said, as I started up the engine.

'But it won't be the last one, Daddy,' I scolded gently, releasing the clutch and steering the car through the gates. 'I shall come and see you in Gloucestershire, and together we can drive back down to Devon and visit all our old haunts.'

'I never wish to return to this place.'

His words shocked me. But how true they were. He never did return to Devon, not until the day he was buried.

I drove down the hill and past the houses of our neighbours, towards the harbour.

'Are we going to Babbacombe?'

'Not today,' Father replied wearily, 'I am tired of looking at the sea. Let's go somewhere else. How about Cockington?'

'All right,' I said unenthusiastically. I had been craving a walk by the sea and had no desire to drive inland, no matter how short the distance. I drove past the sea front and turned right, heading up a narrow, hilly road. Presently we came to a small hamlet of four or five thatched houses, of wattle and daub, with lead windows and golden walls. It was a sunny day, with no wind, and the village was quiet, nestled by trees all around. Ours was the only vehicle.

We walked through the village, towards Cockington Court and the cricket pitch, but we did not go up to the house, standing instead amongst the trees.

'This is where I courted your mother,' my father said quietly. 'I was friends with a chap who lived in that house. Not any more, though.'

I turned to Daddy and looked at his profile. He still had a thick head of hair. I could see strands of ginger in the grey, like fiery embers in the ashes. His cheeks were lined with tiny red veins, and the tip of his nose was red. His pale-blue eyes were watery and the rims were pale pink. I realized, with a mixture of fondness and sadness, that he had the face of a drinker.

'Your mother was engaged to him.'

He took out his pipe, thrusting it into his mouth, and hunted around in his pockets for matches.

'Mummy was engaged to another man?'

'Oh, yes. Poor Alexander. He ripped up his kid gloves when your mother ended things with him. I believe she even had a couple of fiancés before him. She collected us, like trophies.'

He laughed bitterly.

'But maybe, my dear June,' he added gently, 'I am being a little unfair to your mother. She always told me she was never sure, until she met me.'

'Sure of what?'

'Sure that she wished to be married.'

His answer surprised me, for Mummy had always given me the impression that the pinnacle of any girl's life was to be married, and to a wealthy man. Had she desired something other than that, once?

'I should have let Alexander marry her, and not interfered. He was desperately in love with her,' Father continued, lighting his pipe and sucking furiously. 'He would have been a much better provider, but I suppose she preferred me in whites. Your mother always claims that she fell for me while watching me play cricket – apparently I cut quite a figure when I bowl.'

I looked at the empty cricket green, with the small white pavilion facing us. I imagined my father and mother, flirting, with cups of tea in their hands, and little plates with crustless cucumber sandwiches. He was tall, with golden hair, and dressed all in white. The only patch of colour on his clothes were pink smudges on his right leg from where he had rubbed the ball. She was wearing a red dress, exactly the same shade of deep red as the cricket ball. Amid all those men in white, and ladies in pink and pastel, she stood out as hard and dangerous as the ball.

Father sighed. 'I liked it here in Cockington. I would have liked us to live here, but it was a little too close to Alexander for comfort. Besides, your mother insisted on Torquay. She liked the idea of the society that an English seaside town provided. I think she thought it almost as grand as living on the French Riviera.'

He chuckled and, linking his arm through mine, we began to stroll back to where we had parked the car.

'Do you not like our house, Daddy?'

'I do not mind it, but I would have preferred to live in a country manor, a fine neoclassical pile. If only I had had the right background, with a handsome estate to inherit, and a private income.'

'I loved growing up in Torquay.' I gripped his arm fiercely. 'And so did Min. We adored being able to look at the sea every day, and being so close to the beach. It is very important to who we are, Daddy.'

He stopped walking and looked at me curiously. 'Yes, it is, isn't it? You are two beautiful mermaids, and I am so very proud of you both. But I have always loved the countryside inland, and I look forward to Gloucestershire and living in a cottage, maybe like one of these.' And he indicated one of the small thatched cottages we were passing.

'But all those low beams, Daddy, you would constantly be banging your head!'

'At least it will keep me awake.' He smiled woefully. 'For I hope I shan't die of boredom, teaching Latin to twelve-year-old boys.'

'Mummy will be there with you for company.' I tried to sound cheerful.

'Ah yes, your mother.' His tone implied something. 'She is so looking forward to Italy. You are a very lucky girl.'

'Yes, Father, I am very grateful.'

'You shall be able to see all those wonderful buildings.' He squeezed my hand. 'Make me a promise you will draw some pictures, so that you can show them to me when you return.'

We stood outside the car door and my father looked up at the sky.

'Summer is over,' he announced and dipped his hand into his pocket, producing a small hip flask and pressing it to his lips. He did all this so neatly and quickly, as if he thought I mightn't notice. But what if I did? Where was the harm in a quick nip on a Sunday-afternoon walk? 'Maybe, one day, you will be a schoolmistress too? I think a history teacher.'

Daddy's eyes twinkled, for he was teasing me. He knew I found the idea of teaching as repellent as he did.

'No, you will be a classical scholar, my dear.' He nodded.

'Remember we are only telling stories. It is as simple as this, the telling of tales. As the human race progresses we spiral into each other, generation after generation, repeating, and reliving again and again. Who is to say that I were not a Roman emperor once, and you my daughter?'

He put his hands on his hips and laughed loudly. All the rooks took off from the trees behind, and his voice echoed across the silent village. Then he took the flask out of his pocket again, and took a longer drink, before opening the car door and getting in. Father sat waiting for me, a mask devoid of expression suddenly covering his face.

THE ADULTERESS III

She comes at twilight when all the sun that is left burns in her eyes. Always the same way she stands outside his house, pausing, tempting herself to turn away. She hopes the shadows conceal her, but really she doesn't care any more. She knows it is a dangerous game, but all self-control has long since been shed.

Why does she want to make love with this man who is not her husband? Is it because she wants to believe in something, or that someone else could love her? Or is she just like her mother, self-obsessed and vain, constantly wanting male attention? No, her lover is not an aristocrat. Her mother would never have gone near him. But this is what she likes.

The texture of his hands seduces her, rough against her skin, the nails engrained with paint, unkempt. These are hands that know what it is like not to hold many coins in their palms. These are hands that have clung onto the edge and know how to climb, inch by inch, determination overcoming pain. Her husband's hands are soft and careless, wandering without any particular purpose across her stomach, half-heartedly brushing her breasts. But this man, he knows what to do with his hands. He touches her with conviction, picking her up, brushing against her as if she is one of his paintings.

She opens her bag, takes out her compact and looks at her lips. They are as red as when she last looked at them, but still she takes out her lipstick. She wants to mark him when she arrives – his shirt, his chest, his bruising chin. She lifts the compact up to her eyes. They glitter like a cat on a hunt, and for an instant she doesn't recognize herself. She hesitates. She could still turn back, go home, but already she knows it is too late. He is watching her from his studio. She looks up to the top of the house. Its windows stare back blankly. How is it possible this one house could hide their secret? A love, she thinks, that is bigger than the two of them. A love she believes to be immortal. This is why her lover is an artist. He too believes that, like art, some things can last forever. Even if their bodies perish, what they share – love – is for always.

It starts to rain, and pulling her coat more tightly around her she runs up the steps, pushing open the front door. Up the staircase, three floors to the top, until she stands breathless and edgy on the landing. She doesn't have to knock. The door is open. She walks inside, takes her hat off and smooths her hair.

She arrives, the artist's muse. He says.

He has not shaved, and she is attracted by this audacity. His hair is unruly, and his skin looks even darker than usual, as if he has been abroad. But she knows he has been nowhere. Just here, working, since the last time they met.

She holds back from the embrace, her throat tightening, unable to speak. This is always the way. They never touch, not at first, but eke out this moment for as long as possible until they are two electrical wires fizzing and sparking.

He has never drawn her, but now his eyes trace her contours as she slowly undresses. She feels bold and wanton, as if she is in one of the films she so adores. Her coat falls to the floor, and then her dress. He kneels before her, tugs at her stockings and knickers, until they are rings around her feet. He begins to lick her and she closes her eyes. His lips, his touch transports her, and suddenly she is no longer there. Instead of the smell of his damp studio, with its bitter scent of oil paint and sweat, another aroma circumferences her. Somewhere dry and warm. Crisp pine dilates her nostrils, and in the inner chamber of her ears she hears a sound, distant but distinct. It is the sound of the sea.

JUNE

My mother met her lover on the steps of the Duomo, her eyes cast skyward, entranced by the glittery spectacle of the fairy-tale cathedral. It seemed like a building that ought to belong to a princess. These were my mother's thoughts as she walked, head craning backwards, straight into the back of the tallest man in Milan.

It was one of those rare moments in the history of love when the fusion is immediate. Nature will do her work, yet neither party dares believe it. He stumbled forward and turned. She stepped back. He apologized in Italian. She in English. He smiled, a rich embrace of a smile, which lifted the small dark moustache above his thick broad lips. She clutched her purse with both hands as she beckoned for me to follow her, and hurried past him into the cathedral, looking once out of the corner of her eye. Yet it only takes one cast to hook a fish.

I decided to climb to the roof of the Duomo on my own. Mother claimed she wished to stay inside the cathedral, to pray. I walked past the confessional boxes lined up in a row down one side of the nave, like bathing houses at the sea. I compared the spiritual abandon of stepping onto the beach, lightly clad, the sea air tickling my bare flesh, with the choking world of the submissive penitent, on one's knees facing into the dark boxes. I had been brought up as a Catholic, but in England this meant something different from the

rest of Europe. I felt no identification with the interior of the cathedral. Its high vaults forced me to crane my neck, and yet for all
its height it made me feel suffocated so that I longed to be out in
the sunlight.

I wondered if my mother would confess her sins. What did she
think when she prayed? I looked at her, on her knees, lit up by the
reflections from the stained glass. A blazing violet light diffused the
gloomy air, splashing onto the side of a grey pillar and crowning
my mother's head. I turned and marched quickly out of the cathedral, stepping into the brilliant sunshine.

The piazza was busy. It was late afternoon and the September
sun was dipping down in the sky, bathing the city in a golden light.
The trams circled the piazza, and pigeons took off at mixed diag-
onals. To my right cars sped up and down, in front of an arcade
milling with people. The buildings were grand, with classical proportions, reminding me of what I had seen in Paris, yet the
atmosphere was different. I felt more at home in Italy. And yet,
breathing deeply, I was aware of the ache inside me, of how I missed
my father, the sea and Min. Everything had changed. I was now my
mother's only companion, and had received more attention from
her than ever before. My mother had even expressed admiration
that I would wish to go to university.

'You are wiser than Minerva,' she had said and then, shaking her
head, she added, 'I am very disappointed in Min.'

I felt disloyal when I said nothing to defend my sister, but then
I was disappointed, too. In the last letter I received from Min she
referred to her wedding night as an 'awakening'. Min assumed I
wanted to know these things, but I didn't. As far as I could deter-
mine, all men did was throw you off-course. What had happened
to Min's plans to become a painter?

Charles and Min were in Rome. In a couple of days Min was

The Adulteress

going to join us in Milan, and from there we would travel south with Mother to Tuscany and back to Rome. My stomach tightened with excitement when I thought about Rome. Finally I would see the architecture of my dreams. I had brought a small sketchbook with me, and, although not as talented as Min, I had promised my father I would document everything I saw.

I began to climb the steps of the Duomo. It surprised me how short the ascent was, for such a monumental structure. After a few moments I was standing on one of the parapets, its marble gleaming in the sunlight. A few couples perambulated in a circle around the edge of the roof, pausing every now and again to look at the view. I was the only woman on my own, but I did not feel strange or odd. I felt serene.

It was very warm on the top of the Duomo, no wind whatsoever. The sky was bright blue, and the marble dazzled beneath my feet. All of the buttresses, which had looked spiky and chiselled from a distance, now appeared gently moulded, with soft contours. I looked at the saints hiding in their miniature turrets, and thought about all the drama of their worlds. I sat on the roof in a pool of stillness and, taking my hat off, I let the sunlight beat down on the crown of my head. I listened to the sounds of the streets below echoing up into the clear air, which surrounded me. I cupped my face in my palms and wordlessly moved my lips, but I knew it was pointless to pray.

From the day we departed I suspected Mother might leave Father, but I had likened myself to the role of guardian, and believed my presence would be enough to contain her. We had travelled by train from Paris to Italy, my mother's fluency in French astonishing me. In every town we stopped in, some man had made an advance, under many different polite guises, some even in front of their wives. All of these gentlemen believed I was my mother's sister, and Mother said nothing to correct them. She had brushed

167

off each of these potential suitors, but not until after she had enter-
tained their advances, even for a short while. It unnerved me that
Mother could not be more aloof.

By the time I descended to the piazza, I saw my mother at the
foot of a large statue of a man on a horse, talking to the tall Italian
man. My heart sank. How had she found him again?

'Signore Giovanni Calvesi has invited us to take an ice cream
with him,' my mother announced, half-turning from her admirer
to speak to me. She was as sparkling as the day, dressed in a long
jade coat over a blue patterned dress, with a small jade hat cocked
teasingly on the side of her head. She brought her gloved hands up
to her face, to keep the sun out of her eyes. They were the same
colour and fabric as her coat. Her black hair glistened, coiffured in
perfect waves, and her lips were painted plum. I pulled the loose
strands of my own hair away from my face, and wondered if I had
put my hat back on straight. I felt like a buffoon beside Mother's
sleek sophistication.

Giovanni Calvesi turned towards me and smiled warmly. I
noticed he had kind eyes, liquid brown with long lashes like a
horse, and smooth pale fingers as he delicately picked up my hand
and pressed it to his lips.

'*Piacere di conosceria.* I am so pleased to meet you. It would be an
honour if you and your sister would like to join me.' Without waiting for an answer, he continued to speak. 'Please . . . come.' He
indicated for us both to take either arm so that we could safely
cross the piazza and avoid the trams.

'How wonderful it is to be in a city of culture,' my mother said
gaily.

Giovanni Calvesi turned to look at her, and her eyes twinkled,
her smile wavering and mysterious. He nodded, completely
entranced.

'Signore Calvesi is a painter, June. He has requested I sit for a portrait.'

'Your sister has a most unusual visage,' said Giovanni the painter. 'The colouring of her skin and its texture. It is such an English rose, and one I would wish to paint.' He paused, a little breathless. 'It is hard in Milano to find a subject who has such fair skin.'

We walked through a monumental arch and beneath a glass dome, people milling about us. Now we were in the shade. Trams passed by us, and we walked swiftly back out into another piazza. Giovanni Calvesi pointed to a building on his left.

'La Scala. One evening I will take you to an opera, I think. Oh, it is quite absolute you must come with me!'

My mother laughed lightly, the notes tinkling like coins dropped on the cobbles.

We turned and walked up a narrow street, cars and trams creating a confusion of noise beside us. I wished Signore Calvesi would not walk so fast. I could feel my cheeks blooming and my forehead dampen. Suddenly he stopped opposite a wide building with dark awnings, and small wooden tables and chairs clustered outside.

'This is the *caffè* of my friend, Giuseppe Castellano, and it is where you will find the best *gelato* in Milano.'

Giovanni Calvesi spread his arms wide and then, again taking each of our elbows, he guided us across the busy street.

'Can you believe Signore Calvesi doesn't like the Duomo,' my mother said to me as she sat down on one of the spindly chairs that our host had pulled back for her.

'It is vulgar, like a wedding cake,' he said, pushing her into it and waving his hands in front of his face. 'To see a beautiful church, you should go to Santa Maria delle Grazie. It is a place that inspires . . .' he paused and waved his hands about again, '. . . the divine, with simple classic proportions, and the frescoes. All you can do in the

Duomo is look up. It is designed to make you feel small, too small for me.'

He laughed flamboyantly, and Mother joined in. I felt dread rise up inside me. This man was different from all the others. I could see it in my mother's face. She was going to betray Father. And what could I do about it? I was useless, and a traitor too.

Yet I had never seen my mother like this before. I had seen her flirt with Captain Sanderson, and all those other poor husbands, and the men we had met on our journey so far. My mother attracted such attention effortlessly. She was always the light around which they gathered, yet sometimes I suspected Mother felt bored, weary of the whole business. Here, in a Milanese *caffè*, delicately spooning vanilla ice cream into her rosebud mouth, my mother was like a child again. The little girl who craved her own glamorous mother's notice and never got it. So who will give it to her? Who will feed her heart, lost in the dark since she was so small? Giovanni Calvesi. He was her light, and my mother was lit by him. She was instantly younger, gayer. Like the first tiny snow-drop pushing its way up through the hard frost, there was something quite beautiful about it. It was the only time I saw my mother's heart in her face, and it was soft.

NICHOLAS

Nicholas takes Hopper for a walk in the Ramor woods in Virginia. The old dog is still limping, but it doesn't seem to bother him. He does look happy, even though he is wounded. Hopper accepts that's the way he is and carries on. They cross a little stone bridge over a rushing brook and climb down to it, through the reeds. Hopper isn't keen to go in the water, but drinks from the puddles on the muddy bank.

Charlie would like it here. Nicholas knows it. For years she had been saying she was tired of Dublin and, if they were going to start a family, she thought it best to move to the country – more room, a better lifestyle. But no children came. He didn't like to plan, and so each day just led into the next, and they were still in Sandycove three years after that first discussion.

Even buying the Fanning house had been by chance. He had got in his car one day, brimming with heat and anger, knowing that he couldn't stay under the same roof as his wife any longer, and started to drive. Hours had passed in a blur, and he had had no idea where he was. He had ended up in Oldcastle, of all places, and by then it was dark so he went into the hotel, booked a room and got drunk at the bar. The next morning, after attempting to cure his hangover with a fried breakfast, he had walked past the estate agents and saw a picture of the house in the window. Something made him stop.

Before he knew it, he was walking through the door and arranging a viewing. Within the week he had made an offer. Charlie had been astonished. She had begged him to think things through, not to make a rash decision. But at the time he couldn't bear to look at her.

Hopper and he come back out of the woods and onto the golf course. He walks back up the hill to the hotel car park and puts Hopper into the car, making sure the windows are all open. The sun has gone in now, and it is chillier, but even so he doesn't want to risk the dog getting dehydrated. The hotel appears deserted. He goes into the empty bar and picks up a menu. He sits on a big red sofa by a fireplace that isn't lit. A girl in a black skirt suit walks in and asks him if he would like anything. He orders fish chowder.

He is on his own in the large, empty lounge of this hotel, look-ing out of the big sash windows at the garden, and it feels so wrong. Charlie should be here with him. The two of them having lunch after walking the dog, maybe a baby in a sling across his chest, and he would be passing him or her to Charlie now so that she could feed the baby. Nicholas clenches his fists. She thought that he hadn't felt anything when she had the first miscarriage, but he had. She hadn't told him what was going on. She had gone to the hospital on her own and rung him to say that she had lost it.

'Why didn't you call me earlier? I could have been with you,' he had said in panic to her, down the phone.

'I'm sorry. I just knew if you were with me, I would have fallen apart. I was better on my own.' She sounded so aloof and distant.

It was only when she got home that she cried. He held her in his arms and wished he could change their destiny.

'We can try again,' he whispered into her hair. 'It'll be all right.'

Three more times Charlie had got pregnant, and three times she had miscarriages. They were good at conceiving, but the babies didn't want to stay. Charlie lost weight, couldn't sleep, and painted more and more furiously. During the daytime he was always trying to comfort her, cooking her food, bringing her cups of coffee to the studio, paying all the bills and cleaning up. But he had lost the babies, too. He knew it wasn't the same, because he hadn't actually been through the physical trauma of being pregnant and then the pain and bloodiness of losing the baby; but he still felt bereft, powerless and a failure. Gradually Charlie became so touchy he thought it best not to mention it any more. Sometimes at night he would wake up and she wasn't in the bed with him, and he would tiptoe across the hall and see her sitting in her studio, rocking backwards and forwards, crying like a child, and it frightened him. She never seemed to see him, so he would creep back to the bedroom feeling like a coward, but convincing himself that if he spoke to her it would only make things worse. She was possessive about her grief and she didn't want to share it with him. What Nicholas couldn't get out of his head was that maybe she had slept with that other man hoping to get pregnant. Maybe she thought his seed was no good? Another man's baby might succeed to full term, whereas his hadn't. It was ridiculous to think this way, but he couldn't help it.

The girl in the suit brings him his bowl of chowder and some home-made brown bread. He looks around the room as he eats. There is a large painting of horses at a fair, with a dog in the foreground staring at him. It is a wiry grey-and-white hound and it reminds him of Hopper. There is a strange light shaped like a duck on the mantelpiece, and a plaster tableau on the wall of Cupid offering Venus a cup of love. Nicholas believes that if he were offered a cup of love right now, he would drink from it. No matter who gave it to him. He is so lonely.

'Hello, Nick.'

Nicholas starts. He hadn't noticed anyone coming into the lounge. And, of all people, it's Geraldine, with her little girl.

'Hello, Geraldine. How are you?'

'I'm grand. This is my daughter, Grainne. Grainne, this is my piano teacher.'

The little girl smiles shyly and then looks at the rug. She must be about eight. She is dressed in riding clothes. She looks like an old-fashioned little girl, her brown hair tied in plaits.

'Grainne's just been riding. We were coming in here for lunch.'

'Would you like to join me?'

'Do you mind?'

'Of course not.' He puts his spoon down. 'As you can see, I'm on my own.'

'Oh, your friend went home.'

'Yes.'

Geraldine and Grainne sit opposite him on another red sofa. Geraldine orders soup and sandwiches for them. She is wearing a lacy white smock dress. Her legs are bare and she has on a pair of pink flip-flops. It is an odd-looking outfit, something a little girl might wear, which looks incongruous on her ample frame. They talk about the weather for a few minutes. Maybe the temperature will stay high and they'll get a bit of summer now before school is back. Grainne says nothing, nibbling her sandwich when it arrives.

'Do you like school?' Nicholas asks her.

The child looks mortified and nods.

'She has a lovely teacher next year,' Geraldine says. 'She's an old schoolfriend of mine. She's really good, does interesting things with the children. More than the usual you get on the curriculum.'

Nicholas nods.

'Sorry,' Geraldine apologizes. 'That's not very interesting for you. Not if you don't have children.'

'Yes. Well, we wanted to.'

Geraldine stops eating, stunned by this admission. 'Oh, I am sorry. I . . . er . . . I didn't mean to pry.'

'That's all right. So how's the practice going?'

She smiles, still pink with embarrassment. 'I don't think you're going to be very pleased with me tomorrow. I'm afraid I haven't had the chance to do much at all. Ray's sister and family are coming to stay at the weekend and I have to get the house ready, laundry and baking.' She sighs, looks at Nicholas. 'It's been non-stop.'

'You know, I think you're a natural.'

'At the piano?'

'Yes. You've really progressed in such a short time. We'll have you playing Beethoven's "Moonlight" Sonata by the end of the year.'

Geraldine looks genuinely thrilled. 'Do you hear that, Grainne? Now wouldn't you like to learn as well? We could play duets.'

'Okay,' the little girl says, dipping her crusts into her soup.

Geraldine beams at Nicholas. 'I can't tell you how much your lessons mean to me. I don't know what I'd do without them.'

He can tell she means it, and it worries him. What kind of life must she have, if the highlight of her week is his piano lessons?

JUNE

The weather turns and the rain comes again. I have been walking down by the lake every afternoon, bathed in autumnal shades, feeding my growing belly with humble November sunshine. Every day I rest on a small cup of shore, and sit on a boulder the shape of a turtle's back, listening to the moorhens coo, and looking at the silhouette of one lone heron. The simple, yet hypnotic quality of nature helps me not to think about what might be happening on the other side of the Irish Sea and to my husband in the skies above Europe.

Now the heavens have opened, and I have to concede that Oonagh is right. It is no weather for me to go walking, as the path down to the lake is slippery and treacherous. It would be foolish to take a chance in my condition, as well as risking a cold, which I am told is always tenfold worse when you are pregnant.

And so I find myself sitting in the bedroom on the cold bed when I should be busy working about the house. I stare out at the rain, those pedantic lines of grey streaking the sky, blocking out the light, imprisoning me, and think I should write my husband a letter. But I have no news to tell him, and I am afraid to write my feelings down for they would surely dismantle me. As the rain pounds into the thatch, and I curl up in my cave, I realize I ought to find something to occupy my mind. Either that or lose my sanity.

I could easily spend all day working on the farm of course, and my chores fill many hours. Sometimes I like the clear simplicity of making butter, feeding the hens, gathering eggs, or just washing the yard. I try to clear my mind of all despondency and I look with satisfaction at my hands, the skin reddened and hardening. These are a farmer's wife's hands.

When I lie down during the day I am so very tired, yet I cannot sleep. Oonagh says it is early pregnancy that makes me so exhausted, and soon I will have energy again. She says this happened to all of her sisters, and sister-in-laws, when they had their children. When I feel sick in the mornings, Oonagh gives me a small dish of grated apple to make me feel better.

I close my eyes, but sleep doesn't come, and instead I daydream of times before the war, before I came to Ireland and the blackout curtain was dropped between my sister's world and mine. It was only a few years ago, and possibly I look back on it all with rose-coloured spectacles, but the world we inhabited then was more colourful, and joyful. I am sure of it. My musings take me back to Italy, and the day Giovanni Calvesi bought Mother and I ice creams in Milan. I watch Mother slowly eating her ice cream, savouring each delicious scoop, her eyes fixed on Giovanni Calvesi's, her spirit detaching from mine and all that she belonged to back home. My ice cream turned to brown sludge in the bottom of my glass bowl and all the time I was thinking: what has kept our family from cherishing each other?

It terrifies me to think I will be a mother soon. I am not ready. But I suppose I would never have been ready. Perhaps it is better this way, to have motherhood forced upon me. And so I try to wear myself out. I work my body as hard as I can, yet still every night I am restless. My mind is racing, and flying off in myriad directions; unfettered, uncontrolled. All the physical work in the world is not going to give me peace. I need to do something with my brain, keep it ticking over, and thinking of other things apart from the past, apart from Robert and the war.

This realization brings me up to the loft, and one small box I had placed in the far corner when we first moved here. I have not opened this box since the day I got married, more than five years ago. I bring it down to the kitchen and place it on the table, standing back and just staring at it. It is a large brown cardboard box, with my name written on the label – *June Sinclair, University College, Gower Street, London*. I step forward, untie the string and slowly lift off the lid. Inside is a stack of papers, notes for my final dissertation, which I never finished. The box is a summary of my failure, and a reminder of what my universe had been before I met Robert.

I was the one to follow in Daddy's classical footsteps, yet his love of Greek and Roman architecture was transformed into literature for me. I loved the anarchy of the Roman authors, their scathing, biting tongues, their elegiac poetry and the epic – a story, part legend, part history, which can bind you for a lifetime. My grasp of Latin grammar was always shaky, but what attracted me was its emphatic structure, phrases that you could picture carved in stone, with a clear beginning, middle and end to them, no lingering, no maybe, just absolute.

Et Mihi Cedet Amor.

That phrase would spin inside my head as I worked in the library on a fresh, blustery spring day in London, cherry blossom knocking on the windowpanes, the air sparkling around my head, becoming a jewel-laden halo, inspiring my endeavours.

Et Mihi Cedet Amor.

And Love Shall Yield to Me.

What did it mean?

I applied it to one woman's life, a Roman princess called Julia, who was the daughter of Emperor Augustus. I thought that phrase of Ovid's was like a gauntlet to women of her time. I believed she should have been a warrior in a different lifetime. Julia was a man in a woman's body, and love was her only chance for combat.

When I met Robert I believed I understood what Ovid meant. Now I was yielding to love, so surely what Ovid had written meant the opposite? His challenge to mankind was: never fall in love. But what human being could ever possibly want *not* to be in love?

My tutor tried to persuade me to focus on Tacitus's *Histories*, and the more respectable verses of Horace, and Virgil. He thought I should be studying the ideal of the Roman hero, and his devotion to the Empire, the repetition of myths and legends, but I wanted to know about the underbelly of Roman society, to try to get a feeling for how the Romans really lived. And so I read Juvenal's *Satires*, and Ovid's *Art of Love*. More than anything I wanted to understand Julia, because she was an adulteress, too.

I sit at the kitchen table, sift through my notes and close my eyes. I am in the library again in London University, finishing off a sentence in haste, about to pack my books away. I have exactly five minutes to walk from the library, across the courtyard and to my tutor's rooms. I am nervous. I have more to prove than my fellow students, for I am the only girl amongst them. My tutor doesn't completely approve of my presence as a woman at the University of London.

Every morning when I woke up as a student of London University I doubted myself. What right had I to be there, safe inside the walls of the university when my father was suffering, and needed me? Yet it was my father's belief in me that continued to motivate me every day. As children, Min was always the dreamer, but strangely our roles had been reversed and now my sister was taking care of Father. It was over six months since I had been in Italy with Mother, and I had not heard from her since Christmas. What good was a degree anyway, when as a woman in our world I was expected to marry and be a wife and a mother? Yet I was passionate about my studies. I happily spent all day in the monolithic library. I craved the safety I found in the building's silent corners, where I had a purpose, and where no one could disturb me. My favourite spot was at the end of the long mahogany table, covered in green baize, opposite one of the large sash windows, affording me a view of the grey rooftops of the college buildings, and three cherry trees, which in the spring were delightfully pink, and gay, lifting me out of my brown world of study and the rows of cases filled with books.

I was not lonely. I saw my sister sometimes, and my father not so often. Mother was in Milan. I had no friends, for it would have been inappropriate to socialize with the other male students on my course. But I didn't mind. I populated my life with characters from the past. In my tiny bedroom, when I could block out the noises of the family I lodged with, I thought only of Rome and of Emperor Augustus's daughter Julia and her many husbands and lovers. More than anything I wanted to know how it felt to be her, and to be adored by men to such an extent?

A patch of blue sky pushes through the clouds. I stand up and walk to the window of my Irish kitchen, holding the sheaves of papers to my chest as if they are a child most dear to me. I remember visiting the island of Ponza in 1933 when I was in Italy. It was the beginning of my obsession. How the beat of the waves on the brittle Mediterranean shore summoned a picture in front of me. I saw quite clearly the exiled Julia, standing on the beach, craning to see land, her hands shielding her eyes, and her figure blurring as if there was a mist rising off the sea. It was only for an instant I saw this, but it was like a call to me, as if Julia herself had whispered into my ear, *Tell me the secret loves of Julia Caesar* so softly it made me shiver.

How could I have told my tutor that I believed I was on a mission to vindicate Julia? He was a cold practical man, hiding behind a pair of steel-rimmed spectacles, with thin lips and a sharp, ironic

wit. He believed my research on Julia to be frivolous, and irrelevant.

'Rome was a patriarchal society,' he kept telling me. 'The lives
of these women were marginal, and did not affect the main political events of the day.'

But I didn't agree with him, and I hoped to prove this to him one
day.

Two weeks in Italy. It changed my family's destiny forever. I pick
up the blue-and-white jug from the draining board and pour some
milk into a teacup, taking a sip. I don't like the taste, but I feel weak
and need some sustenance. The milk is a pale creamy ochre colour,
although it doesn't taste sour. I dip my finger into the milk, and all
of a sudden its colour and texture bring to mind the art of Giovanni Calvesi. The last time I was in his rooms he showed me his
paintings. They were odd. Small and austere pictures of vessels –
bottles, jars, vases, boxes, bowls, all of them brown, cream, yellow,
white, the odd one blue or orange. The objects were always lined
up on a dark-brown table, against a creamy ochre wall the colour
of curdled milk. He called them all *Natura Morta*. Giovanni Calvesi
showed me where he had set up his studio, and there was the same
brown table, littered with lots of different objects, mostly stone
jars, or ceramic bottles and vases.

'Why do you paint these things?' I asked him.

'Because I like what is ordinary. To find beauty in what is plain,
this is my challenge.'

'Then why did you ask to paint *her*?' I asked him sharply.

'Ah,' he smiled slowly, pushing his long fingers through his thick
dark hair. 'That was only an excuse to talk to your sister.'

'But she is a married woman,' I said hotly.

'Yes, I believe that is so. And I, too, I have a wife and child.'

I looked about me. 'Where are they?'

I could see no evidence of a wife in the artist's plain rooms, no womanly touch. The floors were bare, with no rugs, and although the room was not dirty, it was higgledy-piggledy, with books and crockery all mixed up on tables and chairs.

'They are in my home town, Bologna.' He smiled and bent down, picking up a small piece of charcoal. 'I was a boy when I married, and she was a girl. Together we grew up.' He laughed. 'Such innocence. But it cannot last forever. We walk through many circles of love, I call it my *piazza del amore*. Your sister and I. We have entered a new one.'

I could not stop myself, although I had promised Mother I would not tell him. 'She is my mother, not my sister.'

Giovanni widened his eyes, stopped drawing. He roared with laughter.

I uncrossed my legs and stood up.

'Please.' He waved his hands towards the stool. 'Please . . .'

Reluctantly I sat down again.

'You are very young,' he said, suddenly serious. 'I can see this in the texture of your skin, and the whiteness of your eyes. And your mother, hah! She is a goddess!'

'But why did you change your mind and decide to draw me instead!' My eyes blazed. I was angry with myself for agreeing to be this philanderer's subject matter.

'*Sì*, this is true. But she understands why.' He swept his hands behind him, indicating his stacked paintings. 'When she saw what I paint, she knew why I prefer to draw you.'

'I am not a bottle, or a vase, or a jug, Signore Calvesi.'

'No, Signorina June, but your form,' he swept his hand, fingers spread, like the wings of a bird, over my chest, so close to my blouse that the skin beneath pimpled. 'It is all the same, a vessel waiting to be filled.'

He paused, looking directly into my face, smiling kindly, and I felt myself blush, the slow creeping bloom of pink spreading up my neck, across my cheeks, while at the same time a knot untwisted inside my belly. I felt trapped under his knowing gaze, and wanted more than anything to get up and refuse to let him continue draw-ing me. What had he said before? He was interested in painting the ordinary? This was a wicked trick of my mother's, revenge for all the lecturing I had given her the night before. She wanted me to know she believed me dull, and incapable of the grand love she could so easily inspire. For why else had she left me alone in the rooms of this Italian wolf for over one hour, knowing quite surely that he would never touch me?

Giovanni Calvesi picked up the charcoal again, saying no more. I closed my eyes, and then slowly began to unbutton my blouse, thinking all the time of my sister Minerva and what she had done to try to save my parents' marriage.

I drop my notes. The papers scatter and fan out across the flagstone floor. The sky is dark again, and I can hear the rain beating against the door, the wind howling down the chimney. I shiver and crouch down, picking up the papers. I pause and wipe a tear from my eye. Still the humiliation of that moment returns to me. Giovanni Calvesi had stopped drawing, and taken my hands in his. I opened my eyes, expecting him to ravish me, but instead he quickly did up my buttons and kissed my forehead.

'No, no, sweet *signorina*,' he said shaking his head before return-ing to his drawing.

I clench my fists. What quality do my sister and my mother have that eludes me? Yes, Robert married me, but he has never made me feel idolized. No man has ever looked at me as if I were a goddess, as Giovanni called my mother. How do they do it?

I gather my work about me, looking at the words written in a steady slanting hand. I feel better just to look at it. I see a picture of myself running up the staircase in the college, to the second floor, and knocking breathless at my tutor's door. As always my throat is tight, my mouth sticky and dry, my heart is pounding, and I am shaking slightly, gripping tightly onto my books. Yet for all my fear, I have never felt so alive. When I remember this feeling of conviction, I know I need to start what I never finished. I need to write my thesis, even if I am a farmer's wife living in the middle of nowhere in Cavan.

NICHOLAS

Driving into the yard, Nicholas notices a bicycle leaning by the gate to the orchard. It definitely wasn't there this morning when they left. He lifts Hopper out of the car and the dog hobbles towards the bike, sniffing around it.

'Who does that belong to? Hey, boy?'

He opens the gate and walks through the trees. He can see there are more apples to pick. At the back of the orchard there is a diminutive figure with curly white hair, reaching up and filling a plastic bag with plums. Nicholas coughs, unsure what he should say to the old woman.

'Ah, there you are,' Oonagh Tuite says, turning. 'Don't worry, I wasn't going to run off with all your plums. I was going to ask if you minded, but you weren't here, so I decided to pick some and offer to make you some jam in return.'

Nicholas joins the old woman and starts to pick some of the plums.

'Well, that sounds like a good deal to me.'

'Grand so,' she says, stepping back and putting her hands on her hips. 'Well, you get picking then and I shall take a little break.' She breathes in and out deeply, a smile of satisfaction on her face. 'I can barely remember what happened last week, and yet I remember being here during the war as if it were yesterday.'

'What was she like? Mrs Fanning?'

'She was a lady. Not a snob, or above herself, but just a lady. She read lots of books – that used to intimidate me at first, but she knew so much about history and art.'

'So what happened to her?'

'Nothing dramatic. She was here until she died.' Oonagh scratches her head. 'She was quite young when she died. Sometime in the Sixties, it would have been. The place was sold after she went. That was when the land and the farm were split up.'

She leans against the tree and stares wistfully into the woods.

'You know, I don't think she ever got used to living here. She used to talk about England and the seaside where she grew up, all the time. I think she always hoped she would go back home.'

'But if she was here on her own all those years, why didn't she go back?'

'Well, you see, she was waiting. Waiting for him to come back, and I don't think she ever gave up hope.'

Oonagh snaps out of her reverie and claps Nicholas on the back.

'That's why I always say to my granddaughter not to wait for anyone to change. You've to get on with things, because life can pass you by so fast. One day you're a young thing, and next you're a grandmother.'

Nicholas turns to look at Oonagh and her sparkling eyes.

'But I'm still a young one inside,' she says, banging her chest. 'I get surprised when I look in the mirror and see this old wrinkly face looking back at me.'

'Well, you don't look your age,' Nicholas says politely.

'That's very kind of you, young man,' Oonagh says briskly. 'Well, I think you've enough plums there for a gallon of jam. I had better be pushing off. I've tea to get for Paddy. The poor old fella's hips are gone. That's why I keep cycling. I said to him: if you don't use it you lose it.' She laughs heartily and picks up one of the bags full of plums.

Nicholas watches Oonagh cycling back up the lane, two big bags full of plums in her front carrier. There is still a good stretch in the evenings. He knows he should go back inside and do more work on the house, but it smells so good outside and it is so rare for the sun to be out, and the evening mild, that he goes back into the orchard, Hopper at his heels. He enters the wood and it feels like a balm to be walking on his own, in such private tranquillity.

He looks at his watch. Charlie will be home by now. Will she sense he was in the house? He has to stop thinking about her. But he finds thinking about the future without Charlie frightening. He wishes she had never told him about her adultery. He remembers the moment she confessed, the look on her face as if someone had died, and the snap inside his heart as she said the words: 'Nick, I've slept with someone else.'

His reaction had been a gut one, fierce and angry, unforgiving. He believed in fidelity, but was he so naive as to believe you could stay with the same person forever? Was that just a myth? He wonders about June Fanning and her story of the Adulteress. Was she talking about herself? Oonagh had said she was a lady, a faithful wife waiting for her husband to come home from the war. How on earth could she possibly betray him?

JUNE

I am in the orchard picking the last of the windfalls. The overgrown, sprawling mess of the trees make it a hard job. The orchard's abandonment cloaks me, making the place seem even more eerie and miserable, especially on a misty morning like today. I ponder why it is that Robert's family have been unable to bury their grief for so long, year after year, and allow the wreck of the orchard to remind them of their loss. How could they bear it? It is not a place I like to linger, yet ghosts or no ghosts, our orchard is a valuable asset in these hard times.

When every corner of our small larder is packed with apple jelly, apple chutney, pies, tarts, cordial and sauces, and when even I begin to tire of the tart bittersweet tang of apples with nearly every meal, I discover, through Oonagh, that I am able to use my apple harvest to barter for other things. The season for apples is short, and thus they are precious commodities and I have been able to get some more tea, and cigarettes – the two things I miss so much – and a little oil for the lamp so that I can read at night.

This morning we have had the first frost tipping the blades of grass, and ringing the ditches between the fields. As I work I can smell winter coming, and this anticipation knots inside my stomach. How will I cope here all on my own? Again I wonder: should I return to England? At least I would be closer to Robert. Yet he has forbidden me to come. Two weeks ago we spoke on the telephone.

It was an awful conversation, so short and disjointed. I was self-conscious, for a start, standing in the post office, aware of Miss Daly behind the counter, of Oonagh who had walked down with me and was waiting outside the box, and of other neighbours coming in and out. And although I was separated from them by a wooden partition, I was afraid they would hear.

He didn't sound like Robert at all. His voice was more formal – 'English', I suppose, like when I first met him. I missed the soft thrum of his home accent, which I have become accustomed to now. I could hear other voices in the background, and I knew he had no privacy, yet I felt annoyed that he could not say more to me, and tell me he loved me. I almost wished something terrible might happen to me, something to do with the baby, so that I could jolt a reaction out of him.

'Are you warm enough?' he asked me.

'Yes . . . and you, what are your quarters like?'

'Oh, they're grand. How are things with the foot-and-mouth?'

'It's fine,' I replied, irritated he wanted to talk about such things when we had so little time. 'Nobody is affected here.'

'That's good,' he said. And then there was a pause. I could hear all the crackles, and pips on the line, and my breath short and fast against the handpiece, and I realized, astonished, this was the first time we had ever talked to each other on the telephone. The first time, and we had nothing to say to each other.

'Are you flying yet?' I asked, panicked that Robert would say goodbye too soon and end the conversation.

'No.' His voice sounded flat and wooden, and I immediately regretted mentioning it. 'It will be soon, June.'

'When are you getting leave?' I asked, my voice trembling.

'I don't know, June. Not for a while.'

'Can I not come over to you, Robert, and find somewhere to stay, so that we can be near to each other?' I asked hopefully.

'God, no, June! It's far too dangerous for you. There are raids nearly every night here.'

'Oh,' I gulped, and whispered, 'but I miss you, Robert.'

'What? Speak up, will you, there's so much damn noise going on here—'

'I . . .' But I couldn't bring myself to say it again. 'Are you lonely, darling?'

'I'm all right . . . bored mainly.' His voice warmed a little and he sounded less tense. 'There are plenty of dances, though. The chaps know how to have a party. You would laugh to see me, June, stamping on some poor nurse's feet. But it's better than staying in the barracks. Christ, they're freezing!'

I was astonished. Not since we were married, over five years ago, had Robert taken me to a dance. After we were engaged he admitted to me how much he hated them, and I had never asked him to take me to one since. I *love* to dance. Who were these nurses who induced my husband to dance with them?

I was furious, and although I had not intended to mention Phelim Sheriden, I could not help myself. 'Mr Sheriden called to see you,' I said tartly.

'Phelim?'

'Yes, he thought he might catch you before you went. I didn't know you called on the Sheridens,' I continued, hissing into the receiver as quietly as I could. 'Why didn't you bring me? There are so few people for me to meet here, and they are people like me, Robert.'

'I don't want you going there,' he replied stiffly.

'But why?'

'It's not important why.' He paused, his tone softening. 'Please, June, trust me and do as I ask.'

'Oh, Robert!' My voice broke, and I forgot how angry I was. Tears began to prick my eyelids, and I missed him so dreadfully. 'When will this awful war be over?'

'Not long, Junie. Be a brave girl, now.'

There was more noise, in the background, and I could hear someone calling, *Hey Fanning, stop gassing, will ya'*?

'I've got to go, June,' Robert said hurriedly. 'Be good.'

And before I had a chance to say goodbye, to tell him I loved him, to hear him tell me the same, the line had gone dead.

Be good, this was all he had said to me. It was an instruction, not an endearment like be loved, be safe, be well or be happy. I stood with the telephone still in my hand, my lip trembling, and on the verge of tears like a small child. None of this was fair. I wanted my husband back, and I wanted things to return to the way they were before the war, when we first met and we all lived in London. I picked a splinter out of the wood in the telephone box and pushed it against the palm of my hand. I could hear Miss Daly behind me, her low gravelly pitch, and Oonagh's light treble, like a piccolo in comparison. I wondered: was Robert going to a dance that very night? And who would he dance with? A girl he preferred to partner than his own wife? I wondered: would she be a pretty young thing, would she tempt him to stray? The thought made me prick my finger with the splinter, and I stood motionless watching a bud of red blood pop out.

I shuffle through the trees, bending slowly and checking the windfalls for damage. I am in my least favourite part of the orchard. The trees are more closely planted together, and as I move through them, my coat catches on their branches, as if they are pulling at me like demanding children. This place is a million miles away from the war, and yet it makes me think about the tragedy of Robert's brother's fate. I wonder: does his soul wander here?

The gate creaks behind me, a twig snaps, and I jump like a cat. But when I turn it is not the ghost of Robert's dead brother who stands before me, but Phelim Sheriden, a cigarette hanging out of his mouth, a lock of ginger hair flopping across his forehead and his hands shoved into his pockets.

I straighten up, embarrassed that he has caught me in an old pair of Robert's trousers, with my hair tied up in a huge knot on top of my head.

'Apologies for barging in,' he says, 'but Oonagh said you were out here.'

'Is she still in the house?' I ask, looking at the winter sun beginning to sink into the hills.

'She was just leaving.' He stubs out his cigarette on the trunk of the nearest tree. 'Can I give you a hand?'

'On one condition,' I reply.

He looks at me expectantly, his blue eyes wide and mischievous like a schoolboy's. 'And what condition would that be?'

'You take some of the apples off my hands,' I smile at him.

'Delighted to,' he says cheerily, 'it will do Claudette good to eat these apples from the Fanning orchard.'

'How is she?' I ask, feeling suddenly tense at the mention of her name.

He doesn't look at me, but bends down scooping apples up and loading them into my basket. 'She is quite unwell,' he says quietly.

Silence drops between us, and I do not know what else to say. I wonder why he has called round to me.

And as if he has read my thoughts, he says abruptly, 'I brought you some honey.'

'Oh, how wonderful.' I clasp my hands together.

'I was given some, and it is too much for us,' he says.

'Well, that is very kind of you. I adore honey.'

'Yes, I thought you might.'

The basket is brimming with apples. I pick it up, but Phelim leans forward and takes it from my arms. Our hands brush, and his skin feels soft, so different from Robert's rough farmer's hands. He lifts one of the apples out of the basket and smells it, and then holds it for me to smell. I inhale.

'God, I love that smell,' he says. 'It is the perfect combination of bitter and sweet. And it smells so new, unblemished.'

It is almost dark, and now the sun has set and his face is cast in shadow. I feel something enveloping us. Is it the old love-lost ghosts of the orchard? Or is it us – is this the beginning of our desire? I shiver.

'You're cold,' he says.

'Yes, yes,' I stutter. 'It's getting chilly. Would you like to come into the house for a cup of tea?'

We sit either side of the hearth and I offer Phelim a cigarette with his tea.

He takes one, smiling. 'You managed to get a supply?'

'The apples are proving very useful.'

We puff on our cigarettes, and it makes me feel I could be in London sitting in Lyons' Corner House, having a cup of tea with my sister Min, as free as a bird.

'Any word from Robert?' Phelim asks.

'I got a letter this morning. He is flying now, stationed some-where in Sussex. That is all I know.'

Phelim has touched my sore spot. After the disappointment of our telephone conversation I was so excited when I received the letter, hopeful it would uplift me, and practically tore the one single sheet in half when I opened it. The letter was bound to be an anticlimax. I convinced myself my husband would hardly have the time or the inclination to write his wife a love letter when he is in the middle of a gruelling cycle of 'ops', as he calls it. But still his few words seemed inadequate. He wrote about the food and the rationing, how dreadful it is, and how he missed the butter and cream of Cavan. He talked about the other 'chaps', and what good men he was with. Then his writing trailed off in the middle of the page as if he was trying to rack his brains for something to tell me, and finally the letter ended with a few enquiries about the house. Was I warm enough? Not to forget to ask the Tobins to bring in the turf for me.

It was the kind of letter I might expect to receive from an acquaintance, not from a husband to a wife, the woman you cherish and adore, because surely that is what I am to him? There was no mention of the baby or talk of love. Neither did he say when he might be on leave.

The letter made me cry. I fell back on the bed sobbing until I felt weak and sick, and had to stumble into the yard to empty my stomach of breakfast. I sat in the shed for a long time, my back pressed against the wooden stalls, my knees into my chest, shaking my head. Could it be Robert didn't love me at all? Had he joined the war as a way of escaping our marriage?

I needed his letter to feel like he was reaching out to me, so that I could conjure up his scent, his embrace, and know that he was carrying my love for him in his heart wherever he went. I needed him to know this so that it would keep him safe like a talisman. Love is not a hardy thing. Did Robert not know this? How capable it is of disintegrating without reassurance.

'What do you do most evenings?'

Phelim's voice breaks through my distraction. Without thinking I tell him about my thesis. 'I am doing a little writing, some research,' I say uncertainly, afraid he will think me strange.

'I see.' He looks interested, leans forward in his chair.

'When I met Robert I was at university studying Classics.' I take a deep breath. 'I had the intention of writing a study on the life of Julia, the daughter of Emperor Augustus.'

'Oh, the bold Julia!' Phelim laughs.

I am shocked. Here is someone who has heard of Julia, sitting right in front of me, in the last place I would expect, so far from college and London!

'You know about Julia?' I ask excitedly.

'Yes, I am rather interested in classical literature myself. I love Suetonius's *Twelve Caesars*, and all his wonderful gossip. I do believe he wrote quite a bit on Julia.'

'She is a colourful character, and such a wonderful contradiction of beauty and refinement, yet, of course, with very loose morals . . .'

I trail off, not wanting to be too specific.

'Didn't her own father banish her to an island for committing adultery?' he asks, sipping his tea.

'Yes, although I think her stepmother, Livia, was behind her banishment. She wanted to get rid of Julia, and all of her children, so that her son, Tiberius, could become the next emperor.'

'Well, how fascinating to have discovered a classicist, on my doorstep in Cavan.' Phelim chuckles, offering me another cigarette. 'I would love to read your thesis,' he adds.

'Oh, it's not finished,' I answer nervously. 'You see, I never completed my degree . . .' I hesitate, blushing, 'I met Robert, and so then – well, it seemed irrelevant at the time to continue . . .'

'But now it is relevant?' Phelim asks softly, looking at me under lowered eyelids.

'Yes, now it is,' I reply emphatically, inhaling deeply and letting a plume of smoke drift out of my nostrils, and quite by chance I catch Phelim's eye. His expression is encouraging, as if he believes in what I am doing.

The teapot goes cold, yet still we talk on.

'So what is your theory on Julia?' Phelim asks. 'Was she really as depraved as they claim?'

'No, I don't think so.' I shake my head, and feel my heartbeat quicken. 'I think she was frustrated.' I continue, passionately, 'I believe she was in fact a very intelligent woman, and that was her downfall. She had no outlet for her intelligence and so she grew bored. Her adultery was an act of rebellion. I think she used her body as a political tool.'

'But what about love?' Phelim asks, his penetrating gaze making me feel slightly disconcerted. I wonder if I am being disloyal to Robert because I am talking about love with a man I hardly know.

'She wasn't interested in love. Like anyone seeking power, she wanted men – and women – to adore her so that she was always in control. She needed to conquer them.'

I take a deep breath and look to Phelim for reassurance.

'For instance, she registered as a prostitute not for any masochistic reasons, but because a new law had been brought in, making it illegal for any Roman woman to have sexual relations with anyone other than their husband unless she was a prostitute. That is why Julia, and her friend Phoebe and many other Roman women, signed up as prostitutes, not because they were particularly promiscuous or debauched. It was a political act of defiance.'

'So she considered it was her right to be an adulteress if she so chose?'

Are these not dangerous words to say to another man's wife? I look into Phelim's face, his bright blue eyes and boyish smile, remembering the last words Robert had said to me. *Be good.* I look away quickly, out of the window at the full silvery orb of the moon, which has risen while we have been talking. It is wrong, I know, but so very nice to talk to a man and sense that I am being admired.

'Do you think ancient Rome was very different from how we live now?' Phelim's crisp voice breaks the silence.

'Yes, and then no.' I remember the nights I lay in bed when I was at university, wondering about how my Roman characters really lived. 'It is hard to imagine the concept of the gladiatorial games, and the enjoyment of the death of other human beings as a sport, but then maybe that was one way of culling their enemies . . .'

My voice drops, as if someone might be outside the cottage door listening to us, although it is ridiculous to imagine that. We are alone, quite completely, with only the animals of the night outside rustling in the undergrowth, and the trees as silent sentinels.

'I have heard of death camps created by the Nazis. And of course there is the systematic bombing of cities where civilians are living. Is it so different?' My voice trembles. 'Is it maybe even worse?'

We sit without speaking and I grip my hands, for I have frightened my very soul with images of the modern world outside the sanctity of Cavan. Phelim pushes his foot across the flagstones and back again, to rest against his chair leg. I shake myself, thinking of Rome again.

'In many ways,' I say, 'most Roman women experienced more freedom than women do now . . .'

'Especially in Ireland,' Phelim adds. 'I am finding it hard to adjust to society here after Paris.'

'Any word on your daughter and her husband?' I ask, feeling guilty that I have not thought of asking before.

'No,' he replies briefly. 'Claudette and I keep the candles burning and the prayers flowing.'

'You must be so very worried about your daughter,' I say gently, thinking of how much I have been fretting about Robert and Minerva.

'I am. Although it is worse for Claudette.'

I look at him, not sure why he says this. He takes a cigarette out of the packet, plays with it between his fingers and looks up at me furtively.

'Danielle is not my daughter.'

I colour, embarrassed at his disclosure, and wondering why on earth he has told me. I say nothing.

'I am sorry,' he stands up suddenly. 'I'm afraid I must go home. I should not leave Claudette on her own for so long.'

'Of course.' I get up as well, and shake his hand. His grip is firm, his palm warm and engulfing.

'Well, I look forward to hearing more about your studies of Julia,' he says cheerily in an attempt to break the gloom that has descended upon us.

I sigh, still feeling his fingers tipping mine. 'It shall be a hard job, since I am missing most of my books, but I hope to have it finished before the baby comes.'

He squeezes my hand, looking surprised. 'I had no idea – why, congratulations.' He keeps shaking my hand fiercely, nearly dislocating my arm, a bright smile plastered on his face. 'Robert must have been dismayed to leave you.'

'Yes,' I say in a small voice. 'He was.'

He hesitates, looks at me closely. I can feel myself begin to blush and, confused, I stumble towards the door, tugging at it with my right hand.

'Don't forget your apples,' I say, flustered, hoping he will be distracted and not look at my face.

'I'll just take a few,' Phelim says, bending down and reaching into the basket. He shoves some apples into his pockets. I tug at the door, which is incomprehensibly stuck. He puts his hand on my shoulder. 'Please, Mrs Fanning, let me get the door for you.'

I stand aside, and he is next to me. I am surprised to notice that he is not much taller than I. 'Please, call me June.'

He pauses on the threshold, and I shrink back, dreading that he will ask me again about Robert or the baby and that I might disintegrate, as I have so often in recent days.

'I have a library,' he says suddenly. 'You know, I do believe we have quite a few classical authors. Would you by any chance like to come over and see for yourself?'

'Oh, my goodness, I'd love to.'

'Yes,' he continues. 'And I shall introduce you to Claudette. She would be delighted to meet Robert's wife.'

'That would be lovely,' I reply timidly, suddenly intimidated by the idea of meeting Claudette, and yet needing to, desperately needing to.

'Well, then.' He slaps his thigh boisterously, and his breath puffs into the chill air. 'Shall I expect you tomorrow morning, at around eleven o'clock, shall we say? Or maybe that is not convenient . . . come any time. We are always in – always in . . .'

'Eleven is fine,' I reply shyly.

'Excellent,' he looks pleased.

I watch him walk across the garden. He treads in a path of moonlight, his back glinting dove-grey, against the black night. He pauses to light a cigarette, and for a second his face is illuminated and it makes him seem otherworldly. I watch Phelim Sheriden disappear into the trees, and I wonder whether I now have a friend. It is only then that I remember Robert, and his instruction to me while we were speaking on the telephone. Oh, hell, I am not supposed to visit the Sheridens.

THE ADULTERESS IV

He takes up a clean paintbrush and brushes each of her eyelids shut. The soft, dry bristles hush her, and she lets him lead her to the bed like a small child. She lies down.

A sudden bang against the windowpane jolts her and she sits up, her eyes wide open. He stands in front of her, shirtless.

It is only a bird, he says.

She stares at him. He is swarthy and dark, like the pirate in her dreams.

Close your eyes, he says softly, lie down.

She does as she is told. She can hear the floorboards creaking as he moves about the room. She lies on the bed, her eyes closed, naked and reborn, trusting him. Then she feels his breath above her, and she knows he is leaning over her. Her body tightens with anticipation.

She feels a tiny drop land on her forehead, like a speck of rain, and then the brush comes down, this time wet. He pulls a line from the tip of her head, across the bridge of her nose, down her lips to her chin and neck. Then he pauses. She hears the brush dip into water nearby, the tinkling of the handle against the glass, and she imagines his arm as he quickly mixes colours, the way he always does so fast, as if without thought. Back the brush comes and this time he trails it between her breasts, down the centre of her, all the way to her navel. Back to her breasts, and he paints around her nipples; excited by the cold, wet paint, they become hard and she tries to guess what colour they are: green from the forest, blue as the sea, yellow from the sun. He is painting her stomach now, and she senses his delight in her small, round belly. She can feel the brush spiralling around her stomach and then spraying off in all directions onto her hips and thighs. She is reminded of a game she used to play with her sister, when they would take it in turns to lie on their tummies while the other traced a picture on her sister's bare back and the challenge was to guess what it was. They could spend hours like this on the beach in the summer, making temporary pictures, gradually becoming more and more intricate, tattoos of shapes and images, which they carried on their backs until they ran into the sea, kicking spray at each other and enjoying the ecstasy of movement after the still moments of concentration on the sand.

She trembles. He is painting her inner thighs now. Up from her knee, he trails the brush across her skin, until the watery paint mixes with her juice, creating oily curls around her pelvis. The soft tip of the brush teases her, sliding up and down her slit so that she groans and opens her legs wider. He paints an oval, round and round, until the brush comes to one spot, and suddenly its tip is softer and it is a brush no more, but his tongue licking her in adoration. She says his name, tells him she loves him. He raises himself up, and then puts his lips to hers, lowering his body onto her, pressing into her.

I am making a print, he whispers. You are the art, and I am an edition of you.

She opens her eyes as he sits back on his heels and she sees her colours on his skin. She looks down at herself. He has made her an ocean. Her chest is painted Aegean blue, and jade seaweed swirls up her legs, so that when he finally pushes into her, he is at the bottom of the sea, and so is she, drowning.

NICHOLAS

Finally Nicholas sends Charlie a text. Immediately after he presses the send button he regrets it.

Sorry.

It is pathetic. He doesn't even know why he is saying he is sorry, because she is the one who committed adultery, not him. But somehow he feels like it is his fault, although he doesn't know why.

He sits at his kitchen table, squeezing his mobile phone in his hand. He hates it. How easy it is for him to communicate with her, when he is so far away physically. It is tortuous waiting for a reply. He stares at the phone. Puts it down on the table, busies himself by clearing up the breakfast things and even washes them. Still no sound from his phone. He picks it up, checks it isn't on silent, and places it on the dresser now. Half-heartedly he moves tiles from around the bottom of the dresser to the spare room so that he can get into the cupboards. He looks at the stacks of building materials already dumped in the room and feels immediately overwhelmed. He and Kev never did dry-line the house. If he doesn't have it done before winter, the place will be freezing, but he can't afford to pay someone to do it, and he can't face it himself.

Nicholas puts off going back into the kitchen to check his phone for messages and instead goes into the back room and plays the piano for about an hour. He plays *Danse macabre*, loudly banging out the notes and vaguely planning Geraldine's lesson in his head. Eventually he can stand it no longer and goes back into the kitchen. Still no messages. He is shocked. He thought Charlie would respond. Evidently she no longer wants to know him. Nicholas stands white-faced in his bright kitchen, clenching his fists. So this is it, he thinks. This new life is permanent.

Later that morning Geraldine arrives for her lesson, but something is wrong. She twitches on the seat, and her fingers stumble over each other.

'Shit,' she hisses under her breath each time she misses a note.

'Let's take a break,' Nicholas suggests.

They sit side by side at the piano, but neither of them moves. Geraldine stares straight ahead, the clock ticks in the corner. Nicholas shifts on his chair, preparing to get up to make coffee when he hears her sniff. He leans forward to look at her face, but her long hair covers it. She sniffs again.

'Geraldine, are you all right?'

She says nothing.

'What is it? Geraldine, what's wrong?'

She sniffs again, and brings her hand up to pull the hair away from her face. 'It's my birthday.'

'Well, happy birthday! It can't be that bad, can it? Come on, how old are you?'

'Thirty-five.'

'Well, you're younger than me!'

She shakes her head. 'He forgot. The bastard forgot again. When it's his birthday, I always make such a big deal. A meal out with his family, and I bake a cake and get Grainne to make a card. I always buy him something lovely. Last year I got him gold cufflinks. They were real gold, not plated. I saved up for months. And this morning nothing – he forgets . . .'

She takes out a tissue and blows her nose.

'I'm sorry, Nick. You don't want to hear about this.'

She sighs and looks so defeated that Nicholas feels a wave of compassion for her. 'No, it's okay, Geraldine. I'm sorry, but your husband sounds like a complete idiot. You're a beautiful woman who deserves to be cherished.'

She turns to look at him, and he can see in her eyes that she really doesn't believe this and there is a look – a familiar look he recognizes. It is the way Charlie sometimes looked at him. Oh God, he feels suddenly sick. He did this to Charlie. He remembers with cold clarity that he forgot Charlie's last birthday too, and he had thought her so childish in the way she reacted. He had told her they needed to save money, and why did she want a big show when didn't she know that he loved her anyway?

'No,' Geraldine is shaking her head. 'Nick, I'm not attractive at all. I'm an overweight housewife. Rays says I'm a useless lump of a woman.'

'Geraldine, your husband is blind – you're beautiful.'

Nick holds her hand in his. Her fingers are long and tapered, perfect hands for a pianist, he thinks. She doesn't pull them away. They look at each other. He kisses her gently on the lips.

Geraldine blushes, and Nicholas can't think what has got into him, but he just wants to kiss her, so he does so again. This time Geraldine begins to kiss back, they curl around each other on the piano stool, and he puts his arms about her. It has been so long since he has kissed someone like this. With Charlie they had stopped taking time over their kisses. In the past year she had turned her back to him and he had made love to her, looking at the back of her head, her neat curls and the mole on her neck. When was the last time they had closed their eyes and pressed their lips together? Just a kiss.

Geraldine is different from Charlie. Fuller lips, her mouth tasting of cherry drops and her cheeks plump and downy, her soft flesh, full breasts pushing against his body. She is warm and sweet and welcoming. He doesn't care that he is still married or that she is married too. These facts seem ridiculously irrelevant in the light of the important business they are engaged in – two human beings comforting each other in their loneliness. What could be wrong with that?

Geraldine stops. She puts her hand to her chest, and breathes fast. 'Oh God,' she says, her pupils dilated, her irises glittering, 'I . . . I haven't been kissed like that since I got married.'

And then she cries again, this time heartily, against Nicholas's shoulder.

JUNE

I am going to Phelim Sheriden's house. I am disobeying my husband. I tell myself it is the books that lure me, and the task I have set myself of documenting Julia Caesar's life. Or I convince my conscience that before Robert went away, he promised we would call so that I could play the piano. How can he expect me to be without music for so long? If I am honest, it is something altogether different that takes me to the Sheriden house. It is a mixture of curiosity to meet Claudette Sheriden and the need for company. Phelim. I have found within me a strand of wilfulness, something my sister Min had plenty of. I am cross with Robert. He has left me and gone off to war, leaving in his wake a bundle of secrets. I try to hush these thoughts, and push disquiet to the back of my mind. I let Debussy triumph and the plaintive notes of 'Clair de lune' twist in a spiral through my memory into my heart. To be able to play it, just once, would bring me such pleasure.

I dress carefully. I want to look sophisticated, but not too over-dressed for the countryside. I ignore the fact that my clothes are already tighter on me, and squeeze into a bottle-green skirt, along with a cream blouse. I have taken to wearing trousers around the place, so it is nice to put a rare pair of stockings on again and feel a little more feminine. My morning sickness has abated, thanks to the apples and, as Oonagh promised, I no longer feel as tired as I

207

did in the first few weeks. In fact I have never felt so hale and hearty
— no different from how I felt before I became pregnant. I forget
that a few months from now I will be a mother. All my farmer's
wife's chores are done, and therefore I am free to spend several
hours reading books if I so wish. I am free to be the old June.

I put on the gold locket Robert gave me when we became
engaged in London, over five years ago now. I know his picture is
inside, but I daren't open it in case his gaze is censoring. There have
been no letters from him for at least a week. I say a little prayer to
the black bog-wood crucifix on the wall, my hands shaking as I do
up the clasp.

I should be missing you more, I whisper to the primitive figure
etched on the cross.

Since the day we were married I have gone nowhere without
Robert. The bluestocking girl from London University, who
happily gallivanted off on study expeditions to Italy, quickly transformed into the perfect wife. I exist through him. And in company
I became afraid of speaking out — not because Robert didn't want
me to, but because I felt I had nothing interesting to say. All of
Robert's opinions seemed more articulate than mine. My husband
has been gone over a month and I am remembering the girl I once
was. This is my last chance to be who I truly am, before I become
someone's mother. Is this why I am going to see Phelim Sheriden?

I take the road rather than the woods, not wishing to snag my
stockings. I walk the mile into the village and it feels good to swing
my legs, and breathe in deeply, my shoulder feeling the weight
of my bag full of books and papers. I remember the satisfaction
of strolling into college from my lodgings in Euston, all the way
down Gower Street, keeping an eye out for my sister going in or
out of the Slade. I never did see her.

The Sheridens' house is one of the best in the village. It is tall
and austere with, I am counting, at least three floors. I can see that

the roof is sagging a little, and the walls are covered in ivy. The place has a look of desertion about it.

Phelim meets me at the door, and takes me through a dim, draughty hall into a small study. I shiver. The room is cold and cheerless, although there is a fire crackling in the grate. I look about me and see thick dust on the mantelpiece above the fire, cobwebs hanging from all of the lampshades, and dustsheets on the furniture. There is a strong musty odour, and it makes me sneeze.

'I do apologize. This room is awfully cold, for we never use it, but the fire has just been lit, so it should warm up soon.'

Phelim brings me over to the corner of the room and points to three tall, dusty bookcases stuffed with books.

'I am afraid there is no order to them.' He scratches his head, and looks apologetic.

'Please, don't worry. I'll hunt through them.' I rub my gloved hands together, trying to warm up.

'Excellent.' He shoves his hands into his pockets and smiles at me boyishly.

We look at each other, and I do not know whether I should start searching through the books or say something. His eyes are cobalt-blue, so different from Robert's. His hair is the colour of a red setter's, with no grey, again unlike Robert, and his face looks almost brown, there are so many freckles scattered all over it. It strikes me yet again how similar his colouring is to Father's.

'Well,' he says eventually, taking his hands out of his pockets and smoothing his hair down. 'Work away. I am afraid Claudette needs me upstairs.' He goes towards the door, and then turns hesitantly. 'You will join us for luncheon?'

'I'd love to,' I reply immediately, although my stomach contracts with nerves. He looks pleased, making me feel as though the room is warmer already.

*

I am alone in Phelim Sheriden's study and I am shaking so much, as if I am doing something illicit. I take off my gloves and press my palms together. Where to start? My eye is drawn to a blood-red book on the shelf above me. I reach up, take it down and read the gold lettering on the spine.

'*Sexual Life in Ancient Rome* by Otto Kiefer.'

I drop it like a hot brick on the carpet. I look furtively behind me to check that Phelim hasn't slipped back into the room. I pick the book up, and open it randomly.

> We may remind our readers that just at this time Ovid's friv-
> olous *Art of Love* was popular among the gay youth of Rome –
> that is, in the very circles where Julia took pleasure behind her
> husband's back. And did it not describe how to seduce the young
> wife of an ageing husband?

I feel hot and cold at the same time. Are these words a warning to me? I put the book back on the shelf, finger the spines of a few others and finally pull out a slim edition of Ovid's *Art of Love*. I sit in the armchair by the fire and hold the book in my lap. I close my eyes for a moment.

29th September 1933, the island of Ponza, Italy. That was the day I first discovered Julia the Elder, daughter of Emperor Augustus. I had not wanted to go to the island until Min told me Julia's story. Ponza was Julia's place of exile. Found guilty of adultery, she had been banished to the island for life. The word 'adulteress' was still ringing in my ears. It was the word I had used when I left mother in Milan with Giovanni Calvesi.

Harlot! Adulteress! Traitor!

I had screamed at her as I stormed out of Giovanni Calvesi's rooms. On Ponza it was just my sister and I. Charles was in Rome with business associates. We were to meet him in Sorrento in two days' time.

'What shall we do about Mother?' I asked my sister. Now that she was married, would she have some wisdom on the matter? But she shook her head.

'It's too late, Juno. It's too late.'

Min held my hand and we looked over the side of the old fishing boat at the disappearing shore. I saw a Roman villa on the hillside. Later I learned it was the last place Julia stayed on mainland Italy before she was put to sea in a boat and made the same journey that we were making from Terracina to the island of Ponza. I looked at the choppy blue sea and wondered how she must have felt. Did she believe she deserved her punishment? Was she ashamed? Or was she still defiant? Did she regret her affairs? It made me think of Mother again and whether my own flesh and blood possessed a conscience.

We went to the hotel first. I could hardly wait to unpack, but Min insisted that she needed a nap. I couldn't stand it. I just couldn't wait a moment longer. So I went on my own. I walked briskly down the road to *Chiaia di Luna*, the crescent-moon beach. I entered a Roman tunnel, named Julia's Tunnel after my princess, and began to run down it. After a few moments I spilled out into the sunshine onto the glittering beach, breathless and exhilarated. I had never felt so alive in my life. Here I was present in the past. With my own eyes I saw what my ancient princess saw, all those hundreds of years before. Only those who love history can understand my emotions at that moment. I stood in the cup of that half-moon beach, the cliff vertical and golden behind me, cut off from everything but the abandon of the blue Mediterranean Sea. All of my time with Mother slid from my shoulders and felt like a bad dream. I laughed out loud, for suddenly I did not care at all about Mother and Giovanni Calvesi. Instead I felt a sense of how it was to be a Roman. I took my shoes and stockings off. My bare feet were pressed firmly into the sand, and I stood tall, looking at a crystal-clear horizon, the hot sun beating on my head, and the presence of gods and goddesses all about me – the sea, the sky, the sun, the wind, the heart.

That night was the last one before we left to meet Charles, and Min wore her Jezebel dress. It was pure silk, long, bias-cut and simmering crimson. Her hair was covered by a black chiffon scarf, emphasizing her pale and exposed neck. She had long black gloves, though they were hardly needed in the warm evening. I remember thinking what a shame it was that Min was a married woman and I the unmarried one, for she put me completely in the shade. But I wasn't jealous.

We walked back down to the harbour before dinner. The day was still bright, and my sister became quite childish, sitting up on the dock, and swinging on an old rope. She began singing. It wasn't anything classical like her adored Strauss. No, it was something naughty, an old sea shanty. Even when singing a dirty song, my sister's charm was so infectious that I felt some of her beauty rubbing off on me, so that I glowed as well.

We drank far too much Prosecco at dinner, as if we were celebrating. Maybe we were. It was the last time we were free together on our own, we two sisters, although we weren't to know it at the time. For one night only we were nobody's wives, nobody's daughters, nobody's lovers.

We danced after dinner with foreign gentlemen, dark and mysterious, probably Fascists, but with impeccable manners. We let them ply us with drink and cigarettes, but it wasn't hard to shed them later, pleading that it was time for our beauty sleep as we nipped outside for one last nightcap before bed. It was deliciously warm still, jet-black, not even a sliver of the moon in the sky. We sat on the terrace fascinated by the fireflies, overwhelmed by these tiny illogical miracles of light, which blinked around us.

'What happens to fireflies in the morning?' I wondered.

'They go out.'

My sister's voice sounded suddenly serious in contrast to our earlier frivolity. It made me think of Charles and how things would be different when we went to Sorrento, because he would come first, not me.

'Are you happy, Min?' I whispered into the soft night.

'Of course,' she said, taking my hand.

'I wish I could fall in love.'

'Don't worry, big sister – some men find bookish dons most attractive!'

'You beast!'

I leaned over and pulled a strand of Min's hair, which had come loose from her scarf. She laughed, and squirmed lower in her chair.

'Stop now. Stop, Juno, you're hurting me.' Min pulled away, and stood up. 'It's so warm for September. Why don't we go swimming?'

She walked down the stone steps to the edge of the pool. I watched incredulously as Min slipped off her red sheath. Her skin looked like alabaster in the dark.

'There's no moon. No one will see us,' my sister said confidently.

I shook my head, afraid of her audacity. 'We oughtn't to.'

But Min ignored me and sat on the edge of the pool, slithering in.

'I don't think Charles would want you do this!' I called after her.

'But Charles isn't here, is he?'

The water snapped over her head and she was gone, gliding underwater all the way to the other side of the pool. A moment later she came up, sleek as a seal, her dark hair glossy.

'Come on, Juno, the water is wonderful!'

I shook my head, frozen like a statue, afraid we would be found out, that someone from the hotel would come out and see my naked sister at any moment.

Min swam back towards me. She rose up below me, her head bobbing up and down in the water, her eyes like burnt almonds in the dark.

'Sometimes you just have to jump in,' she whispered softly beneath me. 'It's like life. If you don't, nothing will ever happen to you.'

But I turned around and walked back into the hotel. I was cross with Min. When I think about it now, I wish I had got into the water and swum naked with my sister under the hot black sky. I wish I had felt the warm water caressing my skin. I wish I had floated on my back, my breasts exposed to the sky, and not been afraid.

The next day we travelled back to the mainland, going further down the coast until we reached Sorrento. Charles had booked us into the Grand Hotel Excelsior Vittoria, an imposing and majestic hotel that was perched on the edge of a cliff overlooking the Bay of Naples. As my sister and I strolled through the front gates and walked into the gardens of the hotel, between the fragrant orange and lemon trees, I felt her becoming someone else. My salt-water sister, my wild one from the sea, was transforming into a demure young wife with each step she took.

Charles was waiting for us in the glass lobby. He embraced his new wife, showering her with kisses. 'Oh, how I've missed you, my darling,' he exclaimed.

I stood awkwardly on the marble floor, the bellboy disappearing up the staircase with our cases. Charles looked at me.

'But where's your mother?'

'Don't ask,' Min said, putting her arm around his waist. They walked ahead of me up the staircase, and I felt like a foot soldier, an unwanted intrusion on their private love. I paused in the stairwell, letting them go ahead, and looked at the stained-glass window, the large Chinese vase full of flowers, and the plasterwork on the wall in front of me. Two mermaids were facing each other with naked torsos, the nipples of their breasts almost touching, their dance joyous and abandoned. I remembered Father's words before we left Devon, and how he had described Min and I as two mermaids. All that was gone now. Father and Mother, Min and I. I stood on the sumptuous carpet on the staircase of the Grand Hotel Excelsior Vittoria and felt quite bereft, so lonely that not even in Cavan have I felt as desperate as that day.

When Phelim returns to the study I am sitting on the floor surrounded by books, dazzled by history.

'Well, I can see you've settled in,' he says, smiling down at me. 'Would you like to join me for some food?'

He offers me his hand, and I take it, standing up rather awkwardly. I hold onto his fingers for another moment and then pull away, embarrassed.

'Gosh, is it so late already?' I dust down my skirt.

'Indeed. It is just past one.'

'Heavens! I can't believe I've been reading for over two hours!'

He smiles again, and I think what kind eyes he has, summer sky-blue, with laughter lines creasing the skin around them.

'I know how that is,' he says throwing a couple of logs onto the fire. 'When I start painting I forget all other bodily needs. I can work for hours with nothing to eat or drink. I could paint all night sometimes, with no need for sleep.'

'You are like my sister, Min.' I follow him out of the room and into the hall.

He turns, and looks at me questioningly.

'She is a painter, too.'

'Really?'

'Yes, she is in London. She studied at the Slade.'

'You must be worried about her at the moment.'

'Yes I am.'

I am unable to look him directly in the face. How could Phelim guess I cannot stop thinking about my sister – thoughts of her are more present in my mind than of Robert. Why is that? Am I a bad wife?

We walk the length of the hall, alongside a grand mahogany staircase. The walls are covered in dark-green wallpaper, with faded gold stripes.

'I hope you don't mind eating in the kitchen. The dining room is positively arctic.'

Phelim lifts the latch on a large door covered with cracked paint. We enter the kitchen and I am momentarily blinded by brilliant sunshine.

'Oh, what a beautiful day,' I gush. 'I had not noticed in your study.'

'Yes, it is a little dark in there.' He shows me to a seat. 'These old stone houses can be a bit gloomy.'

'I think it a beautiful old house. It reminds of where I grew up in Devon. I do miss staircases.'

'But your cottage is so quaint.' He ladles soup into two bowls. 'And much warmer than here.'

'That's true.' I put my napkin on my lap. 'Although it is lovely and warm in this room.'

'I have the range going night and day. And the sunshine helps.'

I notice the table is only laid for two.

'Is your wife not joining us?'

He pauses, the ladle suspended over the pot.

'No, I'm afraid she is not feeling up to it. But possibly after luncheon she might be feeling strong enough to meet you.'

It is on the tip of my tongue to ask what ails his wife, but manners prevent me from doing so. I notice Phelim's hand is shaking as he brings my bowl over and places it before me on the table. Maybe I have upset him.

'So, did you find some useful material?' he asks, unfolding his napkin.

'Yes, I have. It has been most helpful,' I reply enthusiastically.

'Well, please do feel free to come back again and take more notes.'

I nod, smiling at him gratefully.

'I hope you like pea soup. It is my favourite.'

He dips his spoon into the soup, and I watch him as he sips from the side of it, the way Father used to do.

'Oh, yes, lovely.'

We eat in silence for a few moments. I watch Phelim and he seems so familiar, as if I am back home. I am incredibly warm, a heat rising from my belly. All I am doing is having lunch with a neighbour, and yet it feels as if I am doing something wrong. Phelim stops eating and looks up. We stare at each other for a long moment. I feel my heart beating faster, the colour rising in my cheeks. I tear my eyes away from his face and look back down at my soup.

'So, you fought with Robert's brother, James, in the Great War?' It is the first thing that comes to mind.

'Yes,' he replies, dabbing his chin with his napkin.

I pause, my spoon hovering over my soup bowl, and look again at Phelim Sheriden. Here is a man, just a year older than Robert, and an experienced soldier. Why is he not fighting against the Nazis, like Robert?

'I have had enough of war,' he says suddenly, as if he reads my thoughts. 'I don't think I could kill, again,' he adds quietly.

His words sound shocking, here in the sanctuary of his country house, looking out on the soft drumlins of Cavan, and the downy

sky, where violence is a thunderstorm, and death a natural occurrence. But there is a war going on. I have to remind myself. I try
to picture London in the middle of the Blitz, and our old flat in
Hampstead. Is it in ruins?

And then there is Robert. Is he preparing to fly right now, leaving the English shoreline far behind and thrusting himself, exposed,
into the middle of the German skies, looking down on tiny dolls'
cities and towns, and flashes of fire from his bombs, looking like
splashes of bright paint – their destruction, their carnage, incom-
prehensible to his soul? Is he frightened of what he does? Or of
what might happen to him if they get hit? Does he pray, holding
onto the tiny gold cross I gave him for his wedding present, wrapping his lucky white silk scarf around his neck with a bravado that
is contagious among all of his crew? When my husband is in his
bomber plane doing his duty, does he think of me?

'James D. and I were very young, unmarried and very stupid,
when we joined up to fight.'

'Robert never talks about his brother James.' I blush at this per-
sonal admission, yet feel unable to stop myself from confiding in
him. 'I don't like to ask him, although he did tell me it broke his
mother's heart when he was killed. Apparently she never recov-
ered, and died just one year later.'

Phelim stops eating and looks at me pensively. 'Could that be
why he has chosen to fight now? To live up to the memory of his
brother, as a hero?'

'But both his parents are dead. To whom could he be proving
himself?'

'You, of course.'

'No.' I shake my head vehemently. 'He knows I would rather he
stayed home. I think he joined up because he believes in the Allies.
He is passionately against the Nazis.'

Phelim clears away our soup plates and takes a joint of meat out of the oven.

'The first time we went into action it was at the recapture of Gouzeaucourt in November 1917.' He speaks without looking at me, cutting the meat and sliding it onto two plates. 'I remember, just before we went in, dear old Father Browne from Cork gave us a blessing.' He pauses, and shakes his head sorrowfully. I feel sorry for him.

'Please, you don't have to talk about the war.'

'No, I would like to.' Phelim brings two big plates of food over to the table. 'Claudette can't bear to hear me speak about that time. She was there, in France. It upsets her to talk about it. But sometimes I wish I could talk to someone about it. Do you mind listening?'

'Of course not.' I feel honoured that a man like Phelim Sheriden would wish to tell me about his past.

'I remember I was on a horse, which was absolutely idiotic. But when I saw chaps being shot, I got off the horse. It was a pretty bloody battle, but at least our attack was successful and quick. There was a rumour that the zeal shown by the Irish Guards in the attack was because we knew the enemy held the supplies of the division, which had been evacuated.'

He chuckles softly, but his eyes look sad, their blue faded.

'Indeed, when we got through, we found a couple of supply trains untouched, and a number of guns were recaptured, and most importantly the rum supply was largely intact. When this fact came to light, rum jar by rum jar was borne joyously though the dark streets. The weather was cold and bitter, and I remember James D. that night. At first we drank the rum to get warm. We were so cold in our bones. But then we got more and more intoxicated. A mixture of adrenaline from the battle and the rum. I don't think either of us had ever been so drunk in our lives. If the enemy had rerouted, they would have met little resistance, for we were as helpless as babies from the drink.'

'What happened to James?' I asked hesitantly.

Phelim lets out a deep breath, and stops eating. 'During a lull in the war in 1917 we both attended a training course in gun school, and then we returned to the front in April 1918. In August the advance from Saint-Léger to Ecourt took place. There were extremely heavy casualties – your brother-in-law was one of them – and I was seriously wounded early on in the battle, and that probably saved my life. I was invalided to England and never returned to the war.'

Suddenly the kitchen feels cold, as if someone has opened a door, and I shiver.

'I apologize,' says Phelim suddenly. 'This is a rather gloomy conversation. Let us talk about something other than war.'

We slip into lighter chat easily, for talking with Phelim is like opening doors. As soon as one topic is exhausted, he leads me effortlessly into another. I find myself telling him about my childhood in Devon and the idyllic summers I spent by the sea when I was a girl. I tell him about what happened to Father. I even talk about Giovanni Calvesi and Mother. It is a topic I rarely discuss with Robert, feeling ashamed of her actions, as if it will make him think less of me. But talking with Phelim is easy, and I find myself gushing forth, as if I have been on a desert island for four weeks. We talk about my sister Minerva and art. I tell him about her dream to be an artist, and he tells me about Cubism and the life of the artist in France. It sounds so thrilling that I am envious of those lady artists. How free they must feel! Finally I bring up the subject of Claudette.

'Did Claudette work as an artist's model before she came to Ireland?'

'No, it is I who introduced her to that. No, Claudette was a war orphan. I know very little about her family, apart from the fact that they were all killed during the Great War. It was all so tragic – Claudette's mother, father and sister were killed. Every time I have tried to speak to Claudette about it she gets upset, and confused, telling me she can't remember properly. It is a tragedy that Claudette has carried with her all her life. It is no wonder she is so ill.'

'How did she come to be in Ireland?'

Phelim looks surprised. 'Did Robert never tell you? It was down to James D. He rescued her – was her knight in shining armour, so to speak – and brought her back to Ireland in 1917.'

There is a hint of something in Phelim's voice.

'We all loved her. She is the kind of woman who inspires men to fall in love with her. But Claudette was only in love with one of us: James D. And, unluckily for her, the wrong man was killed.'

He holds my eyes steadily.

'She couldn't resist calling the baby after him, although I married Claudette so that people would think Danielle was mine. That is what friends do for one another.'

'I don't understand.'

'James D. The D stands for Daniel. It is a Fanning name, for their father was called Daniel as well. Did you not know that? I am sure, if you have a boy, Robert will want to call him Daniel.'

'Oh.' I am shaken by how little I know about my husband's family. I remember my vision of Claudette in the woods, calling for Danny. Was it her lost love to whom she was appealing, rather than her daughter?

'So you see, your family and mine are connected through Claudette's daughter. She is Robert's niece. Nobody knows of course, apart from Robert and I. Even Danielle never knew.'

He coughs and looks uncomfortable, getting up suddenly, his napkin dropping to the floor.

'I must apologize, June. It is wrong for me to talk to you about such matters. I assumed Robert would have told you . . .' He trails off, and walks towards the door. 'If you wouldn't mind waiting for a moment in the study, I will find out if Claudette is feeling up to seeing you.'

We walk back down the corridor. Phelim leaves me to go up the staircase, while I enter the study. The room is warmer now, and my books are still spread out on the floor. I pick them up one by one and return them to the shelves.

Butterflies dance inside my stomach, for I am not sure I want to meet Mrs Sheriden now. I need time to think about what Phelim has told me, and to figure out why Robert never spoke about his brother and Claudette. Was this why he did not want to visit the Sheridens? Surely he could not be angry with Phelim for marrying Claudette to protect her reputation, and to take care of his brother's fiancée. To marry someone whom you knew did not love you seemed such a huge sacrifice. But there is something else that bothers me. My academic instinct tells me there is more to the story. Phelim had said, 'We all loved her . . .' Surely he should have said, 'We were both in love with her', if he was referring just to James D. and himself? Who were 'we'?

Phelim comes back into the room. 'I am afraid she is asleep. I wouldn't like to disturb her, but maybe you can meet next time you call round. It will be soon, won't it? Do you need to do more research?' He looks hopeful.

'Yes, if that's all right with you.'

'Absolutely, June.' He covers his mouth and coughs. 'Would you like to see some of my paintings before you go?'

'I would be honoured.' I am reluctant to go home to my empty house.

We climb the stairs. The carpet is threadbare and looks dark grey, although Phelim tells me it was once evergreen. The house is completely silent, in the hushed way houses of the sick are. The only sound is the tick of the grandfather clock on the landing. We pass three doors, and I wonder behind which one is the bedridden Claudette, the woman who inspires men to fall in love with her. Phelim turns a corner, and I follow him to an emerald-green door. He opens it, and it leads to more stairs.

'I am afraid my studio is at the top of the house. Can you manage?'

'Yes, thank you.'

His studio is in the attic. It is small, but neat, not how I would expect an artist's studio to look. An easel faces the door, with an unfinished canvas on it. The piece is similar to the small painting he showed me the first day we met, but this time the tones are blue and green, and linking into each other in interweaving half-moon curves.

'I am softening up. It is slightly less geometric than my previous work.'

I notice a gramophone player in the corner of the room. 'Oh, you have music!'

'Yes, very important. I play music as I paint. It is very much a part of my work.'

I look at him, curious at what he says.

'I paint in keys. Each colour is a key, so if you know a little bit about music, when you look at my art hopefully you will also hear it.'

'What a beautiful idea.' I look closer at his blue painting.

'It is my way of reflecting the divine.'

As my eyes get lost in the contours of his work I can suddenly imagine its sound, full of longing, mirroring the surge of loneliness that washes through me.

'Oh, it's so sad,' I burst out, unable to stop myself from saying it.

Phelim puts his hand on my shoulder.

'Yes,' he whispers almost in my ear. I can feel the warmth of him standing behind me, shielding my back, his breath on my neck. I have an urge to step back and let him wrap his arms about me. Just one step – that is all it would take.

NICHOLAS

Nicholas teaches Geraldine some simple duets. Mrs Kerr's book of duets, the same melodies he used to play with his mum. They sit side by side on the piano stool, and Geraldine is laughing, and he feels quite jolly as their fingers move in and out of each other, not quite touching. His chest is tight with the excitement of playing the duet perfectly. Geraldine stretches across him and he breathes in. They have only kissed the once, on her birthday. But now there is something unspoken between them. He doesn't want her, and yet he does. She is not his type, but despite that there is something attractive about her. He doesn't want to get involved with a married woman who has a child. It is wrong. She is a countrywoman, and apart from the piano they have nothing in common. And yet it is such a relief not to have to prove himself, but to be admired so absolutely. It is easy to see that Geraldine has a crush on him. Nicholas has to be careful. He doesn't want to take advantage of her.

Now, when Geraldine and Nicholas drink their morning coffee and eat apple-and-cinnamon muffins she has baked with the apples that he gave her, Nicholas finds himself telling Geraldine about Charlie.

'I was only going to spend one summer in Ireland. My father was Irish and I wanted to check out my roots. I was staying with a cousin in Dublin, planning to head west, but there was no work at all. So I thought I'd better go back to London. Just the day before I was due to go, I met Charlie. Love at first sight, like they say. I stayed. Got a shitty job washing up in a restaurant kitchen. We moved in together about six weeks after we met, and then we got married a year later.'

'Is Charlie short for Charlotte?' Geraldine asks, pouring more cream into her coffee.

'Yes, but she prefers to be known as Charlie. She has this theory that there are certain assumptions made in the art world, if people know what gender you are. You see, she's an artist. So that's why she calls herself Charlie. I think it suits her more than Charlotte.'

'What does she look like?' Geraldine asks quietly.

'Tall, skinny, long black hair. A bit like a witch.' He laughs, rather too bitterly, and Geraldine looks at him enquiringly, but says nothing. 'She cheated on me. That's why we broke up.' Nicholas speaks bluntly. He gets up and puts their dirty mugs in the sink.

Geraldine follows him, places her hand on his shoulder. 'She must be crazy,' she says softly.

Eventually Nicholas gets a text message, but it is not from Charlie. It is from Kev, telling him that a friend, Simon, is playing a gig in Cavan. He can't go, but he thought Nicholas might be interested. Nicholas invites Geraldine without thinking.

'I'm just asking you as a friend,' he explains. 'You can bring your husband.'

'Oh God, no,' Geraldine laughs. 'He hates that sort of thing. Are you sure you don't mind? I mean, don't you want to hang out with your own friends?'

'It's just Simon, and he'll be playing. I'd love you to come.'

The gig is in a small venue at the back of a pub in Cavan town. It has stone walls, with long trestle tables, and is lit by candles.

'This is lovely,' Geraldine comments. 'I never knew this place was here.'

Nicholas gets them both a pint of Guinness. He bumps into Simon at the bar.

'Sorry about Charlie,' Simon says. 'Is that the new woman in your life?' He indicates Geraldine.

'No way, she's just a friend.'

Nicholas notices Simon taking a good look at him and Geraldine before he goes on stage. He realizes guiltily that he wanted to bring Geraldine with him so that Simon would see him with another woman. Maybe word would even get back to Charlie. Geraldine is beaming. She is in blue tonight, and it suits her better than her usual choice of pink or white.

'You look nice,' he says.

'Thank you.' She wriggles in her seat. 'This is so great. I don't think I've been out to see music since . . . since before Grainne was born.'

'But that was over eight years ago! Surely not?'

'You have no idea how boring my life has become since I've been married.'

Nicholas stays sober. He is driving. Geraldine's cheeks get rosier and rosier, the more she drinks. She is fun to be with, witty and interested in what he has to say. They talk about music and his attempts at composition, her childhood dreams of performing as a pianist.

'It's never too late,' Nick says. 'You have come such a long way in such a short time. You definitely have a talent, Geraldine.'

'Really?' She puts her head on one side. 'You're not just saying that now, are you?'

'No, I mean it.'

'Shit!' Geraldine suddenly sits back against the wall and pulls her hair over her face. 'I don't bloody believe it.'

'What's wrong?'

'Only the biggest gossip in Cavan has come through the door. What the hell is she doing here?'

Nicholas looks at a tall blonde-haired woman who is making for the bar.

'Who is she?'

'Susan Smyth. She's Ray's first cousin. Christ! Has she seen us?'

'No, I don't think so. Did you not tell your husband you were going out to a gig with me tonight?'

Geraldine blushes. 'No . . .' she stutters. 'He can be a bit jealous. I thought it best not to.'

'Right.' Nicholas silently curses himself for being such an idiot. 'Maybe we should go.'

'Wait till she sits down, then we'll sneak through the crowd.'

Geraldine is giggling as they weave through the throng and out the back door. Nicholas tries to be discreet, but it is a small place. The chances are they will be seen. How stupid this is. What does he think he is doing, taking another man's wife out for the night?

'I better get you home,' he says, opening the car door.

Geraldine is standing in the car park, shivering, her bare arms covered in goosebumps. 'But it's still early,' she grumbles, 'let's go for another drink.'

'I think you've had enough.'

They get in the car and Nicholas turns on the ignition. Geraldine puts her hand on his arm. 'What's wrong, Nick?'

He shakes his head. 'I'm sorry, Geraldine. This is wrong. I shouldn't have taken you out. I shouldn't have kissed you. You're married . . . I'm still married . . .'

She leans over and kisses him on the lips. Then she pulls her head back and looks at him, her eyes black and glittering. Their breath steams up the windscreen, and he can feel desire filling his veins again.

'Kiss me. Please,' she whispers.

He tastes the beer on her breath, and feels her damp legs pushed against his in the front of the car.

He kisses her back, she holds onto his shoulders and he looks at her closed eyes, the make-up sparkling on her lids. He gently pushes her back into her seat.

'Geraldine,' he says, 'we can't do this.'

JUNE

The night is black here in Cavan, darker than anywhere I have been in England. The woods keep out any light that might stray from the village or the road. Sometimes I feel like the house is an island, and I am the only one left behind, not only by my husband, but by everyone. I think back to my bustling university days and I see a different me, a young woman with only her studies to think about. I could indulge myself, spend hours poring over books, making notes on Julia Caesar. Now, when I go to pick up where I left off, I feel faintly guilty. I am a wife, soon to become a mother — surely I should be doing something more suited to these roles? Here I am hidden away in Ireland, as if caught in an enchanted glade, and beyond my periphery the world is killing each other, my husband a part of it. Yet that is why I have to write my thesis. It is a means of survival if I can escape from our time into the past.

Sometimes I long to dream about Robert, see his face rise above me as I sleep, so that I can embrace him, imagine his touch once more, but he never comes . . . and then I fear the worst. Maybe at this moment, as I am tucked up safely in our bed, he is flying to his death. Is it possible our child will never know his father?

Instead of Robert, I dream about my sister Minerva. I see her the way she looked the day of Daddy's memorial Mass, pale and thin, married just over a year and yet looking ten years older. In my dream she appeals to me, but I have become Mother and, to my horror, I lean across the tea table and slap her face. I wake up shocked by what I have dreamed.

I sit up in bed and light a candle. I carry it to the window and look out into the dark night. I go back in time and I am looking out of another window, watching snow disintegrate into the angry sea. The sky is milky white, and the water looks dirty against it. Min and I are in the tea rooms in Brixham sitting by the fire. Soon we will have to go back outside and walk to the train station in thin coats. We are not prepared for the snow, yet the unwelcome bleakness of the weather conditions is entirely appropriate for the day's events. The sleety wind's icy bite against my flesh is a similar pain to the hurt that gnaws at my heart. How forlorn we look. Two abandoned, grieving daughters, sitting inside a scene from a picture. Everything is fuzzy around us – the kindly lady serving our tea, the gingham tablecloths and the floral teacups, plates and saucers, linen napkins and silver spoons – yet the sad story playing is our own, in sharp focus.

Min pours the tea. Her cheeks are flushed and the tip of her nose is red.

'Gosh, it was cold out there,' she gasps, putting her hands around her teacup and blowing on it.

The gold wedding band on her finger slides off and plops into her tea.

'Oh, hell,' she says and dips her finger in, fishing it out.

'You don't want to drink your tea now.'

'I'm so cold I couldn't give a damn.' Min sips her brew while she puts her ring in her coat pocket.

'Be careful – you don't want to lose it.'

'It's a wretched thing. It just won't stay on.'

'You ought to have got it fitted.'

'We did, but it seems I have lost a little weight since the summer.

I shall just have to order more cake, Juno, and fatten myself up again.'

Min smiles weakly and digs her fork into a large slice of coffee cake. Her hair, damp from the snow, sticks to her face in wet curls, her cheeks are shiny and flushed, and she looks far too young to be a married woman. She is a girl, yet her eyes are dull with dark circles under them, and it is true she has lost a lot of weight, for her cheekbones are more pronounced.

We are sitting beside the window, but the glass is steamed up and I can no longer see outside. I clear a small pane of glass with the tip of my finger and peer into the gathering dusk.

'It's still snowing. Perhaps we should take a taxi to the station.'

'Good idea. We can take more time over our tea.'

The fire crackles beside us. It is ghastly that the room is so bright and cheery, after the bleak gloom of our father's memorial Mass. The ceilings are low, with original beams, and the walls are covered with small prints of wild flowers and birds. We sit on spindly chairs, with red cushions, at a small wooden table in the window, and beside the fire. Over the fireplace hang small brass pots. They gleam warmly in the pale afternoon, and I can see our distended reflections in them.

This time two years ago we were in school together, and the thought is quite preposterous that our lives could have changed so much in just two years. We are schoolgirls no longer, nor have a home to speak of, for the house is sold, Father dead, Mother in Italy. I close my eyes for an instant, summoning memories of home in the summer. I can hear it. The dog barking, the bees buzzing around the foxgloves, clippers snipping as they trim the hedge, and the serene momentum of the hourly chime of the church bell. I can smell it. Honeysuckle, and roses, and the tang of the sea, constantly in the air, luring me and Min to play on its shore. All of this is gone, forever. I open my eyes wide and search the face of my sister. All our lives we have been like twins. One half of each other, but since Min has become a wife I cannot help but feel estranged, for I am no longer my sister's closest confidant.

'Why are you so thin?' I am suddenly disturbed by my sister's bony fingers as she spoons more sugar into her tea and stirs it.

'Oh,' Min sighs, looking at me for a moment as if she is thinking of what to say. She turns away to look out of the window. 'I have had a busy winter. Now that I am a housewife I seem to have less time to eat than when I was at school. Half the time all we thought about was food, and the other half we tried to eat as much as we could. Remember treacle-pudding nights?'

She smiles softly, and hums to herself for a moment.

'But now, with Charles's new business ventures, I have had a lot of entertaining to organize. We are making many new friends in London, Juno, and all of the socializing takes up a great deal of time. When I am so very busy, it affects my appetite.'

I study her for a moment. She is lying, but why? There seems to be an unspeakable barrier between us now, as if we both reached a crossroads at some point and walked away from each other in quite different directions. It is Min who did this first, when she got married.

'Sometimes I do envy your life, Juno,' Min says accusingly. 'All you have to worry about is yourself. You are so preoccupied with your studies that you haven't been to see me in months. I am only the other side of London.'

I look down at the tablecloth, and twist its lacy fringe between my fingers.

'And what about Father? You never came with me to visit him,' Min says harshly.

'I'm sorry, Minim.'

Min relents, leans over and squeezes my hand. 'It doesn't matter now, does it? And you shall come to see me more often, shan't you?'

I look up and seek out the old Min in her eyes. But my sister evades my gaze, leaning down, opening up her bag and taking out her cigarette case.

'Well,' she offers me a cigarette, 'I have news for you.'

I freeze, my arm outstretched to take the cigarette. For one moment I think Min is going to tell me she is pregnant.

'I am going to study painting, like I always dreamed of.'

'But what about Charles?'

'He approves,' she says gaily, lighting our cigarettes. 'He thinks I am too young to start a family yet.' Min leans forward, her cigarette in one hand, the smoke pluming behind her towards the door. 'Juno, I am going to the Slade!'

'That's wonderful! Oh, Min, you will be right next door to me. We can meet all the time! We can go to the pictures together.'

'Of course,' Min replies, her eyes shining. 'It is a shame you can't lodge with us, for then we could travel together on the Underground.'

When my place at University College had been confirmed, Father had asked Charles if I could live with him and Min so that they could keep an eye on me. His request had been turned down, much to my father's chagrin.

'Maybe I could,' I venture hesitantly.

Min stops and stares at me as if I am stupid. 'Oh no, Juno, you would not want to live with us. Oh gosh, no, Charles can be quite contrary – I wouldn't like you to.' She becomes flustered, and stubs the cigarette out, looking at her watch. 'We had better get a move on. I shall see if we can organize a taxi.'

She gets up from her seat and her coat falls open. She is wearing a black crêpe dress, which hangs off her hips.

I inhale sharply. My sister looks so frail I wonder if she is sick.

And why isn't Charles here, to be by her side at Father's memorial Mass?

Min walks over and talks to the lady behind the counter. I look under the table and Lionel, Father's dachshund, looks up at me sadly. I bend down and stroke the dog, and he licks my hand, grateful for the attention.

'Oh, Lionel,' I whisper, 'what shall we do with you?'

I want desperately to take him with me, yet I know my landlady would flatly refuse to have him in the house. I can't hide him, for he would probably bark all day while I am out. But I want Lionel so badly. He is Daddy's dog, and I want to take care of him. He could keep me company.

Min comes back over, buttoning up her coat and putting on her hat. 'She says we shan't find a taxi at this hour, but her husband will bring us to the station.' She bends down and unties Lionel's lead from the table leg. 'What do you think? Does he suit me? Do I look like a Hollywood starlet with my fancy pooch?'

She puts her head on one side and smiles seductively at me. Her lips are painted dark red, in a neat bow, and her skin looks even paler than usual in contrast. Her hat is pulled down low, so that it covers her forehead and frames her eyes. She has heavy eye make-up on, which make her eyes look even larger, framed by thick black lashes.

'Yes, you do, Minim. You look like a proper vamp.'

Min laughs and Lionel jumps up at her, barking. 'Sit, Lionel! Sit!' she commands, and the little dog goes back down on his haunches, panting, the tip of his pink tongue lolling out of his mouth. He is chestnut-brown and sleek, with shiny black eyes. His red lead hangs limply in Min's hand, and he looks up at her expectantly.

'Are you taking Lionel with you? What about Charles, will he allow you to keep him?' I ask, suddenly panicked that Lionel will be discarded by Min as well.

'Well, if I can't have a baby, he shall have to put up with Lionel,' Min says defiantly.

I laugh, but my sister looks quite serious as we walk towards the door. The little bell tinkles as we step outside into the cold. The snow is falling even heavier now, cascading out of the swirling sky and falling on our eyelashes and lips. Min turns to me, her dark coat covered in white spots, her face opalescent in the gleam of a snowy dusk.

'Everything bad happens at once, doesn't it, June?' She picks Lionel up.

'Why, what else has happened?'

Min pauses, but just as she is about to speak the car pulls up, beeping its horn, and we have to hurry so that we don't miss the train back to London.

We drive down the main street in silence. I peer out, looking at the shop fronts, forlorn and grey. The street is deserted, apart from a lone shopper running hastily in the snow, collar up, head down, so different from the cheerful summer facade I prefer to remember in the holidays, when there were so many people on the streets, gaily dressed for the sun. I wonder if I will ever return to Devon.

'Why do think Mother didn't come?' I ask my sister.

'I am glad she didn't.' Min pulls Lionel up to her chest, laying her cheek against his soft face. 'I never want to see her again.'

Min's words burn in my memory. What was she going to tell me that day? If only I could talk to her now. Her pale face disappears into the black Cavan night. I shiver, fearful I will never see my sister again. I get back into bed and blow out the candle, press my face into the pillow. I think about Lionel. The poor little dog must be terrified of the bombs. I cannot let myself think about my own sister's terror, trapped in the London Blitz. I imagine her brave and strong, helping others. And then I think about Mother.

NICHOLAS

Hopper is barking manically. *The trees*. Nicholas hears June Fanning whisper into his ear. *The trees*. He struggles out of his sleep and looks blearily around the room. What is that noise?

The windows are open, and moonlight floods into his bedroom. It is a full moon. Nicholas gets out of bed, pulls on a sweater and steps into the silvery light. He looks out the window, but the yard is deserted. Hopper is still barking. Nicholas whistles and the dog comes charging into the room. He pants, looking at his master expectantly. All is silent apart from one sound. Echoing across the empty fields and woods, harsh and violent, it is without a doubt a chainsaw.

Nicholas pulls on a pair of jeans and runs into the kitchen. He shoves his bare feet into his boots, and puts Hopper on the lead. The noise is so loud that the chainsaw user must be on his land. He opens the kitchen door and steps out into the yard. He shivers, although it is not so cold, but he feels a thread of fear down his spine. He walks forward cautiously, pulling Hopper back, wondering if he should have brought the dog.

The yard is still empty, but Nicholas can see movement in the orchard. He approaches the apple trees, slowly realizing with horror that some maniac is amongst them, chopping them down. He can see the metal blade of the chainsaw glinting in the dark, and hear the crash and thud as branches festooned with apples land on the ground.

'Hey! Hey!' Nicholas shouts, fury consuming him.

The vandal continues, oblivious to his presence. Nicholas runs back into the house, grabs a torch and a big stick, although it will hardly be much good against a mad chainsaw-wielder. He brings Hopper back out with him. The dog is far from ferocious, but it gives him confidence to have the back-up of his hound.

'You there!' Nicholas shouts, aware that he sounds very English. 'Hey, what do you think you're doing?'

He is at the gate to the orchard now, and he can see the destruction before him. All of the older trees have been battered and chopped to bits. He pushes through the gate.

'Stop, I tell you. Stop!'

The figure turns around, and now Nicholas can see who it is. Nicholas hesitates, then takes a step back, for coming towards him – chainsaw raised and still going – is Ray, Geraldine's husband. He has an insane grin on his face, and his eyes look murderous.

'I've called the Guards. Get off my property.'

But Ray can't hear him above the noise of the chainsaw. He walks towards Nicholas. Hopper senses his fear and starts barking again. Ray is only a few feet from him. He holds the chainsaw out in front of him between the two of them, and Nicholas thinks of Charlie – whether she will cry when he is found chopped to bits in a pool of blood in his destroyed orchard. Ray turns off the chainsaw and stares at Nicholas. He says nothing, just stares him down.

'What the fuck are you doing?' Nicholas blusters, relieved that the man is not completely psycho. 'I've called the Guards. You'd better not touch another thing.'

Ray laughs at him. 'Go ahead, call the Guards, or my mate Pete, because I know them. He's a great believer in family values, be very interested in the fact you've been sleeping with my wife!' Ray spits.

'No, no, you don't understand, we're just friends.'

Ray doesn't believe him for an instant. 'Oh, I have to make Nick some apple muffins today . . . Nick is a great teacher – I just love going over to his house . . .' He imitates Geraldine, mincing around the orchard swinging the chainsaw to and fro. 'Nick is such a great cook . . . I love eating his baked apples . . . and his apple crumble . . . and his cock!'

Ray's voice drops an octave and he eyeballs Nicholas menacingly.

'So you fuck up my marriage, and I'm going to fuck up something on you, even if it is a crappy old orchard. No more apples for you and my wife.'

Ray starts up the chainsaw again and glowers at Nicholas. He can't stop Ray, it's impossible. Nicholas begins to retreat and Ray laughs at him, splicing through the aged bark of his beautiful apple trees.

Nicholas runs back into the house, bolts the door and calls the Guards. He waits, sitting with his back to the kitchen door, the lights off and Hopper between his legs, both of them shaking with shock and fear as they listen to the chainsaw growling relentlessly through the night. By the time one lone Guard eventually arrives, the orchard is butchered and Ray has driven off into the rising sun.

'Do you want to press charges?'

The Guard, Ray's mate Pete, squints at him.

'Well . . .'

'I should warn you, in a small homeland like this, word spreads fast. Ray Mulraney's actions might be seen by some as the result of provocation. You could lose your piano pupils, Mr Healy.'

Nicholas looks at the Guard incredulously. He actually believes that Geraldine's crazy husband is justified in destroying those beautiful trees. What kind of place does he live in? Nicholas feels confused and exhausted.

'I don't know, I'll ring you tomorrow but you know he was very threatening.'

After the Guard is gone, Nicholas goes back out to the orchard. The sun is still rising, and there is a gentle mist lifting off the land, birds are waking. Nicholas looks at the massacred trees.

'Oh God!' He puts his head in his hands. He imagines he can hear the confusion of the birds. *Where are our trees? Where are our trees?* Nearly the whole orchard is destroyed, just a handful of trees remaining untouched, as if Ray Mulraney left them there to taunt him. The ground is littered with apples, not quite ripe, small little bullets of blood-red and bright green. Nicholas walks through his raped orchard picking up hacked branches, and touching trunks that have bark ripped from them. It feels like a battleground. He shakes his head. Is this his fault? Was Ray right to attack his property when Nicholas kissed his wife? His logical brain tells him that of course Ray is wrong, but then he thinks about Charlie and what he wanted to do to the man who slept with *his* wife. There was a moment when he wanted to kill him. At least Ray had kept to the trees.

Eat an apple.

June Fanning speaks to him. He leans down and picks up one of the abandoned apples. He takes a bite out of it. It is sharp, not ready for eating, but he continues to bite into it, and it makes him feel better.

Is it not natural to want to take a bite? The voice in his head says, and he can feel June Fanning's presence beside him, her sadness and her solace.

Nicholas falls on his knees. 'I can't take any more!' he says to the phantom in his orchard. He imagines June reaching out to him and taking his hand, pulling him up to his feet again. He imagines her words, although are they not in truth his own thoughts?

Nobody owns anyone or anything. You do not possess her, and she does not possess you. He doesn't possess her and she cannot possess him. Love is like the apple. It is sweet, yet bitter. It can be innocence and temptation. It belongs to nature, and nature we cannot control.

When Nicholas turns around to go back to the house, Geraldine is standing there. He doesn't know how long she has been in the orchard, or whether she saw June Fanning too, but he can see that she has been crying. Her hair is wild and flaming red in the light of the rising summer sun, and she wears a white nightdress over green wellies. She raises her hand to her mouth and points at the orchard in horror.

'Oh, Nick! Oh, I'm so sorry. I told him we didn't do anything.'

Nicholas walks towards her and takes her hands in his. 'Maybe we should?'

Geraldine looks back at him intently. Nicholas bends down and kisses Geraldine, and he can still taste the apple in his mouth. Then he leads her behind the five remaining trees, and beneath them they make love. Broken twigs from the trees dig into his back, and the ground is hard, damp with dawn dew. He is not comfortable, and yet these moments feel intensely pure. They are beyond all flesh, beyond all emotion, just the distilled essence of two lovers. When he comes he cries, and she holds his head in her hands and gently kisses his forehead. Despite the cold ground, the bumpy earth and splinters from the trees beneath their limbs, they lie in each other's arms beneath the last remaining apple trees until the sun is high in the sky and they are no longer in shade. Then they get up and begin to collect the apples. Geraldine is still in her white nightie and green wellies. It takes them all day and, when they have finished, every vessel in Nicholas's kitchen is filled with apples.

'What will I do with them all?' he asks Geraldine, as they stand side by side looking at the draining board overflowing with apples.

'We will think of something,' she says, and holds his hand.

JUNE

Every day I wake with the determination I shan't go to the Sheriden house. But as the morning progresses I find myself rushing through my chores, thoughts of my Roman Julia filling my head, and it is hard to concentrate on what I am doing. I make a dog's dinner of the churning, and drop eggs on my way into the house. I forget to feed the chickens, and leave the pigs' feed boiling away on the range, so at least twice I return to a stinking, blackened mess of burnt cabbage and potatoes. I try to blame my pregnancy for my scattiness, but I know it is something else. I am pulled towards my neighbours' house, and its sanctity affording me hours of study and peace. How I look forward to seeing Phelim Sheriden opening the door. He appears as a tall golden-haired gentleman, like one of my Roman gods. He is happy to spend time in my company, just talking, and sometimes he will sit with me in the library reading while I work, the two of us comfortable with each other as if we have always known one another. I cannot understand it: how I feel more at home with a man I have known a matter of weeks rather than with my own husband of five years.

I met Robert through my sister Min. She and Charles were having a dinner party. A few of Charles's work colleagues and wives were invited, and Robert was the only bachelor there. He was the first man I met who seemed more interested in me than in Min, for my sister's beauty always outshone mine.

It was December 1935. Just over a year since Father was buried and, out of loyalty to him, I decided not to spend Christmas with Mother. Min refused point-blank to talk to her. Mother had recently moved back to England with Giovanni to escape the Fascists and blackshirts of Milan. She appeared devoted to her artist, and did not complain at the drop in her standard of living or at the simplicity of their little terraced house in Maidenhead. She did everything she could to support his career as an artist, organizing small art exhibitions in London and inducing old friends to buy his pictures. Nonetheless her relationship was tarnished. We knew other women judged her. We were her daughters and even we judged her.

Mother had wanted me to spend Christmas Day with her and Giovanni. I couldn't bear the thought, so as a compromise I went to see her on Christmas Eve. I could not persuade my sister to come with me. I was still angry about Daddy, but Mother refused to mention him. It was as if he no longer existed for her. As always, she was dressed exquisitely, in what she described as an old dress picked up in Italy. The dress was the same colour as her eyes, and it was made of rayon, which Mother said looked like silk, but was a lot cheaper. She had a dark-blue sash tied around her waist, her sleeves billowed out from just above the elbow and the dress fell in wide folds from the waist, giving an impression of soft innocence. Ironically, her clothes were the colours of the Virgin Mary. We stood awkwardly in the hallway as she took my wet hat and coat and insisted on hanging them in front of the fire, so that they would be dry by the time I left. I asked her whether she had visited Father's grave yet, and she said no, she felt there was no need to now. It stunned me how brutally she spoke about Daddy's death. I nearly grabbed my coat off the chair and walked out right then, but something stopped me. I can't say what.

I was shocked at how small the house was, and how few belongings they seemed to have. However, the walls were covered in paintings – Giovanni's – and thus the overall ambience of her new house was bohemian. I realized, with a lump in my throat, that my mother looked more at home here than she had ever done in our grand old house in Devon.

We stood stiffly as Mother enquired after Min, without asking why she hadn't come. 'Is Captain Sanderson treating her well?' she asked.

And I said yes, told her how he had allowed Min to study art and how much she loved the Slade.

'That is good. I am glad both my daughters have found their callings.' She looked at me oddly, her blue eyes steady and unblinking. I could not reply, for I felt as if I were standing in front of a stranger. This was not my mother, surely. This softly spoken creature seemed to have no memory of her former self. The way she used to criticize us, and belittle us, and hit Min. Yet, for all her anger at that time, it was what tied us together, and now I felt an awesome distance between us. She must have felt this too, for there was an awkward silence – strange for a mother and daughter who had not seen each other in over two years.

'Sit down, June,' she said indicating a chair at the table, and I plonked myself down, my head hurting with confusion and desperate to leave, although I could not yet.

Mother spread before me a sumptuous tea, serving Italian pastries along with a home-made fruitcake. She made a pot of tea and called Giovanni in from his studio to join us. As soon as he came into the room she changed. Her body seemed to relax and she leaned back in her chair, the features of her face softening, the tone of her voice lighter, more girlish. They touched a lot. Her fingers tipped the back of his hand as he cut the cake, and he reached over and gently pushed her hair off her forehead. He was in good spirits and appeared delighted to see me, as if it was only the day before that he had drawn my picture in Milan. Gradually I began to feel invisible, for it did not matter who was in the room with Mother and Giovanni Calvesi. They could not contain their relationship, and it spilled over everything – the conversation and the food – making me feel as if I was drenched in our mother's love for another man. It made me feel sick.

I stayed for as short a time as possible, and by four-thirty it was already dark and I was getting up to leave.

'Do you have to go so soon?' Mother looked a little disappointed.

'Yes. Captain Sanderson is picking me up at Paddington.'

Mother and Giovanni exchanged glances.

'A happy Christmas to you, June,' he said, embracing me before I had a chance to step back. 'We will see you again, soon?'

I looked into his smoky brown eyes and could understand why Mother loved him. He was a man who was firmly rooted like a sturdy tree, sure of himself and his love for this woman, unaffected by society or what others thought. He had confidence in the map of his life. As far as he was concerned, my mother was his, and he hers, no matter if they were married to other people. He eschewed moral codes.

'Of course,' I replied lightly, turning away and hastily picking up my bag and gloves.

Giovanni left the room, and Mother rose from beside the fire. She was flushed from the warmth of the flames, and her eyes sparkled in the gathering dusk.

'Before you go, June,' she said, going over to the bureau and opening a drawer, 'I have something for you, and for Minerva. A little Christmas gift each.'

I coloured, for I had not expected a present from Mother, and I myself had arrived empty-handed. Mother handed me two small packages, wrapped in brown paper and tied with string. She had wrapped a silver ribbon about each one and tied a bow.

'Thank you.' I slipped the packages into my bag.

'I hope it will make you smile,' Mother said, turning her back to me and looking into the fire. 'I chose the colours especially to suit each one of you.'

She sighed, and bent down to poke the fire. I looked at the back of her head, and wondered why it was that Mother could show so much tender affection to her lover and yet not to me.

'Goodbye, June,' she said, 'Merry Christmas.'

And that was how I left her, staring into the embers, her back still to me, as I opened the door and stepped out into the dark afternoon.

On the train back up to London I opened my package, not wanting to wait until Christmas Day. And I did smile when I saw what she had given me – a beautiful pair of evening gloves. They were made of the softest silk, and were silvery grey in colour. I put them on my hands and, pulling back my sleeves, drew them up my arms to the elbows. They were the height of elegance. If only I had occasion to wear them. Often over the next few weeks I would take those gloves out when I was on my own in my lodgings, and parade up and down my bedroom in my nightdress with just the gloves on, pretending I was a beautiful, glamorous and desired young lady.

Mother gave Min gloves as well, but they were completely different from mine and more suited for day-wear. They were wine-red, and made of kid. She remembered how red was my sister's colour. There was a hat Min used to wear with them. It was a red Tyrolean-style hat with a feather, the brim of which swept over the left side of her face, hiding her left eye. It pleased me to see my sister wearing the gloves Mother had given her. At least she did not throw them away.

I fingered my silk gloves all the way back to London, as the train sped through the darkness. Charles, Min's Prince Charming, met me at the station. He talked non-stop about how successful his importation business was, and how he believed that soon English people would catch on to eating spaghetti, and Italian pasta and other foods. Then he would be very wealthy. I believe he was showing off to me, as if he wanted to prove something. Quite odd, since he had never before been too interested in my opinion. He didn't ask me about Mother, although he knew that I had just been to see her.

It was a damp drizzly evening, mild for December, and as we pulled up at my sister's house in Highgate, all the lights were on inside. On the doorstep I stood still for a moment, for I could hear Min's sparkling voice singing. Strauss. Charles opened the door and we were greeted by Lionel as he raced towards me across the hall, jumping up with excitement. I bent down and rubbed his ears, kissing the tip of his nose as Charles took my coat and hat in the doorway. He took forever to hang them up. He is such a careful man, so neat and punctilious. How funny to think my sister married someone like him, when she is unable even to keep her own hair tied up for more than an hour. Opposites do attract.

I almost skipped for joy up the stairs. Three hours with Mummy and Giovanni Calvesi had felt such a long time. When Min saw me she stopped singing in mid-flight, let out one loud peal and ran across the room to hug me. Her audience was one lone man sitting on the sofa, and he started in surprise at her outburst. Min squeezed me so tight I could hardly breathe. I could feel her ribs and was shocked at how thin she still was. Over her shoulder I could see her guest, woken out of his musical reverie, standing up and looking curiously at me, his hazel eyes reminding me of a deer, wary and used to solitude. But something about me held his attention, for instead of looking back at Min when she began to speak, as all the other men did, his gaze did not falter.

My husband's eyes are able to do all sorts of things to me. They can fill my belly with warmth, and let me know how he wants to be alone with me. They can criticize me silently, reminding me to be modest. They can cut me down, making me feel ashamed. I suppose Robert is a little old-school, like his chum Charles. How strange that those two old-fashioned men should end up marrying modern girls like Min and I.

Min was so excited to see me that Charles had to tell her to calm down, or else she might have another fainting attack.

'Are you not well, Min?' I asked.

'Oh, I am fine, darling. Just sometimes I get a little tired, dizzy. It is the lot of the hard-working artist, so caught up in their creativity they forget to eat!'

Charles raised his eyes to the ceiling. 'Robert, let me introduce you to my sister-in-law, June Sinclair. June, this is an old colleague of mine, Robert Fanning.'

Robert stepped forward, and we shook hands. His touch was warm, and his hands large, so that mine felt like a small child's. He looked about the same age as Charles, but his expression was less stern, his smile broad and youthful.

'A pleasure,' he said, a small blush spreading across his cheeks, and I could feel myself colouring too.

'Come on, Robert; let's leave the girls to their chat. I have a fine malt whiskey in my study.'

Alone at last, Min and I sat down on the sofa to talk, but my heart was still thumping after touching Robert's hand. Min noticed immediately, of course.

'Oh, he is lovely, isn't he, Juno? And a bachelor too, with a very good job, quite a match.'

'He is a little old, though,' I said cautiously.

'Don't be ridiculous!' Min squealed, 'He is the same age as Charles, or thereabouts. No, he is just right for you. Young men can be so possessive, and impetuous. Older men give one a little more freedom, I think. Besides, they have more money.'

'Min!' I exclaimed with false shock.

'Charles used to work with Robert, and he thinks Robert is an excellent fellow. We shall have to fix you up. I do believe you need a little romance in your life.' Min flicked the hair out of my eyes. 'Too much study makes Juno a dull girl.'

I suddenly felt self-conscious, and a little worried. How could I possibly think this man would be interested in someone like me? 'Where are the other guests?' I asked nervously.

'Oh, they are coming, soon.' Min glanced at her watch. 'Poor dears, Charles wants us to try out some new Italian pasta. He calls it *farfalle*, and it is quite beautiful, like bows or butterflies. But I don't think it will be what our guests are expecting on Christmas Eve!'

We looked at each other. Min leant forward, took my hands in hers and squeezed them. Not for the first time, her lovely face took me aback. Even I, her sister, was sometimes swept away by Min's effervescence. Her beauty was such that, though manifested on the surface, it came from within as well and made her the centre of attention everywhere she went. Yet it was the kind of beauty that made her lonely, for no girl had ever wanted to be Min's friend, and every man wanted to make love to her. It was why she was married before she was out of school, and I believe it trapped Min. I never envied my sister.

'We should see each other more.'

Min pursed her rosebud lips in mock admonishment. 'We live in the same city, for heaven's sake!'

'I know, I'm sorry. How's the Slade?'

'Oh, the Slade is splendid!' Min looked out of the window suddenly, so that her thick, inky hair tumbled out of its loose bun. 'I meet so many talented artists, people from all over the world: Frenchmen, Polish, German. You know, they are saying the Fascists are planning to take over Europe. I have a German friend and he decided to leave Germany because he is a Jew. He told me Hitler and the Nazis plan to force all the Jewish people to leave Germany. He says he thinks he will try to take over the whole world. Can you believe such a thing might be, Juno?'

'I don't think that could ever happen,' I said.

'But look at the British Empire – we did it.'

I had not thought of it like that before. I suppose because I am English and one always thinks the side one is on is right.

'You know Robert is Irish?' Min smiled slyly at me. 'So it is just as well we were reared good Catholic girls!'

'Min, stop teasing me.'

But my sister was right. She could see it more clearly than I. How Robert and I were destined to be together. I believe I fell in love with Robert that very night. He sat next to me at the dinner table and gave me so much attention that my head was in a spin by the end of the meal. In the New Year he called to my lodgings constantly, taking me to the pictures, out to dances, whatever I wanted. Then, on Valentine's Day, we went walking in Hyde Park, and he got down on one knee. Producing an engagement ring from his pocket, and stuttering the words like a teenage boy, this mature man, nearly twenty years my senior, asked me to be his wife. I think it was in that moment that I loved Robert so completely. I could sense the utter humility in his actions, and it overwhelmed me with a compassion I had never encountered in my whole life.

We were married two months later. It was a simple ceremony in London. His father couldn't come because he was busy on the family farm back in Ireland, and Robert's mother was dead. Of course my father was dead too, and I didn't want to invite Mummy and Giovanni. I could not bear to compare Robert and myself to her and her lover.

But she found out anyway and acted as if she cared, demanding to know what Robert's background was. I saw a flash of her old superior self, for she could not help but let it surface. When she discovered he was Irish she was even more patronizing.

'For goodness' sake, June. What are you doing, marrying some bog man from the back of beyond? You have no idea of his breeding.'

I wanted to shout back at her: And what of your Italian artist? What is so special about his pedigree?

'I believe Robert's family is very respectable,' I replied. 'Devout Catholics.'

'But what about your degree, June. What would your father say?'

'I don't think it appropriate for *you* to tell *me* what you think Father would say, when it is evident that you did not consider his feelings for a long time.'

That silenced her.

But it did not matter what Mummy thought, not one whit. Min and Charles were our witnesses, and what with friends from Robert's work and a few of Min's acquaintances, we had a grand day.

We spent our honeymoon in a hotel in Babbacombe, and I had planned to show Robert Torquay, and walk with him by the sea. But it rained the whole weekend. What did we care? We had been waiting three months to consummate our love. It had felt so long, although everyone called it a whirlwind engagement.

What did I feel when Robert first made love to me? I am trying to remember.

Very happy, that was the first sensation, and a little nervous too. I never knew whether he was a virgin as well, but I doubted it because he was so much older than me. I remember nearly laughing in the middle of it, because I suddenly had a picture in my head of Lionel, the dachshund, having sex with Delia, the black Lab that belonged to the Judges. It had looked so ridiculous. I couldn't quite believe humans did this too, and then called it love.

And how did I feel when it was finished? Unfinished, I suppose.

I bloomed with pride though, because now I was a married woman and I was happy to walk away from university, and ancient Rome. I had my own story now and I didn't miss history. I was so delighted to live in another kind of world. London was new to me all over again. We rented a small flat in Hampstead. I spent each day cleaning it until it shimmered, pressing and starching Robert's work shirts and reading *Modern Woman* for more tips on housekeeping and new recipes. My college books were packed away, and I filled my mind with fashion and film stars. Sometimes I would walk down to the Finchley Road, hop on a bus into Oxford Street and then get on another bus back up again. I don't know why I did that. I didn't want to go shopping or see anything in particular. I just loved sitting on the bus as it trundled down the road, watching everyone living their lives, listening to the humdrum sounds of this great city. It made me feel a part of something.

London. Just a few years ago, but everything was different. Robert was happy for it to be just the two of us. He liked London as much as me. Three years flew by in a whirl. After I was married I saw my sister more often, and even though we never regained the symbiosis we had as children, we spent lots of time together. Min took me to art exhibitions and concerts, and I took her to the cinema. We fell in love with Clark Cable together. Min fancied herself Vivien Leigh, and I was Carole Lombard. We discussed fashion, and new dishes to cook for our husbands, and in between it all Min managed to paint. She never stopped painting. Sometimes she asked me about my classical studies and Julia. I would shrug my shoulders and tell her I had lost interest in my Roman princess. Min would cock her head and tell me off.

'No, Juno, you are just taking a break from your studies. You will return to them one day.'

She seemed so certain that I would.

It was strange that each time we met neither of us discussed Mother. Since I had married I did not want to visit her, because I was afraid of what she might think of Robert. Or did I think he would fall for her, too?

We lived each day one at a time, carefree and gay, loving our new husbands, and pushing the idea of children to the back of our minds. We had plenty of time, or so we thought.

Then war broke out, and everything changed. Robert was offered a job in Dublin, and he took it. He said he wanted us to be somewhere safer, somewhere we could think about starting a family. It was the first time he had mentioned children, and it broke my little bubble of contentment. He said we would try Ireland for a while, and return to England once things were back to normal.

Who would have thought the war would still be going on now?

I remember we took the ferry to Dublin. It was packed with people, and none of us on the boat could look each other in the eye because we felt as if we were all running away. There was no laughter, or singing, just the depressing cloud of guilt suspended above us all.

If we had not returned to Ireland, I would have been in London with Min when the bombing started, and things would have turned out differently in the end.

Now it is worse than ever, because Robert is fighting and, instead of being closer to him when he is on leave, I am stuck here in the back of beyond. The Blitz doesn't frighten me. I would rather be in it, living on the edge, right up on the precipice of life. Min once wrote me that when death is such a hair's breadth away she feels so alive. Everything looks like a painting by William Blake, like a startling vision from God. She wrote that danger brings you closer to the divine.

THE ADULTERESS V

Does sex reach a plateau impossible to maintain? If they were not committing adultery, would it fade faster? If they were married to each other, would they have even taken themselves to such heights of passion?

She never experiences such lovemaking with her husband. She never craves him as much as she craves this man, so that she might be about her daily business and the sudden thought of him makes her damp, agitated, counting the hours to their next rendezvous.

Is their love art? Is it something exquisite, which they have created, but which is an illusion of what is real? If only she could hang their feelings up on the wall of her house, they would remind her that it is possible to let a kindred spirit into her heart, even temporarily.

JUNE

I tread a pathway through the orchard and head into the woods. Things do not seem so bleak, because I can spend the afternoon in Phelim's company and forget my husband is in England, flying planes, risking his life every night while Phelim and I laugh and chat and sometimes he plays me the piano. The way through the woods feels like a well-worn path, as if others have taken this trail before me and will do so in many years to come. There is a sense of not being alone, and again I think of Robert's parents and of James D. Are their disapproving spirits silently censoring me?

The time of year assists my daily desertions from our farm. It is mid-winter, and I am told there isn't much to do until February when they start to plough. Besides, the Tobins have been looking after me well, for they view Robert as one of their own.

Oonagh comes as regular as clockwork, three mornings a week. Slowly we are becoming more comfortable together, although we are from such very different worlds. I find her a strange mixture. Some days she will chat about the fairies as if they are real, talking of the banshee, and the pooka – the shape-shifter, she calls it sometimes – and how they can creep up on you if you're not careful. In the next breath she will talk about 'Our Lady', and finger the medallion that she wears around her neck.

The best night is Sunday in the Tobins' house, when all the Mass-going is over for the week. Everyone appears lightened of their sins and determined to let their hair down. Oonagh and her two sisters sing, her father plays the fiddle and her brother the tin whistle. Everyone else dances. It is not the kind of dancing I am used to. They do it in their shoes, stamping their feet up and down on the flagstone floor, like a form of tap dancing. All the dancers – men and women – stand as rigid as poles, their arms clamped to their sides and their faces completely expressionless. It is the legs that say everything, leaping, and stamping and twisting in the air. Then they twirl each other round and round, and it makes me dizzy even to watch, for I could not try to do this type of dancing. Oonagh's mother stands by the stove, laughing stoutly and declaring that the dancing is grand for cleaning the stone floor. It is a kind of folk dancing. When I watch Oonagh and her sisters dance, I wish I could join in. I wish Phelim were here with me to show me how to do it, for I could not imagine my husband jumping up and down on his toes and twirling me around. But Phelim Sheriden is never invited to the Tobins'.

Last Sunday they had a visitor from the north of the county. I believe he was an uncle of Oonagh's, and this man performed lilting. It is quite an incredible thing, for Oonagh told me there was a time when people were so poor here they couldn't even afford musical instruments, and so they made up all of the sounds themselves. We rode the waves of this man's effortless lilting, and I believe my sister Min would have adored it as much as her beloved Strauss. For me, it was the essence of what I have come to be fond of in Cavan. A pure simplicity in what you hear, see and feel, which can be transcendent. It binds me to the land, where my emotions unravel. It is easy to keep them fettered when you live an urban life; not so out in the countryside, where all of nature is a metaphor.

After the song everyone was quiet for a while, and Oonagh's

mother got up slowly and began to make the tea. Oonagh signalled for me to go outside with her, and we stepped out into their yard under a full moon. I could hear their cows restless in the byre, but all the other animals were quiet.

'I saved this,' she said to me, producing a red apple from her pocket. We had spent the day before collecting the last apples, and storing them in pits with sand so that they might last the winter. Oonagh smiled at me conspiratorially. 'Let's do an apple spell.'

'What's an apple spell?'

She looked mildly surprised, but her dark eyes glittered mischievously. 'Myself and Teresa do it every year, but now she is going to marry Brendan. She doesn't want to do it in case . . .'

I raised my eyebrows. 'In case what?'

'It's mad to think you've never done an apple spell,' she said, taking a small knife out of her pocket, 'and you with a sister and all. I can't believe the two of ye never did this.' She began to peel the apple, speaking all the time. 'What you do is, under a full moon,' she raised the knife up to the sky so that it glinted silver in the dark, 'you peel an apple all in one go. You don't break the apple-skin peel. You throw it over your shoulder, and then you see which way the peel falls, and it should spell the initial of your true love!'

'Oh, I see.' I tried to sound interested. It seemed quite silly to me, but I was touched that Oonagh thought I might like to play this little game with her.

'And you say this as you're doing it.'

She paused, lifting her face up to the moonlight, and I was struck by how pretty she actually was. When I saw her every day, with her hair scraped back, bending over the stove, doing something rather gory such as skinning a rabbit, she looked quite ordinary, but now her natural features appeared much softer than in daylight, and her thick hair fell in glossy waves down her shoulders.

'Food of the fairies, guardian of love, sweet apple, most sacred fruit, barer of the silver bough, and spinner of the music that lulls, under the full moon's gaze and her maternal care, show to me my true heart's companion.' She threw the peel over her shoulder briskly. We turned quickly and bent down, peering at the ground in the dark.

'I can't really see it, Oonagh.'

'Oh, can you not? Look.' She pointed at it with her finger. 'Don't you think that is a P?'

I stared for a while. As my eyes grew accustomed to the shadows, I could see the peel lying in a straight line, with the top curled over to meet itself in the middle. 'I suppose it could be,' I said uncertainly.

Oonagh seemed thrilled. 'Sure it is, as sure as the baby Jesus himself. It's a P.'

I smiled to myself, thinking of the boy called Patrick of whom she speaks all the time.

Then she turned to me and, fishing into her pocket, pulled out another apple. 'Will you not try it?' She smiled sweetly as she crunched into her peeled apple.

I stood up, shaking my head. 'Why would I want to do the apple spell, Oonagh? I already have a husband.'

'Please . . . I'll know then if it works, if you get an R.'

'I can't imagine how an apple peel can fall in the shape of an R, Oonagh.' I drew my shawl up about my shoulders. 'Come on, let's go back in and have a cup of tea.'

'It will only take a moment,' she begged, pushing the apple into my hand and passing the knife over.

I sighed. 'Oh, all right, but I think this is just a load of old rubbish.'

She nodded, her eyes gleaming excitedly as she watched me peel the apple. I was surprised by her enthusiasm for this sort of thing.

She was no longer the sensible, practical Oonagh of my daylight hours.

'Don't forget the spell,' she encouraged.

'You'll have to say it with me, I can't remember it.'

However, when I started speaking, the words flowed instinctively off my tongue as if I had always known them.

'Food of the fairies, guardian of love, sweet apple, most sacred fruit, barer of the silver bough, and spinner of the music that lulls, under the full moon's gaze and her maternal care, show to me my true heart's companion. There,' I said as the peel fell to the ground and we both crouched down.

'Where is it?' Oonagh searched the cracked mud with her fingertips.

'I don't know.' I peered down at the dirty yard and fingered the ground. 'Oh, here it is . . . it's a—' I suddenly felt a wave of dread, for how could I have been so stupid as to let myself play this game.

Oonagh finished my sentence. 'P,' she said quietly.

'No, that's yours. That was your peel from before.'

Oonagh wobbled on her haunches, stared down at the ground and shook her head. 'How strange,' she said thoughtfully.

'Yes, I don't know where mine fell. It's just gone.'

I clicked my fingers and stood up. 'Come on, at least we found out what you wanted to know.'

I leaned over and squeezed her hand and she looked at me with wide eyes, as if surprised I would touch her.

'Let's go in, Oonagh. It's cold.'

She got up as well, picking up the P apple peel and scanning the yard once more.

I went towards the door. I could hear more music, and I was longing for a hot brew, but Oonagh hung back. I paused on the threshold and felt her hand touch the back of my shoulder. I turned around. 'What is it?'

She held her peel like a tiny adder in her fingers, and looked at me curiously. 'Have you met Claudette Sheriden yet?'

'No, she is too sick to see me.'

She nodded solemnly. 'I heard she was sick with the cancer. Mammy told me she was once very beautiful, like Claudette Colbert, you know, like in *It Happened One Night*. She had a very modern look, and she used to frighten Father O'Regan with it.'

I didn't know what to say back, so I said nothing, and we stood in an unusually awkward silence. I sensed Oonagh wanted to tell me something and I felt irritated as if she, and all her family, knew something I didn't know.

'What is it, Oonagh?' I asked impatiently.

She looked away from me, fingering her apple peel and then lifting it to her nose and smelling it. 'Father O'Regan says she is the biggest sinner in the whole parish.'

She looked back at me, and her eyes locked on mine, and I could see she knew more, but all of a sudden I was afraid, and whatever she was going to tell me I didn't want to know. I turned around and lifted up the latch, hastily going into the room where the light was, and there was so much noise that she could no longer speak to me.

This chilly afternoon I scurry to the Sheriden house to read classical literature. I run through the orchard. There are no more apples. I have scouted the ground, but all the late windfalls are gone. The orchard looks bare, and bereaved. I wonder should I tidy it a little, cut back some of the brambles, so that the trees can be admired in the spring. But I feel no enthusiasm to do this. The place is forlorn. This is how it needs to be. Besides, I am in a hurry. I run through the woods. I have long since abandoned skirts and stockings, and arrive breathless on Phelim Sheriden's doorstep wearing a pair of slacks. He opens the door and we say nothing to each other. He takes my hand and brings me into the study. We look at each other and we smile. I am a child in a sweet shop. He knows this and understands my desire for learning more than Robert ever did.

I leaf through Virgil and Horace, pick out pieces of Tacitus and Seneca, and devour Ovid's *Art of Love*. I prefer this world of the classical pagans to Oonagh's sprites and spells, and her mystic brand of Catholicism. I crave logic, not superstition, and Ovid's reasoning intrigues me. This poet believed love was not something that just happened to two people. There was nothing predestined to it. Love is a craft, which had to be learned, and mastered. It is an art, like any other, like music, dance and painting.

My desire for the past overwhelms my fear of encountering Claudette. I no longer want to meet her. Each day Phelim greets me, I pray he will say what he has said the day before, that she is too unwell to see me and sends her apologies. He leaves me to my work, while he goes upstairs to paint. But I like to imagine the thread of creativity that links us, running from the study out into the draughty hall, up the empty staircase and down the echoing landing, up again, and up once more, to the tiny garret attic, where he listens to music and paints. We always meet for luncheon, and although the food is often far from splendid (one day we dined on boiled potatoes and lumps of cheese, much to Phelim's embarrassment), I do not care what we eat for it is the conversation that fills me. Sometimes I even forget there is another person living in the house. Last week I nearly jumped out of my skin when I collided with Father O'Regan on the staircase. He looked as shocked as I, finding me in the Sheriden house.

'Mrs Fanning,' he said, nodding coldly, and staring at me with his glassy grey eyes like a seagull's.

'Good afternoon, Father.'

'I did not know you were a friend of Mrs Sheriden – so kind to call on her when she is this weak.'

I nodded, wondering what the priest was doing in the house of the 'biggest sinner' in the parish.

He coughed, and picked up his skirts. 'Well, I must be on my way, there is another needy member of the flock I must administer to.'

I mentioned meeting Father O'Regan to Phelim later on, when we were having tea, and he roared with laughter.

'I'd say you gave old Reggie a fright. He must have been wondering what on earth you were doing creeping around the house.'

'But you don't go to Mass, do you?'

'No, well, I don't. But Claudette did. She is too sick to go now, so Reggie comes here to give her the sacrament. I think, at this stage, her faith gives her something to focus on, rather than worrying.' He sighed, looking suddenly sad.

'Any word on Danielle?'

He shook his head, and bowed down over his plate, saying nothing.

'I am sure you will hear something soon, I am sure it will be all right,' I said as optimistically as I could.

'And you?' He looked up. 'Have you heard from Robert?'

'No,' I tried to sound chirpy, adding, 'I am due a letter from him soon.'

We carry on like this, keeping each other company. For that is all we are doing. There is no harm in kindness, is there not? He is a lonely husband, whose wife is slowly dying in front of him, and I am a lonely wife, whose husband is away at war. We are each other's solace.

And then one day everything changes. I am in the dark woods on my way to the Sheriden house and daydreaming about ancient Rome, and the island of Ponza. I imagine the crashing Mediterranean ocean, the sparkling light and the black rocks. I can see the cliffs of the island like scoops of white clay, everything exposed and brutal, unlike the safe hollow of my Cavan trees. I am lost in my reverie, but as I pick my way across the marshy ground I begin to hear an unfamiliar noise. I stop, on the rim of a tiny bog, and I can hear it distinctly, a sweet singing. Immediately I remember Oonagh's warnings about the Watershree, one of the most deceiving fairies, who with her innocent songs lures unsuspecting travellers into bogs, only to drown them and devour their souls.

I stamp my feet, and speak to myself. 'Don't be so completely ridiculous, June Fanning.'

But I have never met anyone else in these woods, apart from the time I saw Claudette Sheriden, and now she is bedridden. I wonder idly why Phelim never comes here.

I start to walk again. This time more quickly, and yet as carefully as I can over the soggy ground, scanning it for particularly boggy parts. It is not my imagination. I can hear the voice, quite distinctly, and it is getting louder.

I whisper a little prayer for protection and hold onto Robert's locket as if it is a holy amulet. The weak winter sun breaks through the branches. Up ahead I can see a figure, walking towards me.

'Be careful,' Oonagh had warned me. 'The Watershree can appear as a very beautiful woman, or how you would imagine a fairy to look: small, delicate, with gossamer wings.'

The woman who approaches me certainly has the quality of a fairy about her. She is tiny, with the frame of young girl, so that I am not sure of her age until she comes closer and I can see her face. It is Claudette Sheriden.

I am shocked to see her in plain daylight. She has become a fictional person over the past few weeks, never well enough to see me, always in her bed. How is it that she is here, walking towards me, in the woods between our homes?

She moves very slowly and is wrapped up in a long black cape.

Her face is oval, pale and pointed. She looks incredibly sick. Her cheekbones are pronounced, and there is so little flesh to her cheeks that her eyes and mouth look large in her face. It is her eyes that transfix me. They are immense, like the painted eyes on the wings of butterflies. Despite her obvious frailty, there is an intensity to her gaze and I recognize in her expression the look of someone who is not too far from death. The overall effect is one of astonishing beauty.

She reaches me and holds out her hand. It is tiny, and white, the veins raised, the skin slightly yellow. 'You must be June,' she says slowly, taking a breath between each word.

'Yes.' I shake her hand. I am unable to think of anything else to say.

'Phelim has told me much about you.'

I nod, wondering in what way he has explained my visits.

She takes a breath. 'I wonder whether you would be so kind as to help me?'

'Of course.'

'It is my husband, he is so very protective, and he wants me to stay indoors. But . . .' She pauses, and coughs, taking a handkerchief out of her pocket and bringing it up to her mouth. '*Mais les arbres . . .*' she whispers.

'Pardon.' I lean forward, and she catches my arm and loops hers in mine.

'Would you mind if we went back this way a little? I need to see the sky, and the trees.' She sighs. 'I need to hear the birds outside once in a while.'

'Of course,' I reply politely, confused by the Frenchwoman's request. It is obvious Phelim does not know his sick wife is wandering about in the woods. Should I try to persuade her to go home? But I sense this woman is on a mission. She is pitifully thin, but that does not stop her determined step back through the woods towards my house.

'Will you, *ma chérie*, take me to the Fannings' lovely orchard?' Her heavily lidded eyes plead with me.

'It's not quite so lovely now,' I say, but I know in my heart that Claudette doesn't mind how the apple trees look. Now I understand that she wishes to visit James D., and why it is she can't be with Phelim.

We walk in silence, but just as we reach the gate to the orchard, she turns to me and grips my gloved hands. 'You are the same age as my daughter Danielle,' she says softly. 'I am so very happy for Robert. He has found you, at last.'

We pass through the gate, and I try to steer her through the undergrowth without tripping on tangled roots and briars. We circle the orchard, but just by the plum trees Claudette lets go of my hand and begins to walk around them.

'These were James D.'s trees,' she says, touching them gently as if they were the man himself. She turns to me, her thin face one of pain, haunting and ethereal. 'And the apple trees, some of them were Robert's father's, and some were Robert's, of course.'

I feel as if a very cold hand has suddenly been placed over my heart.

'I believe *all* of the orchard was a gift from Robert's father to his mother?'

Claudette sweeps her hands over to the other side of the orchard. 'Yes, of course, that side of the orchard, but can you not see that these trees are younger?'

I look about me. I had noticed that the trees here were a different type of apple when I picked them, but it is not until now that I can see they are not quite as wizened as the other trees, their bark is smoother, their posture more erect.

'I lived here for a year,' Claudette says, her eyes misty with tears.

'James D. planted me plums. He proposed to me under this very tree.' She sighs. 'But then he had to go back to war, and I was left here all on my own.'

She begins to cough again and, taking out her handkerchief, she sits down suddenly under the plum tree. I cannot imagine how I could have heard her singing in the woods, just a short time ago, for now she can hardly speak.

'I think it might be damp . . .' I begin to say, coming towards her, but she shoos me away.

'I think I am a little past caring if I catch a cold.'

She laughs suddenly, and her face is illuminated, and I can see that she once had filmstar looks, big dreamy eyes and creamy white skin, just like Claudette Colbert, as Oonagh described.

'The Fannings looked after me. Robert is a good man.'

'Yes, I know.' I am annoyed that she should feel she has to tell me this.

Claudette sweeps her hand in front of her, as if she is introducing the orchard to me. 'All of these sweet little pippins were planted for me. This orchard is mine.'

And when she says these words I feel as if she has stabbed me. Her words wound me deep down in my soul.

Claudette bends over, coughing, and this time it is as if she cannot stop.

'Are you all right?' I ask, walking towards her, although all I really want to do is run away.

She looks up at me, and bright red blood gushes out of her nostrils. Her expression is one of a small child the first time it has a nosebleed, terrified and helpless. Despite everything, I go over to her and, pulling out the end of my blouse, I rip it off and staunch the flow.

We sit under James D.'s plum trees, and I wonder: does the love of this man still exist here, planted firmly like roots in the earth?

Will he come to meet Claudette, this woman who is so plainly dying minute by minute, and bring her with him? I have never even seen a picture of James D. and yet I can feel him around me. It is a change in the air. It is a sensation hard to describe. We sit quite still and when I hear the sweet singing once again I recognize the voice immediately. Of course it is not Claudette, for it was my sister all along. Claudette and I are sitting in the ether, which floats between this world and the next, and what I long for most is my sister's voice, and this is what it brings me. I pray it is not Min's swansong.

I put my arms around Claudette, the wife of the man whom I desire, and wonder whether my husband still loves her. To plant a whole orchard of apple trees tells me that once he most surely did.

NICHOLAS

The summer is nearly over. Nicholas sits on the doorstep of his house and looks at the destroyed orchard. Now that he has cleared up the broken branches and the fallen apples, the place looks bereft, a few skeleton trees left standing, all the leaves on the ground before they are due to fall, as if they have been dropped by the shock of their bearers' desecration. Some of the trees were so old it breaks his heart to see the massacre. Even if he were to begin replanting today, it would take generations to recreate the orchard. And then there is the chaos of the house behind him. He has made a mess of the roof and, when it rains, water comes into the attic in three places. He needs professional help, but he can't afford it. He knows he should get down to work. There is so much to do – tiling, dry-lining, decorating – but he feels completely overwhelmed. Fixing up a house is something most men are well capable of, but all Nicholas wants to do is play the piano. The past week his head has been invaded by music. When he comes to play the piano, his notes find their own way out, and for the first time in his life he is composing music. He even digs out his guitar and tries adding lyrics to the melody. It is slow work, but it makes him happy, and he hasn't been happy in such a long time.

Nicholas gets up, flings his cold dregs of coffee into the bushes and goes back into the kitchen. A bee struggles to get out of the window, and Nicholas opens it for him. It is a warm day, the sun coming out from behind the clouds, so he leaves the window ajar while he packs the last few bottles of home-made cider into the box. He is proud of his produce. He wouldn't have been able to do it without Geraldine's help. She had actually found out how to make cider and had gone up to Dublin and bought the equipment. It had been a joint venture. They called the cider 'Fanning Orchard Home-Made Cider' in honour of the Fanning orchard. Nicholas has been selling it at local farmers' markets. He probably needs a licence, but it is only a short-term thing. They have nearly run out of apples now. And he isn't sure if the orchard will ever recover, or even if he will be here next year, although he has never said that to Geraldine.

Nicholas glances at the clock. It is still early and he doesn't need to leave quite yet. He goes into the back room and opens the curtains. Sunlight enters this room in the evening, so the light is still dusky in here. He sits at the piano and flicks on the lamp. He strokes its glossy lid, looks at the reflection of the lamp on the wood and opens it. He touches the keys. He has always had a piano to play ever since he can remember. The first couple of years in Dublin they had been too poor to afford one in their flat and it had nearly killed Nicholas. He used to go to a friend's parents' house twice, sometimes three times a week so that he could play, much to the amusement of the couple, who saw Nicholas more than their own son. When Charlie had got her first big grant, she had bought him a piano as a surprise. It took up the whole of their tiny flat and left her hardly any room in which to paint. When she did that – put him before her art – he knew she had really loved him.

Where had all that love gone? How had he lost her love?

Nicholas thinks back to the terrible fights that blighted the last year of their relationship. Days of not talking, and avoiding each other, and then some little thing would spark it off and, before they could stop themselves, they would be rowing. They would say things to each other that no two people should ever say to one another. They had crossed boundaries you should never cross; stomping roughshod over their hearts with less consideration for each other than they would have for a stranger. And whereas previously they would always make up, make love and regain their harmony, those last few months neither of them could make peace. What did Nicholas think would happen? That suddenly Charlie would stop being angry, would shut it all up and not expect him to talk about being childless? He had become afraid of sex, because it had lost its spontaneity and he felt she didn't desire him any more, just wanted him for a purpose. He was afraid she would get pregnant again. He didn't think he could bear one more miscarriage. So he kept walking away, ignoring her attempts to reach him, and her tears and her loneliness. No wonder she found herself in the arms of another man.

Nicholas presses his middle finger firmly down on A, boom, and his ring finger on G, boom, and his index finger on B, boom. Boom. Boom. He bangs on the piano, his fingertips thrumming with emotion.

Of course. It is so much clearer now. Charlie hadn't slept with someone else to hurt him. Whoever that man in London was, he had offered something that Nicholas hadn't been able to give Charlie at that time. Comfort. And she had taken it because she needed to.

Nicholas enters the universe of his music, and he plays his regret on the ivory keys. What an insane institution marriage is. He had prided himself on being the faithful husband, the injured party, but hadn't he more or less pushed Charlie into the arms of another man so that it was her fault, not his, that their marriage ended? He and Charlie had been on the rocks long before she had been unfaithful.

What Charlie did was not the cause, but a symptom of their failed marriage.

Nicholas can hear a car pull up. It must be Geraldine. He continues to play. He can't stop. He closes his eyes and lets the music elevate him, the notes articulating his heartache in a way that words never could. He senses the door open, a gentle summer breeze on his face, and knows Geraldine must be standing there, looking at him. But he cannot stop. He continues to play, following his instincts and at last finding an ending for his song.

He opens his eyes, and jumps up from the piano in surprise. Standing in front of him is not Geraldine, but Charlie. She is holding a large canvas wrapped in bubblewrap and is looking at him in astonishment. She looks so different, yet it is her. It is Charlie.

'Did you write that?' she asks him.

'What . . . what are you doing here? I . . .'

'Did you write that music?'

'Yes.'

She steps into the room, leans the picture against the wall below the window. He walks forward. They stand just a few paces from each other. She is the colour of honey, from Greece, with more freckles than ever spattering her nose, and her black hair has strands of red in it. She looks nothing like a witch.

'It's stunning, Nick. Please play it again.'

'I can't . . . I . . . what are you doing here? How did you find me?'

She smiles. 'I got your message. And Kev told me where you lived.'

'Why didn't you text back?'

'I didn't know what to say. I decided I should come to see you. I was bringing you a painting for your new house. It's taken a few weeks to build up to it. Sorry.' She looks down at the floor, pushes her foot across it. She is wearing flip-flops and Nicholas can see she has painted her toenails azure. She has such tiny feet, and he longs to hold them in the palms of his hands.

'I've missed you.'

The words are dragged from him, but he has to speak. He can't let his pride betray him now. Charlie looks up at him. He feels a warm hand pressed over his heart (could it be June Fanning?), pushing in and out, making him feel. He begins to see a delicate thread between Charlie and himself, a faint connection. It gives him hope.

'Please, play the music again,' Charlie says.

June Fanning takes his hand and leads him back to the piano. *Play for her, play for her.* The phantom's breath tickles the back of his neck. Charlie walks further into the room and stands by the side of the piano, looking down at him. He breathes in and summons the notes back to him. He has only played it once before, and yet the music rushes into his heart and pours down his limbs. His fingers begin to stretch across the keys and he lets his body sway with emotion. Charlie stands quite still, but he knows she can see it. All of what he wants to say, but can't in words, and so he lets the music communicate his loss, his regret, his love for her. When he has finished, he sits with his hands in his lap, breathing deeply, looking down at the piano keys. They look different to him, iridescent and powerful. Charlie leans forward and gently cups his chin in her hand. She forces him to look at her, and at the tears that glitter in her eyes.

'Nicholas,' she demands, 'forgive me.'

JUNE

What are kindred spirits? Is it possible that every single person in the world has a soulmate? How do you know? How do you know if it is the man you have married?

I cannot stop thinking about love since I have been researching Julia, and I am confused. She had so many lovers that it is hard to like her, and easy to judge. Was she really such a lascivious creature? And yet maybe it wasn't sex that Julia craved, but love. Every time she let a man fornicate with her, maybe she wanted a piece of his love, but she never got enough and was never satisfied. Could it be that all she was looking for was intimacy? In her age, in her society, such a thing was as a rare as an exotic bird. It makes me think possibly I have been too hard on Mother.

The last time I saw her she said to me, 'You know, June, your father broke *my* heart first.'

This enraged me. How could she say such a thing when it was she who left Daddy, and only after years of humiliating him, carrying on with every available man in Torquay. I imagined I could see quite clearly how it was when we were little: our mother so vain, and caught up in the adulation of other men, no time for her small children, or her husband.

'Remember how he used to be,' she persisted, and I shook my head, trying to deny her words. 'The way he used to shut himself away in the dark, and not get up for days.' She reached over, across the table and took my hand. 'I felt like he was burying me alive.'

We were in Fortnum & Mason's having tea. Mother had insisted on bringing me here as a treat to celebrate my marriage. She had finally come round to the idea that I was now a wife. I had been relieved not to have to go to Maidenhead and see her with Giovanni Calvesi again, and I did not want her coming to visit us in Hampstead. I did not want Robert to meet my mother. Just in case he fell under her spell, too. It was ridiculous to think such a thing when we had only been married for three weeks.

I pulled my hand away. 'No wonder he hid away from society,' I said hotly. 'He must have been so ashamed of you.'

'No, June.' Mother's forehead creased into a frown. 'You must understand that your father was always that way, from long before. Periodically he used to turn his back on us all and sink into this awful, dark lethargy. No matter what I said to him – whether it was affectionately, compassionately, angrily, even screaming sometimes – it seemed to have no effect. His melancholy was impenetrable to me, and after a while I found it unbearable. You girls should understand this. It was he who broke my heart, for he never loved me as I did him.'

I put my hands over my ears and squeezed my eyes shut. I didn't want to hear her. It was preposterous for her to say such things. All lies.

Why had I agreed to meet my mother? I am the soft one. Min is right to refuse to correspond with Mother, for all it brings is pain. I regretted that we were now in such a public place, because I wanted to stand up on my chair like an angry child and point my finger at her, screaming, 'Harlot! Jezebel! Adulteress!'

'June,' I heard her urgent whisper. 'June, please open your eyes and look at me.'

But I shook my head and through clenched lips said, 'Mother, I think you should go.'

'Please, June.'

I opened my eyes reluctantly. It is true her Italian lover had changed my mother. If I had not been her daughter, I would probably have liked her now. The flint in her eyes was no longer there, and her Ice Queen heart had melted. The light in Fortnum's was golden and warm, and seemed to wrap her up in its glow. Her red dress matched a small pendant of a red heart, brilliant against her pale skin, as if this was what she stood for now. The heart. Her lips were full and curved in a gentle smile and her cheeks were flushed the colour of the cherry blossom I had passed in the street. She looked anxious, as if she did care what I thought of her. I had never experienced such power before in the company of my mother. I looked at her long and hard, and my glare must have been fierce, for she recoiled as if hit.

I put my gloves on, stood up and, without a backward glance, strode out through the door. I heard the last words she said to me. They were the flotsam and jetsam of my departure. 'I am sorry,' she said. 'I am so very sorry.'

But for whom? For my sister, whom she beat; or for me, whom she could not love; or for Father, whom she betrayed? Or maybe she was sorry for herself, in her belief that Father broke her heart.

Now I can't help wondering: how many times is a heart supposed to be broken in one lifetime? Should it be broken at least once? What if it never happens to you? Does it mean you do not deserve to be loved?

Robert was the only man I have loved. We are married, and our love is supposed to last forever. This should mean that my heart will never be broken, for it will always belong to my husband. He will keep it safe and sound.

Yet I remember how I felt when Robert left to join up. On the morning he walked out our front door he did not even hesitate. He didn't come back, not for one second to kiss me again and reassure me. Were the feelings I experienced that morning heartbreak? It felt physical. A tight pain in my chest so that I could hardly breathe. I was drowning in the bed, gulping to come up to the surface. Something broke.

I have a picture in my head of a pretty porcelain figure of myself. She is dewy-eyed Juno on her wedding day in her fawn two-piece, and brown velvet hat, holding a bunch of yellow daffodils with a pure, wide-open heart. The day my husband left to fight she cracked, right through the middle, and I am afraid she might never be fixed.

There is something else, too. When I am reading about Julia it makes me think about sex. I shouldn't. I am a married woman, pregnant, yet I can't stop wondering: is there more to making love than what I am used to with Robert? Min told me things about her marriage bed, and I wished she hadn't. I was too embarrassed to say so at the time, but I have never experienced those physical sensations my sister described to me. Will I ever? Are Mother and Min different creatures from me? Are they two sensual divas satisfied by sex, and I the frigid one? Or are we all the same? Are we cast from the same stone and it is just that I am with the wrong man?

Phelim Sheriden. I am trying not to think of him, but often during the day he just pops into my head, and I imagine him painting in his studio, and I wonder what it would feel like if he were to hold my hand. Would it feel the same as Robert? Or, if he kissed me, how would his lips feel? Then I am all hot and bothered and try to do something else – work with Oonagh in the house, sweep the yard ten times, anything to banish these awful thoughts from my mind. Is this what pregnancy does to you? Turn you into a creature that craves something beyond all morality? It is dreadful, really.

Yet when I think about it, my feelings for Phelim Sheriden are not purely physical. Yes, he is attractive. But there is something else we share. It is a sort of kinship, an understanding of each other, with no effort required. I find it so easy to talk to him. Sometimes sharing a conversation with Robert makes me nervous because he is so quick to criticize. He wants to talk about politics, and farming, economics and the war. The damn war. He thought he was marrying a college girl, with a mind of her own, who could discuss these things, but really I have no interest. I love classical literature, art, music, and so does Phelim. None of these things can I share with Robert.

The other day I was working in Phelim's study, writing my story about Julia, slowly piecing her life together like a jigsaw, when I heard music. It lured me out into the hall and, astounded, I realized Phelim was playing 'Clair de lune' by Debussy, one of my most favourite pieces. I followed the magical sounds down to the back of the hall and pushed a door open. Phelim was sitting at a tiny grand, playing the music I play, swaying the way I do, engrossed in the poetry of the keys, his heart capitulating the way mine does, fallen on its knees by the expressive power of the music.

He did not see me watching him play or, if he did, he pretended not to. He looked like a god to me, with his rich golden hair, blazing on his head. I closed my eyes and let the music wash over me. Oh, it pierced my heart so, because it brought me back to my sister's front room in Highgate and playing the piano for her. I could see her face clearly, and the tips of my fingers tingled as I saw myself playing the keys, holding each note long enough, tantalizingly, until I tip onto the next one, vibrating into our souls, so that my own eyes and Min's lock and we are speechless with emotion. I dug my fingers into the paintwork of the Sheridens' sitting-room door and quelled my raging heart. I pulled back and stood in the dark shadows of the corridor, holding my sides and crying with such longing for my sister. Phelim had finished playing 'Clair de lune' and was now playing Arabesque No. 1, and I remembered how Min loved me to play this also. We were other girls then.

I took a handkerchief out from the cuff of my pullover and wiped my eyes, tucking it back in. I shuffled back down the narrow corridor and into the Gothic hallway. I wondered at the transcendental nature of music, the closest thing to heaven that man can make. I was not thinking where I was going, for I was surprised to find myself suddenly at the top of the staircase, with no memory of having walked up it. The landing was as dark as the hall. The long, narrow windows were shuttered, with tiny slithers of daylight scattered about the dark rug. If I had a house with such grand windows, I would pull back the shutters and open them wide, let the light flood in. I realized this was one thing I missed so much in Robert's house. The tiny windows kept the place perpetually in a dull half-light. It was depressing. If I were mistress of the Sheriden house, I would try to steal as much as I could of the dreary Cavan daylight, and I would paint the walls ivory, and have tawny carpets on the floors. I would not mind if it were cold, for my furnishings would make it feel warm. I would fill vases with honeysuckle and apple blossom, and the place would smell sweet, and fresh. I stood on the landing, sucking in the smell of Phelim's house. It was musty, and damp, but beneath that there were other smells, medicinal and stuffy. Intuitively I knew which door Claudette Sheriden slept behind. I stood and faced it. The white door was greyish in the gloom.

It opened. I gave a tiny yelp, jumping back in surprise. Claudette Sheriden faced me. She was hanging onto the handle of the door, and was dressed in a voluminous white nightgown. She looked more like a ghost than anything I could have imagined. She was even thinner than when I was with her in the orchard, and her eyes were huge, like a sea creature's, glimmering and pearly. She looked as if she had no strength at all, as if she might crumple to the floor at any moment.

'Can I help you?' I asked her, stepping forward.

She did not appear surprised that I should be standing on her landing, a virtual stranger, and nodded.

I took her arm. 'Shall I take you back to bed?'

She nodded again.

I led her back into the bedroom. Unlike the rest of the house, there was an open window, and I could hear the birds singing in the trees outside. The room was not one you would expect a lady to appreciate. It appeared to be decorated to the taste of a bachelor gentleman, with heavy dark furniture and dark-green drapes.

'I wanted to hear the music better,' she whispered to me, as I helped her up into the bed and pulled the linen sheets up to her chin.

'Shall I leave the door open?' I asked, and she nodded her assent, closing her eyes as we let Debussy wash into the room. I sat on the end of the bed, clasping my hands, feeling that it would be rude just to leave without saying anything else, yet not wanting to talk over the music. I did not look at her, for her eyes were shut, and I felt it was invasive to do so. It was shocking how sick she looked. It frightened me.

Finally the music stopped, and the piano was silent. Claudette sighed and opened her eyes. 'Thank you,' she said slowly. 'You are very sweet.' She paused, her breath rasping between each word. 'I am so very happy for Robert that he has found you, at last.'

I felt, as she said these words, as if she had some kind of knowledge of my husband, a past ownership. I remembered Phelim's words at lunch one day – 'We all loved her' – and what Claudette had said to me in the orchard. Robert had planted all those trees for her. I wanted to ask her, more than anything, whether my husband had loved her once, but it seemed cruel to question her when she was so ill, and of course terribly impolite. Yet I had to know.

'The apples are all gone,' I said. 'It is getting quite cold.'

'Yes,' she said looking out of the window, 'I smell it.'

I knew I should leave, but I sensed she was about to say more. There was a bowl of plums on her bedside stand. She picked one up and weakly offered it to me.

I shook my head. 'No, thank you.'

'Please,' she insisted. 'I cannot eat them any more.'

I took it to placate her and bit into it, feeling the purple juice spurt inside my mouth. It was slightly bitter, but I continued eating it, feeling that it was giving the dying Claudette pleasure to watch another person eat one of her sacred plums.

'Soon,' she sighed, her eyes cast towards the ceiling, 'I shall see James D. again. Soon.'

I said nothing, unable to think of a suitable reply. She glanced over at me.

'You are the same age as Danielle, but I think you look a lot younger.' She brushed my cheek with her cold hand. 'Those freckles, they are so very fetching.'

I blushed.

'I wish Danielle were here.' Her voice cracked. 'Phelim is so good. He promises he will find her. He promises war will not get her as it did James D.'

'Her father . . .' I whispered, unable to stop myself saying it.

Claudette's eyes widened, and she said, 'Oh no, James D. is not Danielle's father.'

'But Phelim told me—'

She interrupted, speaking painfully and slowly, 'Can I confide in you? You are, after all, Robert's wife.' She paused, as if thinking to herself. 'Did he not tell you?'

I shook my head, my heart pounding.

She hesitated. '*Non*, I should not tell you, *non, non, non*. I do not want to come between a husband and his wife — *secours, merde, secours, secours*. It is up to him.' The length of this sentence seemed to have exhausted her and she lay back against the pillows, half-closing her eyes.

'Phelim told me he married you because you were having James D.'s child. He did it for his friend, and for your reputation,' I persisted quite impertinently, but I could not let her go now. She had to tell me everything.

'Yes, yes,' she said, looking at me again, with her luminous grey eyes. 'Dear Phelim, such a good man, like Robert, too. He wanted to marry me as well. He told you this?'

I nodded, although I felt my cheeks burning, the shock of this information causing my heart to race.

'Such good men, and I had to choose one of them. You see, how hard it was for me? I could not tell Phelim the truth, but Robert knows, he does. I believe he must hate me now.'

'I don't understand . . .'

But Claudette appeared exhausted from her conversation with me and waved me away with her hand. 'I am sorry, later we will talk . . .' Her voice trailed off, and I watched her drift towards sleep. 'James D. and I . . . *comme les cousins* . . . so innocent . . . I was keeping myself pure for him.'

I watched her sleep, my body shaking and my heart pounding. I hated her. She lay in front of me, and even so close to death I could see the exquisite creature this woman was, delicate and fine, something I will never be. I should feel compassion for her. She must be in terrible pain, and the torment of not knowing where her child is. All these things should have filled me with empathy. But I couldn't feel them, for all I was thinking was that Claudette was a seductress like Mother. She had a part of my husband, and I wanted it back. As I sat with my back to the window, the birds twittering behind me, and looked out of Claudette Sheriden's bedroom door, across the landing to the dusty banisters and cracked ceiling, a realization suddenly dawned on me. Could it be that Danielle was Robert's child?

It is possible isn't it? Min would tell me to buck up, and stop being such an idiot to think such things. 'Robert is mad about you,' she always told me. But why then did he leave me all on my own in Cavan? Was he running away?

If only the war were over and Robert was safely home. Everything would be back to normal. We could continue to ignore Claudette Sheriden. But I know that's not true, because porcelain Juno is slipping through my hands, and I cannot even try to catch her as she smashes onto the floor.

NICHOLAS

'You have a dog,' Charlie says as she sits down by the range in the kitchen. Hopper hops up to her and she strokes his ears.

'He was abandoned. I found him on the road, nearly dead.'

'I always wanted a dog.'

'I know.'

Nicholas had heard it many times. How much Charlie had wanted a dog when she was a little girl, but her mother wouldn't allow it.

He makes coffee for them and they sit on either side of the range. Charlie looks at the boxes of cider.

'What's all this?'

'It's a little business venture. I made cider from the apples in the orchard.'

'That's a great idea.'

Nicholas gets up and takes a bottle from one of the boxes. 'Here, take a bottle. Try it.'

He hands it to her awkwardly and she takes it, resting it in her lap. 'Thanks. Yeah, sure, I'll try it.'

Nicholas looks at Charlie. She is still beautiful to him.

'The house is lovely, Nick,' she says, and he knows she means it.

'Do you want to see around it?'

He takes her through the downstairs first, from the kitchen

down the little hall into the back room again, then the spare room and the bedroom.

'It's small, but there's a great attic. You could do so much with it.'

They walk up the tiny little wooden staircase. She is in front of him, and he is conscious of her warm body as he leans over and pushes the trap door open. She feels different, familiar and yet new.

Charlie pokes her head through the trap door. She turns around and smiles at him. 'This is fantastic.'

'It used to be thatch, but the previous owners put on the slate roof and put in dormer windows, so you've a great view.'

They climb in and Charlie walks over to the window and looks out of it. 'So do you own all this land?'

He goes over and stands next to her. 'No, not all of it. The woods belong to the people who live in that house. All those fields are owned by a local farmer. But I own the yard, the field in front and the orchard.'

'What happened to all the trees?'

'It's a long story.'

Charlie looks at him, and he knows she knows he doesn't want to talk about it. She steps back into the attic and spins on the floorboards, sunlight sprinkles her skin and hair. He wonders for a moment: has he conjured her from his imagination, or is she real? She looks like a celestial vision.

'The light is great in here. This would make a fantastic studio.' She stops spinning. 'For small works. It's so quiet here. You'd have to find a space outside for larger pieces.'

'I have sheds I can convert.'

They stare at each other. For a moment there is so much between them – all the years of love, the months of hurt. The air is full and brimming with the past and with what might be to come.

Charlie is standing by the window again. She suddenly sees something and points. 'Who's that?'

Nicholas looks down at the yard. Geraldine's white Ford is parked outside. He didn't even hear her arrive, and Hopper didn't bark. She is getting out of the car, her red hair loose like a snake down her back. Grainne is sitting in the back of the car, reading a book.

'Oh, that's a friend.' Nicholas can feel himself blushing as Charlie scrutinizes him. 'I'd better go down. You stay here . . .' he pauses, 'if you like.'

Nick has never seen Geraldine so excited. Her eyes are sparkling, her cheeks blooming, and she sounds as if she has just run all the way to his house, she is so breathless.

'Oh, great . . . I thought I might have missed you,' she gushes. 'Aren't you supposed to be gone by now? Here, let me help you.'

She picks up a box of the cider and starts towards the kitchen door.

'Is your car open?' she asks over her shoulder.

'Yes,' says Nicholas, gathering up a box.

Charlie has parked her car down the side of the house, so it isn't visible from the yard. Geraldine rests the box of cider on the roof of his car and flings open the boot, placing the box inside. She turns to face him, grinning, and Nicholas is conscious of the possibility that Charlie is watching them from the attic.

'I have come to a very important decision,' Geraldine announces.

Nicholas shrinks back. He doesn't know what to say. All he knows is that he doesn't want Charlie to see him and Geraldine together.

'Are you all right?' Geraldine asks him.

Nick carefully puts his box of cider in the boot. 'Yes, it's just—'

Geraldine interrupts. 'Oh, Nick, I am *so* excited. And it's all down to you. It's you I have to thank.'

Before he can pull back, she has flung her arms around him and hugs him.

'Thank you. Thank you.' She pulls back and stands smiling at him. 'For the first time in years I feel so alive. Now Ray has moved out, I realize I had made myself a prisoner. I didn't *have* to stay. Life is too short to be trapped in an unhappy marriage.'

'Maybe my apple trees were worth the sacrifice then,' Nicholas says softly.

'It's terrible, I know, but it highlighted who I had married. After that, I had no choice but to ask him to leave. But it doesn't stop there, Nick, because today I have come to realize something. And I am so very, very happy!'

Again she bounds forward and hugs him, and Nicholas can feel the elation off her, and he can't help but hug Geraldine back. Nicholas wants Geraldine to be happy.

They separate again and she glances at her watch. 'You'd better hurry up. You're going to miss the market.'

They go back towards the house to collect more boxes.

'And so this is what I have decided . . .' Geraldine is saying as they walk through door. 'Oh, hello.' She stops dead.

Charlie is standing by the sink, empty cup in hand. She puts it in the sink and stretches out her hand in greeting. 'Hello, I'm Charlotte.' She pauses. 'Nicholas's wife.'

Geraldine turns crimson. 'Hello . . . pleased to meet you,' she stutters.

Nicholas cannot bear to look at Geraldine's face, but he can sense her disappointment and it makes him feel awful.

'I'm Geraldine. One of Nick's piano pupils . . .'

'Is he a good teacher?' Charlie asks.

'Very.'

Geraldine looks at Nicholas. He raises his eyes to meet her face. Her expression is a question. He stands between the two women and knows in his heart that he must make a choice.

JUNE

We huddle outside the church. It is bitterly cold, the first fierce day of winter. I push my gloved hands deeper into my pockets and watch the door of Phelim's house. A few people talk in hushed whispers, but most are silent. They have little to say about Claudette, for I would guess that we are all here out of duty, rather than friendship. Claudette waits for us in the church. Her shell is hidden in the casket, her spirit hovering around us. Her longing is palpable. It bites me like the tiny hailstones that begin to pelt out of the sky and force us into the church, a building suddenly full of strangers to mourn her passing. Those who should be here — her daughter Danielle, the rest of her family in France, and her lost love James D. — are painfully absent. Would she wish that Robert were here too?

We shuffle into the pews. I sit between Oonagh and Teresa. Father O'Regan waits patiently at the pulpit, and we listen to the sudden squall of hail batter the windows. The candles flicker as Phelim finally arrives. Instead of letting in more light as he opens the door, it feels as if darkness shadows him as he walks up to the top of the church. I am afraid to look at him, but cannot stop myself from glancing up. He walks past me, but I do not think he sees me. He looks taller, and paler than usual. His narrow face is drained of colour, shaded by sleepless nights, aged by witnessing his wife's journey out of this life. Had she slipped away peacefully, or was she dragged each step of the way, desperate to see her only child just one more time?

I feel suddenly choked, and tears start to flood down my cheeks. Oonagh looks over at me. I can see the surprise in her eyes, but she takes my hand and squeezes it. I cannot bear to think of Claudette, and her slow, desperate end. When Father died I could not cry. During the whole funeral I sat tearless in the front pew. Yet I can cry for Claudette Sheriden. I think of Mrs Sanderson and what happened to her, and suddenly I feel punched in the stomach. My knees buckle, forcing me to sit down on the bench and search for a handkerchief in my bag. I miss my sister. And yet it is Mummy I want now. I want the caress of the woman we never got to know. I want her safe arms holding me, telling me everything will be fine. But Mummy has never been able to do this, even when we were tiny tots. I grieve for something I have never known.

It is time to go to the graveyard. Phelim walks the length of the church, Claudette's coffin following, carried by six local men. We tilt our faces in sympathy towards Phelim, but he looks straight ahead. We follow, milling around outside the church, while Claudette's coffin is secured in the back of a cart. A bay cob puffs into the freezing air and we shiver, shifting our cold feet on the wet ground. The hailstorm is over, but small white pellets of hail can still be seen littered in the flowerbeds and along the path. The slate roof of Phelim's house sparkles across the street. It is nearly the same colour as the sky.

Everyone is going up to Phelim and offering their condolences. I watch him smoking a cigarette, dragging comfort out of it, his gloveless hands shaking, his mane of hair as golden as an angel's, politely nodding as his neighbours talk to him.

'Have you spoken to him?' Oonagh asks me.

'No, do you think I should?'

'Of course.' Oonagh gives me a little push towards Phelim.

I weave through the crowd. Most of the people I do not recognize and assume are distant Sheriden relatives. I come up behind Phelim and tap him gently on the shoulder. He turns and I take his hands, squeezing them in mine.

'Thank you for coming,' he says, his teeth chattering.

'But of course I wanted to be here.'

'You never did get to meet her, did you?'

I hesitate, for now is not the time to tell him about Claudette's visit to the orchard, or mine to her bedroom. I wonder if I will ever tell him.

He offers me a cigarette and takes one for himself, lighting them both with difficulty in the cold wind. He puffs for a minute. 'I don't know what's taking so long . . .'

'I think everyone is waiting for you.'

He nods. 'Yes, of course.'

I am so close to him that I can see his nose is dripping, and I long to pass him a clean handkerchief. It is a strangely intimate urge. I am still holding his hand, and I put my fingers through his.

'Would you like me to walk with you to the graveyard?'

He looks surprised, and for the first time I see a hint of the man I met a few weeks ago, a warmth in his eyes and the glimmer of a smile. 'That is kind of you, June, very kind. But Claudette wanted it just to be family at the burial.' He bends down and whispers in my ear, 'She wanted a picture of James D. to be placed on her coffin and buried with her.'

I look at him, astonished, feeling a stab of hurt for him in my heart. 'Oh, Phelim!' I wish I could do something to help him feel better.

But I know nothing will. In fact the best thing he can do is hold his grief in both hands. Let him feel the shape of it, its hidden contours of secrets and regrets, its moments of words and looks, which are locked in time now as permanent as the headstone on the grave.

Phelim looks about him, and gently pulls his hand away. 'I wish you could come with me,' he says softly, and then walks quickly over to the hearse, along with a straggle of relatives.

I step back and stand with Oonagh and her sister on the side of the road, watching the small group of relatives, led by Father O'Regan in a black cape, walk into the chill wind. Hats are held on by hands, coats are blown open, the heads of some of the flowers shoot up into the sky, and the priest's skirts billow like a black balloon as the procession goes up the town and out again, down the hill into the cemetery.

Oonagh takes Teresa's hand and the two sisters walk ahead of me out of the village and along the road home. I dally behind them, wanting so urgently to be with Phelim and to comfort him. These emotions confuse me, and I wish I had a sister walking next to me, in whom I could confide. Would Min give me the right advice?

I remember Min's twenty-first birthday. I was surprised my sister wanted to spend it with me rather than her husband. I had hoped we might all go out to dinner. Robert and I, Charles and Min. We would make a happy foursome. It was a dream of mine. This harmony between couples. For what could be better than sisters married to best friends?

But Min had not mentioned the possibility and, besides, Robert didn't like socializing. I put it down to shyness, and self-consciousness because his background was very different from that of his friends and colleagues. Sooner or later, he said, it always came up. Once they found out he was an Irishman, no matter how English he sounded, they behaved a little differently with him.

Min and I met during the day for a matinee showing, because I had to be home by six o'clock to prepare Robert's dinner. Min made no mention of similar duties.

The picture was called *Nothing Sacred* and was a comedy starring my favourite Carole Lombard. I adored her. She was able to combine Garboesque beauty with lightness, and humour. But what astounded me about the picture was the fact that it was filmed in Technicolor. It was the first time we had seen a colour picture, and I found it particularly unsettling. I was used to applying colour myself. Now this autonomy had been taken away from me. The picture appeared gaudy; the colours garish and jarring. My picture world was in black and white, detached and removed from the real world. The grey tones of my favourite films gave them an ethereal quality, and a mystery. Technicolor ruined all of this. I thought it far too vulgar. The images were not those I liked to dream about. But Min disagreed.

'How thrilling,' she exclaimed as we came out of the cinema into the sunshine, 'and exciting, to be able to create moving images in colour. This is the way forward, June.'

'I prefer the old pictures.'

'Oh, how could you? For a picture to be in colour is bringing it as close to the real world as possible. Soon they will be able to make mirror images of us, and the world will be able to look at itself. I wonder what we will all learn then.'

'But I love making up the colours myself. Remember when we saw *Jezebel*. We both knew she was wearing a red dress, even though the film was in black and white, but I am sure my shade of red is different from yours.'

'I suppose.' Min skipped a step and then, linking her arm through mine, she said, 'Let's have a quick cup of tea and a bun, before you have to get back.'

We two sisters walked past Leicester Square Tube station, the dark and the fair. Min had cut her hair recently, and thus we both sported bobs. Min's was waved into soft black curls at the nape of her neck, whereas my mousy bob was tucked behind my ears, thick and straight, with a heavy fringe hanging above my eyes. Min always knew which colours suited her best. She was wearing a dress the colour of bluebells, a seductive shade halfway between purple and blue, and as she moved it gave off a shimmer like a haze of flowers in a woodland glade. The day was hot, and she had her jacket – blue as well – slung over her other arm as we walked along. I stuck to muted shades. I was wearing a pale-grey sweater and a brown skirt, which were both too warm for the weather. The wool of the sweater stuck to my body. I longed for a cool breeze to soothe my prickly skin.

Min paused and looked into the window of a bookshop on Charing Cross Road. I glanced at our reflections. How different we looked now.

'I cannot be only twenty-one! I feel so old,' Min suddenly exclaimed, squeezing my hand. 'It should be exciting to be twenty-one, but instead it's boring. I can see each year just the same. Day in, day out.'

I glanced over at my sister's profile. What had brought on this outburst? It was Min's birthday and we should be celebrating. But then birthdays were difficult times, especially when it was a reminder of past birthdays as a small child. The sense of anticlimax because Mother would never quite make you feel she cared, and Daddy would forget. I searched for something to talk about that would cheer Min up and make her sparkle again.

'What about painting? I thought you loved studying art.'

Min brightened up. 'Yes, of course, that is something which keeps me going.'

We proceeded up Charing Cross Road until we came to a small tea house, with tiny latticed windows, like one that you would expect in the middle of a country village, not in the centre of London. I went first, pushing the door open. It was packed, and the air was thick with cigarette smoke and noisy chat, but we pushed into the throng and were able to find a table for two in the corner. We sat down opposite each other, and a waitress came over and took our order. Although the place was busy, the service was extremely fast and within a few moments we had our pot of tea for two and a selection of cakes, sticky buns and pastries on a plain white dish. I unfolded my napkin and placed it on my knee.

'Shall I be mother?' I picked up the teapot. Min nodded, and I filled our cups with steaming brown tea.

Min opened her bag, took out a little mirror and, looking at herself, she sighed. 'All those people in the film. They are so glamorous.' She produced a lipstick from the bottom of her bag and repainted her lips plum-red. 'Imagine living in America, Juno, and being a rich divorcee!'

She put her lipstick away and pursed her red lips together, arched her eyebrows and put on a face like a femme fatale. She made me laugh. The idea of going to Hollywood was as ridiculous an idea to me as flying to the moon.

'Will you ever go to America, do you think?' Min continued, dropping her act and looking normal again, one eyebrow raised, her smile asymmetrical.

I shook my head. 'I haven't really thought about it. If Robert wanted to go, I would.'

'Maybe we might go together one day,' Min said dreamily, stirring her tea. 'We'll sail to New York, and then we'll drive across the whole country to California and Hollywood. We'll get spotted on the street, and next thing you know, we'll be watching ourselves in the pictures! Oh, what glamour-pusses we will be.'

'Oh, how silly you are, Min!' I bit into my sticky bun, but the idea appealed to me somehow. There was so much space in America.

'Will we do it, June?' Min's eyes were gleaming.

'Oh, yes, let's go ahead and book our passage today,' I answered sarcastically.

'I mean it, June, let's run away,' Min said urgently, her lips quivering and her cheeks flushed.

'But, Min, we would be away for months. What about Charles? What about Robert?'

'Yes,' said Min, shaking her head. 'I couldn't ask you to go, not now you've met Robert. I shall have to do it on my own.'

I felt my heart quicken. Min was actually serious. 'This is one of your fantasies, Min. What on earth would you be doing in America, and without Charles?'

'I would paint the Wild West desert. I would go somewhere so wholly different from here. A big, blank canvas. I want to burn the soles of my feet on the red earth, and my soul on the sizzling orange sun. I would look up into a gigantic sky, watch the eagles circling, and feel free.' She raised her arms and spread them wide, causing a few glances in our direction. 'America is the new world, June, and I want to be part of it.'

'But Charles . . .' I stuttered, reddening with confusion. 'You are married to Charles.'

Min dropped her arms and bowed her head over her teacup. 'He doesn't love me,' she whispered.

I bent my head down, close to my sister's face. I could see a tear trail down her cheek. Her lashes were laced with them. 'Oh, Min, of course he loves you, how could he not?'

'I stole him from Mother, and now this is my punishment. I am always to be compared to her.' She shook her head, and took her handkerchief out, began to dab her eyes. 'What good did it do anyway? For she left Father all the same.'

'Min, that was a bad reason to marry Charles.' I was appalled that my sister would do such a stupid thing, but at the same time I had always known deep down it was the reason why Min had married so young, and to Captain Sanderson.

'I know, I know, but I did believe I loved him. Why, Juno,' she said, a twisted smile on her lips, her eyes watery, 'he was always my Prince Charming, remember? It's just that he can be so cruel.'

I looked at my sister in alarm. She was so delicate, more so every time I saw her. I looked at her slender white arms and shoulders, the soft-capped sleeves of her blue dress making them look even more delicate, like narrow white stems. She had no strength whatsoever.

'Does he hurt you, Min?' I spoke sharply, anger rising in my belly.

'No, not in the way you mean – no, Charles would never touch me. It is just that he makes me feel so frivolous. I am an artist, June, but he doesn't take me seriously. He thinks it is my hobby and that I should just be his decorative wife, hanging off his arm. Sometimes I wish I were ugly, because then if he really loved me, it wouldn't matter how I looked.'

'Only someone with a face like yours could say such a flippant thing,' I replied crossly. 'I have always wanted to be as pretty as you.' I softened, tucking one of Min's black tendrils behind her ear. 'You have no idea how very fortunate you are.'

'It is a curse, Juno, believe me,' Min said bitterly.

We sat in silence for a moment. I poured another cup of tea and spooned one sugar into it, stirring the spoon round and round, watching the brown liquid swirl.

'When you have a baby, it will be different, Min.'

'Oh, but even that is not easy.' Min's voice shook. She looked away from me, out of the steamed-up window of the tea rooms. 'We have been trying for so long, and . . .' She hesitated, and seemed unable to say any more. Tears flooded down her cheeks again.

I took my sister's tiny hands and squeezed them within my own.
'It will get better. It will, I promise.'

'Should I leave him?' Min asked suddenly, turning her face and
looking straight into my eyes.

She sniffed and dabbed her nose with a handkerchief, and
although she had been crying, she looked pale and tragic, rather
than red and blotchy. Her dark eyes were deep violet, and her gaze
was a plea, haunting and brimming with the pain of her question.
I winced. I knew my sister was so lost she would do whatever I told
her to do.

But this is what marriage is, I convinced myself, a veteran of a
mere year. There are ups and there are downs, but it is for life. I
had seen the way Charles looked at Min. He was devoted to her.
Min could be very demanding. Maybe Charles wasn't actually being
cruel, but was just standing up for himself. I considered Min lucky,
for Charles had allowed her to go to the Slade. When I had mentioned the possibility of returning to university to complete my
degree, Robert had appeared stunned I would think of such a thing
now that I was his wife. Min was a little depressed because she had
still not had her longed-for first child. Soon she would be pregnant.
I felt sure she would be happy then, and would laugh at the idea of
running off to America to be an artist, or a film actress. How could
she possibly survive over there, so far away from me? I couldn't
bear for her to be all that way from me.

'No,' I said emphatically. 'You oughtn't to leave Charles.'

NICHOLAS

Charlie takes a kitchen knife out of the drawer, rips the bubblewrap off the painting and slashes it right across the middle.

'What are you doing?'

Nicholas tries to grab her arm, but the knife blade sparkles in the light and she attacks her canvas again.

'Stop,' he shouts. 'Charlie, stop.' He sobs.

She drops the knife. 'You're crying.' She stares at him. Her eyes look wild, the pupils dilated.

It has started again, the crying that has attacked him over the past few weeks, unforeseen, without warning. All the years he never cried – with repressed grief from losing the babies and, before that, the loss of his father – are now being documented down his cheeks.

'Nicholas!' Charlie is horrified. She rushes to him and, even though he is so much taller than her, she manages to hold him in her arms and let him cry.

'Don't destroy it,' he manages to say.

She holds him cradled in her arms for a long time. Nicholas feels the breeze through the window falling on their faces, brushing the sorrow away.

'Please, Charlie, don't rip up your painting.'

'I have to,' she says tightly.

'Why?'

She releases him, picks up the picture and holds it up. 'Look!' she commands him.

He wipes his eyes, and stares at the painting. It is the same one he saw on the easel the day he broke into their flat. Yet she has done a little more work to it. There is a figure moving slowly through the fog. It is walking away from the viewer, he can see that clearly now. And there are tiny little leaves floating about the figure. They are red, the colour of blood, and they stand out against the grey, white and blue swirls of paint. The picture is bleak.

'I was going to give you this, to make you feel bad,' Charlie blurts out. 'I was doing it again. Hiding behind my art. I wanted you to know how much your rejection hurt me, and to tell you that you rejected me first.'

Nicholas looks at the picture and he can see how it would have tortured him to have it on his wall, in his lonely house in Cavan, looking at it night after night. He is the figure in the painting, and he is walking towards a void – he is becoming nothing.

'Is that what I am to you?' he asks her. 'Am I nothing now?'

'No!' Charlie says vehemently. 'Oh, no!'

Nicholas can smell the baking again, and he knows June Fanning is in the kitchen with them, busy cooking, trying to bake love into her apple pie so that they can eat it.

No one is nothing if they are loved.

The phantom whispers in his inner ear, until her words become a song, binding his heart.

Have no regret.

This is their moment of truth. Nicholas and Charlotte Healy have been married for over ten years, but it is only now, in her husband's Cavan kitchen, that Charlie can see who her husband is and what she has lost. She asks him with her eyes. Does he still want her?

Nicholas considers his anger, his pride, his betrayal, and how hurt he has been by what Charlie did. Could he ever trust her again? But if he lets her go out of the door today, he knows he would regret it. They have too much love between them to desert it. He steps forward and embraces his wife, and Nicholas knows he has made the right choice. For a second he wonders what Geraldine was going to say just before she met Charlie, but he is glad now she never had the opportunity to say it. It had just been that one time between them in the orchard. Geraldine had waited for him to say something to Charlie, but he had placed himself beside his wife at the stove and then she had known. She had left. He wishes her well. He hopes she meets someone one day with whom she can share the same kindred connection that he and his wife have. It is a rare and precious thing. He is a man who is going to learn to forgive his wife, as long as she can forgive him.

JUNE

Here the water rises up from beneath the land to create small lakes. It is a sorrowful place. The water is always there, no matter how dry it might be. It emerges from within the earth's crust, making small, still pools of cool blue, dips in the green land, which swell around me like the sea. Up and down. I can never see too far. The land and trees shelter the house, so that I have to walk out onto the road to get a sense of distance and see the Iron Mountains, their top the flat back of a crouching lion, their ginger mane of reeds visible even from here, in the wet, grey Cavan mist.

We are on the borders of Leitrim and Cavan, and never have I lived in such a melancholy landscape. Robert told me many people suffered here in the last century, particularly at the hands of the English, and many people have left. There is a sense of abandonment in the very fibre of the place. The air is heavy, particularly at this time of year, when the leaves fail to defy gravity and turn to mulch. I can smell the decay all around me, filling my nostrils, making me sense the heavy, cloying world that I live in. Will I remain here for the rest of my life?

I can't help remembering the light and air in Devon. So different from here. Bright, sparkling sunshine, like fresh lemonade, the sea air tasting fizzy on my tongue, and even though it was not actually hot, like in Italy, it was still warm enough to brave the frothy sea, wilful and excited as my sister and I were.

I am trying to follow the war on the wireless, but in the end I turn it off. I tremble at the images that are conjured inside my head when I think of Robert, in the middle of it, and my sister too. When I go walking in the woods I manage to calm my beating heart, and think of other things. How my body is feeling, and how it is changing. My breasts are even fuller, and my belly is a tiny little dome. I feel a sense of something else taking over my body. Sometimes I resent this.

The earth is almost black here, and our woods are full of beech trees with crisp red leaves, a valiant few still clinging on, fluttering in the breeze. My favourite place is a small dip in the middle of the wood like a miniature valley. It is completely covered in leaves, yellow and brown, with a ring of beech trees around its circumference, and one huge upturned root slightly off-centre. I could look for hours at those roots, and the intricacy of their interlacing. It gives me as much pleasure as looking at a painting.

I come here most days and sometimes I just let my mind wander free, and daydream. I close my eyes, sitting on the edge of the root, and I fantasize. The trees whispering around me highlight my longing, because that is what it is, a deep ache to be touched, caressed. I pick up a couple of twigs and curl the lichen under my fingers, pulling it away. It is soft, and fuzzy, too fragile to leave in the woods, and I wish I could make a small nest of it and hibernate here. Hide inside the woods until the war – no, my temptation – is over.

As I am sitting in my tiny valley it begins to rain. That is how it is here. No warning whatsoever. You never say: it looks like rain today, because it always looks like rain every day. Bands of grey clouds lock out the sun, apart from a rare hour or two, and sit aloft the mountains. The rain comes down like a cloak, shrouding the land, the houses and all the people. Sometimes it can be gentle. A comforting drizzle, its tiny drops separate particles, which glisten in your hair. But some days it comes down in sheets, suddenly and with an intense chill that cuts into your bones. It begins to rain like this. So I run.

It is a moment of exhilaration and some small release of my self-pitying pangs. I am a fortunate woman, I tell myself as I race down the path, slippery with leaves and out the other side of the woods.

Why do I decide to come out onto the road? It is quicker to go home through the back of the woods, and the orchard, but instead I am standing on the road, in the strange grey half-light that exists most of the day being pelted by rain. I run down the road towards town, and away from Robert's cottage.

And then I am standing opposite Phelim Sheriden's house. Something other than shelter propels me to his door, and before I can stop myself I am banging his knocker, catching my breath.

The door swings open, and Phelim stands there. I have not seen him since Claudette's funeral and he is like a bright spot of light on this dull, dark day. His hair is gleaming gold, and he is wearing a sea-green jersey, spattered with paint. It is a colour that goes straight to the heart of me.

'June!' he says in surprise, and pulls back the door.

'I am so sorry to intrude,' I begin, 'but I have got caught in the rain.'

'Come in, come in.'

I stand on his threshold, dripping with rain and blowing the water off the end of my nose. He looks at me curiously and then, I don't know why, I begin to giggle. I imagine how I must look. Like a drenched sea-turtle in my dark-blue coat and dripping wool beret, but I cannot help my laughter. It is so inappropriate. Is it nerves or is it abandon?

He smiles at me, and I know he doesn't think I am insane. 'Quickly, come into the kitchen, the stove is lit.'

Phelim takes my coat and hat and hangs them above the stove. Then he takes a bottle of whiskey from a shelf over the sink.

'I believe hot whiskey might warm you up.' He indicates that I should sit down by the fire. 'I have a tiny bit left here, for special occasions.'

I am shivering a little, and he comes over and touches my sleeve. I jump as if branded.

'Apologies,' he says hastily, 'I just wanted to see if you were wet through. We do not want to risk you getting ill.'

'I'm fine.'

He hands me a rug, which is hanging on the back of the chair. 'Please warm yourself a little with this.'

I thank him, wrapping the rug around my shoulders and feeling like a little girl. I am safe here. In fact I am happy. I do not care that maybe it is not so appropriate for me to call here on my own, with no real excuse other than a wet winter's afternoon.

'I have not seen you in a while.' He pours whiskey into two glasses and places the kettle on the stove.

'After the funeral, I thought you might want to be alone.'

He doesn't mention Claudette, and instead asks me brightly, 'So, you finished reading all my books?'

'No, of course not, but I began to think maybe my studies are all a little frivolous.'

'Why would that be?' He looks at me earnestly and continues to speak. 'History is an essential in life. Without knowledge of the past, how can we learn to live in the present, learn from what happened before?'

'But we haven't, have we? Look at the world now – hundreds of years after the time of Julia we are still fighting each other. One empire trying to dominate another. And we are still judging those who won't, or can't, conform.'

'So is that what you think of Julia? That she is an anarchist?' He sits down opposite me and hands me a hot glass of whiskey, a napkin wrapped around its base to keep me from burning my fingers.

'I am confused by her,' I say, taking my drink. 'Sometimes, when I read about what she actually did, how she ignored her children and corrupted Phoebe, and prostituted herself . . .'

I am suddenly nervous. This is a scandalous subject, and I am not sure how Phelim will react to me saying such things.

'I cannot understand how any woman would want to do what she did in the end. How could she sell her own body, unless she was desperate for the money? How could she enjoy it?'

'It is surprising what some people find themselves craving.' Phelim speaks quietly. 'For many it is because they cannot love themselves, and so they believe this is what they deserve. Maybe, for Julia, the defilement of her body by strangers was an expression of her self-hatred?'

'Or maybe she was a warrior?' I counter, looking up at Phelim's sapphire eyes, thinking how much I have missed him these past two weeks.

'Like any soldier, she used her body as a weapon, to dig at the roots of the Roman Empire and to make a political point. She must have known she would end up exiled or, worse still, executed. So she was brave. She sacrificed her life so that she could expose the truth, the hypocrisy of Rome.'

'All very good,' Phelim laughs, 'but it didn't work, did it?'

'No, I suppose not.' I smile back, and sip the sweet hot whiskey. 'Oh, this is delicious.'

'It's flavoured with honey.'

We sit in silence for a while. I already feel better, warm from the whiskey and stimulated by our conversation about Julia. Robert has never been interested in my classical studies. He would often ask me: what relevance did it have to the modern world? I could not explain it to him. How it is that I can lose myself in the voices of a distant age, and then actually walk into it. That is what happened to me when I was in Italy, on the island of Ponza. I felt as if I was able to pull back the curtain and walk in Julia's footsteps across the spine of the island, look at what she saw, smell it, feel it, completely imagine how it must be to live another life. I could feel how that parallel world felt. It is a way of escaping and at the same time coping with the present. Unlike Robert, with Phelim I sense a level of understanding.

'Are you painting?' I ask him suddenly.

'Yes, it is helping me,' he says falteringly. 'I am working on a concerto of colour. I am trying to create music visually, it is . . . a little strange.'

I shift my legs. Rain still lashes against the window, and suddenly I am so nervous I am afraid to speak. I do not know why Phelim says what he does next. Maybe it is the mixture of whiskey, loss and loneliness, for each word he utters sculpts itself inside my heart.

'June, I must tell you, I am in love with you.'

I start as if shot, stunned into silence.

'There, it is said.' He looks sheepish, gets up nervously.

'But Claudette . . .' I whisper shakily.

'I stopped being in love with Claudette a long, long time ago. When the love you feel for someone is not returned, then it is like a plant without water. It slowly withers and dies.'

'You are upset.' I cannot look at him. 'You hardly know me—'

He interrupts me. 'I know, and you are married to another man. But, June, I need to tell you I have never met a woman whom I have felt this way about. As soon as I saw you . . . everything about you: your face, your eyes, your lips are just for me.'

He sighs and shakes his head.

'Don't worry,' he says forlornly. 'You are married and with Robert, but I have to go away soon, and it is important for me to tell you this, that I love you . . .' His voice peters out and I stand up, the rug falling off my knees.

'What do you mean, go away soon?'

'I am going up North in a few days, signing up. Now that Claudette is gone, I should do my duty. If your husband is prepared to leave you, and I have no one, well then, I have no excuse.'

'Don't mention him!' The anguish of Robert's absence incenses me.

Phelim stands uncomfortably, shaking his head, looking down. 'Robert . . .'

'Don't say his name!'

I am an inch away from Phelim's face. I can see laughter lines around his eyes and the flat, brown freckles across his nose and cheeks. Our desperate needs rattle inside our hearts, screaming for us to touch. He steps back from me. His eyes are wide open, and his pupils dilated.

'June?'

But I am unable to speak for a moment. I step towards him, take his hand, drop it, stare at the flagstone floor. 'Please, Phelim. Please don't go.'

THE ADULTERESS VI

His room is brown. Brown jacket hanging on the back of the door, heavy chestnut furniture, dusty and old, the drawers not completely pushed in, so that she can see corners of things – papers, clothes, forgotten articles. The floor is bare walnut floorboards, uneven, and there are no rugs. He says he doesn't want to get paint on them. There is little light, strange since he works in here. During the day he raises the blind, but the window is so dirty that the light that strays into the room has a dingy, jaundiced air. At night he works by the one bare bulb, too shockingly bright, disturbing the spiders, which scurry to the corners of the ceiling, highlighting the overwhelming masculinity of the room.

She likes to light a candle and turn out the light, for it would be impossible to make love under the bare bulb. There is something too indecent about it.

Who is she fooling? She needs to know why she keeps coming here.

Because she does love her husband.

And then the thought occurs to her. Is it possible to be in love with two people at the same time?

With her lover she shares conversations she could never share with her husband, and their lovemaking is different, more hectic, free. Yet she knows her lover is a selfish man, a self-obsessed artist, who only makes her feel loved through the inspiration she gives him. He would make a bad father.

Her husband has a heart three times the size of her lover. She knows this. He does not deserve to be betrayed. Yet it is her lover who tells her that he loves her, and she doesn't care that it is probably not true, she just needs to hear the words. He looks at her, notices what she is wearing, the shape of her face he finds beautiful, the tone of her skin, its touch, and every little detail about her body he looks at and relishes. Has her husband ever even looked beneath the bed sheets?

Her lover is painting a self-portrait. She is fascinated that he is able to sit here day after day and scrutinize himself. The flesh tones are so tactile that she wants to touch the image, but resists; the paint is still wet. He is wearing brown in the painting, and it makes her laugh, the brown-and-pink colour of it, reflecting his real life, their flesh, naked limb against limb, on his brown blankets in his brown room.

When will it stop? When the world orders it so. She senses they are close to the end now. The war, and death, frames them. They are on the brink of extinction. The streets have become smoky battlegrounds and, as she runs through them, on her way to meet her lover, she is afraid to look into the rubble, see a child's toy or an old woman's shoe, see the debris that war creates, making her want to weep with shame.

Is this what makes her so desperate to conceive, so that she makes love to her lover and her husband in the same night and does not care who the real father will be? She hopes a baby will stop her, make her forget about her lover, settle as a wife. Why has she been denied the one thing she has always wished for in her life?

But maybe she is just like her mother: of the same flesh and blood, mind and heart.

She reaches out to touch her lover's self-portrait, but he stands behind her, pulls her arm back.

'*Noli me tangere*,' he whispers in her ear.

He lifts up her skirt, knowing she is naked underneath, for she no longer bothers with underwear. One simple movement and he is inside her, its directness taking her breath away. The sirens start to wail, but they do not even hesitate. She feels it would be impossible to part them, not even fear of death can stop them now. It adds to the intensity of their lovemaking, and as they hear the bombs dropping on London, they are exploding on the inside.

JUNE

Virtus, or self-discipline, was the backbone to Roman morality. It had three basic qualities: *gravitas*, which was a sense of responsibility, and a denial of sentiment; *pietas*, which symbolized the duty that a Roman owed to the gods, to his country, to his neighbour, and above all to his family; and *simplicitas*, which was humility, and gave the Roman his or her rationality.

Before I met Robert I was able to study these concepts dispassionately. In my first year in college I made a modest study on the causes of marital breakdown in Rome in the first century AD. To think I thought it was a matter for academics! Without any experience from real life, I argued how the erosion of the *pietas* principle during Augustus's reign caused marital breakdown. I wrote a paper on the decline of marriages as an expression of duty and obedience to the family and the Empire. Once a union was imposed upon young people, and settled by a contract that ignored their wishes, marriage had gradually become based upon mutual consent and lasted only by virtue of the couple's joint desire to keep it in existence.

I agreed with the Stoics. The mind must always be rational, the heart feared. Never, ever fall victim to the desires of the heart. Yet I did – all that time I was secretly dreaming of it, and it took Robert to look at me once, and for me to imagine him marrying me, for my heart to reveal itself as idealistic and naive.

In college I put forward the thesis that one of the major causes of the eventual fall of Rome was its own lack of moral fibre. I wrote about orgies, yet I was a virgin myself. I blush to remember presenting my first paper to my tutor, and how I spoke on the demoralization of marriages, not for one instant understanding what marriage was.

When you are little, you are taught that there is only one way to be in love. This first love is the person you must marry. Min and I played wedding days. We would dress up in our communion dresses and take it in turns to be bride, and bridesmaid. It never seemed to matter that there was no groom. The important thing was to be a wife, to be wanted.

But look what happened to Mother.

I remember my own wedding day and how full of expectation I was. Finally I fitted in. I was a wife. I think back to our honeymoon in Babbacombe. Even in our first week of marriage, did the cracks begin to appear?

One afternoon it stopped raining, and we left the hotel for a walk. I imagined we were like squirrels emerging from hibernation, hungry for air, and food, yet at the same time craving our return to the bedroom, and our love nest beneath the sheets.

As we walked down the front path of our hotel, and out onto the pavement, I felt like a tourist in my own Devon, for now I was seeing things through Robert's eyes. It was a sparkling afternoon. The only dry, sunny spell we were to see in the whole week. A row of hotels faced out towards the cliffs and the sea. They looked grander from the outside than they really were within, with large sash windows, classical columns at the door and tall, whitewashed stone walls. Their front lawns sloped down to the road, cut up by neat gravel paths, manicured and mud-free, despite the rain. Some of the trees were already beginning to blossom, although it was still very cold. Robert breathed in deeply, looking up at the sky, and I followed his gaze, looking at the seagulls circling above them.

'Do you like it here?' I asked anxiously.

'Yes,' he said warmly, taking my hand in his and squeezing it. 'It is so different from home. It is perfect for our honeymoon.'

'And what is home like?' I asked, intrigued to hear Robert's description of his birthplace, something he had never spoken about before.

He hesitated, and I looked at him, but his face remained in profile and he looked across the road, towards the sea.

'We don't have houses like yours, for a start,' he said, and paused, then shook his head. 'Not where I live, that's for sure.'

He began to stride briskly down the street, and I had to almost skip to keep up, my arm swinging against his, and he moved as if he had a purpose, as if we had somewhere in particular to go, although this day each moment was ours to squander as we wished.

'Do you know of a nice place to have tea?' Robert asked me.

'We could go to the tea rooms in the Morningside. Sometimes Father and I would go together after Min was married. When he was feeling well, he liked me to drive him out here. He said he liked the view from Babbacombe. He told me the beach was a place that he and Mother used to bring us to when we were small. It was also an excuse for him to give me a chance to practise driving, for Mother did not like me to use the car.'

'Whyever not? I think it grand and terribly modern for you to be able to drive. I cannot think of one girl at home who can drive a car.'

'I think she believed I should be able to find a husband rich enough to afford me a chauffeur,' I said lightly, and then bit my tongue. How foolish of me to say such a thing. Robert said nothing, only coughed, and I opened my mouth to try to erase what I had said, but found I couldn't think of anything to say. 'Here we are.' I pointed at the Morningside. Its tall white walls gleamed in the sunlight. 'Tea here is just the best,' I added cheerfully.

We had dined every night in our hotel, so it was refreshing to be eating somewhere else. We had scrambled eggs and toast, buttered and hot, followed by scones, jam and clotted cream. The tea was piping hot, and strong. We drank two pots.

'Gosh, I had not realized how hungry I was.' I wolfed a second scone.

'We have been missing meals,' Robert said quietly, and caught my eye. I licked the cream off my lips, and held his gaze. All my girlish gawkiness had disappeared. I stared back at him, unafraid. I was a wife now. I was allowed to look my husband in the eye, with desire. He was looking at me in a way that made me feel like someone else, like Min, or even my mother – beautiful, although I knew I was not.

'Have you had enough tea, Mrs Fanning?' He smiled mischievously. He looked to me like a boy of my age, not a man who was old enough to be my father.

'I think so.' I fingered my gold wedding band and felt my cheeks glow. A swirl of warmth in my belly snaked down to my groin. 'Will we go back to the hotel?'

Robert looked out of the window. 'It's such a beautiful afternoon. Why don't we walk along the promenade on the cliff, get a little sea air.'

'All right then.' I was a little disappointed, but then we had the whole evening, all the night, did we not?

Now it was late afternoon, and there was a rosy glow above the ocean. I gazed at the blue sea lapping gently on the beach, and at it stretching across the Channel, at the low white line of the south coast of England, which eventually petered out, leaving an infinite expanse of deep blue like the sea in Italy, even though it was the

English Channel. The air was cold, but very still. We could hear the waves breaking against the shore, even from up on the cliff. They were swathed in the chill bands of an early English spring, and I believed there was nothing so pure on the face of the earth.

Robert led the way, and we began to wend down the path, towards the beach. The colour of the sea reminded me of Italy – being on Ponza in particular – and I noticed that Babbacombe beach was shaped in a tiny half-moon, not nearly as big as the *Chiaia di Luna*, but still a crescent shape. Closer to the shore the water was a paler blue, where spindly rocks fingered out into the sea. The approach to Babbacombe, however, was completely different from Ponza. Here we were surrounded by downy English shrubs on our descent, and the beach had an utterly homely and familiar feel to it, like the landscape of my childhood, soft and safe.

We walked on the shingle-and-sand beach, sheltered from the wind by a large red sandstone cliff protruding out to sea. We were the only people there, as the light was quickly leaching out of the sky and the temperature was dropping. I shivered.

'Are you cold?' my husband asked me, pulling me closer to him.

'No, I'm fine.'

He planted a kiss on my lips, and we stopped walking for a moment. As he bent down to me, the kiss gradually became longer, more passionate.

I couldn't stop thinking about my Roman Julia. How she fed her soul on being touched, on letting someone – anyone – right inside her. I kissed Robert back with force. I loved him utterly. He was the only man I desired and I wanted him to fill me up, again and again, all of my days, every day. We pulled away reluctantly, and Robert looked into my eyes, as if he was asking me something. He took my hand, and led me along the beach. A breeze came across the waves, lifting my hair off my face and flushing my cheeks.

Robert pulled me with him, around the red rock into a tiny

cove, hidden from the clifftop view. I followed him behind a boulder, and he turned me around by the shoulders so that my back was to the sea and I was facing him, with the cliff behind him. His lips fell onto my skin, kissing my forehead, and my cheeks, and my neck, feverishly. I put my arms around his waist and clung onto him. I imagined I was a limpet and he the rock, wet with passion from the ocean. I closed my eyes and smelt the salt in the air, tasted the tang of it on my tongue, my open mouth, as Robert pushed his lips onto mine. I felt his hands about my waist, and how they gently pushed beneath my skirt, unfastening my stockings, so quickly, and letting them fall about my ankles. A distant voice inside my head whispered, *What if someone sees you? Someone who knows you, your father or your mother?* But no one could, for we were hidden from view, from the whole wide world. I squeezed my eyes fast, afraid of the expression on Robert's face, convincing myself I was half-asleep and we were both in a dream. I held onto him, tighter, tighter, and then I felt his nakedness brush against my thigh, and I quivered with anticipation.

This was different from our wedding night. Different from all the days afterwards in our honeymoon bed. This was like the elements. How I imagined Julia felt when she coupled with another man. He parted my legs with one hand and lifted my skirt with the other, and then quickly pushed inside me. He gave a low moan. 'Open your eyes,' he said in a hoarse voice. My fingers dug into the back of his tweed coat, as he pushed deeper inside me. I lifted my eyelids slowly, but he was not looking at *me*. It was as if his gaze was looking directly through me, as if he could see someone else inside me. It was unnerving. He appeared completely different. The dusky glow in the sea made his skin darker, and his hair had fallen forward and was tousled by the wind, his lips curled, pushed out by his teeth so that they seemed fuller. For one second I thought of Giovanni Calvesi, and it made me feel sick. But then I could feel my husband inside me. I found myself no longer motionless, but pushing back. An emotion overcame me, whereby I wanted to be here forever, locked into Robert, in our primeval motion by the sea. I found myself opening up, tingling sensations beginning to stir, which I had felt once before, but never with Robert. I began to pant, and then just as I had closed my eyes again and was willing to open my mouth and cry out, he stopped. I pushed against him, once, twice, desperately a third time, but he would not move. He had lifted me up against a rock, and now he was leaning against me like a dead weight. In vain I squeezed his waist and squirmed beneath him, but I could feel him slipping away, and now all there was left between my legs was wetness, and his juice, inside me, all over me. I opened my eyes and he was smiling at me, the old Robert again. He smoothed back my hair and kissed my forehead, before bending down and gently pulling each stocking up my leg and attaching it to my belt. He pulled down my skirt and coat, and then stepped back as if he had just been rearranging furniture. Suddenly I felt very cold, and I began to shiver, yet I could not move. Inside I was still throbbing. Did he not see the look on my face? How could he not know? But Robert was doing up his trousers and pulling his coat about him. 'Come on. We've just time to get back and changed for supper.'

I looked at him, astonished, for he made no reference to what we had just done, what we had shared. The intimacy of our lovemaking seemed wasted, like the limp strands of wet seaweed strewn about the rocks beside me. I began walking slowly, he linked my arm and we moved back the way we had come in silence. My heart was clamouring. I felt betrayed — yes, that was how I felt — to be opened up in such a way and then left stranded. But Min had told me this was how it was for a wife.

'Never expect too much,' she had said, the night before I married. I had been so cross with her for saying that, because I had been brimming with expectation, and my sister managed to cast a shadow on my marriage before it had even begun.

'Stay with him in his desire,' Min had said, 'and then you will be satisfied through him. Never seek your own pleasure.'

After my wedding night, I remembered my sister's advice and had stuck to it all week long. I had enjoyed giving my husband such gratification, because he made me feel attractive, and powerful. I was mistress of all his desires. I had not looked for anything else. But now I felt jarred, and irritated. I no longer felt covetable, but abandoned somehow, although my husband held my arm and helped me up the cliff path as if I was his most precious possession. What had got into me?

And if it weren't for the apple trees, I might have behaved or said something to Robert that would have damaged our marriage for-ever. But when I saw the three wild crab-apple trees, just like the little ones in the lane on the way up to Daddy's house, I thought of Father, and Mother, and how lucky I was to have a husband who loved me like Robert. These were old crab-apple trees, very aged and gnarled-looking, and I only noticed them by chance as they were leaning away from the path at crazy angles, as if they were trying to hide themselves behind the other trees. The trees were not in bud yet, but I remembered their small pink flowers, with a scent simi-lar to honeysuckle, as sweet and innocent as a baby's skin. I stopped walking and dropped Robert's hand.

'Oh, look.' I walked towards the three trees and, reaching forwards, I picked one of the leaves. It was small and almost heart-shaped, glossy and mid-green.

'What is it?'

'They're wild crab-apple trees.' I turned to Robert and showed him the perfect leaf stuck to my palm. 'How odd that they should be here, so close to the sea.'

'I've never seen one of these before,' said Robert, stepping back and shoving his hands in his pockets.

'There were some crab-apple trees down the lane, where I grew up. And sometimes we made jelly with them. Oh, look, goodness – I can't believe it – there is one tiny little apple.' I reached up and picked the miniature yellow fruit. 'You can't eat them raw, very bitter.' I spun it between my fingers.

'I wouldn't want to anyway,' Robert replied, beginning to walk away up towards the promenade. 'I can't stand the taste of apples.'

'How odd,' I remarked, almost to myself. 'I can't imagine not liking apples.'

I popped the crab apple in my pocket and skipped after him. He reached back and took my hand. I felt him holding me tight, the reassuring pressure of his fingers against my wedding band. My frustration by the sea was suddenly gone with the breeze, and I looked up at the sky, my eyes following a group of seagulls fending off a buzzard. The clouds were gathering, and I could smell the tang of rain approaching. Our afternoon of sunshine was a brief, bright interlude in a wet March honeymoon. We walked leisurely back towards the hotel. Happiness began to swell in me again, as I felt the joy of being attached to Robert, the pride of being the wife of a proper man, like my sister was. I was no longer a girl. I had fully graduated into womanhood, and I supposed now that the bewilderment and thwarted desire of earlier was part of my lot as a wife, as Min had warned me. I was determined never to let my guard down again.

I believe in symbols. My father told me that apples were always sacred to the pagan love goddesses, and to share an apple with your loved one was to seal that love forever. That day on Babbacombe beach I was glad I had found the wild crab-apple trees because I thought they stood for our marital love, and the endurance of my partnership with Robert. But my husband does not like apples.

Maybe we are meant to love many times, and in many different ways. Maybe we are never meant to marry?

Possibly the early Romans were right. For them, marriage was a contractual tool, which involved no romance whatsoever, but brought about financial, political and reproductive resolutions. I cannot believe that they were a heartless race, but a generation of people who understood more than we do the vagaries of passion, the fickle nature of our hearts, and that sometimes we believe we are in love with someone just because they are there with us, in a particular moment in our lives. We can share it with them, and not be alone. When I think of this, I think of Phelim. I know by the way he looks at me that he can bring me to the edge of love, a place my husband never could.

MIN

June is late. Her train must be delayed. Min had come down the night before with Charles. They had stayed in a small hotel in Brixham. The same one they stayed in at the time of the funeral. Charles was supposed to come to the Mass with her and drive the two sisters home, but this morning he informed her that he had to return to London unexpectedly, for business reasons, and she would have to get the train back with June. Min was secretly relieved, for they had argued all the way down in the car and she couldn't bear another moment of antipathy in his company. Not when she was feeling so very vulnerable. Besides, he seemed particularly irritated by the presence of Lionel, her father's dachshund, which they had to collect when they arrived. Charles kept saying that he had no wish to keep the wretched animal, but Min was determined otherwise.

Min thought about her husband, and how he didn't look so much like a Prince Charming when he was cross with her. His eyes looked tiny, like an angry pig's. His face became tight, his lips a straight narrow line across his face, and his forehead appeared too shallow. The perfection of his face was a veneer. It was his height, and the way he dressed and held himself, that lent him the aspect of a handsome man, but really, up close, he was not so dashing. Min pinched herself. How could she think such horrible things about the man she loved? They had been married just over a year. They should still be enthralled with each other. Yet so much had happened within that year. Min felt she had aged ten.

She wandered through the churchyard, Lionel at her heels. She was early for the Mass, yet had not wanted to hang around in the town. As soon as Charles had left she had risen. With only a cup of tea lining her stomach, she had set out for the church and the graveyard. She was bleeding still. She didn't know when it would stop. It left her feeling empty and emotional, her thoughts in a turmoil. She hoped to gain some peace here in the place where her father was buried.

It was odd the way she had ended up looking after her father, rather than June, for her sister had always been his favourite. But Daddy had not wanted to distract June from her studies, especially since it was her first year at university. It had fallen on Min's shoulders to visit her father in Gloucestershire, at the boys' school where he worked, and make sure he had clean laundry, and not too much drink in his cupboards. At least he dined at the school, for she would have imagined he might have starved to death otherwise. The headmaster and the other teachers were very understanding, for often her father was unable to get out of bed to teach his classes, and they turned a blind eye, for he was such a brilliant scholar he deserved some leniency. But when he began to turn up to classes stinking of whiskey, something had to be done. That was when Min was called upon. Although she was the youngest daughter, the fact that she was a married woman somehow made her more responsible.

Charles had little sympathy for her father. He saw things from her mother's point of view, and when Min tried to get his help, he said her father deserved to lose his job. He said her father was lazy. But at least Daddy wasn't a coward.

Min had begun to suspect Charles was unable to operate

without a woman behind him, to bolster his ego. He was so very touchy, especially when she asked him about the war. From what she could make out, he had not actually experienced any kind of combat at all. It embarrassed her when he dressed in military uniform and talked about the war in company, for she could see he was just an actor playing a part. And yet she knew that her husband adored her, and this was what made him so cross with her, for he believed she could never love him to the same degree. Again and again it would come up, as it had the previous evening.

'I wonder, will your mother be there tomorrow?' he had said, as they drove south into the gathering darkness.

'I hardly think so,' she had replied tightly. 'She didn't come to the funeral, so why would she come to the memorial Mass? Besides, we don't want her there.'

'How do you know June might not want to see her?' He flicked his eyes over in her direction. She did not look back at him, but out of the window of the car, at the sky losing its colour and the trees swaying in the wind.

'Because she feels the same way as me. We both hate Mother.'

'Min, you should forgive her,' Charles said patronizingly. 'You know your father was a difficult man. She must have put up with a lot.'

'Don't tell me what Daddy was like. You, of all people, have no right to tell me how to behave with my mother.'

'She was first and foremost my friend, Min. I have told you so many times how it was only that one time we kissed, and that was because Meryl had died. She comforted me.'

'How very kind of her. But you know, Charles, it is not the usual way in which people comfort each other.'

She had managed to make Charles cross, something she did frequently. 'It does not become you, Min, to speak in such a way about your mother.'

His face hardened as he looked ahead at the road.

'You mean it makes me ugly?' she spat back, stupidly.

'No, but it makes me wonder why you married me. Sometimes I am afraid it was out of revenge, to take me away from your mother.'

His words stung her as if he had slapped her. She had loved him. Of course she had. She had always loved him, since she was thirteen. But the last few days had been painful, and confusing. She had never expected to lose the baby, although she had been very sick for the first seven weeks, unable to keep much food down, and then she had been bleeding sporadically the last week. She had just hoped it would stop, and everything would be normal. But the night before last she had felt strange vibrations within her womb, and then deep, knifing pains in her abdomen. She had not wanted to tell Charles, for she had not wanted to believe it was true, and so she had crept out of bed and sat on the landing as blood began to pour from her, soaking her nightdress and making a stain on the carpet. Charles had found her there at five in the morning, tearful, and not far from hysteria. He had bathed her gently, and had told her it didn't matter, they could try again, as long as she was all right – that was what mattered to him. He even suggested she go to art school, which she had dreamed of doing before they married, and forget about having a family for a few years. They had plenty of time to make babies in the future.

That was two days ago, and now it was as if, to Charles, the miscarriage had never happened. He was the same brusque man he had been before she found out that she was pregnant, and she missed his attention, the way he treated her as if she was something extraprecious while she was pregnant. As the car accelerated, Min determined that she would try to conceive again as soon as possible, even if it was just to regain the gentle devotion of her husband.

Min shivers and wraps her coat tightly about her. Her hat is pulled down low over her forehead, and she is wearing gloves, but still the cold wind bites into her. She looks up at the sky. It is dark, with heavy storm clouds. She guesses it might snow. She walks between the graves, down the gravel path, until she turns a corner behind the church. She stops in her tracks. Standing with her back to her, in front of Father's grave, is her mother. Stylish as always, Min's mother is wearing a rust-coloured cloth coat with a grey fur collar, and a hat to match. In one hand she carries a black suede bag, which matches her shoes, and a pair of fawn gloves. In the other hand she carries a tiny limp bunch of snowdrops. She leans down over the grave and places them on the mound of fresh earth. She then steps back, crosses herself and stands motionless.

Min is paralysed by shock. She has not seen her mother in over a year – September 1933 – when she had stood in Giovanni Calvesi's apartment and neither backed up her mother nor her sister as they fought over her mother's adultery. She couldn't share in June's outrage, and yet she couldn't understand what her mother had done either, for up until that day she had believed they were both in love with the same man. Charles. However, in Milan, Min had realized they had been competing over nothing. Charles was no match for Giovanni Calvesi in her mother's eyes. Everything Min had done had been for nothing. It had made her so angry with her mother that she had been unable to speak.

Min begins to back away slowly, but it is too late. Lionel rushes forward, instantly recognizing his late master's wife and, barking excitedly, he bounds towards her. Her mother turns round and sees her. She waves to her. Reluctantly Min walks towards her mother. How she wishes June were here.

'Minerva.' Her mother embraces her, and then steps back and pats Lionel, crouching down to stroke his face. 'Hello, dear Lionel.' She straightens up and looks into Min's face. 'Where's June?'

'She caught the train. She should be here soon. I came down with Charles last night.'

Her mother looks about her. 'So where is he?'

'He had to go back to London this morning. Urgently.'

'I see.'

There is an awkward silence. Min feels a dull, throbbing pain in her womb again and wonders if she is bleeding more. When will it end? How long does a miscarriage go on for? She feels as if she has been losing tiny little parts of her baby for days, like splinters being torn out of her flesh. So cruel. Lionel sits down at her heels and nuzzles her legs, as if he senses her pain.

'What are you doing here?' she asks her mother suddenly, harshly.

'I came as soon as I could,' her mother says apologetically. 'It takes a long time to get to Devon from Milan. I was sorry to miss the funeral, but you arranged it so quickly. It was impossible for me to get here in time.'

Her mother is different. Her voice is even different, softer and with a lilt, maybe the result of living amongst Italians for nearly six months. Her hair has grown, and is not so sculpted. It cascades from beneath her hat into rich waves upon her shoulders. She has put on a little weight, and the result is that her face looks less pointed and more heart-shaped.

'That is because we didn't want you to come,' Min says slowly and emphatically.

Her mother looks surprised. A deep blush spreads across her cheeks. Min has never seen her mother look so embarrassed.

'But why ever not? I was his wife.'

'And also the reason he is dead.'

'Oh, Min!' her mother gasps, too shocked to say any more. She reaches out and takes Min's hand, but Min pulls it away from her.

'Please go away, Mother. We don't want you here. If June sees you she will be devastated, for you know how much she adored Daddy.'

'Please, Min, you are being unfair . . .'

'No, Mother, you were unfair when you ran off and had an affair with your Italian lover, and then never came home. What did you think would happen to Daddy after you had gone?'

'I never meant . . .' Her mother stutters and then, mustering herself, she says angrily, 'I am not responsible for what happened to your father.'

'Well, as far as June and I are concerned, you are. I hate you. And, I can promise you, so does June.'

Min waits for her mother to slap her. She wants her to, so that they can shout at each other and then make up, like they used to do when she was younger. Always a tug of war between them, but this time her mother doesn't respond. Instead she looks down at the ground, nodding slowly. She says nothing, putting on her gloves, sliding each finger in, one by one. Min's breath streams out of her mouth in heavy puffs, her chest is tight and her head aches. She waits for her mother to volley with her, but without a word Mrs Sinclair turns on her heel and walks briskly away from her. Min is rooted to the spot, stunned, watching her mother's departing figure getting smaller and smaller, walking down the path and out of the church gates. There is a car waiting for her, and she gets into it. Min cannot see who the driver is, but she guesses it is Giovanni Calvesi. How dare she bring him to Devon. The car starts up, breaking the silent air and causing the rooks to take flight out of the yew trees, screeching, under the leaden clouds.

'Mummy,' Min whispers, 'Mummy.'

She feels incredibly faint, as if the life has practically drained out of her. She holds her sides, swaying slightly, and then calls out, 'Mummy!' Her voice joins Lionel's barks, and he leaps in alarm at her distress, and at the raucous crows that swoop about her head, making a cacophony of sound.

It is too late. Her mother is gone, and Min knows she will never see her again.

'I want my mummy!' She sobs like a little girl, putting her hand on her belly, and with a deep ache wishing she could tell her mother about the baby she has just lost.

It begins to snow, and Min stands like a statue in the graveyard, letting the white blizzard swirl about her. It is only when her teeth begin to chatter that she makes her way towards the church. Lionel follows her, and they enter its candlelit haven. It is here that June finds her praying on her knees, with Lionel curled up beside her, five candles lit at the base of the Virgin Mary. How is Min to know each candle is for the life of a baby she will lose? How is Min to know she will never become a mother herself, although she is more deserving than her own mother, more ready to shower her children with unconditional maternal love? For now all she can think is that everything bad happens at once – her father's death, her husband's anger, the miscarriage and her mother's desertion. All she has left is June. She is Min's comrade in pain, her salt-water sister.

JUNE

I have been sick. It started the day I got caught in the rain. The day Phelim told me he was in love with me. Of course, I was so involved in my emotions I forgot about common sense. When I finally got home that night I sat for hours on the doorstep to Robert's cottage, my damp clothes clinging to me, looking out at the moonlight, praying for an answer to my question. What will I do?

I went into the house, sat at the kitchen table, wrote my question down on writing paper to my sister Min. Tell me what to do, I asked her.

I knew what I *should* do. Be the good wife, and never again set foot in the Sheriden house. But Phelim is our neighbour and, when Robert returns home, he will want to call on him now that Claudette is dead. I cannot bear the deceit. Phelim should never have told me he loved me. It was shocking that he said those words to me. He could not have been in his right mind. He was grieving. He was lonely. But then I remembered the look in his eyes, and knew in my heart that I always saw the love, right from the beginning.

Sitting in my wet clothes, I was thrown into turmoil. Looking out the window at the inky night, the still death of it engulfing me, I was in a rage. No one part of me was in harmony. My head was lecturing me, telling me the impossibility of the situation and at the same time scheming, working out a way of sneaking back to his house in the night so that no one would notice. The audacity of it! But I was a woman on fire, my heart in my mouth. I could taste its ferocious desires. I had not felt this way about Robert since that day in Babbacombe on our honeymoon. Now, in Cavan I was consumed by this keen, primal urge just to unite with Phelim Sheriden physically. If only I had been honest with Robert when we first married, maybe we could have talked about our lovemaking. Robert and I could never discuss sex.

What was happening to me? I went into the bedroom and threw off my clothes, watching the shapes that the shadows of my body made on the walls of the room. I was in the heart of my home, like a princess in the tower, like a demon in his lair. I opened the wardrobe door and looked at myself in the mirror. Properly. I had never done this before. I only surveyed my body if I was dressed, never naked. I was surprised at what I saw. The pregnancy had ripened my body, yet I was not fat. Sometimes, when Robert and I had made love, I would catch sight of my bare thighs, or of my breast as he touched it, and they looked monolithic to me, but now as I stood unadorned in front of myself I saw how perfect I actually was. My breasts were full, and had grown, and my stomach was no longer flat, yet my hips were narrow and boyish in dimensions, my arms and legs were narrow and lean.

How pale you are, I whispered to my glimmering reflection and then, without thinking, I touched my breast. The nipple hardened immediately, and I ached between my legs.

Phelim. His name trickled out of my mouth, like a dying word, and I could not take away the image of his face from my mind. He was just one field away from me, in the top of his house, in his studio, painting, loving me. I had never let my hands touch my own body, and now I let them wander, my mind a feverish confusion. I

lay down on the rug in my husband's bedroom and fondled myself.
I was able to take myself to a place my husband had never taken
me. I gasped, cried out and then, just as suddenly, within the very
same instant, I curled up, desperate with shame. But beneath the
feeling of shame still lay my unanswered question. What will I do?

When our hearts and minds are twisted together in a dilemma,
then the body answers for us. And this is what happened to me. The
next morning I woke shivering on the cold rug. I had fallen asleep,
naked, and now I was cold through to the bone. I got up shakily
and pulled on my nightdress, getting weakly into the bed. It must
have been early still, because the sky was dusky outside.

The next time I woke I was so wet I thought for a moment I
was lying in a bath, although we do not have one. I opened my eyes,
yet nothing was clear, my nightdress was stuck to me and I was
drenched in sweat. Fear began to fuel my thoughts. What
was wrong? What about the baby? It must have been late, because
light was pouring into the room. I tried to get out of bed, but my
body would not obey me.

'Oonagh,' I called weakly. As loudly as I could, I called again. But
there was no answer, and I could hear nothing stir in the house. It
was Tuesday, and this was one of Oonagh's days off. I lay in a fever
all day and all night, and not a soul came to the house. At first I
hoped Phelim would call, but of course he would not do such a
thing.

As the fever took hold of my brain, I dreamed about Robert for
the first time. He was in the air in his bomber, gliding above the
cities of Germany, like a Roman god, his metal wings protecting
him, his face serene, full of forgiveness. I lay on my hot, wet bed
and sobbed with terror. I wanted Robert. He was my familiar and
I needed him now. I did not care if he had loved Claudette and was
the father of her child, for he was the father of mine. Was I so sick
that our baby would die? Is this what I had done? Had my lust killed

our child? I was filled with remorse for resenting my pregnancy, because now, more than anything, I didn't want to lose the baby.

The next day Oonagh found me delirious. She had seen her grandfather like this before he had died, and the vision of my raving, flushed face told her how serious it could be. Giving one of her brothers instructions to run into the village as quickly as possible and fetch the doctor, she then stripped me and bathed me in a basin of cool water in front of the stove. Afterwards she led me back into the bedroom and, peeling back crisp, fresh sheets, put me in the bed. Sitting on a stool beside it, she dribbled water on my tongue, for I was unable to keep anything down. I was hardly conscious, a tiny white sylph in my big nightgown. She looked at my ghastly face and fell on her knees and prayed to God, the Virgin Mary, to all the saints she loved, and then she lit a candle, speaking all the while to sprites she had sometimes seen in the woods at night, because maybe their magic was just as strong as the power of God.

Whatever Oonagh did, it worked. Along with her prayers she fed me apple sauce, made from apples she had saved from the harvest, three times a day. I did not want to eat it at first, for I knew they were the apples Robert had grown for Claudette, but eventually I gave in. Each day I felt the apples nourishing me. Now, just one week later, I am strong again. My feverish dilemma over Phelim Sheriden seems like a distant haze, because I know what I should do. I must wait for Robert. I am having his child. It is simple. I chose Robert, and now I have no right to make any other choice.

No, Mother, I will not hear it. You can whisper all you want to in my ear, but I shall cast all those dreams away. We are human beings invested with a conscience, with a sense of our own morality, and we do have duties in this life. I shall not become what you became. I shall not be an adulteress.

THE ADULTERESS VII

He is pure talent. She recognizes it, knows it in her heart and soul. His art will outlive them all. He paints in his own way, wilfully ignoring both tradition and the new movements in art – Cubism, abstraction, Expressionism – which had so excited her when she was at the Slade. She tries to talk to him about the German Expressionists and Kandinsky's *Blue Rider*. Can they not set up some kind of artistic collaboration themselves and make a book of simple woodcut prints? But he has no interest in anyone else's pictures, not even hers. Art is his.

He paints people. Some are ugly, and some are beautiful, but they are never alone. All of his paintings tell stories, and their protagonists are attached to each other, a jumble of limbs, and twisted bodies that manage to create an overall pattern upon the canvas. His dominant tone is brown, and flesh; he paints it as if it is raw meat. His nudes almost repulse her, the way he reduces the body to what it is, blood, skin, bones, muscle and fat.

She has never let him paint her picture, but now he insists. He is leaving soon, being sent to Africa as a war artist. He wants to paint her a picture as a gift. He does not care that she is married, for that fact has never stopped him falling in love with anyone.

She came earlier this day so that they could have more light. Her husband asked her where she was going, and she did not even bother to think of a good excuse.

'To see a friend from the Slade,' she said.

It was the truth.

The last year has been hard. Two miscarriages, the second one at nearly four months. Over the course of her marriage she has lost five babies. Each failure breaks off another part of her heart. It is awfully unfair. She misses the company of her sister, and can't shake the painful memory of her father's dreadful death. Her husband, constantly moaning about his leg, saying how useless he feels, how ashamed he is that he cannot fight in this war. But she knows deep down he is secretly relieved. She knows him so well. He flies into unprovoked rages over the most trivial thing, taking his guilt out upon her.

And then London starts falling apart around them. Her marriage mirrors the battered and blitzed city. The wreck it becomes. The daily dangers should have brought them closer, but they don't. Instead they have driven her into the arms of another man.

If there wasn't a war, maybe she might never have taken a lover. If her husband had gone off to fight, maybe she would have felt bound to be faithful. The first time she slept with her artist she thought: why not? I might be dead tomorrow.

When she travels across London on the Underground train she tries to guess where the next bomb will fall. You never know. After one has fallen, and she has survived yet again, she cannot help feeling this intense sense of liberation, a rush of energy making her want to live life to the full. It is the same feeling she gets when she makes love to her artist. In the Underground station she looks at other people and their eyes are shining too, and she has this sense of togetherness. The whole of London is connected, one living, moving, breathing entity fighting for its life. This is why she feels no guilt as she steps through her lover's door, for this is part of her destiny.

He paints her in her clothes. She is sitting at the window, in a rose-coloured blouse, a garnet necklace that her sister gave her around her neck. Her hair falls into soft dark curls, and he paints her eyes a brighter shade of blue than they really are. It is her neck that takes so much time. He paints it tenderly, as if it is the slender stem of a Michaelmas daisy, his favourite flower, the one that reminds him of his childhood.

It takes one week to paint Min's portrait. Each day they sacrifice their precious few hours together so that he can paint. She watches his hands move across the surface of the canvas, and the expression on his face as he looks at his painting. She hopes one day a man might look at her with such concentration and attention to each moment. She has not painted since the day she left the Slade, unable to silence the censor in her head. What is the point of her painting? She looks with envy at her lover working.

On the last day, the day he leaves, they finish early. He stands, hands on his hips, and lets her see the painting for the first time. She is startled. It is not the way he usually paints. There is a strange light that seeps across the painting, yet she can't figure out from where it comes. It lifts off the smoky Thames, which can be seen in the background view of a window, in front of which she sits. Her blouse blushes against her chest, and it is so tactile that she can sense its silky surface on her fingertips, and yet it is her skin that surprises her. It is like paper, white and translucent, as if he has painted a spirit.

'I look like a ghost,' she says. 'Am I really that pale?'

He holds out his hands, covered in paint, and she takes them.

'Yes,' he replies, kissing her, beginning to unbutton the tiny mother-of-pearl buttons on her blouse.

*

336

He peels his own creation, for he has made her now. He knows this. He has taken her out of the shade and made her stand under the glare of his love. It is a passing emotion. There is nothing permanent in his world apart from the canvases he paints. He does not own Min. No one does now. Not even herself.

They do not bother to draw the blinds. He imagines their silhouettes projected across the cityscape, as he stands behind her and cups her into him.

Soon it will be blackout and they will have to turn out the lights.

JUNE

Mummy was wrong. Minerva is not the Goddess of War. She thought she was, because she was born clad in armour, but that merely signifies that her virtue and purity are unassailable. Minerva never fought for its own sake. She only took arms to protect the innocent and deserving against tyrannical oppression. In the same way, my sister Min protected me from my mother, although I was the elder.

Minerva was never a rash goddess. She is as wise as her father, Jupiter, and she presides over learning, and all the arts, but most importantly she is patroness of those feminine crafts of spinning, sewing and weaving. Did my sister possess some of the qualities of her ancient namesake?

My mind flashes back to summers we spent in Devon. For hours my sister sat in the harbour in Brixham, watching the women making the fishing nets for their husbands. When we got home Min could not help but pull apart old woolly jumpers and weave them into loose nets. Then we would wear them on our heads and, standing on the beds, with wooden spoons in our hands and a saucepan lid each as a shield, we would imagine ourselves Greek goddesses, tiny Athenes. Bounding between the beds we re-enacted Olympian adventures.

Daddy said to me, 'The world of the Ancients will never be dead.'

He showed me pictures of the ancient buildings in Greece: the Parthenon, and Athene's palace, and the Colosseum in Rome. Picture after picture of the time when he visited Pompeii. The amphitheatre, the forum, the Temple of Isis. Just looking at the perfect symmetry of these structures made me feel calm inside, as if all was in order. Daddy was like the Classics, impermeable through the flood of time, although his wife was a harpy.

I heard Daddy call Mother that. Once.

Have you ever felt the pull of another century? Did you ever consider you might have been born into the wrong age? When I was a girl, I was convinced I was living in the wrong era. I was sure I had fallen into the wrong period. I shirked everything modern. When I was tiny, I thought clothes were stupid and ridiculous. I was forever trying to take mine off, much to Mother's annoyance. The Hebrews wore too many clothes, as did the Christians, but the Romans and Egyptians ran around naked. As a small child, it made a lot of sense to me.

When I was older, my sister and I found our secret little cove, where no one could see us or find us, and this is where we danced, emboldened by symphonic crescendos from the foaming sea. We shed our layers, until we were both naked. The challenge was to stop dancing then. To stand facing into the sea, on our pointy toes, held up by the wind, and let it wash over us. Liberation.

Are we our mother's daughters?

How can we know? Mother never let us near her when we were little. She was rejected by her own mother. She was never loved as a little girl, and so how could she know how to love us? The only time I remember her touching me was to correct me – pull my clothes straight, do up a ribbon, brush my hair and scrub my soapy scalp in the bath. But surely there were other times when she caressed?

I believe Daddy loved Mummy, but she never loved him. She

could not sit still. Like a moth around a light she fluttered about him, criticizing everything he said and did until he spoke less and less, until you would see his sorrowful look of compassion turn cold and redden into rage. She forced him to take to the bed to hide from her. It was her fault he could not get up out of it. When she left him for Giovanni Calvesi, he finally knew for sure that she could not love him, and so he took to drink for comfort. And soon alcohol usurped her place in his heart. Isn't this what happened? Don't you think it was my mother's fault?

Yet if my father had loved Mother, don't you think he should have fought for her? What do you think, Nicholas Healy? Could a man like my father forgive an adulteress?

Daddy had us, his daughters, but he forgot about our love. Yes, the love of your child is a lot, but it is still not enough. You can have a hundred children, all loving you, all needing you, and still feel terribly alone.

I sit in your damp house in Cavan (it is still damp despite all your renovations) looking out at a dead day, so grey it seems the sun never got up. I think about Mummy for once. How must it have been for her when we were away at school? Those silent autumnal evenings in the house in Torquay, with Father in the study for hours, reading and drinking, or else taken to the bed, and no one to talk to, nothing to do. She never had a career, and now she was no longer needed as a mother. So what was she to do? Just fall away each year like a leaf off a tree, just hibernate inside their crumbling old house and wait for summer to come again, or would she choose to ride out into the unknown? We both know the answer.

I close my eyes, and back to my youth I go again. Oh, sweet, sweet memories of my sister and I, blissful in our innocence and companionship. I remember the rocks in Bude. It is the first day of the summer holidays, and I drive Min and I across Devon. We park the car in Bude and climb the hill overlooking the cove. We lie on

our backs in the long grass. We can see the curvature of the earth
as we lie there. The dome of the sky above our heads, like a blue
hood protecting us. As I lie and doze, my sister must have sat up
again, because when I awoke she was painting in her little black
sketchbook, using her tiny set of watercolours that Father had
given her for her birthday.

'See,' she said, handing me the sketchbook.

I looked down at the small watercolour. Min had painted two
boulders, which glistened at the edge of the cove, right beneath the
pink sunset. Both were donkey-grey and smooth, as if they were
the backs of whales. They had similar shapes – two perfect ovals –
yet one was twice the size of the other. The small stone was riding
on the back of the large one. Underneath the rocks Min had written 'Mother and Child'. We looked at each other. In a pinprick of
recognition, we both knew we felt envious of the small boulder. To
be carried on the back of its mother was a comfort we had never
known.

THE ADULTERESS VIII

She doesn't go straight home. It was so hard to leave, knowing it would be the last time they kissed until when? Possibly forever. Her throat is dry and sore at the thought she might never see her artist again, this man who treasures her in a way her husband never seems to. He told her he was infatuated with her. He dreams paintings of her. She is his muse.

She cannot cry. Even at the last, as she walks down his rickety stairs, all the way to the bottom, and can feel his eyes on her back, she doesn't break down. Her lips move in a wordless prayer, some magic cast from within her to protect him. He will not die because he is not a soldier. He is merely a war artist, an observer rather than a participant in the violence that will surround him.

'Is this the end of our affair?' she asked him, finally, as she put her coat back on, adjusted her hat. She tried to sound coquettish, carefree, but he saw through that.

'Dear Minerva,' he said kindly, taking her gloved hands into his. 'I will always love you.'

She holds these words proudly to her chest. She has to clutch them, grasp them, although she is not sure whether she believes them, because hadn't she said the same thing to Charles the day they got married?

The tears are caught in her throat, like small, perfectly round stones, and her face gleams with a false brightness. She walks the charred streets of London, through ruined squares full of detritus, sudden yawning chasms of light where buildings once stood, and fragments of glass littered on the pavement like particles of ice. She imagines she is no longer in this wasteland, but somewhere else, a city at the height of its power, full of life, and heaving with every exotic sight, sound and aroma from the four corners of its empire. She closes her eyes, hears birdsong again, the laughter of children, and voices of other women who live freely like her.

She walks into the city, all the way to Euston, and then down Gower Street, straight and narrow as a Roman road. She goes to the pictures, barely taking in the film at all, but crying in the dark, blinded by tears and heartbreak.

Afterwards she sits in a small tea shop and drinks tea. She wishes June were there, remembering the huge teas they shared in Lyons' Corner House, competing over who managed to pile the most cream onto her scone. And it is in this moment of remembering her old self, with her better half, June, that she decides she can no longer live her deception. Once she had asked her sister whether she should leave Charles. She had followed June's advice that day, but now she realizes her sister had been wrong. She will return home and confess all to Charles, tell him everything. It is the decent thing to do. He is a good man and he deserves better. They will divorce, and after the war maybe she and her artist could go to America and start a new life.

Min stops dead in the street, startled by the sudden knowledge that her mother had been a better woman than her, for she had not deceived her husband as Min had, but had left him swiftly, as soon as she had met Giovanni Calvesi. But what about all the other men, before her Italian lover: had she not played adulteress with them? She longs for her mother to explain to her the vagaries of the human heart.

By the time Min arrives at the Underground station at Russell Square it is already dark, and people are beginning to gather on the platform with blankets and pillows for the night. She pictures Charles sitting in his armchair at home, glass of black-market whiskey in one hand, his walking stick by his side. He doesn't need it, but he has taken to bringing it with him when they go out. Although he never admits it, she knows he is embarrassed that he looks able-bodied and yet is not in uniform. There he is. Charles staring into the fire, at the hot embers, cursing his invalidity, never seeing her, never listening.

She turns the final corner and walks the familiar steps to her front door. It is a dark, moonless night, and the wind rustles through the ash tree in the front garden. It makes her shiver, although it is not cold.

All the lights are on. This is the first thing she notices. Charles is so particular about keeping the house as dark as possible, as if this might save it from the bombs. But tonight the blackout curtains are not drawn. She opens the door, still missing the welcoming sound of Lionel's barks, although he has been gone over three months now. Ever since the bombing started the animal had been terrified, shaking and whimpering in fear every night. She lost him during one of the first raids. She had been standing at the back door, watching the fireworks from the bombing down at the docks one night, and he had flown through her legs and out the back, across the garden and into the hedge. She had called and searched for hour upon hour, ignoring the sirens herself, but to no avail. Lionel had simply disappeared. It had upset her terribly, as much as one of the miscarriages.

Min hurries into the front room, her body suddenly tense with apprehension. The grate is still full of ashes from last night's fire, and up on the mantelpiece, instead of their wedding photograph, is the painting. She screams in shock as she stares at her portrait, the image even more ethereal and ghostlike than it had been a few hours ago in her artist's studio. The bright electric light in the room creates a glare off the still-wet paint, so that the pink blouse now looks gaudy, and her hair is as black as a witch's.

Min runs up the stairs, two at a time.

'Charles!' Her voice has the same urgency as the siren.

In the bathroom, her domain of lost babies, she finds him. She drops on her knees in front of her husband, the breath knocked out of her. She reaches up and touches his bare foot. It is still warm.

The art of death can be as beautiful as the art of love. The doorway creates a frame around the central composition of a woman dressed in a rose-coloured blouse and grey woollen skirt, blood-red glove in one hand, the other discarded on the black-and-white floor, kneeling before the surrendered body of her husband. A Renaissance Deposition.

JUNE

Two letters arrive this morning. Sean Tobin brings them from the village, the tip of his nose blue, puffing out steam from his mouth, unable to look me in the eye as he hands them to me.

It is a foggy morning, a clean white frost layering each wizened leaf, ringing the lawn, pure and perfect. You could almost think you were in a heavenly place.

I go back into the house, and Oonagh stands at the stove, motionless, looking at me. I sit down at the table holding the two envelopes between my trembling hands. One is a letter from Robert, and one is an official envelope.

'Oh, Oonagh,' I whisper hoarsely.

'Open it,' she says emphatically. 'Just open it, June.'

I know which one she means.

And this is how it begins: *We regret to inform you . . .*

Robert's plane was shot down somewhere over France. He is missing in action, along with the rest of his crew. That is all they know. There is so little information in the letter. I want to know where in France. I want to know did they bail out in time? I want to know who was with him, what he said, was he very, very afraid? I want to know did he save the others first, is he a hero? I begin to shake. Oonagh quickly hands me a cup of tea. It is strong for once,

346

hot and sweet, and although it scalds the inside of my mouth, it brings me back to life, a little.

'He is missing in action,' I say to her, fingering the other letter between my hands. 'His plane was shot down over France.'

'So he could be all right?' she asks hopefully.

'I suppose.'

I look away from her face, and her expression of optimism. I cannot bear it. I stare out of the window at the orchard, the fog still heavy and dense, and feel a dreadful sense of fate. Have I brought this on myself? Is this my punishment for not loving my husband enough?

I put the other letter down on the table and get up.

'Are you not opening Robert's letter?' Oonagh stands guard over it at the table.

I walk to the door and take my coat off the peg. 'I can't, Oonagh,' I say, my voice trembling. 'I couldn't bear to, not at the moment.'

'Of course.' She nods her head sympathetically. How can I tell her it is the lack of emotion in Robert's letter that will break my heart. It will be what he doesn't say, rather than what he does. I do not think I could stand to read another short, bald page on what they were eating and the dances he had been going to, not now I know they are possibly the last words he wrote to me.

'Where are you going?' Oonagh asks nervously, watching me put on Robert's old coat.

'I need to go for a walk.' I turn around, shoving my hands into the pockets.

She looks at me, and I can see her concern, and it surprises me how close we have become, although we have only known each other a few months.

'Don't worry, I think Robert will be fine,' I say slowly, to convince myself as well as her. 'I can feel it.'

But I can't, not really, and there is a howling face inside my belly, and I know I have to get outside, just breathe in the stiff, tart air of the frozen woods.

I go to Robert's orchard first. His field of dreams, and I touch each apple tree one by one.

'Tell me,' I whisper, 'is he alive?'

But the orchard is dying. Most of the trees are bare, looking older than their years, twisted as if they would wish to crawl back into the earth. The fog refuses to rise and draws me into its void. I pick one lost apple off the ground, ringed in frost, and put it in my pocket. I open the gate and enter the woods.

Another wife might go to church, light a candle, get down on her knees and pray. But I have never believed much in God. I was reared to follow the Catholic religion, and was always aware of being different from most people in England. I was proud we were not like the others. But our religion made our sins bigger, and although I went through the motions, I felt I had never had a conversation with the Christian God. When I began to study the Roman gods and goddesses, then I could begin to understand divinity. My awe of the ocean as a child was veneration for Neptune, and so nature was the means by which my spirit could be inspired, and the answer to my prayers.

I go to my little valley in the woods, what Oonagh calls a fairy ring. She says there are nymphs that live in the woods, tiny celestial beings. I prefer to think the magic one feels are the tree-souls themselves.

I sit on a fallen tree, shivering with cold and shock, holding my sides, my eyes squeezed tight. I try to summon a picture of Robert in my mind's eye. Wouldn't I just know if he is dead or alive? Wouldn't I feel it? I have never wished so hard for my sister Min to be there with me, holding my hand, and comforting me. I believe I have never felt so completely alone in my whole life. I put

my hand on my stomach. Inside me is a part of Robert. I gulp, terrified, for if I cry I might never be able to stop. Instead I open my
eyes, focus on the intricate lacings of cobwebs, bejewelled with
dew. Such spinning takes my breath away, the beauty of it, and
nowhere a spider to be seen. I think about Arachne's weaving con-
test with Minerva, and how this mortal hanged herself in shame at
challenging a goddess. Minerva brought her back to life and made
her a spider, spinning for all eternity. I think our lives are like
spider's webs — each lifetime we experience one more loop. Could
we scamper along the sticky thread and move between the ages? I
touch the fragile net, for here I am at one point on the web, and if
I touch it over the other side, here I am nearly two thousand years
earlier. Sometimes I think we live our future lives first, only to
return to the past.

A twig snaps, and for one ridiculous moment I think it is my
sister Min, come at last. I turn round and Phelim Sheriden is standing before me. I start, looking at the vision of him above me, his
red hair vivid against the white sky, as if the sun is beginning to
break through the fog.

'June,' he says softly, 'I heard.' He sits down next to me on the
tree.

'I thought you were joining up,' I say flatly, looking away.

'You asked me not to.'

I turn on him angrily. 'I am a married woman, what in God's
name do you think you are doing?'

He takes my gloved hand, but I pull it away.

'I know what it's like,' he says gently.

I look at him, comprehending. He is thinking of Claudette, but
it is not the same thing.

'Robert is not dead!' I stand up and shout at him, immediately
afterwards bursting into tears. It should be Phelim who is crying,
I keep thinking, but his face is serene and his eyes are the colour of

liquid mercury as he steps forward, puts his arms around me. I cannot pull away.

'June,' he whispers into my hair, 'I never thought I would be able to love again.'

I am almost unable to stand, and he leads me by the arm, through the woods towards his house. We live either side of the trees. This is our common ground of discovery. This is our mutual way through. It is nature that connects us.

I am sobbing, and he holds me gently, yet firmly, whispering that everything will be fine. He says he will take care of me, and the baby.

We walk as the fog shrouds our steps, sucks us into its obscurity. I am invisible as we walk up the stone steps to his house and enter its dark haven. He brings me upstairs to his studio.

'It's the only warm room,' he whispers.

Inside everything glows. I look outside the window at the blank white world, while in here the fire crackles and flickers merrily. Phelim is in the middle of working on a painting, a large canvas, full of soft organic shapes, orange, red and gold melding into a decorative icon.

'It's beautiful,' I say, attempting to dry my face with a damp handkerchief.

'It is about you.'

I understand the picture instantly, how he sees my glory as a woman and lets it shine through the undulating curves of his composition. I am shaken by this picture, stunned that a man could want to paint me, could love me so.

I sit down on a small sofa by the fire while Phelim takes out a bottle from behind some books.

'I think you need something stronger than tea.'

He hands me a glass of clear liquid.

'What is it?'

'Poitín. It's strong, but it will do the trick.'

I knock it back, cough and splutter. He smiles at me. 'Are you all right now?'

'Yes,' I say, sniffing and blowing my nose.

'You are in shock,' he sighs. 'It has been a terrible day. Did you hear about Pearl Harbor?'

I shake my head, and he tells me about the Japanese attack on the American warships in Hawaii. It is a horrendous catastrophe, and yet I feel removed from what he is telling me, all the time thinking about Robert and wondering whether I will ever see him again.

'Do you think I should have hope?' I suddenly ask Phelim. 'Or would that be foolish . . . should I expect the worst?' I stutter.

Phelim considers my question. 'You must always have hope, June, for I do believe in the power of prayers. It can make the difference for Robert, between life and death. Claudette's prayers have been answered. Although too late, too late.'

I raise my eyebrows, take another sip of the poitín, which second time around doesn't taste so bad.

'I have heard from Danielle,' he says, smiling.

'Oh, Phelim, that's wonderful.'

'They are in England, safe and sound.'

I get up and hug him. He squeezes me tightly, 'I am so happy for you,' I say into his shoulder, yet shaking at the thought I might soon meet Robert's child. Will I see him in her face? I wonder if she looks like him. I wonder should I confide in Phelim, but it is a fact I want no one to know, not even him.

'I have not told her about Claudette,' he says, pulling back. 'I think it will be better if I tell her when I see her face to face.'

We stand like this, looking at each other, neither of us knowing what to say. Phelim breaks the silence.

'Well then, will I walk you home?'

I shake my head. I cannot bear to go back to the cottage and read Robert's letter. I dread it.

'Not yet. Can I just sit here for a while and watch you paint?'

He looks pleased. 'Of course.'

He throws more peat on the fire and then puts a record on the gramophone. Piano music fills the room. I recognize it as Chopin and I slip my shoes off, tucking my feet up under my legs on the sofa. Phelim takes off his jacket and sits on a stool in front of the painting, staring at it for a long time. I watch him, and at first he keeps looking at me out of the corner of his eye, nervously, but as he begins to paint I sense he forgets I am there. He is lost in the total absorption of his creation. It comforts me, to sit wrapped up in a rug by his fire, like a little girl, depleted of tears, unable to cry any more, and surrendered, just letting be.

I fall asleep, for when I wake later the room is dark and I am being carried out of it, down the stairs, along a dark corridor and into another unlit room. Phelim lays me on the bed, gently. I open my eyes to see the back of him walking out of the room.

'Phelim!'

He turns around, his hand resting on the door knob. 'You slept all day. I told Oonagh you should stay here.'

I nod, and he opens the door. A shaft of light spills in from the landing. I feel dizzy, as if I am drifting towards the light, although I am still lying on the bed, fully clothed.

'Phelim.' I reach out with my arms, as if I am welcoming an old friend.

He walks towards me, with no hesitation, and folds me into his arms. I do not know who begins first, but suddenly we are kissing each other, and it is so tender, and sweet. The touch of his lips on mine sends a shudder through my being. He lies down next to me on the bed and holds me in his arms. We kiss some more, and then we get under the covers. Slowly we take our outer clothing off so that we are just in our underwear. I am shaking with fear and desire.

'It's all right, June,' Phelim whispers. 'You can sleep. I will hold you.'

I lie in Phelim Sheriden's arms and I have never felt so safe in my whole life. I begin to relax, knowing that this love is beyond anything physical. He kisses the back of my neck as I drift off to sleep. The last thing I see before I close my eyes are the curtains in his room. They are deep crimson, the same colour as Min's Jezebel dress, the same colour as her mistress gloves.

MIN

Min crawls out of the bathroom, no tears and no hysterics. Her body propels her down the stairs, and she stands in the hallway, her heart pounding, her head swirling in fear.

How did Charles get the painting?

This is all she can think of, her lover.

She runs back out of the house, leaving all the lights blazing. She doesn't care if the house is bombed, for she never wants to go back. She runs coatless, down the empty streets, her shoes clattering, her whole being shivering with shock, or is it the cold? She runs all the way to her lover's house. By the time she gets there her blouse is drenched in sweat and her legs are as heavy as lead. She stops outside, looks up. The building is completely in darkness.

Up the stairs, something she does every day, had done only this morning, but now they seem to be the staircase into the sky. Why does his studio have to be on the top floor? She pounds on his door. But no one answers. She calls his name, all discretion pointless now. But still the door does not open. She tries the handle and, to her surprise, the door is unlocked.

The room is empty. For a moment she thinks she is in the wrong house, but then she sees the things he has left behind. The marks of paint on the table, a pair of brown lace-up shoes under the bed and the Michaelmas daisies she had brought him that morning in a glass on the table by the bed. She calls him again, but she knows it is useless.

She sits down on the bed, stripped now of its clothes, and looks at the stains on the mattress. Were they the marks of their love? She takes off her red gloves and holds them tightly in her hands. She walks the circumference of the room, fingering everything she always pictured in her head, when she was at home in bed with Charles, reliving making love to her lover, while her husband held her in his arms.

She looks with wide eyes at the debris of her affair, and the wave of her lost love hits her, but it is not for her artist — the man who transformed her and made her feel beautiful — but for her husband, the man who did not need to change her.

What have I done? she whispers in horror to a crack in the wall.

Her adultery has killed her husband. Like her mother killed her father.

Daddy had been drunk, and shot himself with one of his shooting guns. Officially it was an accident. But Min knew otherwise. She had been with Daddy the night before it happened. He had been out of control, raving, fuelled by whiskey rage. He was yelling that he was a failure, and this was the reason why their mother had left him. He kept saying it again and again. It was his fault. Min had tried to reassure him, tell him it was Mummy who let him down, but it had been useless. Only their mother could have saved him. Min had stayed the night, she had been so concerned, and she remembered now that Charles had offered to come down and stay with her, although he didn't like her father. But she had refused. And while she slept in the tiny spare bedroom of her father's house, he had stumbled out into the woods, behind the playing fields, and shot himself. He was found, with Lionel by his side howling, by a sixth-year the next morning on his way to rugby practice. Min would never forget the shame, the humiliation and the guilt of that dreadful day. All along she blamed her mother.

Min walks out of the artist's room, leaving the door wide open, for what is the point of shutting it? He is never coming back. She knows this. What has passed between her husband and her lover she will never find out; all she does know is that her husband is dead, and her lover alive, and if she had to choose she would wish it the other way round.

She steps out into the street, and it feels like a tomb. She looks up into the sky, its utter void, and then closes her eyes and searches deep inside herself.

I can cry now. And even before she thinks it, she can feel the tears cascading down her cheeks and her gulping, raw pain, the heavy weight of shame, dragging her down into a cave where all she wants is to sleep and never wake up again.

She sees the searchlights crossing in front of her, like an X branded in her mind, and then the sirens begin to wail. She drags her heels slowly down the street, as a few stragglers run towards her. A warden grabs her arm.

'The station's this way, love.' He tries to drag her with him, but Min shakes her head, refusing to move.

'I want to walk out of this city,' she says to him. 'I want to sail down the river. I want to go home.'

He looks at her as if she is crazy. 'Suit yerself.'

The warden lets go of her arm and runs on. There are others who want to be saved. He has no time to coax this odd white-faced woman. Min walks steadily away from him, putting on the blood-red gloves her mother gave her, finger by finger, pushing each one in, so that she feels ready for action.

The scene is set. The night sky is illuminated by white search-lights, and artillery. The planes are coming, and the sound of them mirrors the sound in her head, the tension of her heart and mind.

The bombs drop, and fires spring like holy wells out of the smashed buildings. Min walks towards them. She has no choice, because they are on her way home.

'Fire and water,' she whispers.

JUNE

Dear Nicholas, I talked to you not because you were lonely too, or because you play the piano, but because you remind me of him, and when I first saw you in my attic my heart gave a little jump and I thought at last he has returned. But you live in a different world. Maybe you are my loved one in the future and you will come back to the past one day, come back to me, and then there could be a happy ending to my story. We should choose whom we love the most, whether it be our husband or our lover. It should be that simple. But how do you know? And what if you love them both the same? It is only hindsight that helps us see.

My sister Min, an adulteress, walked into the fires of London in 1941 and was never seen again. Her adultery killed her husband and her. My mother, an adulteress, lived a long and happy life with her lover, Giovanni Calvesi. After the war she moved back to Italy with Giovanni and a newborn baby. She wrote to me often, but I never saw her again. And what about me? I will show you a scene from the past, a point on the cobweb of my destiny, a fantasy scene that I pray will become real. Here, in my lonely haunting, I return to it again and again like one of my favourite old movies. I wish for it so hard that it could be the truth.

See a large oak tree in the garden, standing majestically all on its own, its wizened branches twisted and gnarled, but nevertheless it reaches up towards the blue sky, in hope. Despite its great age it is still strong, and since he doesn't wish to disturb the other fruit-laden trees, this is where my husband has hung a swing for the children. They are too small to use it properly yet. The baby is only a few months, one just three, and the eldest a tiny five-year-old, but she likes to be put upon it, along with her sister. I think they enjoy the sense of suspension in the air, their feet dangling above the ground, so that they are somehow free from what binds them to the world.

Push! they command me, but I only rock them back and forth, gripping the rough rope, letting it chafe my palms.

After the children have gone to bed, I come out to the swing on my own. It is still light, but there is a slight chill in the air, telling me August is nearly over and soon it will be autumn, soon the apples will be ready to pick. I sit on the swing for a moment and let my heels drag back and forth on the mossy ground. Perfect red-apple hearts and pale green pears hang in the canopies of our fruit trees. I breathe in and push off, kicking my legs out straight, then bending them as I swing backwards, out and in, out and in, higher and higher I climb. I let my cardigan flap open and push my face forward, adoring the exhilaration of my ascent. Each time I think I will reach the clouds with the tips of my feet as they scamper across the lowering sun.

Over the wall of our garden I can see the dark treetops of the wood, and the roof of the other house. It is in an even worse state since last winter's storms. I remember how it looked in February, when the snow was so high it went up to the tips of the telegraph poles in town, and that house looked like a hoary old wreck abandoned in a blanket of pristine pure-white. I shiver. How cold it must be, wrapped in its abandonment.

Thinking of the snow reminds me of the frozen lake, so thick with ice that everybody went skating on it. It makes me laugh to remember Patrick Tuite twirling Oonagh on the ice in their black boots, her legs skidding out beneath her, clinging onto him as they fall backwards in slow motion, but looking radiant nonetheless, in the arms of her new husband.

I hadn't been able to go on the ice because of the baby, so my husband drove me across it. It had been a strange sensation, like pushing out to sea in a boat, and yet we weren't carried by water, but floating on its solid counterpart. There was an incredible sense of stillness, of peace, as we slid across the vast expanse of shimmering ice. It had been a sunny day, a low winter sun, bouncing off the frozen lake, almost blinding us, but still so icy cold that there was no thaw. It was a celestial moment, our black car frosted and silvery, slowly and steadily entering chalky oblivion. We were all quiet in the car, even the children awed and held back, our breath puffing the air, so that I could not help thinking of all the loved souls I have lost.

I relax my body, drop my head forward and let the swing rock back down to earth. I look at the skeleton leaves, snapped twigs, broken cobwebs and little black beetles below me, and close my eyes. I summon a tiny part of my sister Min. It is the space behind her earlobe, on her neck, and I press my lips against it. For although she has been dead over six years now, I can still smell her just the same, and touch her as she was. And the sensation of her presence beside me inflames my heart, and makes me grateful that I can still hold the pain that makes love. Is it Min who has brought all these fluttering little girl souls into my womb?

A gentle breeze lifts the hair off my forehead and I open my eyes, knowing she is gone. I rock softly back and forth, thinking about my husband's touch, how we still desire each other.

I look across at the tall grey house and think, not for the first time: this is my home.

Phelim comes out of the door, holding the baby in his arms. 'She's hungry,' he calls.

NICHOLAS

Nicholas is up in the attic clearing a space for Charlie. His wife has gone back to Sandycove to begin packing up. They cannot believe it sold so fast. Now they have the money to hire people to restore the cottage properly, and enough left over for a second honeymoon. Maybe they will go back to Hawaii?

He can feel the fluttering presence of June beside him. He wonders if Charlie will sense her, and knows that of course she will. In fact he is quite sure she will embrace the phantom, make her part of her, the way she is able to with most people. No one wants to let Charlie go.

'Thank you, June Fanning,' Nicholas says because he feels that somehow the ghost helped him get back his wife. How different he feels now that his months of exile are over. Everything looks new to him. The house is full of possibilities rather than being a daunting task, and the land around him is all theirs to do whatever they want with it. They can grow vegetables. Charlie wants to get chickens and more animals, abandoned dogs and cats, even a horse. They can create somewhere so private, hidden away from the rest of the world. He cannot wait to see Charlie again, and make love to her under the rustling eaves of the attic.

I have only one regret.

Nicholas feels as if he is being tugged to the other side of the attic, over by the chimney breast. Instinctively he bends down and puts his hand behind the brick, his fingers touching something hard. He stretches his hand in and manages to pull something out. It is a dusty old notebook with a red cover. He opens it and a letter flutters out. He picks it up. It is addressed to June Fanning. Nicholas's heart begins to beat faster. He opens the notebook. Inside the front cover, handwritten in black ink, are the words: *The Secret Loves of Julia Caesar by J. C. FANNING.*

Nicholas sits back on the floor and stretches his legs out. He flicks through page after page of sloping black writing. It seems to be the story of a Roman princess called Julia Caesar. He goes back to the front and reads the first page.

Note from the Author

Julia II, daughter of Octavius Caesar, the Emperor Augustus, and wife of Tiberius, was exiled to an island for life for committing adultery.

This is her story through my eyes. I ask for your forbearance in regards to the historical accuracies of the book. I started along the road of a serious academic study of the life of Julia, but found that I wandered into fictional territory. In the end I gave in to my flights of fancy. This is mere frivolity compared to the measured studies on the history of the period. It is something I have conjured from my imagination, based in small part on fact. Yet Julia has provided me with hours of company and helped heal my heart. I hope this little book may do the same for you.

June Fanning, Cavan, 1947

Nicholas wonders: did June Fanning ever show anyone this book? Was it ever published? Or had it been hidden here in the attic ever since she had finished writing it, unseen by anyone until this day? He can't wait to show it to Charlie. It might inspire a whole series of work for her. Already she has been painting the apples left on the orchard floor. Close-up studies of red, gold and green orbs that were so much more than just apples, their skin so tactile you could almost bite into them. And she was drawing the trees, too. Charcoal studies that were desolate and poignant, making his heart churn with the memory of how sad he had been when he first came to Cavan.

He puts the book down on the floor, deciding he will read it together with his wife. *The Secret Loves of Julia Caesar.* This is a story they should share in bed at night. Suddenly Nicholas remembers the letter. He picks it up off the floor. The handwriting on the front is faded to light brown and the postmark is 1941. He turns it over. The letter has never been opened. Should he read it? He gets up and walks to the window, looks out at the blighted orchard. It is a grey day, the sun never making it into the sky, and banks of clouds press down on the broken trees. He sees a little white-haired lady wearing an orange hat riding her bicycle down the lane into his yard. It is Oonagh Tuite.

'Good day to you!' Oonagh says cheerfully as she parks her bicycle by the side of Nicholas's shed. He steps out of the door hesitantly. Has she come here to berate him for breaking up her granddaughter's marriage and then rejecting her?

'Hello, how are you?'

'I'm grand, young man,' she says clapping together her bare hands, which look slightly blue and cold.

'Would you like some tea?'

'Well, I only came to see the orchard. I heard what that ignorant man did, and I wanted to see it for myself.'

Nicholas takes her by the arm and leads her to the orchard. The old woman tuts and shakes her head as they walk around it. She seems lost for words. Finally she speaks.

'I wish I had a shotgun. I'd shoot the head off him.'

Nicholas can't help but laugh at the image of little old Oonagh Tuite chasing Ray Mulraney with a shotgun.

'I'd like to see that!'

She laughs as well.

'So,' the old lady says as she settles herself at the kitchen table. 'How are you?'

'I'm well, thank you.' Nicholas pours hot water from the kettle into the teapot.

Oonagh fixes Nicholas with her eyes. He feels them boring into him and cannot help colouring a little.

'Did you hear about Geraldine?'

Nicholas feels dread rising up from his belly. 'No.'

'She's left.'

'What?'

'Yes. Sold the house and headed off to London with Grainne.'

Nicholas feels a wave of relief. At least he won't have to bump into Geraldine in the shops every week and feel guilty and awkward.

'She says it was all down to you.'

Nicholas looks at Oonagh and he is surprised to see she is beaming. 'Me?'

'Yes. She is studying music, Nicholas. She has gone back to college. Well now, isn't that just grand? I shall miss her of course, and the wee girl, but I have to say I am delighted she has finally got rid of that awful husband. My girl would be so glad about that.'

A tear trails down Oonagh's cheek and she takes out a handkerchief.

'It was terrible to see the way that man treated my daughter's child. The number of times I wanted to box him, but Paddy told me I shouldn't interfere in someone else's marriage, even if it was my granddaughter. I couldn't help remembering poor June, and how I wished I hadn't said what I did to her all those years ago.'

'What did happen to June Fanning, Oonagh?' Nicholas asks, pouring the tea and sitting down. 'Why do you think she is still haunting this house?'

Oonagh blows her nose, puts her handkerchief away and then takes a sip from her tea. 'There she was, all on her own in this little cottage, missing her beloved sister who was killed in the Blitz, and then Robert was shot down in action. I thought that was why she ran to Phelim Sheriden. I thought it was because she was lonely and grieving, and when you are in that state sometimes you do not know your right mind. You can imagine things.'

Oonagh shakes her head and looks down at the floor.

'After she got the official letter telling her that Robert was missing in action, she went to see Phelim Sheriden and didn't come back. There was uproar behind closed doors. Father O'Regan went to see her and tell her she was committing a mortal sin, and then my father went to see her and tried to convince her to come back to the farm and we would take care of her. There was still a chance Robert would come home. She mustn't give up on him. I thought that too – that she had given up on her husband and was running to the nearest available man to protect her and the baby. I didn't realize she actually loved Phelim Sheriden.'

Oonagh sighs.

'But maybe I did know it, deep down. I saw it the day of Claudette's funeral. I could see that June and Phelim belonged together, but I didn't want to believe it, because it was *wrong*.'

Nicholas puts his hand in his pocket. He can feel the slim letter in his fingers, the paper delicate from age.

'The whole community kept up the pressure, and because it was the war, Phelim and June had nowhere to run to. I called round in the end, and as her friend I advised her to come back to the farm, at least until she knew for sure that Robert wasn't returning. Then she would no longer be an adulteress – a term she used, not I – but a widow. Then she could be respectable. She actually listened to me and did what I suggested. Years later she told me that she couldn't bear to be the same as her mother – a Jezebel, she called her. She would wait, because she believed in Phelim and knew he would wait for her.'

'So why is June haunting this house, Oonagh, if she eventually ended up with Phelim Sheriden?'

'Oh, but she didn't. That is the tragedy.'

Nicholas feels the cold hand pressed against his heart again, the same feeling he had in the woods the day he went walking with Kev.

'Just one week after June returned to this cottage, Phelim Sheriden left to join up and fight in the same war that had taken her husband from her. I don't know what words passed between them, for she never told me, but I cannot imagine how she must have felt at being left a second time. A few months later June had a beautiful little baby boy and called him Daniel, in the Fanning tradition. My family and I helped her through those tough years. She never spoke to me about her lost men. And then, one day, Robert Fanning came back from the war. He had been in a prisoner-of-war camp all that time. Oh, there was such jubilation in the community. I have no idea how June really felt. Sometimes I would see her walking through the orchard, standing at the edge of the wood and looking towards the empty Sheriden house. I think she was waiting for him, despite the fact that Robert was back. I think she still wanted Phelim. But we never heard of him again and I don't know what happened to him.'

'That's awful. I mean, great that Robert Fanning survived, but so sad for June and Phelim.'

Oonagh nods and picks up her teacup. 'Many's the time I tried to talk to June about it, but she just clammed up, refused point-blank, said that she had had a happy life as a mother. She went on to have five more children, three boys and two girls. All those children are gone now, all over the world – Australia, America, New Zealand. They sold the house after she died and none of them came back.'

Oonagh puts her teacup back down in its saucer with a clatter.

'The thing is, I don't think June ever knew how much her husband, Robert Fanning, loved her. All that time she was waiting for true love to return, maybe it was right there under her nose. There are many different kinds of love. I suspect Phelim Sheriden was the big passion in her life, but would it have lasted? Stood the test of time? I prefer the kind of love Robert had for his wife. Steady, sure, faithful. I saw the way that man looked at his wife. She was his world.'

By the time Oonagh leaves, it is dusk. Nicholas gives her a bottle of cider for Paddy.

'Could you give Geraldine a message from me?' Nicholas asks the old lady as she mounts her bike.

'Of course, dear.' Her eyes twinkle and Nicholas knows that she knows about him and Geraldine.

'Please tell her from me that she is going to be a wonderful musician, because she has so much heart.'

Oonagh laughs. 'Yes, she gets it from me.' She pauses, puts on her orange beret. 'I hope you and your wife will be very happy here.'

Nicholas watches Oonagh wobble up the lane, her orange hat a bright point in the gloom, and wonders: should he have driven her home, shoved the bike in his generous boot? But he knows she would only have refused. It begins to spit rain. He goes into the kitchen and wanders back up to the attic to continue clearing it out. June Fanning's red notebook sits on the dusty floor, and again he fingers the letter in his pocket.

Open it.

He is sure he can hear her speak and, even if it is just his imagination, what harm will it do if he opens the letter now, after all these years?

15th November 1941

My dear June

Your letter arrived this morning, and I have been thinking about it all day. When you wrote about Claudette Sheriden's funeral, I could not get it out of my head, although every day here chaps are dying, not coming back from ops. You are afraid to make friends, in case it marks them for death. Our lives are transitory and we try to take each day as it comes. It is hard to think about my other life, with you back in Ireland, let alone the past.

But when you wrote to me of Claudette Sheriden's death, everything came flooding back to me, and I thought how unfair I have been to you. Your letter was so short, June, and formal, and at first it disturbed me a little, but then I remembered how my letters to you have been so short, too. I thought you understood how bad a letter-writer I am, and did not need me to write endearments to you because you would know my true feelings, but maybe I have been wrong.

Dear June, I do love you, and think of you every day here, when I question my decision to join up and fight in this war. In a marriage there should be no secrets, yet I have not revealed to you certain things about my family. This is not right, and I shall now attempt to right that wrong and hope that you will forgive me.

You know Claudette as Phelim Sheriden's wife, yet it was in fact my brother, James D., who loved her first. He rescued her during the Great War and brought her back to Ireland. My

brother had fallen for her completely. It was under the plum
trees, on his last day of leave, that James proposed to Claudette
and she accepted. And so my brother went back to the front leaving his fiancée behind with my parents and I.

As you know, a few weeks later my brother was killed. It devastated my mother, for he was always her favourite, and the poor
woman shut herself away for over a month. My father and I tried
to carry on as normal. Claudette's reaction was strange. She was
very quiet – no tears like my mother. By the time Phelim
returned from the war, recovering from his injury, it was clear
that Claudette was pregnant. It didn't make sense, for my
brother had left eight months beforehand and, to my eyes, she
didn't look that far gone, but no one said anything.

My hand is shaking, for I am ashamed to write of what happened next. You know I hardly speak of my father. It is because
of him, June, that my face is burning with shame as I write. One
day I saw him with Claudette, in the orchard, amongst the very
trees he had planted for his wife. In an instant it was clear to me.
The father of Claudette's child was my own father, and in that
same instant I knew that the knowledge of this would kill my
poor mother, after the shock of losing James.

Once Phelim found out Claudette was with child, he was
determined to make her his wife, out of honour for his dead
friend. I was in an awful quandary, for I could not tell Phelim
the terrible truth, yet I was horrified that he was sacrificing his
life for this woman, who I believed had schemed her way into
our family. I hated her, and still do, June, and I am glad poor
Phelim is finally released, and pray he may find someone more
deserving of his love.

So in an effort to protect Phelim and my mother, I proposed
to Claudette, although I despised her. Of course she rejected me
for Phelim, who must have appeared a more appealing prospect

as a husband, but she used this fact against me while I remained on the farm. She believed I was in love with her. That is why I didn't want you to visit her, in case she led you to believe things that aren't true. I hope you can understand.

It was after the baby was born, a full ten months after my brother had died, when she named it Danielle after my father, and he planted a whole side of the orchard with new apple trees for her, that I finally lost my temper and confronted my father. My mother overheard the row and found out everything. So you see, June, I blame myself for her death, for only a few days later she collapsed, never to recover. Now you can understand why I left my home, not to return until I knew that my father was six feet under.

My darling, please believe it was my utter shame that has stopped me from confiding in you before. Now Claudette is gone, I hope you will visit Phelim, for he is a good man. Please know how much I cherish you, and I miss you, darling. Do not be afraid – I will come back to you and look after you for the rest of my life. You are my one and only true love,

Robert

Three boxes on the other side of the attic topple over and make a tremendous clatter. Nicholas jumps up and looks around him. The window bangs open, but there is no wind. He can see that while he was reading the letter the spitting rain has turned to mist, and as the light disappears out of the sky, a gentle fog rises off the fields. He folds the letter up and puts it back in his pocket and then he tries to close the window, but the handle is wet with condensation and he keeps letting it slip out of his hand. He has the feeling that he needs to keep the window open.

You are my one and only true love, Robert.

Nicholas hears June sigh, and it makes him think: did Robert ever reveal to her the contents of that letter when he returned from the war? Did June go through their whole marriage thinking Danielle was her husband's daughter, and that Claudette Sheriden had been the one true love of his life? Not her, not June. He wonders if two people could live together their whole lives, the length of a marriage, and not tell each other how dear they are to one another and how much they are loved. Nicholas knows it is possible. He knows many couples who live just like that, and he swears he and Charlie will never let that happen to them again. Nicholas understands now that adultery has nothing to do with betraying another, for it is an inquisition upon your own heart.

He looks at the fog and it conjures up the idea of Aristotle's fifth element – not water or fire, earth or air, but something else. An essence that combines all four. The mist looks like smoke, catching in his throat at the open window. Yet it is without substance, an ether like air. It rises off the earth, preternatural, its smell pungent of autumn beginning, and it makes his cheeks damp with condensation. Is fog the place where spirits dwell and feel most comfortable, in its blank oblivion? Does fog have the ability to propel mortals into thoughts of another realm beyond their own? Nicholas thinks this is truly a place where fire and water can mix, and if he allowed himself to be lost in its fumes, he might be able to see beyond himself. He might see a light shining through this invisible field. A crow caws loudly, highlighting the silence of the other birds, of utter stillness emanating from the ground below.

And through the mist swirling above the field Nicholas sees a figure standing, looking at the house. It is a tall man with thick black hair, in a long dark coat, and he stands as still as a scarecrow.

I miss you.

Something brushes by Nicholas, and it feels as if thin muslin has been dragged across his cheeks. A chill goes down his spine and he knows this is a moment of passing, a final passing.

'Goodbye, June,' he says to his phantom companion as she flies out the window, down to the fields to hold hands with her husband. Robert will take June across the mulch and muck and down into the earth, back home, back together. She has waited so long.

Nicholas sees a car coming round the bend in the lane, its lights cutting a path through the fog. It is Charlie returning. He runs downstairs to put peat on the fire, June Fanning's book in his hand. He cannot wait to tell her the story of an adulteress whose husband loved her beyond death, beyond life.

ACKNOWLEDGEMENTS

Thank you to Marianne Gunn O'Connor, my very special agent, to Vicki Satlow, my other very special agent, and to Pat Lynch, Marianne's indispensable assistant. Thank you to my wonderful editor Imogen Taylor, and to her assistants Thalia Suzuma and Trisha Jackson. Thank you to Dave Adamson, Chloe Healy and all at Pan Macmillan. Thanks to Joy Terekiev and Cristiana Moroni at Mondadori, and to Barbara Heinzius at Random House.

Thank you to my first readers and good friends Kate Bootle, Monica McInerney, Jo Southall, Donna Ansley, Ciara O'Hara, Miriam McCabe, Sinéad Nic Coitir, Sally Nelson, Maura McInerney and Jason Irrgang, all of whom gave me valuable feedback at different stages of the book's development.

Thank you to Bernie McCabe for talking to me about life in Cavan during the Emergency, and to Bernie Kellett for her advice on the fashion of the period.

A very special acknowledgment to my darling departed mother Claire Davies, her sisters Ruth Blishen & Joyce D'Silva, her late brother John Blake Kelly, and her late sister Bán Hanlon, whose writings on the history of our family provided me with many ideas.

Thank you to Carol O'Connor for creative inspiration, and to Agata, Roberto and Gaia Purini in Milan.

Thank you to my old Latin teacher Miss Wilcox, who instilled in me a lifelong passion for ancient Rome.

Thank you to Fintan Blake Kelly, Barry Ansley, Page Allen, Jenny Brady, Jill Igoe, Synnøve and Hanna Bakke, Therese Dalton, Bernie McGrath, Tanja and Kathrin Eigendorf, Corey Ansley and Helena Goode.

6